TWO MILLION DOLLAR DEATH

"What I offer you is an opportunity to make two million dollars tax-free plus expenses," said the mysterious man who had summoned Konrad to this meeting. "It could be dangerous," he went on, "but possibly not at all. I would calculate your chances of success at about two out of three. In the event of failure, however, the chance of escaping with your life would be slim."

"I don't have much of a life right now," Konrad said bitterly. "Go ahead. I'm listening."

"Very well," said the stranger. "Your assignment is to take over a country."

Konrad stared uncomprehending; the whole concept was outside his frame of reference. "Take over a country? You mean a *country*, with a government . . . an army . . . ?"

"Precisely, and don't look so stunned; what I propose is perfectly feasible. I want you to take over Liechtenstein." He suddenly laughed. "You will be the next ruler of the Principality of Liechtenstein—in a manner of speaking."

"Or I'll be dead."

"Yes . . . or you'll be dead."

Blood
of the
Eagle

by Fred Dickey

ZEBRA BOOKS
KENSINGTON PUBLISHING CORP.

For my children

ZEBRA BOOKS

are published by

Kensington Publishing Corp.
475 Park Avenue South
New York, NY 10016

First printing: June 1985

Printed in the United States of America

Chapter One

The recon patrol was about to find the enemy, but as so often happened, they didn't know it until the enemy first found them.

Lieutenant Konrad was slouching in a rare dry spot deep in the trackless, endless swamp geographers call Vietnam's Mekong Delta. Konrad and the men of his platoon called it something else. It wasn't much of a place to take a break, but they weren't complaining after hours and miles of a hot, tiresome search for reported heavy Viet Cong movement in the sector.

Konrad ran his eyes over the surrounding jungle while, next to him, a young, buck-toothed replacement who had just joined them a couple of days earlier complained about his new boots. Konrad remembered from his drawl that the soldier was from Arkansas.

"Shit, man, these gawddamn boots do'n' fit. They's too tight an' ah cain't walk without gettin' blisters all over ma feet. Seems to me the fuckin' ar—"

One moment Konrad was idly listening to the man bitch, the next he was gaping at the man's face which had turned into a mass of spurting dark red jelly. An instant later, the ringing report of a rifle shot wrenched his attention back to the plight of his platoon and away from the soldier who was silently sinking to the earth. He no longer figured in the situation.

Konrad threw himself into a stream bed and screamed, "Snipers. Down!" At the same instant, automatic rifle fire seemed to converge in a thunderous racket from every direction. It was joined by heavy mortars and light field artillery that shook the earth and compounded the fear and confusion.

With bullets whining overhead and clumps of earth falling on him from the continuous blasting of the mortars, Konrad's instinct was to bury his face in the earth and wait for it to go away or kill him, whichever came first.

Instead, he forced himself to take command of the situation. This was still his platoon, and he would protect his men. Frightening though the mortars were, he instantly realized the Viet Cong had made a mistake in using them. Since mortar aiming, especially in first getting a target zeroed in, is an iffy thing at best, the V.C. could not be very close for fear of hitting themselves. Had they not used the mortars and concentrated instead on close-range small arms fire, the platoon would have become history in short order.

Konrad started bellowing. "Fan out, men. Expand those perimeters. Push out. Get us some room. Move."

In response to his frantic appeals, the men started crawling forward, toward the blinking light of the concealed enemy guns. A soldier would fire a spurt then crawl forward another couple of feet. Within minutes, the platoon was well-anchored in a defensive circle about

6

one hundred yards in diameter.

Then, as quickly as it started, the firing stopped. But Konrad knew it was only temporary. As soon as Charlie shifted positions to wherever he thought most advantageous, the attack would resume more ferociously than before. It wouldn't be long, because, in an attack like this, the Cong were always aware they operated on borrowed time. As soon as the first helicopter gunship appeared in response to the call for help, they would have to melt back into the jungle.

Konrad screamed loud enough for all his men to hear: "Dig in. Stay alert and blast hell out of anything that moves out there." Konrad knew that his shouting orders could easily allow the enemy to identify his position as the command post and focus their attack on him, but it couldn't be helped. The men had to have a sense of unity and it was his job to provide it.

He turned to his radio man who had been silently lying beside him. "Willie Mac, get that damned thing humming. Contact battalion. In a half hour those bastards out there will be jumping like scalded dogs, they'll have so much lead chasing their asses."

While he waited for the radio man to raise battalion, Konrad used his rifle butt to push aside the green scum lying on top of the stagnant water, then dipped his helmet into the pool and poured the warm water over his head. He closed his eyes and sighed with pleasure as the stinking liquid cooled his head and ran down his neck and back, providing a moment of relief from the crushing, sucking heat.

Konrad lay in the high grass at the water's edge and smelled the rot of vegetation. He winced at the bites of invisible insects hidden in his clothing and which

7

overran his feeble defenses because they wouldn't quit or rest and because they outnumbered him a million to one. He felt the pain of chafed, raw skin in his groin, armpits and neck, anyplace where skin rubbed against skin and ground the wet salt of perspiration back into his body.

As if all this were not enough to complete his misery, just a short distance away, lots of funny-looking little men waited to kill him, to turn him into one of the formless, stinking piles of fly-blown ex-humans he had often carefully avoided stepping on along the serpentine trails of South Vietnam's jungles.

As that reality played on his mind, he thought of the young hillbilly sprawled motionless in the puppet pose of death a few yards away, staring with his remaining sightless eyes as the ants and flies staked claims to the gore that had been his face a few minutes ago.

He turned away and forced the picture from his mind, blinking his eyes in protest to the sting of sweat that flowed into them. He angrily rearranged the heavy ammunition belt trying to find relief from the sticky discomfort. He didn't want to die, and he didn't want to be in this miserable place. Above all, he didn't want to die in this miserable place.

Pvt. Willie Mac Russell, the radio man, slammed the instrument in disgust and turned to Konrad. "Sir, this damned thing won't work. It took shrapnel right through its guts."

"Are you sure?"

"It's deader'n Grandpaw's dick."

Konrad didn't know Grandpaw, but he knew Willie Mac. He stared into the sweating black face of the young man approximately his own age who was his constant companion in the field. He liked Willie Mac, liked him a lot.

Willie Mac Russell was a survivor of Chicago's ghetto. He had escaped that place with his quick smile and sense of humor intact. Maybe he was able to escape because of them. He had already decided to make the Army his career. He had discovered, as had centuries of soldiers before him, that the quickest way out of society's garbage pit is military service. It's an easy step, because it isn't a very big one. But it was enough when staked up against life in a crumbling tenement where the only ones in control are the rats. The Army may take a man's life, but at least it doesn't waste it on street corners.

Willie Mac had been an all-state basketball player back home, and had started college on a scholarship that took him to the first grade report. "I was about as ready for college as a pimp is for a compact Ford," is how he remembered the experience.

An unbroken series of F's resulted in a fast termination of his career as a scholar, and left him with a decision that did not require much learning to figure out: Go back to the ghetto or join the Army. Thus Willie Mac traded the silk uniform with his name and number on the back for an anonymous one made of khaki; he went from hardwood court to the hard-ass corps with no stops between.

Konrad's life contrasted as sharply with Willie Mac's as did his skin color. A degree in linguistics and the student-colonelcy of the R.O.T.C. at a big-name university seemed to confirm the unquestioned optimism that directed his life. The future was an inviting, well-paved highway stretching out before him. Three years on active duty, then service in the State Department, or in the foreign section of an international corporation had been his original intent. Lately, however, he had been thinking more and more of a military career. He loved the power of command, the respect his considerable skills earned him from troops and superiors alike, and the idea he was doing something of value for his country. He even got a kick out of combat, the breathless kind that comes from using wits and skill to overcome danger. Regardless of what he decided to do with his life, Konrad's options were open. His future seemed to be a plum he could pick at his leisure when he found the one that was best-tasting. Konrad's life wasn't terribly exceptional, but it sure was nice.

These advantages plus a buoyant personality that everyone liked gave Konrad his edge. If he weren't so likable, you'd call him cocky.

Konrad, as they say, had all the advantages. He grew up in the prosperous, bucolic Berkshires of Connecticut as clean-cut as the boy next door in a rich neighborhood. He was the offspring of that great, arrogant American boast of the 1950s which proclaimed that its shadows eclipsed the entire world, that God had used gold thread in weaving it into the tapestry of nations.

Konrad was endowed with great dreams of accomplishment. His psyche was tanned by the glow from that bright beacon that illuminated American purity. He memorized the miracles of his American heritage, played football, won the spelling bee, a Sunday School attendance pin, and absorbed the folklore of his class and the mood of his times. In the innocent insularity of his youth, he believed that the magic of his life's mission would bless all lives it touched.

Everything he did was according to the plan of middle-class advancement, and everything he tried worked. So when the ambitions of Konrad and his country inter-sected in Vietnam, the stage was set for the justification of history—or the wrath of it.

As it happened to the nation, it happened to the man.

Why this young lieutenant and equally young private became buddies, no one could say. For their part, it wasn't important. They liked to drink their beer ration together and swap stories. Willie Mac got a big kick out of how Konrad would break up into helpless, rolling-on-the-ground laughter when he described some of the ghetto characters he remembered from the streets. Pimps like Cottonmouth and the Tuba Man were as strange to Konrad as Greenland Eskimos, but they became good friends through Willie Mac's tales.

They didn't socialize off-duty or in camp—that just wasn't done—but the friendship flourished in the jungle where it counted most and was needed most.

The two seemed to thrive on the differences between them, often comparing their life styles, memories, values and dreams, each providing a window for the other's wide-eyed gaze into an alien world. Like the time they were lounging around at the end of a patrol waiting for the helicopter to pick them up . . .

"What you be doin' if you wasn't here, Lieutenant?" Willie Mac asked casually as he leaned back against the roots of a large tree hiding him from the searching, punishing jungle sun. "You be makin' big bread workin' for some rich outfit?"

Konrad twisted his heavy belt around in a constant, never-winning effort to find comfort in the sticky heat. "No, I don't think so, at least not for that motive. I'd like to be doing something of value to others; just chasing dollars doesn't appeal to me. I've always wanted to

11

conduct my life so it counts for the important things. How about you?"

"Man, Lieutenant, you sound like a preacher I oncet knew. He alwuz talk about doin' good things for people, too; trouble with him was, the people he was talkin' about was hisself. Me? Guess I'd be dealin' a little, playin' some ball. . . ."

"Dealing what?" Konrad asked.

Willie Mac looked at him as he would a slightly amusing child, grinning at his naivete.

"Do you mean drugs? Come on, Willie Mac, smoking a little grass I can handle, but *dealing*? You can think of more worthwhile things to do with your life."

"You got to remember, Lieutenant, we come from different parts of town. You can talk about feedin' your soul; I got to worry about feedin' my face. Any bread I come across sure ain't gonna get cast on any waters, like the preacher say."

Konrad shook his head wonderingly at the differences in people. "My parents were immigrants, and this country was very good to them. They were intensely patriotic and God-fearing and they brought me up that way. That's how I was taught, and that's how I feel, and to me, service to others, to my country, and to God is what governs my life. If I didn't believe I counted for humanity, then I couldn't be happy. It would be like I had failed my beliefs, my purpose."

Willie Mac started to say something, then thought better of it.

At that moment, the heavy rhythmic beating of the helicopter's engine swept low over the trees, buffeting the men in a miniature windstorm. As they grabbed their gear and hunched forward for the walk to the chopper,

Willie Mac shouted close to Konrad's ear to make himself heard, "Man, Lieutenant, those ideas sure put you up on a cloud; jes' remember, underneath those clouds is hard ground, and it's a long way down."

Disgusted with the dead radio, Willie Mac leaned heavily against the bank and sighed. From deep within himself, he drew on the humor that had sustained his people through centuries of hardship and fear. He chuckled softly. "Man, I never thought I'd miss the South Side of Chicago. But if I could get out of this fuckin' place, I'd be happy to kiss any dope dealer's ass in the middle of Sixty-Third Street. Man, I am so thoroughly goddamn miserable that the thought of lyin' in this shit one more minute is—"

"Incoming!" screamed a voice just as the freight-train rumble of artillery shells fell from the sky. The men barely had time to duck before the concussion of the heavy blasts squeezed them in waves of heat.

For several long minutes they hugged the shuddering earth seeking to disappear into the shallow contours of their trenches, holding their breaths, fearing that the sounds of their breathing would attract the attention of the monster that was pounding the earth and spreading fire on top of them.

As the explosions gradually subsided, their bodies relaxed in unison to the quiet. Konrad looked over at his companion. Willie Mac's eyes were squeezed shut and sweat ran in streams down his glistening, ebony face. "You OK?"

The round, brown eyes opened in their pools of white. "Compared to what? Compared to sittin' in a cool bar drinkin' a cold beer, naw, I ain't worth a shit. But if you're askin' am I still miserable, itchin' an' sittin' here in one piece, then yeah, I'm OK."

Konrad was scared. Everyone there was scared, but it was up to him to show the guts, to give the others reason to think it wasn't all that bad, after all. He forced his voice to be calm. "Willie Mac, I hope you realize we're in deep shit." He spoke the frightening truth, but he said it in the we-can-handle-it way the men had come to expect from their young lieutenant.

"Ain't no doubt about that, sir."

"Get the squad leaders over here on the double."

Willie Mac slithered over the top of the bank to the next position to pass the word for the four non-coms. Within minutes, Sergeants Williams and Ignalzio tumbled over the bank and presented themselves to the platoon leader.

"Where are Thompson and Padulski?" Konrad asked.

"Thompson bought it when the mortars opened up. Padulski took a rifle round in the leg," Williams said.

"How are the men?"

"Looks like five dead and three wounded. That leaves us thirty-one men total, Lieutenant," Ignalzio said.

"The lines holding?"

"No sweat. The perimeter's secure—for the time being," Williams said.

Konrad forced himself to sound casual. "We've got a little problem here, men, and I'd like your ideas on how to get the hell out of it."

Konrad looked at the sergeants. They looked back, expecting him to continue. "What we're up against is a dead radio and an enemy force that obviously out-numbers us heavily. We have no way to let battalion

14

know we need help." Konrad looked at his watch. "It's almost noon now; they won't start looking for us for several more hours."

Ignalzio asked nervously, "Can we hold out until they find us?"

"Problem is, Ignalzio, it could take them a week to find us in this jungle. This modern army, as we like to call it, is set up to run by radio communications. And right now, we're fucked in that department. Pretty soon, old Charlie out there is gonna figure out that no helicopters are coming over those hills to pull our asses out of the fire."

Williams offered the suggestion that was in everyone's mind. "How about sending someone for help?"

Konrad studied the thought for a moment. "You're talking about trying to sneak through Charlie's lines over unfamiliar terrain in broad daylight. That's a suicide mission. I don't know about you, but I'd hate to ask any of those rookies out there to volunteer for something like that."

"The kids couldn't do it, Lieutenant," Williams said.

"What are you getting at, Williams?"

Williams hesitated, then plunged ahead. "You're the only one with the experience and ability to do it, sir." Williams was a little shocked at the idea of volunteering his own officer, but the thought was out so he elected to pursue it. "Look, sir, everyone knows you're the best soldier in the battalion, probably the regiment. If anyone can get through, you can."

"Williams, an officer doesn't abandon his men."

"Would it be better to see them all get killed? It wouldn't be like running out on them, sir. Ignalzio and I can keep things together here. Please, sir, it's our only chance."

Konrad thought about the Viet Cong who awaited him just beyond the edge of the jungle; he thought of the agony of trying to force his body to endure one hundred degree heat and high humidity for several punishing hours over booby-trapped trails and lung-tearing hills. He also knew it had to be done, and he was flattered by his sergeant's praise. What choice did he really have?

"I'll need to take another man, someone to watch my back and to keep going if I don't make it."

Willie Mac had been silently listening to the exchange from a short distance, but now he took a casual step forward and said, "Well, Lieutenant, I been taking care of you for almost a year, guess I'd kinda worry if I let you out of my sight now. Besides—" he gestured toward the useless radio—"might be kinda nice to take a hike without having to lug that damned pile of junk on my back."

Konrad studied him, then asked quietly, "Know what you're getting into, Willie Mac?"

"No, and don't tell me, either. I might change my mind."

Konrad and Willie Mac filled two canteens with purified water and grabbed handfuls of food. They each took several clips of rifle ammunition, but resisted the temptation to take the grenades thrust at them by helpful buddies. They had to keep ease of movement uppermost in their preparations, enticing though it was to load down with comforting weaponry.

They checked each other's packs, and Konrad gave Willie Mac a sturdy slap on the back to signal approval. "Well, how does a little stroll in the garden sound?" he joked weakly.

"I ain't seen your alternatives, Lieutenant."

"I don't have any."

Silently, as their comrades watched with hopeful eyes, they slipped into one of the stream beds that interlaced the swampy terrain of the delta. This one had a protective covering of vines that virtually made it a tunnel. It meandered in the right direction and seemed a safe path, provided it wasn't also chosen by the Cong for the same reasons.

Konrad and Willie Mac crept through the knee-deep water and held onto the vines along the bank for stability. A slip or loud splash would mean capture or death.

Suddenly, voices sounded almost directly above them. The two men hugged the bank and froze. It wasn't easy to tell how far off the V.C. voices were, but it couldn't have been more than a few feet. Konrad leaned against the network of dense roots protruding from the bank. Through the covering of his hiding place, he could see one of them about fifty feet away. He was a tiny doll-man who wouldn't have stood higher than Konrad's shoulder. He wore only ragged shorts and sandals made of strips of old automobile tires. Looking at the skinny, bedraggled little man, Konrad found it incredible to believe the man was a threat to him, but the ugly, shining AK-47 he was holding said otherwise.

Konrad felt something brush against his arm. He half-turned toward the movement and froze. He stared at the thick, round body; the broad, black-and-yellow bands undulated slowly as the snake moved, its cool, steel-hard body sending chills through him where it touched his skin. Konrad recognized the snake as a krait, one of the most venomous in Southeast Asia. It had emerged from the entangled roots of the bank and somehow wedged itself between Konrad's arm and the damp earth. Konrad

17

slowly shifted his head, knowing with dread that he was about to see dull, black eyes staring directly into his own and a tongue flickering threateningly in advance of the fatal strike.

The nauseous feeling of panic surged toward his throat as Konrad realized that whether he lived or died depended on the will of the ugly, deadly creature that was deciding his fate as it watched him. He felt the thick body slithering more quickly, but the snake wasn't withdrawing, it was gathering itself. It was going to strike, and Konrad was helpless to stop it; any sudden move would only make it happen sooner.

With no warning, a silver flash came out of the corner of his eye and struck the snake. Konrad recoiled in surprise and then realized what had happened. Willie Mac had impaled the snake's head on his bayonet. Konrad watched him straining to keep the deadly head pinned against the soft bank. The blade hadn't caught the snake dead-center, and barely held it by part of its lower head, leaving the krait partial movement, enough so it could twist backward and make its mouth come within an inch or two of Willie Mac's hand.

The powerful muscles of its body convulsed wildly requiring all of Willie Mac's strength to maintain his hold. Konrad saw the terror in Willie Mac's sweating face each time the krait almost reached the hand holding the knife. The snake's entire body began to thrash, beating against Konrad like a whip. He grabbed the tail to still the noise and the deadly struggle acted out in furious pantomime. Finally, with one hand still holding the twisting tail, Konrad drew his own bayonet and severed the snake's head.

The two exhausted men gently laid the dead snake into

18

the water and leaned against each other with the weakness that comes with the release of great fear.

Konrad put his lips close to Willie Mac's ear and whispered, "I owe you."

They rested for only a moment, then the voices from above reminded them that another danger, equally deadly, lurked here. They carefully edged along the stream bed until the voices drifted away and they were confident the V.C. lines were behind them.

Cautiously, they climbed onto dry land and crept through the jungle in an easterly direction. They weren't far enough way yet to use a main trail, but each yard narrowed the distance between them and help. Despite hours of fighting vines, sinkholes and ensnaring roots, the thought of the enemy behind and all around them gave the men the strength to ignore their sweat-stained weariness. Finally, they came to the edge of a trail and fell into a heap.

Willie Mac moaned softly and managed to ask, "How far do you think we've come?"

"Hard to say," Konrad rasped, trying to catch his breath and talk at the same time. "Seems like we've come a hundred miles. I guess it's safe now to use the trail. One thing is sure, we've got to pace ourselves better or we'll collapse before we make it."

"Amen to that." Willie Mac started to loosen his pack, great weariness evident in every tortured, slow-motion move.

Suddenly, from somewhere in the surrounding brush, a stick snapped, a limb rustled and several birds protested loudly. Willie Mac hastily rebuckled his pack. "On second thought, I feel like moving right along," he whispered.

As they drew closer to the battalion and farther from their surrounded buddies, the fear and tension increased rather than lessened. It was as though the nearer they came to safety, to completion of their mission, the more ominous the shadows became, and every sound in the jungle became louder and had a frightening, hidden meaning. The promise of success seemed a lie, the knowledge that safety was just a few miles away had to be a trick. They had passed unaware into that gray state of mind where hope gives way to fear which then compounds into panic. They were spooked.

Exhaustion was forgotten, caution surrendered to the need to hurry. They rushed along the jungle trail, not in pursuit of the safety that tantalized them just over the next hill or around the next turn, but running from the danger that lay behind.

Konrad was leading as they ran along the bank of a rushing river. Half blind from sweat streaming into his eyes, legs protesting their abuse by sending pain waves to his brain, he vaguely heard Willie Mac cry out sharply. Trying to turn and look while he ran, Konrad fell to his knees and desperately fought for breath.

Willie Mac's moaning released Konrad's attention from his own misery and cleared away the fear shadows in his mind. He scooted over to the stricken man. Willie Mac was holding his right ankle and rocking back and forth.

"How bad is it?" Konrad gently forced apart Willie Mac's hands to inspect the ankle. One glance at the obscene angle of the break answered his question.

"Shit," Konrad hissed softly.

Willie Mac anxiously searched Konrad's face for signs of hope. He saw little that comforted him. "How'm I gonna walk, Lieutenant?" He threw a worried glance over his shoulder. "I can't stay here."

"Don't worry, I'll help you. We started this thing together, and we'll finish it together. You have my word on that." Konrad provided support as Willie Mac gingerly climbed to his feet.

"Where's your rifle?"

"I donno, sir. Musta dropped it somewhere back there."

Together they hobbled down the trail. Konrad supported Willie Mac with his arm around the injured man's waist and by holding the other arm over his shoulder. He glanced at Willie Mac's grimacing face, then at the brooding, waiting jungle. He heard Willie Mac's tortured groans, but he also heard the sudden cries of animals on the prowl, the warning shrieks of birds trying to alert all within hearing to danger.

Konrad tried to fight off the fears that battered his mind. "It's just my imagination, it's just my imagination," he kept whispering to himself, but in counterpoint, another voice in his mind said, "Maybe it's not, maybe it's not."

After what seemed like an eternity but must have been about a mile, Konrad was forced to stop and rest. He eased Willie Mac down as gently as he could, then half-fell beside him. They lay that way for several minutes, not talking, not knowing anything appropriate to say. Suddenly, the stupor of their exhaustion was interrupted by the unmistakable sound of a human voice. They were instantly alert, all signs of fatigue and pain pushed aside as the new danger unfolded.

Konrad squeezed Willie Mac's shoulder. "It's going to be all right. I'm going on ahead to that rise and check it out. Be right back." As he scooted ahead, Willie Mac's panic-stricken plea followed him. "Don't leave me, Lieutenant, please don't leave me."

Konrad turned and held his finger to his lips. Then he circled his fingers in the OK sign and winked with a bravado he didn't feel.

Konrad crawled to the top of the rise, then climbed into the lower branches of a gnarled cypress. From there he could see for several hundred yards, but he didn't have to look that far to spot four Viet Cong slowly advancing toward his position. Because they were stretched out in a forage line, Konrad knew they were searching for something. He had no doubts what.

Konrad watched the little men with their silly conical hats and black pajama outfits, but also with businesslike automatic rifles held at the ready, then glanced back to the waiting Willie Mac. As his gaze shifted from one to the other then back again, conflicting emotions started to churn inside him and wrestle for control of his mind. DUTY: I've got to get back to battalion; if I don't, a lot of good men will die. That's my mission, I can't fail those men. LOYALTY: You can't leave Willie Mac. You can take out four Charlies. He's counting on you. He saved your life. You promised not to abandon him. Besides, those men might already be dead, or maybe the V.C. withdrew. FEAR: Get out, get out. If you stay here, you'll die. What if there are more right behind those four? He's only a private and going nowhere in life. Your future is too bright to waste trying to be a hero. Stay alive, run.

The searchers were close enough for Willie Mac to hear clearly. As the sounds reached his ears, his face was transformed into a mask of fear. His lips moved in soundless begging to Konrad. "Help me, don't leave me," was what Konrad could lip-read over the distance.

Konrad looked again at the nearing enemy, at the trembling Willie Mac, then down the beckoning trail that led to the battalion and safety. He hesitated.

Willie Mac's heart pounded with the sounds of the approaching soldiers. He watched Konrad with desperate hope: Konrad would save him. Hadn't he saved Konrad's life? Even with only Konrad's rifle, they could hold out. Battalion wasn't that far. Help could show up at any minute.

The eye contact between Konrad and Willie Mac was electric with expectation on the part of the injured man, and doubts on the part of his leader. Konrad was frozen into place by the look of panic and supplication that came from Willie Mac. The look said, you are my only hope; without you, I die, just as you would have died without me.

Konrad shut his eyes for a long moment—he had to decide. Which would it be, Willie Mac or safety? He took a deep breath and forced himself to move down the trail—away from Willie Mac.

The injured radio man knew the sight of Konrad's retreating back meant his death sentence. Despair flooded his brain and protest burned in his throat. If he was going to die, then his last act would be to brand the man who sentenced him. He screamed out his anguish. "Konrad, you promised. You owe me. You white devil. Remember me, you white devil."

The screams stopped and there was silence, but only for a moment. Different voices, many of them, now filled the air. Laughing voices. Then they, too, fell silent with the ending punctuation of gunfire.

Konrad didn't stop, but as he plunged down the trail, something important to him was left behind.

Colonel Johnson's face lit up and he purred in a soft Southern drawl when Konrad entered the battalion headquarters hut. "Well, well, here's the man of the hour. Did you have a nice sleep, Lieutenant? Lord knows you deserved it." The colonel sprang to his feet and solicitously took Konrad by the arm. "Here, have a seat right over here." He made sure Konrad was comfortable, then reached into a desk drawer and withdrew a bottle. "How about a little sippin' whiskey? After what you've been through, no one's going to quibble over regulations."

Konrad ignored the glass set before him. "Colonel, did you save my platoon?"

The colonel shook his head and grinned. "Boy, you sure were a mess when you stumbled into camp yesterday. But you're gonna look fine when the bands start playing. Fella, what you are is a genuine, certified hero. Yessir, a lieutenant in my own outfit—"

"Colonel, please, my platoon."

"Right. When you staggered in here, babbling about your platoon being trapped, we jumped. Yessir, we had relief choppers on the way 'bout as quick as you could say Ho Chi Mihn. We got 'em all. Twenty-six men rescued. Gave old Charlie a good kick in the ass, too. Just when those gooks thought they had your men just where they wanted 'em, and were moving in for the kill, those gunships came over the ridge and caught 'em flat-footed."

"Thank God."

"Thank *you*! Sneakin' through those gooks the way you did would have been a real miracle for someone else, like the Marines, but for one of my boys, it's all in a day's work, eh? Sure you don't have any Injun blood in you? Man, I sure wouldn't want to try sneakin' through those little devils in broad daylight."

The colonel cleared his throat and paused for dramatic effect. "Lieutenant, it's my pleasure to inform you that I'm recommending your promotion to captain. I'm also starting the paperwork for a Silver Star. I'll give odds both will slide through easier'n a wet rubber. Be a real credit to the battalion."

"Colonel, any word on the man who was with me, a private named Russell?"

The colonel studied some papers on his desk briefly. "Oh, yeah. A patrol found him early this morning, at least what the slopes had left of him. Nasty little bastards when they get a man cornered. They didn't just shoot him, they started at the toes and worked up. He'll get a purple heart and maybe I can arrange a citation. His folks can be proud of him. He must have been a good soldier, shame to lose men like that."

The surprised colonel stared open-mouthed as Konrad abruptly rushed from the room, spilling his untouched drink in the process.

The colonel surveyed the widening stain on the carpet and said a silent prayer for the young officer. He had seen it before.

Konrad left the Army compound in a daze; his mind and body had absorbed to the limit. He wandered into

Khanh Hung seeking some kind of refuge among the stinking, littered streets of what had once been a quiet provincial city of sixty thousand and now was an army town, an uprooted tree in the path of a hurricane. Despite the infusion of American wealth, it still had become a slum, because the people who lived there had patterned their lives to confront the daily dealings with life, death, greed and lust. Next to such apocalyptic issues, cleanliness, tranquility and dignity seemed unimportant and archaic, the dim residue of another time.

Konrad wandered into a seedy bar along a side street that even the hardest acid-head misfits of the Army wisely avoided. It was little more than a shack with a few tables teetering on an uneven earth floor and surrounded by mismatched old kitchen chairs. The bartender watched silently as he threw himself down at one of the tables. Americans who came in this place were welcome because of the money they invariably left behind, but were regarded warily because they usually were the types closely followed by trouble.

At that time of day, Konrad was the only customer, but still the bartender didn't move. Konrad finally walked over to the bar which was little more than a high, rickety table, and ordered whiskey, a whole bottle with an unbroken seal. He did so automatically because the American who would drink from an opened bottle in a place like this was very soon a dead American. Poisoned whiskey and ice cubes with shaved glass buried in them were two weapons the Viet Cong found very effective and which inflicted no casualties on them in return.

Amidst this background—the noise of people on nerves' edge trying to fashion lives out of a sardine-can environment in pressure-cooker heat; squalling children; nauseous cooking smells; slinking dogs who had learned that acting like normal, barking canines was a quick invitation to the cooking pot—in this chosen place, Konrad set about the serious business of getting thoroughly drunk.

With the bartender suspiciously watching him, he choked down one swallow of the cheap whiskey after another. Soon, the liquor made good on its bargain, and Konrad's head slowly slumped to the grimy, bare table top, lost in the dreamless thanatopsis of the drunk. The escape he sought was heralded by soft, uneven snores. It wouldn't last, but it would do.

Someone was calling; he wanted to be left alone, but they wouldn't stop. Finally, he managed to lift his head and peer through fogged eyes to see who dared interrupt his peace.

She was a skinny seventeen-year-old named Que Phi Phan, hardly larger than a child, but she shook Konrad's shoulder with the resolve of one determined to be heard. He finally responded in a slurred voice. "What?"

She was patient; she had done this before. "You want fuck, Joe?" She might have been saying, "Would you like another drink, sir" or "Ten minutes to closing time, sir." She was businesslike.

"What?" he tried again, but the fog lingered.

"You want fuck, Joe?"

"My name isn't Joe."

"What your name? You want fuck?"

Konrad thought about his name, he dwelt on the question for long moments. Finally, he was satisfied. "My name is Death."

"You want fuck, Death?" The girl didn't know the irony of her innocence. With the rot of war all around

27

her, she knew only American words that represented living and pleasure, things that could be grabbed quickly and paid for in cash. The word death was not part of that vocabulary, though she walked daily among its works.

"You come me, Death; good time, much fuck." She tugged him to his feet and led the way out of the ramshackle bar and into midday.

As the brutal heat of the full sun clasped them, he sagged against her, but she didn't even stagger as she maneuvered him toward her pathetic little shack. It was hardly more than a lean-to with a blanket door and she soon had him inside where she let him collapse on her pallet. Working deftly, she unzipped his fly to inspect for venereal disease. Then she pulled his pants down and massaged his penis until he sustained a reflexive erection. Then, still stroking, she demanded, "First money, Death. Fifty dollar."

Half conscious, Konrad fumbled for his wallet and poked among the bills. One by one, he pulled out crumpled bills until she appeared to be satisfied.

She leaped to her feet and in one fast motion lifted the shift over her head. She stood for a moment in front of him, her tiny breasts barely raised from her chest. The nipples were small and dark, totally unresponsive to the erotic scene of her creation. Were it not for the thin tuft of black pubic hair at the crease of her tiny legs, she could have passed for a young child. She stared disinterestedly at the half-aware Konrad and stroked him mechanically to maintain his erection as she sat on her haunches next to him. With her other hand she reached for a nearby bottle of Vaseline, put a liberal amount on her fingers and reached between her legs and inserted it, trying to create artificially the lubrication of passion that her mind and

28

body shrugged off.

Her preparations complete, she lowered herself down atop his body and fitted him inside her. Then, with a practiced nonchalance, she attempted to earn her money.

Konrad, even in his dim state, responded to the pleasure and rode it out silently on gentle swells of warm stimuli. Her impassive, flat face was comforting to him because it belonged to a person who cared nothing for who he was or what he had done.

As the waves of passion neared their crest, Konrad closed his eyes to intensify the effect, but as the woman's face disappeared in darkness, another image entered the frame in his mind.

Now staring at him with a laughing face but with angry eyes was Willie Mac. "I see you're getting laid, Konrad," he said through lips that didn't move from a twisted grin. "Wish I could do that, but I'm dead, you know. The dead don't get laid. Give her one for me, too, will you, old buddy?"

Konrad tried to say something, but he could force no sound through his lips.

Willie Mac laughed, but again the twisted lips didn't move. "I might as well get going, Lieutenant, there's nothing for me around here; the dead can't get drunk or laid. Go ahead and have a good time, but I want you to remember one thing: What you took from me, you yourself will surrender. Everywhere you look you'll see your ugly, evil self."

Willie Mac laughed wildly and started to retreat. As he backed off, Konrad could see he was dressed in camouflage fatigues with dog tags jingling as he moved. Konrad tried to tell him to stay, that he wanted to explain things, he *had* to explain. But as Konrad advanced with arms outstretched in pleading, the laughing Willie Mac started to run. Konrad chased, came nearer, but couldn't quite catch up. Willie Mac ran to a small hill, stopped at the foot for a second to look back and laugh mockingly one final time, then raced to the crest and jumped into a hole.

Konrad ran up the hill to the foot of the hole. It was shaped like a grave and had a mound of earth on the side as though it were freshly dug. Konrad looked down and backed away in horror. There lay Willie Mac. His arms were solemnly folded across his chest and he now wore a neatly pressed dress uniform topped by a shiny helmet buckled under his chin. The smile was gone, and so was the face. What stared back at Konrad through eyeless sockets was a hideous mask of decayed flesh. The face moved, arranging itself into a pattern of a smile across Willie Mac's bare teeth. Konrad looked closer. The smile had been formed by masses of worms.

Konrad tried to scream but nothing came out. He finally forced his eyes away from the grotesque scene inside the hole, attracted by something shining at the head of the grave where the tombstone should have been.

He looked up and saw a light the brightness of which burned through his skull like a laser. He threw up his arms and staggered backwards until gradually he was able to look at it and saw a form take shape. When he saw it, he fell to the earth and sobbed.

It was a Silver Star, glowing with a ghostly luster except where it was crusted over with dried blood. The size was that of a tombstone, but there were no flowers at its base.

*   *   *

The girl had tried everything, and now she gave up. She dropped his flaccid penis, stood up and slipped the dress back over her head. She gazed impassively at the moaning, sobbing man lying on her pallet holding his arms protectively over his eyes. She had seen battle fatigue before and felt little sympathy. If men were stupid enough to try to kill each other, she couldn't worry about what happened to them.

She helped Konrad into his clothes and pushed him toward the door. When she saw that he was still in a daze, she slipped the wallet from his pants and removed the rest of the bills. "You go now, Death," she urged and gave him a firm shove past the blanket door.

She watched him lurch down the street, then turned away. The strange man with the name she had never heard before ceased to exist.

She couldn't have known—and wouldn't have cared— that the man who stumbled away into the distance was heading for a future where the years would pass in agonized slow motion, like a crippled man trying to run, and the pain would not pass at all.

Chapter Two

The prima ballerina is poised to float across the stage, a lithe beauty prepared to conquer difficulty with grace. The gossamer white costume drifts behind like wings of mist. Her face is serene with assurance. She knows that the whirling *tour en l'air* she is about to attempt is at the command of her skill. Her mood is enhanced by the subtle, glowing pastels surrounding her—flowers in her hair and at her waist, the orange haze of the footlight glow.

Honi Miller closed the book and her eyes and imagined the *L'Etoile* painting by Degas come to life. In the background, her stereo softly caressed the mood with the entreating violins of Mozart's *Les Petits Riens* ballet. With the ease of a wish, Honi became the ballerina.

Moments like this made all the work and struggle worthwhile. Her studies of the classics dominated her spare time, took her money and taxed her limited education, but Honi felt repaid when she could look at such a painting and whisper to the artist, "Monsieur Degas, I think I can feel what you must have felt. Thank you for sharing such a private thought with me."

Her reverie was broken by the rude jangling of the telephone.

"Hello, is this Honi?"

"Yes."

"My name is Horst. Do you remember Paul who visited you from Bonn a few weeks ago?" the man asked in a deep, hoarse voice.

"Yes," she answered guardedly.

"I'm a friend of his. He gave me your number. Are you free tonight?"

"I might be, what did you have in mind?"

"Well, I'm in town for a business meeting; it's been a good trip so I decided to give myself a treat tonight." He paused, then chuckled. "I was hoping you could be it."

"Did Paul tell you the size gift I require?"

"He also said you were worth it."

"Well, Horst, where would you like to meet and how much time should I allow?"

"Why don't we meet in the bar at the Cafe Royal at nine? Plan to stay the night. Unless Paul is a liar, this will be a real pleasure."

Honi switched off the stereo, abruptly enveloping the room in silence and changing the atmosphere to her frame of mine—businesslike and resigned. By the habit of long practice, she purged her mind of art, music, pleasure. She stripped off her blue jeans and T-shirt with the mocking slogan, "Innocence is a lost art," and stepped into the shower.

Honi emerged from the bathroom to stand in front of a full-length mirror. What the glass reflected was five-feet, eight-inches of gentle curves tanned to honey gold. The long legs were lean and athletic, but not a muscle interrupted the symmetry of softness that she knew drove men wild. The breasts were small and pert, the size experience told her men prefer in the flesh to the drooping, bovine kind they buy magazines to gaze at. The buttocks were small and tight, the blond hair thick and natural.

Any other woman so lusciously composed could be excused a time of lingering before her own image, but to Honi, this was cold, hard business. She was indifferent to what she saw, it was merely a product to be merchandised, and as such, had to be maintained in a marketable state. She loathed this body that had so cruelly betrayed her. If she could punish it with work that would, at the same time, give her the means to feed her intellect, then she wouldn't hesitate. She turned away from the mirror and toward the tools of her trade: perfume and a clinging silk dress.

The Cafe Royal was one of those enigmas so common in today's Europe. One would like to believe it was whisked across generations and placed here in modern Munich as a reminder of a more glorious day. The fact is, such a place represents as much accurate history as Mother Goose. Europeans know that, but American and Japanese tourists don't, and a firm rule of the tourism business is that you cater to the ignorance of the guy who pays the bills.

The restaurant's theme celebrated the Age of Napoleon with the requisite mural of the Retreat from Moscow as though poor old Boney never wanted to come in out of the cold, or even finish the trip. The antiques were authentic, and paid for by an extra twenty percent tacked onto an admittedly excellent French cuisine menu. Few Cafe Royal customers mentioned the irony of the name—Napoleon's career advanced over the severed heads of royalty. They were more interested in the parfait.

Honi had the method down pat: Stand in the doorway and look around. A beautiful woman does that unnoticed for about five seconds; Horst would find her.

The way he looked at her as he approached told Honi that this was Horst, friend of Paul, who was a friend of Michael, who was . . .

Honi felt a chill as she looked at the brute of a man who advanced toward her with a menacing smile on his face, but her professional smile ignited. "I hope you're Horst," she said giving the impression she had surveyed all the men in the room and settled on him as the one she wanted. She extended a hand limply and cocked her head in a coquettish manner.

He was huge, with features like a plow horse: bulky, bony, and built to be used. His face looked like the work of a sculptor in a hurry on a bad day—lantern jaw, overhanging eyebrows, thick lips, lumpy nose. But the eyes didn't fit the peasant mold, they were too alert, too moving. They were the eyes of a man who lived by guile, not brawn.

Dinner was eaten in an uneasy silence. Contrary to myth, conversations at such times are rarely clever or fun. Honi had developed an ability to talk interminably about the weather, cost of living, even sports, to men more often than not nervously preoccupied with the worry that, when the time came, they'd be a foolishly inadequate sexual partner for the beautiful woman at their table, or else guiltily fearful that their wives, priests or mother would suddenly walk through the door, even if they were hundreds of kilometers from home.

As soon as Honi put the last piece of steak between her lips, Horst suddenly blurted out, "Let's go."

Taken aback by his abruptness, Honi blankly asked, "Where?"

"To my room, of course."

"W-well, if you're ready."

Horst shut the door and poured himself a drink, ignoring Honi standing in the middle of the room. She didn't really mind the rudeness, considering it one of the drawbacks of the profession. Men who resent their wives, mothers, elderly aunts or whatever woman think a prostitute is a handy female on whom to take their revenge. Honi ignored their boorish behavior as long as they didn't try to hurt her. She wanted their money, not their manners. Speaking of which . . .

"I'd like my money now, please."

"What's the hurry, little lady?"

"The hurry is going to happen in about ten seconds when I walk out that door unless you cut out the games."

"Oh, hell, how much?"

"One thousand Deutschemarks."

"God, woman, I don't want to buy it, just rent it."

Honi often thought she'd scream if she heard that stupid comment one more time. Instead, she started for the door.

"OK, OK, here." He peeled off several bills and handed them to her. Before she could count the money, he unbuckled his pants, let them drop to the floor, and pushed his underwear down. He sat back in an easy chair and beckoned to her.

Even Honi, accustomed to the casualness of sex as she was, blinked in astonishment. "What do you want me to do?"

"Jesus, what kind of whore are you? Go down," he said, pointing to his erection which seemed to be waiting impatiently for Honi.

"Just like this?" she asked, gesturing to her clothing which was still completely in place. "Don't you want to get into bed?"

"Do it, goddamn it."

Honi knelt before him. She felt him tremble as she used both hands to caress, knead, stroke. She lowered her head. She knew tricks that would get this over with quickly. But while her hands and mouth were busy in well-practiced, mechanical motions, her mind was touring the Louvre. Tonight she was visiting the works of Cézanne. She was especially interested in his use of vivid greens in *The Bridge at Maincy*.

Her trance was broken by the quivering of the body in front of her. The quivering turned to spasms and was joined by a loud rasping of breath. Then, as he limply collapsed, it was over.

Honi closed the bathroom door behind her. As quickly as she could clean up, she intended to get out. There was something about this she didn't like, something she could feel but not identify. She laid half the money he had given her on top of the sink where he couldn't miss it. A refund for less than full value. As casually as she could, Honi left the bathroom and walked toward the outside door.

Horst's eyes followed her every movement. "Where do you think you're going? Our agreement was for the

37

whole night."

"I've changed my mind. You'll find half your money in the bathroom where I left it."

"Nothing doing. A deal's a deal. You're coming with me. There's someone else who wants to meet you."

Honi let her anger flash to mask the fear that was becoming stronger. This brute could crush her with one hand, and she sensed the requisite sadism. "Listen, you, I'm going to walk out of here right now, and if you try to stop me, I'll see you in jail for kidnapping."

Honi's hand closed around the doorknob, but as it started to turn, another hand, one much more powerful, also closed. On her throat.

Honi heard the muffled footsteps of her own death rushing up behind her. The rough fingers closed over the carotid artery, depriving her brain of blood and leaving her powerless to stop a descending curtain of darkness. The man ignored her clawing attempts to fight him off as a wolf would ignore the struggles of a rabbit in its jaws. He squeezed steadily. He was very good at this, but even so, he knew an extra instant's pressure would kill her.

Horst gathered Honi in his arms like a sleeping child and headed for the service exit, which, as expected for that time of night, was clear of people. There was nothing to keep him from the big black car that waited below in the alley.

Honi awoke to a view of blackness. It took a moment for her to realize that a hood was over her head and her hands had been tied behind her. A painful bite of the rope quickly proved the futility of struggle. "Help! Please let me go!" she screamed and pleaded.

"Shut up, bitch," the too-familiar voice of Horst demanded from the front seat. "The only thing your bellowing will do is piss me off, and I don't think that's a good idea right now."

"Where are you taking me? Turn me loose, and I won't say anything. Please." Every prostitute's fear of a brutal, sadistic death filled Honi's mind.

He laughed harshly, but apparently didn't think her bargaining deserved a reply.

After what seemed like an endless time driving, but must have been about twenty minutes, Honi heard a garage door open. The car turned in and stopped. After one door slammed and hers opened, rough hands lifted her out and she was guided up a flight of stairs, along what echoed like a long, bare-floor hallway, and finally into a room with thick carpeting.

No one said a word, but she felt someone undoing the rope around her wrists. Honi rubbed her numb arms and then tentatively lifted off the hood. All she could see were deep shadows in a room that was almost as dark as her hood had been. She heard a sound and turned in time to see a sliver of light and a heavy door being pulled shut by a huge, gnarled hand she had come to know. She heard a click and the whole room flooded with glaring, harsh light. She turned and winced as the bright floods beamed directly into her eyes and created a blinding barrier to her vision.

Total silence oppressed the room. Honi extended her arms and started groping clumsily for the same door she had seen Horst leave by, but a deep, gravelly voice stopped her.

"Good evening, Fräulein Miller. Please pardon the crude invitation, but I'm afraid it was necessary."

Honi whirled toward the voice, but the lights were a solid curtain beyond which she couldn't see. She didn't

39

move. "Who are you?" her voice quavered.

"A friend who wants to help you."

Honi's composure started to creep back. "For a friend, you have a very unfriendly way of introducing yourself."

"Please sit down and don't try to look into the lights, you'll be more comfortable that way. Try that chair to your right. It's three hundred years old; it belonged to Frederick the Great, but now it belongs to me."

Honi sat on the edge of the chair, hands folded protectively in her lap and legs tight together. "Why don't you turn off those lights so I can see? Why are you hiding?"

"For the protection of both of us. We don't need to see each other to conduct our business."

"What business? I don't know what you're talking about. Furthermore, I don't know why you had to kidnap me, and . . . and . . ."

He chuckled. "And why the sex, eh? Well it was Horst's night off and it seemed only fair to sweeten the pot, sort of like overtime pay. Besides, it reminded all concerned just who you are."

Anger flashed. "Listen, whoever-you-are, you may know *what* I am, but you don't know *who* I am."

"There's no difference."

"Like hell there's not. Now tell me what you want and then let me out of this nightmare."

His voice became crisp. "Very well, *fräulein*, how would you like to earn a million dollars, tax free, for doing next to nothing?"

Honi stood up abruptly, the chair skidding behind her. "This is a cruel game you're playing. The only thing I want from you is out of here."

There was silence for a long moment, then the

40

command came in a tone of ice. "Sit down." It wasn't harsh or loud, but the effect was so ominous that Honi did as ordered.

"Now, maybe we can talk business. I asked you if you would like to earn a million dollars; your response showed me that you don't think of yourself on that scale, but I assure you I'm completely serious—deadly serious. Now would you like to respond in a rational manner?"

Her subdued voice reflected his sudden dominance. "What would I have to do? People just don't give away a million dollars with no catches."

"The only catch is that I need you. You have knowledge of the place I intend to rob."

"Where is that?"

"Your homeland. With your help, some associates of mine could loot it for an amount that would make your million dollars seem like small change. What is your reaction to that?"

Curiosity and bitter memories lessened Honi's fear and she shrugged indifferently. "I assume you're asking if my conscience would bother me. Well, my conscience has been worn pretty thin the last few years; there's not much left. To be blunt—I couldn't care less."

"Good. I had reason to believe you would feel that way. May I take your response to mean yes?"

"Sure, why not?"

"Very well, let me tell you how you will become a rich woman."

The voice behind the lights spent several minutes telling an attentive Honi how his idea would unfold. As she listened, a picture developed of how the plan could work, and how she could become wealthy, both subjects of considerable appeal.

41

"Now, *fräulein*, I suggest you open that drawer in the table beside you if you'd like to see what one hundred thousand dollars looks like."

She did as directed and took out a bundle of fresh, green bills. She examined it with the wonderment and tenderness of holy writ. She finally started to return it to the drawer when the voice stopped her.

"No, not in there. Put it in your pocket. It's yours."

Honi hesitated only a moment then dropped the thick packet into her pocket and hugged it to her.

The man suddenly broke into peals of hoarse laughter. As Honi listened to the man's humorless, cruel mirth, the first small doubts crept into her mind.

Chapter Three

The penetrating persistence of the morning sun and the clatter of bustling San Francisco on the street below shook Konrad out of his snoring, dreamless, drunken sleep. He opened his eyes and squinted; the sourness of cotton in his mouth made him grimace with distaste. He thought of the relief promised by the mouthwash bottle in the bathroom and tried to think how he could make his confused, tired muscles carry him that far.

As he started to move, he saw her lying beside him. She was about thirty-five, sound asleep and snoring softly, her lipstick-smeared mouth hanging slackly open. Her mascara and makeup had smeared down her sallow cheeks making her look like a street mime just stepped out of a rainstorm. Konrad didn't know her name, her face, how she had gotten into his bed, even whether she had been any good—or, for that matter, whether he had been. All he had cared about were the few hours of oblivion the night of drinking had brought him; freedom from nightmares of the mocking face of a long-dead soldier was enough for him.

He climbed awkwardly but softly over her stretched-out body. He wanted to be fully dressed and half out the door before waking her to avoid as much talking as possible. Avoiding his and her clothes strewn haphazardly in the middle of the floor, he padded quickly across his bare studio apartment, or at least what was left of it after the creaky, old double bed took up its fifty percent of floor space.

Cursing silently but earnestly, he stubbed his bare toe against the leg of the cheap kitchenette table that, with the bed, a battered old desk and a misshapen, stained, overstuffed chair, left almost no room on the slippery linoleum floor.

He locked himself into the tiny bathroom with its rust-stained sink and dripping shower and luxuriated in the twin comforts of a gargle with Listerine and a long, first piss of the morning.

Konrad flushed the toilet and walked naked into the other room. She had just risen and stood in the middle of the room in her panties gathering up clothes. He looked at her flaccid breasts and skinny legs widening into hips made rubbery with fat deposits. Konrad turned away and climbed into his underwear. If sex was what had brought them together, it had beaten a hasty retreat and slammed the door on the way out. All he wanted from her now was goodbye, and hoped she wanted only the same.

"Can I use your bathroom?" she asked in a tinny voice with a faint Spanish accent.

"Help yourself," he said shortly and gestured with a toss of his head in the right direction as though it might otherwise be hard to find.

Wordlessly, she took quick, little steps and disappeared, and then only the sound of the shower reminded him of her presence.

Konrad went to the tiny refrigerator and opened a Coke and let it pour down his throat, the cold carbonation easing the wounds in his dehydrated system caused by the raging hangover. He leaned weakly against the kitchen wall and closed his eyes, willing his throbbing head to leave him alone. He heard the mailman noisily thumping through his duties in the downstairs hall and wearily went down to find out what bad news was being delivered to him today.

He sorted through the stack of mail as he pushed his reluctant legs back up the stairs. There was a bulky package that he quickly recognized as a rejected manuscript, hurled back by some jaded publisher in the stamped envelope provided by Konrad. Dirty, cheap bastards even use your own stamps to tell you to go to hell, he mused crossly. Without opening the envelope, Konrad knew the line: "Dear Mr. Konrad:" (with his name typed into the form letter) "Thank you for your submission. While your work has merit, it doesn't fit our needs at the present time. Thank you for considering us."

Well, the hell with 'em, he groused. What do they know about writing?

By the time he reached the door, all the bills and circulars had been sorted; Konrad didn't have money for either, so he threw them into the wastebasket, already half full with yesterday's unopened bills. There would be more tomorrow, too.

That left two letters. One, he could tell from the familiar handwriting, was from his mother. He tore the end off and let the contents slide out. As he expected, there was a check for five hundred dollars and a short letter. Resisting the urge to tear up the check in shame, he sat on the edge of the bed and started to read.

Dear Son:

Just a line to let you know I'm fine and thinking of you. I hope this finds you in good health. I know you probably don't need it, but I'm enclosing a small gift which would please me if it buys you something you would really enjoy.

I don't like to keep harping on it, but I would like so much to hear from you—postcard, phone call, anything that would tell me you're well and happy. Since your father passed away, you're all I have left.

I spend much of my time these days going through old scrapbooks and photo albums. Some might say that's a sure sign of old age, but I don't care. Since I can't have you here, it's what makes me happy. The other day I found an old copy of your Voice of Democracy speech. My! what an idealistic young man you were. I remember how proud I was when you won; I'm afraid I wasn't very modest about it.

I know the years since you left the Army have been difficult, but you can still live the dreams of your youth. I hate to meddle, but I wish we could talk. I don't have all the answers, but I'm pretty good at listening and understanding. Please, son, don't exclude me from your life.

Love, Mom

Konrad let the letter fall to the floor and leaned back with his eyes closed. Hell of a thing, he thought, to depend on your mother for charity in your mid-thirties. But, as he thought about the past few years, he realized his alternatives were zero. Fate hadn't been kind to Konrad. From bright beginnings, his life had tobogganed downward, gathering speed as the failures blurred by.

After he left the Army, political turmoil in the Third World had made the mercenary market bullish, so he had managed to catch on with various tin-pot dictators around the globe. He had been an advisor to General Pinochet's forces before they overthrew Allende in Chile. He had been recruited to try to help keep Samosa in power in Nicaragua. He had served a brief stint in Rhodesia while that country was still fighting black guerrillas. Africa was the source of most of the action for mercenaries, but Konrad found that the British had the choice assignments sewn up, and their cliquishness forced Americans to serve as non-coms in menial roles, something Konrad had difficulty adjusting to. He didn't fit well into such a highly politicized situation; he preferred danger to bullshit.

Konrad had gravitated to mercenary work because he was very proficient in the requisite skills and he had nothing else going. He was so reduced in self-esteem that dangers which would give long pause to most people drew only a shrug from him. But, contrary to popular myth, the pay for such work was meager and infrequent, and those one had to associate with, both employers and colleagues, were normally loutish, sadistic, stupid misfits, about as pleasant to be around as a whore with crabs. Gradually, and in disgust, he drifted out of mercenary work and into whatever was available—usually not much. At various times he found himself laboring as part-time bartender, aluminum siding sales-

man, security guard, and then the latest, most frus-
tratingly laughable of all, mystery writer. It seemed that
whatever he touched turned to shit and he couldn't get
the stink off his fingers.

Konrad's stormy mulling was interrupted by the
flushing of the toilet. He looked up, startled to suddenly
recall he was not alone, and watched the woman who had
occupied his bed walk out of the bathroom self-
consciously straightening her skirt. She walked over and
stood directly in front of him and looked down with big
brown eyes that seemed magnified with circles of fresh
black makeup.

"Hi," she said.

"Hi," Konrad replied matter-of-factly, as though
greeting a stranger who had just walked in from the
street.

"My name's Appalonia. That was Pola Negri's real
name. Ever see any of her old movies?" She stood
shifting from one foot to the other, waiting for a
response. When none came, she tried again. "That was
nice last night." When again there was no response, she
pushed the issue. "Did you like it?"

"Huh? Oh, yeah, that was nice."

"I'm a waitress, but I'm going to start beautician
school pretty soon. My sister has her own beauty shop,
and she says I have more talent for it than even she does.
What do you do?"

"I'm a writer—sometimes."

"A writer? How exciting. What do you write? Maybe
I've read something you've written."

"Eh, I don't think so. Look, er . . ."

"Appalonia."

"Right, Appalonia. Say, I've got to rush to an

48

appointment, so maybe some other time."

Taking the hint, she clutched her tiny purse and headed for the door. "Will I see you again?"

"Yeah, right."

"I work at the Blue Dolphin; get off at midnight. See ya." She gave a little finger wave and was gone.

Konrad sighed with relief and looked longingly at the unmade bed. As he shuffled toward its inviting comfort, he noticed the letter he had forgotten to open. He collapsed heavily onto the bed and ripped open the envelope. His hangover was completely forgotten as he scanned the brief, unsigned typewritten note on plain bond paper:

> Mr. Konrad, enclosed you will find a round-trip, first-class airline ticket between San Francisco and Frankfurt. It is for eight days after you receive this letter. That will give you sufficient time to renew your passport which, as you have probably forgotten, is in the bottom right-hand drawer of your desk. You will be met at Frankfurt airport by a man who will recognize you. Perhaps if you follow these instructions, you will be able to afford your own ticket next time.

Reading things about himself that only he should know made him look reflexively around the room for an intruder. He realized that someone was trying to dramatize their power over him—and doing a damn fine job.

His confusion about the letter led him to his favorite pondering place, Manny's, a smoky joint destined to be considered one thing or another: trendy or dumpy. It was

49

one of those ramshackle San Francisco saloons kept secret from the tourist crowds and thus reserved for the un- and not-very-successful writers, artists and actors who each day and night formed clusters in the small bar, the men's room, and any other place available to discuss the wrongs of the world—mostly as applied to them personally. The only problem with Manny's was that the Bohemian characters who populated it were as numerous in San Francisco as Custer's Indians. Had the place been located in Cincinnati, it would have achieved the privacy and charm one might expect from such a joint. But in San Francisco, Manny's was about as private as a McDonald's at noon. Only some select highly regular regulars and friends of Manny were guaranteed seating at the few postage-stamp tables that offered refuge from the shoulder-to-shoulder throngs that pressed against the bar.

If any footsore tourist attempted to sit at one of the tables, Manny himself would appear, as if by magic, and sternly advise the interloper that the tables were reserved. If the offending party argued that the table was vacant, Manny would bluntly tell him that he was confident of his ability to survive the economic pitfalls of life without selling said person one goddamn beer, and furthermore, why didn't that person remove himself or herself (chivalry had no reservation at Manny's) to one of the tourist traps where he wouldn't have to observe the time-honored traditions of the house?

That's what they invariably did.

Konrad arrived at about the normal time, which meant that Angus O'Callahan would already be bantering with the bartender, the cocktail waitress, Manny, or anyone else within earshot. O'Callahan was a loud, balloon-shaped, sweepingly mustachioed disc jockey for an obscure underground rock station. No one had ever heard his program, or talked to anyone who had, but then they could listen to him every day at Manny's with no commercials, so no one cared.

Konrad had been Angus' drinking companion since they discovered a mutual interest in German which both spoke. Angus said that he majored in German during college as a first step to eventually finding Hitler's buried treasure, which he claimed was hidden in a San Francisco bar, and he was determined to press his search until it was found.

Konrad once asked Angus what his real name was, and why he changed it. Angus had slowly sipped his Jack Daniel's, which he claimed contained magical medicinal qualities to prevent scurvy, and said solemnly, "I was the albino son of Idi Amin, former president-for-life of Uganda and currently planning a comeback. From an early age I was fascinated by torture and plunder so I decided to go into radio until Daddy's spot opened. My name in those days was Mickey Amin, but I changed it because I didn't want anyone saying I made it in radio only because of my old man. I choose Angus O'Callahan because Ryan O'Neal was taken and I didn't like Bernstein."

As Konrad approached the hulking figure from the rear, he could hear the stentorian voice trying to entice a young woman standing at the bar, at least twenty feet away. "How would you like to spend tonight with a man who has only forty-seven years yet to live?" he asked in mock pleading.

Angus was philosophic about his failure with women, even saw the humor in it. He learned very early that getting a girl to laugh was far different from getting her into bed. In a moment of self-examination, he had said, "I score about as often as a one-legged halfback. If they locked me in a phone booth with a nympho, I'd still come up empty-handed."

As Konrad took his accustomed seat at the table, Angus abruptly turned his back on the girl, to her amused indifference.

Another regular named Imogene, whose main concern in life was solving the world's hunger problems but who paid for her own TV dinners and margaritas by clerking for the Social Security Administration, came to the table brandishing a copy of an obscure magazine. "Look at this, Angus," she challenged. "You make fun of my idea about restricting everyone to a diet of two thousand calories per day and sending the surplus to the Third World, but it says right here that half the people of the world go to bed hungry every night."

Angus ignored the magazine thrust into his face and shrugged. "Name two."

As Imogene stomped away sputtering, Angus turned to Konrad with a palm-slapping gesture, "Hey, my man! What's the haps, baby? What's comin' down?" He had recently taken up black jive talk, saying he always had a feel for foreign languages.

"You won't believe what happened today," Konrad said, and proceeded to relate the arrival of the mysterious letter and its invitation.

When Konrad finished, Angus turned serious, as even he was capable of on rare occasions. "And you're wondering whether to go. Well, why shouldn't you? You don't write worth a shit, and you don't have any big publishers afraid you might be killed in a plane crash.

You don't have a family or friends other than here at Manny's, and even here, a lot of folks would like to have your regular seat. You don't really give a shit about anyone or anything, especially yourself. Konrad, old buddy, you don't seem to be going anyplace else, so why the hell not?"

"Ladies and gentlemen, we will be landing at Frankfurt International Airport in a few minutes. Please have your passports and customs declarations ready."

Konrad alternated his attention between the broad German plain below and the droning voice of the flight attendant as she mechanically repeated her announcement in the heavy, faltering accent that American airline companies consider acceptable German.

As Konrad extended his champagne glass for one final refill, the first-class attendant sized him up. She sensed an alert intelligence which was concealed by his plain appearance: early thirties; off-the-rack corduroy suit; slightly scuffed cheap shoes; the full-length average-guy look from his sandy brown, unruly hair, past the open, attentive Anglo-Saxon face with lively brown eyes, and down the six-two length of his slim, muscular build.

He wasn't especially handsome, but neither did he have any visible warts. But behind the friendly manner and crinkly, full-faced smile, she sensed a sadness, a tension that he wore like a pair of ill-fitting shoes— uncomfortable, but almost grown accustomed to. She decided this was not a man one could make snap judgments about.

The attendant did all this evaluating subconsciously and automatically, a mental game learned years ago to relieve the boredom of serving thousands of expense-account types, like this one, who travel first class when someone else foots the bill and who try to squeeze every last amenity out of the trip. Then the matter left her thoughts like so much passing scenery as she prepared for landing.

She was right, to a point. Konrad didn't ordinarily fly first class, and someone else was picking up the tab—the only difference in his case was he didn't know who, and he was about to be met by a stranger to whom he apparently was not.

The contact didn't happen until Konrad had claimed his single suitcase and turned toward the exit, wondering what to do next. The man quickly approached and asked brusquely, "Herr Konrad?" When Konrad nodded, the man allowed Konrad to pick up his own suitcase and then said, "Follow me."

Although the man was dressed as a chauffeur, Konrad could tell he wasn't by the alert shifting of the eyes, the stony silence, and the lack of the professional obsequious manner, and above all, by the tension that seemed to encircle him like an aura.

They rode for several minutes during which Konrad felt as much captive as passenger; he neither spoke nor was he spoken to. The man drove to the front entrance of the Airport Hotel and handed Konrad a key that said Suite 1560. Konrad took the key and got out of the car; he automatically started to reach in his pocket for a tip but the driver ignored him and roared away in a cloud of gasoline fumes.

The Airport Hotel was a short distance from the airport and had been created expressly to cater to the convenience and insensitive indulgence of gray-flannel

European and American accountants and salesmen who ply the skies and airports of the world, selling goods and collecting fees in a sterile existence of chrome and glass.

Konrad barely had a chance to hang up his spare suit and inspect the luxurious suite when the bedside telephone rang.

"Welcome, Herr Konrad. So glad you could accept my invitation. If you would be so kind as to come to my suite, number 1800, your curiosity—and your appetite—will be satisfied." The telephone clicked and the harsh voice was gone before Konrad had a chance to answer.

The door with the gold-plate scroll proclaiming 1800 in a flowing script opened seconds after his knock. A nasty-looking primate who must have weighed over two-fifty ushered him inside with a brusque nod that warned Konrad that the employer of this man was interested in duties more ominous than just opening doors politely. The man did not follow him into the room, but left quietly, closing the door softly behind him, and leaving Konrad standing by himself in the middle of the parlor.

The suite was elegant, obviously the best in the hotel. Although Konrad didn't often indulge personally, he at least could recognize dollar-quality, and this suite had lots of it. As Konrad scanned the rich decor, his eye was attracted to a sudden movement behind a translucent cloth screen set up in a corner near a large window. Staring at the screen, he could see the silhouette of a large man sitting with his back to the light, his mountainous bullet head pointed straight at Konrad. The outline of the man's body shifted and a voice so harsh it could have been filtered through sandpaper came through the screen.

Though Konrad could only see the man's dark outline,

he had the feeling the man could see him very clearly. The man gestured with a massive hand to a nearby chair and spoke in precise, formal German. "Thank you for coming, Herr Konrad. Please have a seat. I trust your trip was pleasant. If you're as enterprising as you used to be, I know you'll find it profitable. Go ahead and pour yourself a drink." He lifted his hand slightly, showing the outline of a glass. "I'm having cognac, which I know you don't like, but how about Dewars on the rocks which I know you most certainly do? The bar's over in that far corner."

Confused, Konrad mixed his drink and returned to the chair, waiting for the mystery to unravel. Through the screen, Konrad could see the dark glass go briefly to his host's lips; in his huge, fleshy fingers it looked like part of a doll set. The man gave a soft gasp of pleasure as he savored the liquor, then spoke. "Please forgive my staying behind this rather ridiculous screen, but as you'll discover in due time, it's for both our protection. I know there are many questions in your mind; let me see if I can provide some answers. First, you wonder how I know so much about you, your apartment, that you're fluent in German, what you drink, and your resources—or should I say, lack of them. That, I'm afraid, must remain a mystery. But don't allow the fact that I have the ability to learn such things escape your attention."

Konrad started to speak, but the man raised a massive hand to stifle Konrad's questions, and said, "Wait, I can tell you more, much more. You are a very interesting man, not a very effective one, but nonetheless interesting. You were born in the Bavarian city of Freiburg and lived there until the age of nine when your parents emigrated to America. You grew up in Connecticut where your father was a successful businessman and you enjoyed all the fruits of a comfortable but rather sheltered youth."

The German's monologue was interrupted by the silent re-entry of the hulking bodyguard/butler pushing a covered room-service cart which he abandoned in the middle of the room. He disappeared the instant the voice behind the screen said, "Thank you, Horst."

As Konrad hungrily smelled the delicious aromas escaping from beneath the covered trays, the German said, "As your host, I am pleased to offer you dinner. Let me remind you that cooking, like many other things, is done best in the fatherland."

Konrad uncovered the trays and gaped in amazement to see every one of his favorite dishes: schweinschnitzle, boiled potatoes, vinegar salad, strudel and a chilled Moselle wine.

As Konrad sat by himself in the middle of the room eating, the man continued. "As I was saying, you had all the benefits as a youth, including a fine education, especially in linguistics. You have an amazing ability to master the spoken word in whatever language you hear it. Not only did you recall German easily, you mastered most of the dialects that are so prevalent in our language, differing from section to section, from class to class. A German wears his dialect like a birthmark. Where he is from and the extent of his breeding and education are normally stamped on his speech like a tatoo. You, however, can jump from dialect to dialect as easily as a whore from sailor to sailor on a life raft.

"After college an army commission took you to Vietnam where you were decorated for valor. Next, you were stationed in Germany for three years, near this very city. You were as fine a soldier in the field as any

57

commander could desire. Your sense of combat was superb, both in comprehension and execution. In short, you were a damned fine soldier. Your only problem was you didn't spend all your time on maneuvers. On base, you specialized in cheating the United States government out of whatever it didn't have the foresight to nail down. For some reason, you went from the ideal officer in Vietnam to a total misfit in Germany, an overnight transformation for the worse."

Konrad shifted uneasily in his chair and started to protest, but the German's voice overrode his own. "The black market alliance you formed with the Frankfurt underground was a stronger bond than NATO, and worked twice as well. Unfortunately for you, your superiors caught on and your military career took an abrupt turn for the worse—worse for you, but better for the Army. After you were cashiered, they discovered that a lot of supplies stopped leaving."

The reference to his departure from the Army prodded a wound in Konrad's memory, and the sinister German voice dissolved into the nasal New England twang of Colonel Cavanaugh sitting behind the big oak desk framed by the U.S. and division flags a few feet to the rear.

"Come in, Captain Konrad, have a seat over there."

Konrad waited nervously as Cavanaugh finished signing a stack of papers and shuffling others. Konrad knew he was up for promotion and stared at the papers in Cavanaugh's hands, wondering if among them was an order creating Major Konrad, United States Army. He couldn't tell from Cavanaugh's manner; the man was an expert at turning his craggy face into a blank wall of inscrutability.

Konrad straightened in the chair as the colonel came around the desk and leaned against it. "Captain, as you're no doubt aware, you have been mentioned for a promotion to major." He glanced over at Konrad who nodded hopefully. The colonel cleared his throat and continued. "I have in my hand an order that affects you, but not in the way you expect. Let me just read a couple of sentences from the first page. 'And said Captain Konrad shall be remanded to the custody of the officer of the day until such time as a general court-martial can be convened to try him on the several charges of misuse of government property, grand theft, dereliction of duty. . . .' Shall I go on, Captain, or have you heard enough?"

Konrad stared at the colonel, speechless in the face of the charges he knew were true but had thought were undiscovered.

Cavanaugh paced the floor slowly. "The fact that you had the gall to actually expect a promotion instead of this—what you really deserve—is quite typical of you. You're incapable of associating duty and honor with your own conduct. From what I've been able to learn, you probably thought you deserved a promotion. And that's the shame of it, because if you weren't a thief, you *would* deserve a higher rank. Too bad you're not as good a man as you are a soldier; a more natural one never entered the Army."

Cavanaugh pointed to the ribbon on Konrad's chest. "Contrary to what you might be thinking, that Silver Star you earned in Vietnam won't help you. In fact, the Army's position is that it makes matters worse because you've disgraced one of the highest honors your nation can bestow."

Cavanaugh slowly shook his head. "I just can't understand it. You became a hero in Vietnam, and then you turn into one of the biggest shitheels in the Army. It's just like you suddenly lost all self-respect."

Konrad started to speak. "No, Captain, don't open your mouth; I'm not through." Cavanaugh looked at him sorrowfully. "What a goddamn shame. You had it all, boy: pleasing personality, liked by everyone, smart as they come . . . an instinctive soldier, one of the few. You could have gone far. But being a good officer requires another trait, one you don't seem to have—character."

The colonel leaned against the back of a chair directly in front of Konrad. He suddenly seemed older, more tired. "Mister, I've been in this man's army for over thirty years. I've seen them all: men whose rifles you wouldn't be fit to clean, others who would make even you seem a saint by comparison. I've known dishonest men; I've known cruel men, but all of them seemed to have some reason, some twisted rationalization, for acting the way they did. But you, you don't have a goddamn reason in the world except your lack of guts."

Konrad protested. "You can't call me a coward."

"There are different ways of being brave, and different ways of being a coward. You certainly wouldn't be a coward if an enemy pointed a gun at you, but when the enemy is yourself, then you fold like a yellow dog. You don't have the courage of your convictions. Hell, you don't have any convictions. When you have to choose between the right thing and your personal comfort or greed, the right thing always loses. You've made some bad choices, soldier, and you don't seem to give a damn."

Cavanaugh straightened as though he suddenly realized he was wasting his time. "Now, Konrad, I'm

60

going to be honest with you, a courtesy you haven't given the Army. The black-marketing charges against you are going to be tough to prove. It's possible a smart lawyer could get you off, but that's a chance we're willing to take."

Konrad sensed an opening. "Is there anyway a trial might be avoided, sir?"

Cavanaugh paced silently, letting Konrad's plea hang in the air between them. "Perhaps. If you gave us the names of the people who worked with you in the theft of Army property, all the supply sergeants, drivers, everyone who betrayed his oath as you did, if we were given such a list we might accept your resignation from the service and give you a less-than-honorable discharge."

Konrad paled. "You're asking me to be an informer, a stool pigeon."

Cavanaugh pushed a pen and paper toward him. "I have no doubt of your ability to rise to the task, if that's what's bothering you."

Konrad picked up the pen as though it were coated with a loathsome germ, but he slowly started to write. . . .

The harsh voice of the mysterious German shook the daydream out of Konrad's mind. "Herr Konrad, I expect your attention. I didn't bring you over here to let your mind wander."

"Sorry, but something you said reminded me of the past."

"I have no doubt. As I was saying, you invested your youth in the military, and what did you get out of it? An expertise in guns and black-market hoodlums. Neither of these things is frequently mentioned in newspaper employment advertisements.

"So, having no contacts in the American underworld, and no relatively safe opportunities to earn a dishonest dollar, you first turned to two-bit mercenary assignments, and then eventually to what else you *thought* you could do." He paused for dramatic effect, and then laughed. "Herr Konrad, you became a *writer*. The only difficulty with that decision is the painfully obvious and unalterable fact that you can't write worth a damn."

The resentment erupted in Konrad. "Now wait just a goddamn—"

"Herr Konrad," the man interrupted in a patronizing tone. "Don't force me to prove your incompetence with the written word. Although I have no intention of— what's the saying?—of putting you down, would you like me to recite some of your less flattering rejection notices? Do you remember the rejection of your manuscript, I believe it was called *Offshore Conspiracy*? As I recall, it—"

"Never mind," Konrad sighed. "I know it better than you. But if I'm such a klutz, why bother to gather all the information on me? Why waste your money bringing me over here? What possible value am I to you?"

The man didn't respond immediately. Through the screen, Konrad could see him pour more cognac and take a slow, pleasurable sip. "Ahhh, a good cognac is one of the true arts of Western civilization."

"The hell with the booze; I asked you a question, whatever-your-name-is," Konrad snapped.

The man froze behind his screen and Konrad could feel his eyes bore into him. "We must understand each other. Although I appreciate your apprehensions at this very unusual encounter, you must realize there are certain persons whom you cannot address in such a manner. I am such a person.

"I have selected you for this assignment—provided you approve, of course—because of certain traits that recommend you: You have no family except an aging mother; no ties of any kind; there's no one who would be curious about your whereabouts or activities. Except for your drinking companions in that disreputable San Francisco bar, and a literary agent who might temporarily notice you were no longer pestering him, you are quite alone. You are a military tactician of rare talent. You are expert in the language and customs of Germanic peoples. You are a failure at what you are now doing with no prospects for a change of fortune.

"You have in the past displayed a sufficient amount of dishonesty to demonstrate that you place gain above honor. Finally, you are intelligent enough to carry out the plan I may reveal to you, but not intelligent enough to conceive it."

"Where is all this leading?" Konrad demanded.

"Patience. Herr Konrad, I am about to give you the opportunity to say yes or no to the chance to become a multimillionaire. If you say no, then fine, you are free to leave. If you say yes, you will be given the means to make your success probable. But first allow me to observe that I believe you are bright enough to realize that if you ever breathe a word of this meeting or any subsequent to this, you are, at that moment, a dead man. And I think you know enough already to believe that."

"What—"

"One other thing, Herr Konrad. Assume that I am an unscrupulous man in pursuit of what I desire. Assume further that I am a very deadly man when anyone tries to keep me from those desires. I suggest you think about my nationality and where and from whom I might have learned such qualities. I say this so you know you're not dealing with an amateur, nor are you dealing with a man of pity.

"Now to the point. What I offer you is an opportunity to make two million dollars tax-free plus expenses. It could be dangerous, but possibly not at all. I would calculate your chance of success at about two out of three. In the event of failure, the chance of escaping with your life and freedom intact would be slim. What do you say?"

"What do I say about what?" Konrad asked blankly.

"Do you accept the assignment?"

"What assignment? I don't know what the hell you're talking about."

"Let me spell it out for you," the man replied in a patronizing tone. "You don't really think I would give you details in advance of your acceptance? If I were to do that, and then you refused, well, don't you see, I'd have to have you killed. No, the decision you must make is whether you want the job with the rewards and risks I have described. You must answer one way or the other with no further details. If you answer no, you may leave immediately, but if you answer yes, you are staking your life on carrying it out to the best of your ability. I await your decision."

Konrad nodded, put his face between his hands and stared at the carpet. On the one hand, he thought, this guy is bad news. He had come to the obvious conclusion that he was an ex-Nazi, and probably a damned efficient one with friendly fellow ex-Nazis throughout Germany and the world, ready to obliterate suckers like himself at the crook of a finger and the point of a gun. This was indeed pretty fast company.

On the other hand, what did he have to lose? He didn't think much of his own life and no one else seemed to either. If you're going to live a shitty life, might as well live it in comfort. Besides, there were some assholes in his past he'd like to show a thing or two about what he could do.

Konrad leaned back in the chair, removed a cigarette and lit it with his very best steady hand. He exhaled the first puff slowly, looked directly toward the screen and calmly said, "I accept."

"I congratulate you, Herr Konrad. You have taken a very big first step toward becoming a comfortably rich man, and in the most supportive of company, I might add. Now let me tell you of your assignment."

The man paused for a long moment, as if to make a final assessment of his choice, then spoke slowly, like each word was weighed down with sandbags. "Herr Konrad, I want you to take over a country."

Konrad stared uncomprehending, the whole concept outside his frame of reference. "Take over a country? You mean a *country*, with a government . . . an army . . . ?"

"Precisely, and don't look so stunned; what I propose is perfectly feasible. I want you to take over Liechtenstein. You will be the next ruler of the Principality of Liechtenstein—in a manner of speaking."

Konrad scanned his memory for the few things he knew of Liechtenstein. A tiny country just a few miles south of his birthplace in southern Germany, he could imagine it on a map of Europe tucked between Austria

65

and Switzerland. He knew the country was German in language and customs, but knew little else. Actually, *nobody* knew much about Liechtenstein. He had driven through a couple of times, but paid little attention and the memories were vague.

The German sensed his thoughts. "Don't feel bad if you don't qualify as a Liechtenstein expert, very few do. However, your education is about to undergo a dramatic improvement. Unfold that map on the table, please."

Konrad unwrapped a large map and spread it over the table. "Confused?" the German laughed from behind his screen. "You are looking at Liechtenstein. Very few persons ever see it like this. Usually all they see of this tiny land on a map is a black dot to the east of Switzerland. But look at it for a moment." He paused to give Konrad time to study the map. "See, the country is very narrow, with the Rhine River on the west bordering Switzerland, and the Alps on the east next to Austria. The whole country is about twelve miles long and only three or four miles wide in its inhabitable valleys."

Konrad took in the details easily and rapidly because of his military map-reading training. The German continued with a steady stream of data about Liechtenstein. "There are about twenty-three thousand residents, but only about sixteen thousand are citizens. The rest are foreign workers, mainly Swiss and Yugoslav. The country is ruled nominally by a crown prince named Frederick, but real power is vested in the parliament, called the *Landtag*, and a prime minister.

"Liechtenstein is oriented toward the West, but is officially neutral. In fact, Liechtenstein is an expert among countries at remaining neutral. It hasn't been involved in a war for more than one hundred years, and has no army whatsoever. Also, it has no defense treaty with any country."

The German droned on with his recitation about the makeup of Liechtenstein as though he were a professor and Konrad his pupil. "Although Liechtenstein is completely independent, it does have a treaty that permits Switzerland to conduct its foreign affairs and manage foreign trade and customs. One can freely enter the country through Switzerland, but there are Swiss customs guards at the Austrian border crossings. These are the only armed Swiss officials stationed in the country, and they have no police power other than customs."

Konrad resumed his seat and listened intently as the German droned on. "Don't misunderstand the significance of the treaty with Switzerland. It is a convenient working arrangement, nothing more. A few years ago, a Swiss army patrol mistakenly wandered onto Liechtenstein territory for a few hundred meters. All hell broke loose, as you Americans would say. Liechtenstein demanded, and received, a full apology. They are, indeed, very jealous of their sovereignty."

Konrad was listening but not hearing much that made sense to him. "This is an interesting travelogue, but you don't just walk into a country and take it over. What makes you think the police, or the Swiss army for that matter, wouldn't just throw my ass in jail like a Saturday night drunk? I've heard of some far-out schemes, but this—"

The German's voice hardened. "Don't patronize me. To flippantly pass judgment on what I am suggesting is to presume greater knowledge than my own. Are you prepared to make that assumption?"

Konrad's silence provided the answer, and the German continued. "There are, of course, many other details, but those you will be learning for yourself. Now, I'll explain the strategy that will make all this possible. Assume for a moment that you controlled the Russian or East German foreign ministry or intelligence operation. What would you desire above all things? I'll tell you. You would want a puppet state in the heart of Western Europe. One from where you would have freedom to monitor activities of NATO nations surrounding you, and to serve as a base for propaganda and espionage assaults.

"Therefore, if you were to receive an out-of-the-blue plea from a tiny nation in Western Europe that suddenly announced a leftist takeover and appealed for your protection, what would you do? Would you turn your back on that appeal and leave those valiant revolutionaries at the mercy of their capitalist neighbors? Of course not. In the name of socialist brotherhood you would jump to their defense and warn all others away. All out of ideological comradeship, of course."

The German recited his strategy non-stop and confidently, as one well-rehearsed and confident of his reasoning. "And if you were the Swiss, or the Austrians, or the West Germans, or the British, or the Americans, would you risk a confrontation with the Soviet Union and the Warsaw Pact nations over a tiny pinpoint on the map? Of course not, at least not for a few days until you had the opportunity to fully assess the situation. And a few days, Herr Konrad, is all you will need."

"Need for what?"

"To conduct the most lucrative, daring raid on a nation's wealth that has ever been attempted by a private band. You, Herr Konrad, are going to rob Liechtenstein blind. You are going to strip her of her national wealth and proudest possessions." The German's voice grew excited in a fervor of greed. His voice came in a rasping whisper. "You are going to redefine international piracy."

The German became quiet to regain his composure and continued more matter-of-factly. "Your primary goal will be one of the great art collections of the world, the heart of which are twenty-four works of Peter Paul Rubens, the great Flemish master. You will also raid the two banks located in the capital city of Vaduz and the stamp museum, also located there. Your secondary targets will be additional works of art and the files of several key lawyers."

"What's the big deal about a bunch of stamps?" Konrad asked.

"Some of the world's most rare and valuable stamps are in the stamp museum in Vaduz. One of the very profitable industries of Liechtenstein for years has been the limited production of unique postage stamps. In that museum are kept the most rare and valuable of all. I want those stamps; they're worth a big fortune."

"Why would anyone pay for hot stamps he wouldn't be able to show anybody?"

"My dear Konrad, to answer that you must understand the mind of the dedicated philatelist, or as you would call him, stamp collector. He is a slave to the stamps he doesn't have. The pursuit of them dominates his soul. He worships gummed gods about an inch square. There are men who would give sizable fortunes to possess the stamps held in Liechtenstein's museum for even one day. To own them completely, they would give their wives, maybe even their lives.

"Whoever might possess those stamps would be the greatest stamp collector in the world. Being able to show them to others would be almost incidental. It would be sufficient for the collector himself to know he possessed them."

Konrad was slightly amused. "Hell, I'll be more appreciative the next time I mail a letter."

The German continued talking like a shopkeeper describing his wares, but in reality, he was describing what art connoisseurs the world over have come to regard almost as a shrine—the Liechtenstein art collection. Dating from the fourteenth century, the collection grew slowly and discriminately. The ancestors of the crown prince used exquisite taste, vast sums of money and an acute sense of cultural history to compile the staggering array of genius and beauty that Frederick had decided to share with his countrymen and visitors in a small museum in the center of Vaduz.

The German directed Konrad to a colorful brochure lying on a table top. "That folder is a tourist's guide to the museum. I've marked the art objects I want, mainly the Rubens, but also works by Raphael, Bassano, Tintoretto and others. Understand that many of these are quite large and will have to be crated. Crated very carefully, I might add.

"Attached to it is a list of six international companies. I want the files of those companies. They are kept in the offices of the two Vaduz firms noted on the list. Memorize and destroy this paper immediately. It is not so innocent looking as a musuem tourist's guide."

Konrad scanned the list with a puzzled look. "What's so valuable about a bunch of legal files?"

"Herr Konrad, too bad you wasted your time stealing

things like cigarettes, gasoline and tires. The finer things available to steal completely escape you." As with all the German's humor, it was short-lived. He quickly returned to the subject. "Liechtenstein is a haven for foreign corporations in much the same way Delaware is in the United States. I have reason to believe—in fact, I know—that the files I have indicated contain confidential information that would greatly embarrass those companies. So much so that they will buy them back at considerable expense to themselves, and considerable profit to me.

"As for the banks, that speaks for itself. The amount of cash on hand varies, as with all banks, but you should find a substantial amount of gold bullion in the vaults of the National Bank of Liechtenstein. Get it all."

"How am I supposed to do all this, and what do I do it with?"

"How you do it is up to you, you're the expert. All I ask is that you deliver it to me at a designated place in Germany. Speaking of that, I assume you'll remove it from the country by helicopters?"

Konrad thought for a few moments, rapidly computing in his mind what he knew of the terrain of Liechtenstein, and the distances involved. "I'll need plenty of men, so helicopters are out. I couldn't get ones big enough to do the job without attracting attention." He thought a moment longer, then plunged ahead. "I'd say use DC-3s. You know, the old American transport plane from World War II. There are a lot of them still being used by air freight companies and small charter outfits."

"Unfortunately, Liechtenstein has no airport."

Konrad flashed a smile, this was his end of the game and he was starting to get into it. "Let me worry about things like that."

The German didn't like being kept in the dark, but he could hardly question Konrad at this point after lauding his status as an expert. Instead, he chose to change the subject. "When do you think would be a good time to act?"

Konrad picked up a small calendar next to the telephone and studied it. "One thing's certain, we'll have to have a large number of personnel involved. That means time will be necessarily short. The more who know of an operation, the less time you have before rumors start to leak."

Konrad concentrated on the calendar, leafing pages back and forth until he seemed satisfied. "Let's see, this is the end of October. I think around Christmas would be the best time. People tend to relax during a holiday, and the tourist traffic would be at a minimum during winter, right?"

The German roared with laughter. "Let's give Liechtenstein a Christmas present: a new government, led by none other than Crown Prince Konrad."

Konrad waited patiently for the laughter to die down. "One thing I want to get straight is that this has to be done my way. I don't want a bunch of second-guessing and you looking over my shoulder."

"Herr Konrad, do I seem so amateurish that I would hire an expert and then tie his hands? No, you do the job right and you'll never even know I exist until you deliver the goods."

"And where is that to be?"

"There is a small, abandoned airfield two kilometers north of the village of Karlsfeld in Bavaria. That's where you'll bring the loot. When is the only question. An hour before you fly out of Liechtenstein, send this radio message: 'Every possession implies duty.' That's from a Rockefeller, appropriately, and it'll also remind you of your obligation. Once that is transmitted you can expect to find me at the Karlsfeld airfield."

"Sounds simple enough. Now, one other thing: I'll need a new identity to use for the operation."

"Why not use your real name?"

"Now just a minute," Konrad protested.

"For this reason," the German's voice overrode Konrad's objection. "When this is over, there will be no concealing your real identity. You'll be an international celebrity, the most wanted man in the world. It makes much more sense to create a new identity *after* the raid is over, that way you can spend your millions in peace and anonymity. With your contacts in the German under-ground, a fake I.D. should be simple."

"OK, I'll buy that," Konrad agreed, "but another thing I want to make clear is that I don't want to be followed everywhere I go by any of your boys. You either trust me or you don't."

"Herr Konrad, my contacts are so extensive that I don't have to rely on anything so clumsy as a 'tail.' I'll know what you're doing without that. No, if you see someone following you, it won't be one of mine."

Konrad nodded with satisfaction. Then his look turned slightly quizzical. "The stuff you described must be worth an incredible fortune. How do you know I won't double-cross you? I could just take it all and split, right?"

The German was quiet for a moment. "There are two reasons why you won't do that. One, you wouldn't live long enough to get the least bit of satisfaction out of such treachery. Two, you couldn't dispose of what you had stolen from me. What would you do with Rubens' *The Dedication to Death*, run an advertisement in a newspaper? I can just see it: 'For sale, one painting, very old, by well-known artist. Priced below market value. Call this number after five.'"

Konrad held up both hands and waited for the German's laughter to subside. "OK, OK. But more important from my standpoint, how do I know you won't double-cross *me*?"

"Because I'm very professional and businesslike in this line of work. I won't deny that I have no scruples against cheating you, none at all. But in this case, I would be foolish to try to cheat you out of a comparative pittance that might risk the whole thing. When we get to the point of payoff, that will mean everything has gone smoothly. I won't risk a foul-up at the edge of success. You can trust me, because a smooth ending to this affair will mean a very happy ending—for all concerned."

Konrad knew that was all the assurance he would be given. He had to trust this strange man, not the most comforting of thoughts. "OK, I can live with that—I hope. But how about money? This little party is going to be expensive."

"As I said, money will be no problem. Two million dollars for expenses has been deposited in a numbered bank account in Zurich. That's your budget. I'll give you the account number which you must memorize and destroy. Also, a dummy corporation has been established for whatever use you may find necessary. It is called Trans-Europe Oil Corporation, and you are its president. Congratulations. When you deliver the loot from Liechtenstein, you will be paid two million dollars; your partner will receive one million."

74

Konrad interrupted in alarm. "Wait a minute, you didn't say anything about a partner."

The German picked up a telephone and spoke into it. "You may come in now."

Konrad had opened his mouth to protest, but it snapped shut when he looked toward the door. Staring suddenly became more important than talking.

Honi Miller recognized the look on the stranger's face; she had seen it on the faces of more men than she cared to count. But this time she didn't mind what her own eyes saw in return. He was tall, slim and young with alert brown eyes set in an angular face that featured a crooked nose that looked pushed slightly off center. He was dressed cheaply, but with care. He struck her as a guy who wasn't doing too well, but was still giving it his best shot.

Konrad couldn't—didn't want to—stop staring at the tall blonde suddenly standing before him. She was about thirty, slim but curvaceous, in the way of Bacall in her prime. Her mouth was full, but perhaps a little wide for her nose, a small imperfection that seemed to add to her beauty. Most interesting were her eyes, not because they were smoke gray, but because they returned his stare unblinkingly.

The German broke the spell. "Herr Konrad, this is your partner; please meet Fräulein Miller. The *fräulein* will work with you in the activities you are about to undertake."

Konrad spoke to the woman. "I'm sorry, *fräulein*, but this is the first I knew you existed. I still don't understand how you're involved."

She opened her mouth to speak, but the German responded. "Fräulein Miller is a native Liechtensteiner who at present is somewhat at odds with her native land. She knows the country and she knows the objective, and she knows she will suffer the same penalty for betrayal. She is your ticket to Liechtenstein." The German's tone grew lighter and he snickered. "Now, I have the honor of introducing Herr Konrad and Frau Konrad, husband and wife, young lovers returning to the bride's homeland to pursue the soon-to-be brilliant success of the young husband's writing career."

The German's snicker turned to a snorting laugh. "I now leave you two to your life together. May we all live happily ever after."

Realizing they had been dismissed, Konrad politely guided Honi by the elbow and started for the door. Knowing nothing else to say, he lamely added, "Well, I guess I'll be seeing you."

"No," the German replied, "I'll be seeing *you*."

Konrad thought the elevator would never arrive, so awkwardly conscious was he of the woman waiting patiently at his side. Both concentrated on the ascending light of the elevator floor indicator, using it as a diversion for the uneasiness that enveloped them.

Konrad tried to break the ice. "Uh, let's get a drink— or two or three. And since we're going to be married, it seems, we might as well get acquainted."

She stared at him icily. Honi was quick to anger when she thought a man was dictating to her. "Don't get carried away with that marriage idea."

"Sorry," he answered contritely. "I didn't mean it that way. It's just . . . well, in one afternoon I've had an entire country and a beautiful woman thrown at me. The whole thing requires some getting used to."

To his relief, the elevator arrived and he pushed the button for the penthouse bar.

After the waiter took their drink order and left, Konrad smiled and lifted his hands in a bewildered gesture. "Well, here we are, just met and already we're partners. I can only assume you're as trustworthy as I am."

"Funny, but I was thinking the same thing. It seems we've become pretty dependent on each other."

Konrad nodded. "Our host back in that suite said you had a falling out with Liechtenstein. What did he mean by that?"

"I'd rather not say; it's nothing for you to be concerned about."

The tension both were feeling made Konrad react peevishly. "Nothing for me to be concerned about? For chrissakes, woman, I'm literally putting my life in your hands and you say it's nothing for me to be concerned about. We'd better get a few things straight."

Honi compressed her lips in anger, but she knew he had a point. "Look, let's just say it was a misunderstanding about a medical problem. It concerned no one that you'll have to be involved with; if it did, I'd tell you, OK?"

Konrad wasn't completely convinced, but he nodded and changed the subject. "Let me ask you something: Are you aware of how dangerous this could be?"

She sensed a challenge and replied defensively. "I think I have an idea."

"Have you ever been shot at, or have you even shot a gun?"

Her expression answered the question, but she came

77

right back. "As I understand it, you can hire people to do those things. My job is to provide you with a base of operations inside Liechtenstein. That's something no gunman could do."

"I'm just trying to give you an idea of the kind of people you'll be dealing with. What do you know of mercenaries?"

"Just that they're soldiers for hire. What else is there?"

"Plenty. The mercenary movement has become one of the better growth industries of recent years. These are men—and some women—who've developed a specialty of taking from others what those people don't want to give up. Sometimes they resist, and that's where the mercenary's real value comes in: He's very good at killing people. Now, killing is a time-honored profession, to be sure, but you don't meet many of the tea and crumpets set among people who do it for a living. When your profession primarily means being prepared to blow someone's brains out, it's bound to affect your personality. Unless you're familiar with the type, being around them can be a bit disconcerting and definitely dangerous."

Honi wasn't terribly impressed. In her line of work, catering to men not known for their gentility was an everyday occurrence. "I think I can take care of myself, but tell me, why is the mercenary business so big all of a sudden?"

Konrad gradually relaxed; he was now in his element. "It's the old principle that a vacuum never goes unfilled. In this case, it's the power vacuum. With so many new and weak countries being established in the Third World, there are lots of governments that don't have the know-how or strength to rule. When that happens, there's always someone with the money and guts to make a power grab. They go out and hire some professional soldiers—you'd be surprised at how few it takes to get the job done—and take what they want. Where you have strong governments, you don't have mercenaries. It all comes down to the fact that when you have something valuable and attractive, and you can't defend it, there are always people around very happy to take it from you; it's as simple as that."

"What kind of people are they? The mercenaries, I mean."

"All kinds, some are the salt of the earth, some the scum of the earth."

"Are you a good mercenary?"

"I have been, but it's a business where yesterday's victories won't keep you alive today."

The conversation drifted to Liechtenstein, and Honi spent a leisurely two hours describing details of her homeland that she hadn't thought of consciously for years. She found herself enjoying the task, and the frequent visits of the waiter bringing fresh drinks attested to the growing ease with which they regarded each other's company.

As the liquor warmed and relaxed him, Konrad found himself looking at Honi more than listening to her. The soft lights of the cocktail lounge heightened her beauty and made him doubly aware of how desirable a woman she was.

It was an old story to Honi. More than once she had seen a combination of liquor and her ability to excite men create the same effect it had on Konrad: an obviously lagging interest in the conversation; appreciative glances at her body; bold, sustained eye contact. She had seen it all before. She also knew that if they were to have a successful partnership, the sexual tension would have to be dealt with. Konrad's male curiosity and urge to conquer would have to be eliminated, or at least temporarily satisfied.

Honi suddenly looked boldly and suggestively at Konrad. Their eyes locked in mutual searching. She smiled demurely and reached over and softly ran her finger along his arm. "Haven't we discussed enough business for one day? I'm tired of this. Why don't we have some champagne sent up to your room?"

Konrad's mouth fell open as though she had been reading his thoughts, which of course she had. He spilled what remained of his drink, started to mop it up with a napkin, then glanced again at her and abandoned the effort. He stood up unsteadily and said, "Today is too unreal, it didn't happen. But just to be sure, I'll give it one more chance." He reached for her arm and they headed for the elevator.

In his room, with the door closed behind them, both dropped their posturings and stared directly at each other. Each realized they were now confronting, not a situation, but each other. They were two strangers thrown into intimacy like a small boy tossed into a pond to teach him how to swim.

Konrad thought of saying something to put her at ease, to bridge the clumsy span between stare and caress. He had the words formed in his mind, but they never found voice. Instead, his hand slowly reached for her face as though it acted independent of his thoughts. In fact, his mind was a partner to the act, focused on the softness of her blond hair and the soft white down on her full upper

80

lip above an open mouth.

As she slowly stripped, he stood with mouth agape as her luscious body was gradually revealed to him. The firm breasts and long, slim legs converging in a tawny triangle made his desire a thing of sweet pain demanding to be soothed. He reached for her.

Honi did nothing, simply stood awaiting his pleasure. The only change was a softening of the eyes; they no longer glinted with gray purpose, but focused over Konrad's shoulder, transporting her to another place, another time when this same scene was enacted, but with more meaning, with a man who was not a stranger, and with a feeling that she was certain she would never know again.

She was a superb actress. She had learned that what most men want from a woman during the act of love is a statement. A statement expressed usually by sighs, gyrations and paroxysms of passion, each reaffirming their manhood.

Honi regarded herself as a fortress which had often been scaled and assaulted, but never conquered. She had prevailed out of willpower and because she had mastered her feelings. No man had ever stormed the battlements of her mind, no man had ever surmounted the barricades of callus with which she had surrounded her psyche like a moat.

Honi was in control. Almost. As this strange and unfamiliar body heaved and thrust into her, a crack appeared in the wall of her indifference, and as she slowly encircled his back with her arms, her lips formed a name and repeated it silently, over and over. . . .

Afterwards she slept. Konrad got out of bed and slipped into a robe. He paced the floor and tried to analyze the events of the past few hours. "I guess there's no point in trying to figure out how I got into this, since I can't get out of it," he mumbled.

On an impulse, he picked up the phone and dialed the hotel operator. "Hello, this is Herr Konrad in 1560. I was just dining with the gentleman in Suite 1800 and wanted to send him a thank you note, but I'm not certain how to spell his name. Would you spell it for me, please?"

Konrad could hear the operator shuffling papers. "I'm sorry, sir, you must be mistaken, no one's in Suite 1800. It's vacant."

"No, operator, there's a man staying there," Konrad attempted to argue.

"I'm sorry, sir. Goodbye."

Konrad looked curiously at the dead receiver. He suddenly felt a chill and removed the robe and climbed back into bed. He looked down at the sleeping Honi. Who is this woman? he wondered silently. My life may depend on her, and I have no idea who she is.

If Konrad could have joined Honi at that moment on the passage of her dreams, back to that yesterday place of enduring pain, he might have understood.

Chapter Four

It is scenery from which travel posters and Alpine fairy tales are made. The rocky fields overlook a silver, shimmering river far below. The green undulation of the pastures rolls upward toward craggy, snow-tipped peaks. Fat cows graze lazily in fields spotted with white and red barns and bordered by fences constructed from the gray granite lying in the fields.

It was to such a scene that Honi Miller's dream returned her, to a little farm near the mountain-side village of Planken, Liechtenstein.

She was the only child of industrious Catholic farmers, good people who weaved hard work and rigid faith into a fabric of life that, though it wasn't colorful, proved durable to the demands of their environment.

Village society of Liechtenstein offers a sheltered life with clearly defined boundaries and directions for social conduct, ambitions and beliefs. The unwritten philosophy is of contentment, frugality and, above all, fitting in, belonging. Most of those born into this setting slip gradually and easily into the life style and mind-set. Oh, certainly, young men are expected to foray on Saturday nights across the Rhine into Switzerland or up into Germany to taste the fruits and spill the seeds of youthful exuberance. But wistful tolerance quickly turns into stern disapproval if such conduct is brought back home.

Young women are not so liberally indulged. Perhaps this is out of a belief that liberality toward women, possible in an urban society, would be unworkable here. Survival in a small, closed society depends heavily upon clearly understood rules, and the avoidance of situations that may give rise to passions that could threaten the social order. The Liechtensteiner may read dispassionately of the liberated women of London or New York, but to him it is a foreign thing, never to be imported. To him, a permissive or free-thinking neighbor living just down the street would be a daily threat to him, his family and the community. And in his protective society that still denies women the vote, the ideas of feminism would challenge the roots of his power.

Not everyone adjusts—Liechtenstein is near the top in per capita suicides, the departure of willful spirits who find the prospect of going along more painful and frightening than leaving forever.

Societies everywhere are like herds of wild beasts, protective of the inner circle, finding comfort in massed numbers, quick to cull from the group those who don't keep up or those who stray. There is no compassion to survival, and survival is the ultimate purpose of any society.

This was the world into which Honi Miller was born, a blond child of the mountain meadow, a long-legged tomboy nurtured on the freedom found in the fields and

the open curiosity in her bright mind. Heidi of the Alps.
But a real Heidi with a desire to reach out and touch.

Frau Miller rustled mechanically about her sun-filled
kitchen performing three functions independent of each
other: her hands preparing breakfast for her small
family, her eyes looking out the window at her husband
performing his morning chores, and her mind wondering
how best to talk about womanhood to her daughter.

"Honi," she began hesitantly, "I'd like to talk to you."

"OK, Mama, what about?" The tall girl turned toward
her mother with the bounce that comes so easily to an
eighteen-year-old filled with the energy of life-
anticipation, even at seven in the morning.

"Honi, baby," the mother began, using the endear-
ment after the girl's name as she did only when feeling
especially close to her daughter. She sat at the kitchen
table and gestured to Honi to take the chair opposite. "I
thought we could have a little chat about your future.
Have you made any plans yet?"

A little wary of her mother's manner, Honi answered
cautiously. "Not really, at least not in the way I think
you mean."

"Well, you're eighteen now, and it's time to be
thinking about it. Sometimes your papa and I worry that
you aren't as serious about things as you should be."

"Such as?"

"Things like settling down and beginning a family.
When I was your age—"

"Mama, you're not me," Honi interrupted in exasperation. "I just want to be young for a while, that's all. Why

85

should I rush into something I'm not ready for? Heck, you can always get married."

Honi's mother groped for words, searching for a way to tell her daughter of the lessons that life had taught her. "Dear, we live in a small place, very close to other people, and it's not wise to be too different. A farm girl your age is expected to show some interest in the right values and not be so rebellious." Seeing the hurt look of surprise on her daughter's face made the mother reconsider. "Well, not rebellious, you're too good a daughter for that." The mother, searching for the elusive right words, looked out the window at the scenes she could best relate to. "You're like the *fohn*, the strong wind that blows down from the mountains. Or like that frisky young calf running around the pasture, just doing what she wants, letting her whim lead her. But calves grow up to become milk cows. And that's what I'm trying to tell you; it's time to get serious about life. You're a very headstrong girl, and a lot of people think that's not the way a young woman should be."

Honi reached across the table and took her mother's hand in both of hers. "I guess I know what you're trying to say," she began softly. "I've always been a little different. In school, I'd question what the other kids just memorized. While they studied paintings of mountains, I'd gaze out the window at them in the distance. My teachers used to get upset with me, but I was just listening to the questions in my own mind and dreaming of things that seemed important to me. I guess I'm different from other girls around here; I don't want a husband and children, at least not right now, before I'm ready. I want to live my own life until I understand it better. I don't want to have to pretend to feel things that aren't in me."

86

Honi gripped her mother's work-roughened hand for emphasis. "Mama, I'm eighteen years old, and I've never been anyplace. Sometimes I lie out in the meadow and daydream of being in a place where the people are different from me and those I've been around all my life. Everything about me is average and kind of blah. I'm such an unspecial person, yet I feel special things, things I don't understand but I know are inside me. I want to look for the meaning of those things and see if they're real."

Her mother shook her head resolutely. "You have to get rid of that itching for independence and replace it with a desire to belong, and become a serious, responsible adult. All young girls feel that way sometimes—I did, too—but they get over it and grow up."

Honi's voice took on an edge of defiance. "Well, maybe that's the real difference about me, I don't want to grow up at the expense of my dreams. I'd never forgive myself for that."

"My dear," her mother said softly, "I just don't want you to get hurt. Maybe I haven't seen the world, but I understand happiness and I understand unhappiness. And believe me, happiness is worth whatever price you have to pay; it's worth whatever dreams you have to forget. Happiness is knowing you belong, it's being surrounded by warmth and love on a dark winter night when the cold wind blows just beyond the walls that protect you."

The older woman sighed in resignation. How could she possibly explain to a girl of eighteen all the things it had taken her a lifetime to learn? She changed the subject. "How are things between you and Hans Haas? He's such a nice young man, so steady and serious. You two must be getting pretty serious by now."

"Oh, Mama, Hans is nice and all that, and I've dated him since the beginning of time, but as much as I care for him, he's—well, he's boring. All he ever seems to think about are his cows and that farm."

"Well, what's wrong with that? Most young men his age have other things on their minds when it comes to girls, and farming isn't one of them. His family has a nice place that'll be his someday. That's a lot of responsibility for a young man. He has to think of the future, and look for a proper young woman to share it with."

"Mama, isn't what *I* want important? Besides, Hans doesn't want to rush into anything, either. He's a very cautious fellow, hardly the type who jumps into marriage or anything else before he's ready." Honi leaned forward toward her mother. "Do you know something, Mama? Not once in this whole conversation have you asked me if I love Hans?"

"Do you?"

"I don't know. He's the only boy I've ever really known so I don't have anything to compare the feeling to, but even if I do, why does love have to tie you down before you're ready?" She laughed softly. "One thing I know for certain—I don't like being an afterthought to a cow."

Honi placed the full picnic basket at her side and slowly rocked back and forth with her chin resting on her forearm which embraced her knees. She was still massaging feelings of guilt and resentment from the breakfast conversation with her mother. Maybe they just want a puppet for a daughter, she thought as she sulked, a daughter who dances on their strings, who'll meekly follow all their silly rules and obediently give them a litter of grandchildren to parade through the village marketplace on a Saturday afternoon.

Despite her resentment, it bothered Honi deeply to know that her parents had doubts about her. She didn't want to disappoint anyone, especially the two persons she loved more than anything or anyone in the world.

Honi was waiting for Hans to join her for a midafternoon picnic in a quiet place they had come to regard over the years as belonging to them. It was a small copse of oak trees on a plateau formed out of the hillside by a millennium of carving rivulets of rain water and melted snow pausing to leave their signature on the hill before resuming a mad rush to join the river. In the distance to the west and about two thousand feet below lay the valley of the Rhine, jewel-encrusted with the florid colors of late autumn, the clustered towns of Liechtenstein on the near side of the river and those of Switzerland on the other. In the distance was the capital of Vaduz—only a village, really—and directly above it, on a bluff of about two hundred feet, stood the castle of the crown prince. The castle was old but well-maintained and had lost none of its sentry self-assurance, the purpose for which it had been built many, many generations ago.

In the intervening distance, farmers were working their fields, moving briskly between cattle contentedly munching; toy-size automobiles were making monotonous progress traversing the narrow ribbon of highway along the river and over the bridges into Switzerland.

But Honi was seeing none of this, her gaze was still turned inward as she pondered the things her mother had warned her about. She wanted the best possible future for herself, but she wasn't certain she loved Hans because she wasn't certain what love was. Was it the feeling of security she felt as Hans so earnestly told her of his dreams for developing his family's dairy farm? Was it the quickening of pulse and the flushed feeling that came over her when he took her into his arms and caressed her with such feeling, kissing her gently while patiently awaiting the gathering momentum of her response, and then enduring the wrenching apart before things went beyond that passion point which she knew would mean an irreversible commitment? Irreversible, at least according to the way things were done in Liechtenstein where sex not only signified love, but also a deep, lifelong pledge. Love was a mystery to Honi because she had experienced so few of life's alternatives.

Her reverie was interrupted by the swishing of tall grass and low whistling of Hans as he came over the rise, trudging along in that steady, heavy-footed gait common to farmers everywhere who develop it by plodding through the soft soil of plowed ground.

"Ah, my little nymph of the forest. What deep thoughts occupy your pretty head?"

Honi smiled. Hans tried so hard to sound romantic, like in the Hollywood movies they saw together, but his stilted and clumsy attempts were only cute at best, making him lovable for the effort, if not the result.

"I'm just thinking about love. Do you ever think about that, Hans? I mean *really* think about it?"

"Sure, all the time. Come here and I'll show you what love is." He made a wide-embrace grab for her which she nimbly avoided with a pseudo shriek. The obligatory jest completed, Hans immediately lost interest in his response as well as her question. "What's in the basket?"

he asked, raising the edge of the cloth and inhaling the escaping aromas with an exaggerated expression of ecstasy.

Honi accepted the obvious cue and began spreading the lunch as Hans leaned his lanky six-foot frame against a tree, placing the stem of a weed between his teeth. As he surveyed the countryside, scrutinizing the state of the fields and condition of the cows, Hans became a stereotype in the scene he created: He was a farmer and this was his place. The diverse elements of green fields, wind- and sunburned face, idling cows, rough work clothes, stout fences, and unruly brown hair tossed by the breeze neatly fit together to solve the puzzle of Hans' life; not a very complicated puzzle, but one where all the pieces were present and fit. He saw the same scenes as Honi had earlier, but with entirely different vision.

They sat and passed the fried chicken, potato salad and thick black bread smeared with butter to each other in a wordless feast. Finally, Honi, absently picking a loose thread on her skirt, asked, "Hans, do you ever think about traveling, about just getting away from here and seeing what the rest of the world is like?"

He slowly finished a piece of chicken while intently peering at her as though trying to see the thought behind the question. "I guess I'd like to see the world, why not? I'd like to see how other farmers operate, check out some of the things I've seen on television, like Disneyland, Japan, places like that. But when I finished, I'd come home and go back to work." He gave a sideways glance at Honi. "But if you ever went far away, I wonder if you'd come back. Maybe you'd just want to find something you like better and stay."

The resentment bubbled inside her. "There you go

91

again. Just because I ask a lot of questions and wonder about things I've never seen, you think I'm some sort of irresponsible child. Hans, sometimes you remind me of an old man. You sound just like my mother."

Hans slowly wiped his fingers on an embroidered napkin and then slowly scooted over to her side. He lowered his voice as he spoke close to her ear. She stared frostily into the distance as he talked. "I admit I'm only a simple farmer. I won't say that's all I've ever dreamed of being, but that's what I am, and I've grown to like it. A farmer is the type of man who's got to feel good about his land and the things he shares with it. He's got to love them and depend on them, and they on him. That's why I don't jump into things. I have to be sure."

Honi sobbed with frustration. Why was she continually confronted by the doubts of people who refused to understand her? Everyone seemed so worried about making her the way they wanted her to be, they ignored the person she really was. She yearned to be a free, happy, strong woman, but that desire seemed threatening to the people she cared about and wanted to please. In her heart, she knew that the real Honi was a person they could love and admire, but how to reveal that elusive, mystical person who hid in the restless fiber of her girl's being?

Hans, feeling guilty about causing her tears, put his arm around her and squeezed consolingly. She looked so vulnerable, so soft, so beautiful; he buried his face in her soft, fragrant hair and surrendered to a powerful desire that he normally was able to keep pent up in his practical, common-sensical soul. His youthful lust took control of him like an airplane on automatic pilot, dictating that he must have her . . . at any cost.

92

"I'm sorry, baby. I didn't mean to be critical, it's just that you're different from any farmer's wife I know and that sort of scares me. But I love you, I really do. I would . . . I would like to marry you."

The words had a magical ring to Honi and in their echo she felt her cares fade away. In marriage she could find approval, belonging, her irresponsible longings would disappear. She felt an outpouring of warmth toward Hans for providing such deliverance. She was ready for love, her mind sought it and her body demanded it. It was time.

Hans pulled back and looked at her with pleading, feverish desire. His hand gently caressed her soft breast, and he uttered just one word. "Please?"

Honi turned to him with a mysterious smile. Her arms encircled his neck and she pulled him gently down to her on the soft, lush grass. Slowly, feelingly, she kissed his lips. Her fingers reached inside the coarse workman's shirt and lightly caressed his strong chest.

In response, Hans massaged her soft face with his calloused hands. His desire was swept along by the urgings of her hot, uneven breath and the pressing of her body against his. His fingers started to fumble with the buttons of her clothes, and far from objecting, her own hands joined in a frantic rush to explore the forbidden unknown. They attacked each other's clothing as though unwrapping Christmas presents, the closer they got to the gift, the more excited they became.

It was the Great Discovery and they pawed impatiently, inexpertly at each other to reach it. Doubts, better judgments, and the stern teachings of strict upbringing were thrown aside in the onrush of youthful wanting.

"Oh, Hans, love me," Honi whispered as they teetered

on the brink. Then, with a great surge of wonder, they fell together off the edge, losing forever that tenuous, slippery foothold on the narrow ledge called innocence. They found that their dreams had not been mistaken, and their longings did not exaggerate.

Afterwards, as they lay exhausted and contented in each other's arms, Honi asked dreamily, "Hans, when do you want to get married?"

He was silent for a long moment, then he moved away a distance and started to get dressed with his back to her. "As soon as it's practical," he mumbled."

As the weeks passed, Honi's body sent her signals of change that confused her at first. Even though she was raised on a farm amid the everyday workings of nature, it didn't occur to her to apply those same life-cycle signs to herself. So she didn't recognize the indications of beginning pregnancy. She wasn't alerted by missing two periods, nor by the increasing nausea. Much later, she would be bemused by her naivete, but at the time, it was as though desiring a continuance of innocence would make it so.

Finally, she could no longer ignore her swelling belly and the lingering, frowning stares of her mother. She was forced to face her plight, but she didn't know to whom or where to turn. Certainly not to her mother, that prospect was simply too humiliating to bear. Her condition seemed a threat with only one hope of rescue—Hans.

Hans was waiting at a rear table in the small cafe in Planken where they often met after dinner for a glass of warm German beer to wash down slices of *saurcase*, the Liechtenstein peasant cheese. Since that afternoon on the hillside when they had known the intense feelings that sex between them had brought, and which had not been repeated, Hans had been strangely aloof and always seemed to find a reason not to discuss the marriage he had proposed on that same afternoon. Their relationship had become a mixture of awkwardness and shyness, often manifested by a nervous or averted glance, as though each wanted to pretend they still shared the innocence of an earlier time.

No sooner had Honi removed her heavy leather and fur coat and pressed her palms to rosy cheeks to warm them from the bite of the winter wind, Hans began.

"I was talking to Herr Gobel, the veterinarian, you know, and he said my cows are so healthy that he would be bankrupt if all the livestock in Liechtenstein were as well cared for. Boy, you should have . . ." His voice trailed off as he noticed that Honi was very upset and ignoring him. A strained silence followed as he traced his finger through the ring his beer made on the table top and studied the watery patterns, feeling as clumsy as a confused rhino, and fighting a vague uneasiness he couldn't identify.

"What's wrong?" he finally asked.

Honi avoided looking at him and struggled to calm a trembling lower lip. Even though responsibility for her pregnancy obviously had to be borne by both, she felt guilty as though her swelling body was a dirty trick she was willfully playing on the nervous young man sitting opposite her. She braced her voice to keep the tremor out. "Hans, I'm . . . I'm going to have a baby."

He stared at her silently in wide-eyed shock. "Why?" he asked dumbly, then shrugged off the idiocy of the question, and the two lapsed into strained silence. Hans was the first to speak, and with an angry edge in his voice. "Why did you let it happen?" he demanded in a hissed whisper, suddenly aware of other customers sitting nearby.

Honi was lost for words and shook her head incredulously. "You don't think I . . ."

Hans' anger was rooted in fear, fear that his carefully laid plans for life's orderly progression were about to be smashed. "Everyone knows you've been pushing to marry me. Just the other day you were talking about furniture and the kind of house you'd like."

Hurt and disbelief stung Honi. "*Hans*," she protested, "you know that's not true. *You're* the one who said you wanted to get married, and I believed you. All you wanted was to have sex, and I thought you loved me."

Embarrassed by the reminder of his proposal, Hans covered it up with anger. "Damnit," he swore at her between clenched teeth. "I said we would get married when the time was right. You *know* that won't be for several years. Now, be honest, did I say we were going to get married right away? I think you just tried to hurry it along."

Honi's mouth fell open in shock. "How *dare* you think I'd try to trap you like this. I wouldn't have told you if I thought—"

"Well," he said decisively, "an abortion is out. We just don't do those things here."

"I never said anything about an abortion. I only—"

Hans cut through her words like a fist through paper. "You'll have to have it, that's all there is to it."

The morbid fear of loneliness started to ebb from Honi's beleaguered mind. "Hans, do you mean it? Do you really?"

"Certainly. I have enough money saved to pay for it. We'll go to Zurich and find out where those places are."

"What places?"

"Why, the places where you can go to live and have your baby. They'll give it up for adoption as soon as it's born, and then you can come back home. You'll never have to see it. If we're lucky, no one'll be the wiser. I guess your parents will have to be told, but—"

"Hans—" the word was part plea and part curse—"I'll do no such thing! Whether you like it or not, this is *our* baby in my body, and I won't let it be born just to give it away like . . . like it was some calf on your precious farm." Her voice trailed away as the loneliness of her plight threatened to suffocate her with a cold, clinging panic.

"Be sensible," he scolded, "there's no other way. Marriage is certainly out of the question. Maybe in a few years, but—"

With a sudden convulsive sob, Honi surged to her feet, spilling a mug of beer into Hans' lap. She grabbed her coat and bolted for the door. Down the snow-slick sidewalk she ran, dodging shoppers who looked back in surprise, past friendly shopkeepers whose greetings from their doorways went unanswered. Honi ran all the way home with the speed possible only in one possessed or pursued. Past her startled parents, she flew into her room, collapsing against the back of the slammed door.

For two days Honi eluded the world outside her room and writhed in the tormenting grasp of the world she had caused within. She spoke to no one, ate no food, ignored every appeal from behind the protective locked door.

At dawn of the third day, the depression came. It came slowly, tiptoeing like a playful child, intent on lulling her

97

into unawareness. It didn't seize her, it caressed her into the calm of a shielding trance. It gently lifted the burden of her agonies and kindly substituted a becalming voice. Medicine may recognize acute depression as a double-crossing cruelty of strained emotions, but Honi knew it as a caring friend that cooled the fevers of her mind, that gently gave her nothing, peaceful nothing.

Hour after hour Honi lay in bed protected from her conscious mind, but at the same time, terribly vulnerable. Deep within the shadows of her subconscious other forces were at work, imploring her to end her miseries, to return to the sweet peace she knew before all this started. The voices touched a responsive chord by providing answers where before there had existed only hopelessness.

What happened next can be viewed as inevitable, a remorseless wolf finally catching his prey in deep snow. Honi acted as an automaton, the mechanical slave to the false promise of release made by the voices in her benumbed mind.

She raised herself from the bed and went to the closet as though to get dressed. Instead, she took a single wire coat hanger down and examined it slowly, turning it in her hands like a strange tool. She unwound the tight wire steel wrapping at the neck and straightened the hanger. Studying it curiously, she knelt on the bed and grasped the hanger in both hands and drew it in to her, into her. Though deeper and deeper it penetrated, there was no sign on her face of the terrible wound she was inflicting. Pain that would have been intolerable in a normal state of mind did not exist for her.

The first sign was a small trickle of blood which ran slowly down the inside of her thigh and onto the white sheet where it blotted into a widening Rorschach pattern. Honi paused, then thrust upward, quickly and hard. The blood gushed forth, turning her legs bright scarlet and cascading into a pool on the bed.

Honi calmly let the wire slip from her grasp and looked at what she had done. Then, in a voice strangely devoid of emotion or pain, she turned her head upward and screamed shrilly, as though those strange voices at whose behest she had acted were cheering their success as they retreated victoriously into the recesses of her mind.

She awoke, not with the languid easiness that follows an untroubled sleep, but with a start, fully alert and wide-eyed. She didn't recognize the room she was in, but the sterile whiteness and spartan furnishings told her that she was in a hospital. Honi caught a movement in the corner of the room and turned to see a young nurse staring back at her. The nurse didn't speak, but turned abruptly and left the room.

A few minutes later a stern-looking middle-aged man entered whom she recognized as Dr. Werner. He approached and took a position at the foot of her bed. She sensed this was not a particularly friendly visit; if it were a more kindly mission, he would have come to her side.

Dr. Werner looked at her sadly and then spoke in a very proper, formal voice. "I see you are awake, *fräulein*. Good. I'm pleased to tell you your progress is very satisfactory."

If he were pleased, he certainly concealed his joy, Honi told herself. She was mystified by the doctor's attitude. He had delivered Honi at this very hospital; she had cared for his children when he and his wife wanted an

99

evening out.

"Why am I in the hospital, Dr. Werner? What's wrong?"

The doctor seemed to find it awkward to speak. "Well . . . well . . . you mean you don't know what happened to you?"

"I have no idea," she said, which was true as far as it went, but didn't explain the dark foreboding she felt.

"No?" he repeated her response and seemed to ponder it a moment. "Well, you were found in your bedroom, hemorrhaging quite heavily. We brought you by ambulance to the hospital where you have been treated for loss of blood and shock. We then—"

"Doctor, what happened? Please get to the point," she said urgently.

"*Fräulein*, you aborted yourself. Using a straightened wire coat hanger, you—you destroyed the life you were carrying."

Hearing the truth spoken drove it sharply into Honi's conscience, leaving her no way to avoid confronting it. "No, no, I couldn't have," she sobbed. Honi attempted to raise herself and reach out to the doctor, but she was stopped short by a sharp pain in her abdomen. She gasped, moved her hand protectively to her stomach and fell backward on the bed.

"You've had a severe abdominal trauma. If you hadn't screamed, you would have bled to death," the doctor explained like he was pronouncing a sentence.

"How long will you keep me here?"

"About three days. You've suffered no permanent damage, except you'll never be able to have children. You should be on your feet by tomorrow. About the only thing you won't be able to do for a few weeks is the thing that got you into this situation."

Dr. Werner seemed to search for words. "Young lady, I'm neither a priest nor a psychiatrist. I don't know why you would do such a thing, and I don't have any pretty, scientific words to describe it. All I know is that you've committed a mortal sin, and for that I have no treatment." The doctor turned to leave, but with his hand on the door, he said, "You can plan to leave Friday morning. Pardon my abruptness, but we need the bed."

Other than the young nurse who seemed to regard her as a leper, and an older nurse who showed her disdain by rattling dishes more forcefully than necessary and by pounding her pillow when she made Honi's bed, Honi was alone with the person she least wanted to be with—herself.

For three days she stared at the white walls, trying to grasp the tragedy she had caused, trying to comprehend how she could have done such a thing, and examining her feelings as thoroughly and gingerly as she would a ripe melon in the market. For three days the black telephone next to her bed never rang. For three days the door never swung open to reveal the face of family or friend. She was alone with her guilt.

On a gray and cold Thursday afternoon she was resting in a state of semi-sleep, the type that comes with having slept too much, with having thought too much, but with nothing else to do, when the door started to open. Honi was used to the bustling, officious comings and goings of the nurses, so the slow, self-conscious way the door was opening told her this was someone different, that she finally had a visitor.

Into the room came a familiar, reassuring sight: the round, red face of Father Hammerschmidt. This was the

101

kindly man who had represented goodness and authority in her life for as long as she could remember. Her family had lived within a mile of his since before either kept records. For her, he represented not only the church, but also a neighbor; he was as much a part of her lifescape as the forests or mountains. But most of all, he now represented someone with whom she could talk, someone who might have the answers that she could not find in herself.

With unrestrained joy, she cried out, "Father! How wonderful to see you. Please come in."

The plump, sweating priest pushed his way into the room, wrestling two suitcases through the door. Honi thought she recognized her own luggage, but made no immediate connection. The first sense of foreboding she received was the uncharacteristically nervous and formal way he spoke.

"Good afternoon, Fräulein Miller. I'm told by the doctor that your progress is satisfactory."

"Why, yes, I think so. They say I can go home tomorrow."

The grim priest hesitated, then his shoulders seemed to square in resolve. The words poured forth in a well-rehearsed rush. "What I am about to say, my child, gives me no pleasure. But I long ago realized that doing the work of God and His church often requires things that pain us, but which must be done if His will is to be served. It is my sad duty to inform you that you no longer have a home to return to. You have been cast out of your father's house in the same way Cain was cast out of his family, for he, too, took a life that God had seen fit to bring forth."

"What do you mean? My father and mother . . ."

102

Honi's voice trailed off as the priest's words began to sink in.

"They have turned from you, their only child. Regretfully, there is no longer room under your father's roof for one with the blood of a dead child on her hands."

"My mother—what does my mother say?"

"Your mother is a dutiful wife; she stands behind her husband."

"Father," Honi began in the half-reasoning, half-pleading voice used to penetrate a closed mind. "I know what I did was wrong and evil; I wish I had died instead of that baby." She paused and added in a small voice, "My baby." She shuddered and looked at him in appeal. "But please believe that I didn't know what I was doing. All I remember is that I was scared and angry with no idea of what to do or where to turn." The tears streamed down her cheeks and splashed on the sheets she gripped tightly around her throat. "Please tell me why this had to happen. Won't someone say they love me and understand?"

"Daughter, the love is still there, but I'm afraid there can be no understanding of what you did."

"I always believed that love *is* understanding. It has to be. What good is love if it doesn't help me now?"

Father Hammerschmidt cleared his throat loudly. "The church is very clear on matters such as this. There is an abundance of scripture that tells us you must be punished and sent forth into the wilderness of your own creation."

"Father." Honi's anger at the priest helped dry her tears. "I'm already in a wilderness, and I can't escape. As for your scripture, I remember reading some that mentioned other things—like forgiveness and understanding. But I think you choose your scripture to suit your purpose."

The priest was growing uncomfortable with Honi's unexpectedly strong response. He motioned toward the suitcases and reached into his coat for a plain white envelope. Placing it on her bedside table, he said, "In there are two thousand francs. It's all your parents could gather. In those two suitcases are your clothes. It is my earnest suggestion that you leave Liechtenstein and this experience behind you and seek a new life elsewhere. I would be willing to hear your confession before I leave."

"No, thank you. My confession belongs to me, and I think I'll save it for more sympathetic ears."

"As you wish, *fräulein*." The priest started for the door, but was stopped by Honi's voice. "Father, what does Hans say?"

"Hans denies it was his baby."

Honi leaned back in the bed and squeezed her eyes shut in a hopeless attempt to block out the ugly words. The priest was almost out the door when she said, "Father, if there is a god and you're his priest, why did he give you such a dead heart?"

The door closed quietly.

There are times in life when things become so despairing that the only recourse left is to fight back, when the only thing that seems possible is to save one's self-respect. Honi spent the rest of that bleak afternoon gathering her strength and the will to go on.

Before Father Hammerschmidt's visit, her reliance for recovery lay in her faith that the love of her parents and Hans would bring her through. Now, since she had been denied that support, her only salvation was in her own strength. The marrow of will power is thought to be

104

determination, but often it is desperation, the knowledge that it is the last hope and all that remains.

When the floor nurse made her late rounds, she entered Honi's room and was shocked to see the young patient sitting on the edge of her bed, fully dressed in a plain blue dress, her long blond hair tied in a bun, and with a heavy winter coat folded across her lap.

"Fräulein Miller, what're you doing? You aren't scheduled to leave until tomorrow."

"I'm leaving tonight. Immediately."

The nurse lifted one of the suitcases. "You can't possibly carry this. Is someone coming for you?"

"I'm alone. I can manage." Honi struggled to her feet, lifted the suitcases and walked out of the room. As she slowly made her way into the gathering gloom of the winter night, the words echoed in her mind: I'm alone. I can manage.

Konrad leaned on one elbow and studied the sleeping woman next to him. He watched with sympathy as she tossed her sweat-matted head back and forth, mumbling words Konrad could not quite catch. He gently patted the perspiration off her forehead with an edge of the sheet. Boy, he thought, I don't know what it is, but she's really carrying around a lot of baggage. He gently shook her. "Hey, wake up," he urged softly. "We've got a lot of work to do."

Chapter Five

Konrad studied the outside of the old inn, *Der Stern*, The Star, as he locked the rented Mercedes. He had chosen this out-of-the-way small inn in the quiet town of Bad Helsfeld because he knew Owl wouldn't feel comfortable this far from his regular city haunts.

If Owl and his kind were predictable in adhering to established patterns, then the police were aware of it, too, and wouldn't be expecting him in such a rural area. Strange, he thought, for all their shrewdness, men like Owl could be stupidly predictable in their habits.

The front door jingled musically as Konrad entered the inn. There was no bar, so he went into the almost-deserted dining room and took a corner table. The only other occupants of the room were two elderly ladies wearily sitting on the far side who, judging from their bundles, were taking a break from shopping. Konrad ordered a beer and settled back to wait.

Within minutes, a quizzical, round face peered cautiously around the hallway corner. Konrad quickly reacquainted himself with the once-familiar features:

thick, round glasses, tufts of white hair emerging from ears and nostrils, and a heavy overcoat that was misplaced even in the chill of early November. The man located Konrad and hurried across the dining room.

"My dear Konrad," he croaked obsequiously, "I wondered what happened to you. I'm glad to see you again—" he glanced around nervously—"even in such a spooky place."

This was the Owl. Real name: Meyer Franken. Occupation: black market dealer, specifically, fence for stolen supplies taken from the abundance of military bases of all nationalities located in West Germany. When Konrad had been active in the black market during his duty tour in Germany, the Owl had purchased most of what he lifted from his posts, everything from hand grenades to tractor tires. Konrad knew him to be honest only when it was good business. When the double-cross was a sound investment, then Owl could be counted on to stab the nearest back.

"Where have you been?" Owl asked, then quickly recognizing his violation of underworld protocol, said, "What do you have to sell me today? Just like the old days, eh?"

"I'm not selling today, Owl, I'm buying. But first let's get a couple of things straight. When we did business before . . ."

There was an awkward pause as the waitress came to take Owl's order. He acted so obviously suspicious toward her that the woman scurried away as soon as he muttered, "Mineral water."

Konrad picked up the thread of his comment. "When we did business before, it was because the relationship was mutually profitable. I expect the same conditions now. Without going into detail, I'm aware of certain information leaks that your customers have been plagued with in the past. Those leaks seemed to turn into floods when the police were willing to pay enough. The result was usually unpleasant for those customers, people who had dealt with you straight up."

Konrad held up a hand to silence the protest Owl was beginning to sputter. "I've always had my own questions about a certain truckload of frozen meat which I offered to sell you. I almost lost my ass when army investigators seemed to know just where to look. But I don't want to dig up unpleasantness. I just want you to know that, in the matter I am about to discuss with you, lapses of good judgment could be very unhealthy. Especially—" and at this point Konrad laid his combination bomb and smoke screen—"considering that the people I represent are known for nasty tempers that sometimes make them do disgusting, uncivilized things when they think they've been double-crossed. Maybe it's the hot sand and the smelly camels that give them a bad disposition, but they seemed very agitated when I told them I thought we could trust you, even though you're Jewish."

"Jewish?" Owl moaned. "I'm not Jewish. I've never been Jewish."

Konrad sounded almost contrite. "You're not? Oh, I'm sorry. But I'm not sure they'd believe me if I said I was mistaken. I'm really sorry, Owl. Oh, well, if everything goes smoothly, it'll be OK."

Owl gulped down his glass of mineral water, took a deep breath and exhaled slowly. Finally, he said, "Tell your friends they can trust me completely. My sympathies have always been pro-Arab. Why, I never—"

"Thanks, Owl, I'm sure they'll find your reassurances

very consoling. Now, let's talk a little business."

"What is it I can do for you, friend Konrad?"

"I need fifty M-16 rifles, ten thousand rounds of ammunition, one hundred extra rifle clips, ten pounds of plastique explosive, twenty detonators." Konrad paused to allow the scribbling Owl to catch up with him. "Also, one hundred yards of detonating wire and two signal pistols with ten flares of various colors."

Owl studied the list. "Why M-16s? I could get you Russian AK-47s or Israeli Uzis."

"Because, despite what you hear from people who don't know any better, the M-16 is the superior, all-purpose weapon. It's more reliable than the AK-47 and more accurate than the Uzi. The rifle had some problems when it was first introduced in Vietnam, but that was traced to a malfunction of the self-cleaning mechanism caused by the wrong gunpowder being used. It was easily corrected, but the impression remains. And besides, I don't think my clients would be interested in a weapon made in Israel.

"I also know, Owl, that with so many American bases nearby you can deliver the M-16s for half the price of the others, and still make a profit that would make an oil dealer blush."

"Ah, Konrad, but you have to realize that the Americans have tightened security on their bases. It's no longer an easy thing to, shall we say, share their abundance with them."

Konrad leaned back and laughed, drawing stares from the elderly women across the room. "Owl, you're as full of shit as a constipated pig. If the price were right, you'd deliver the general's false teeth. Since the first stone was thrown in anger, armies were made for two things: to win battles, and to make men like you rich. No, Owl, I have complete faith in your greed being more than a match for the security of any army."

"Thank you for those kind words, Konrad, but be that as it may, the task is still difficult." Owl began scratching some numbers on his list. He laid his pen down and studied the figures for a moment. "I think I could deliver the items you request for sixty-five thousand dollars. I assure you, this price is based partly on sentimentality for the good relations we've always enjoyed. I couldn't possibly take one penny less."

Konrad sadly shook his head. "Owl, Owl, haven't you been listening to me? These folks don't want to pay retail. They hired me because they thought I had some good wholesale contacts. Now why do you waste my time and insult my intelligence by quoting a price that you know goddamn well is double what you'll take?"

"Double?" Owl blanched. "Double? Do you seriously think?" Owl suddenly relaxed and smiled. "Konrad, why do we haggle like Arabs—I mean, like children, over such a trivial thing as price? Old acquaintances should never let money come between them. How about forty thousand dollars? That's twenty-five below my asking price."

"And ten thousand more than fair. All right, but delivered."

"A deal." Owl extended his hand which Konrad took briefly and reluctantly.

Konrad removed an envelope from the breast pocket of his jacket. From it he removed a slip of paper and handed it to Owl. "Here's the address of a warehouse in Munich. Deliver the merchandise three weeks from today. I'll be there to take delivery. Crate it in wooden boxes marked farm machinery."

Konrad removed another envelope from the pocket that was considerably thicker. He glanced around to make certain they were not being watched, and removed a stack of large-denomination bills from it. He counted out forty thousand-dollar bills. He took the remaining ten bills and put them into his pocket. Owl accepted the money, but his forlorn eyes were on the pocket where the other bills had disappeared.

Konrad chuckled. "Don't worry about the ten that got away, just think about the forty that didn't. And remember, until the goods are delivered, that money is just in your possession, it doesn't belong to you until you earn it."

Owl sighed. "Don't worry, Konrad. After all, didn't you name me the Owl because of my wisdom and understanding of how this business works?"

Konrad stood up and placed a five-mark bill on the table. "Owl, my man, I gave you that name because you look like a fucking owl."

As Konrad and Owl haggled over their deal in the inn, the town square outside was a tableau of village tranquility. The ornate stone fountain, rhythmically gushing beneath the facade of the town hall, was playing host, as usual, to enterprising pigeons whose ancestors had, countless decades ago, staked this place out as a reliable picnic ground. And it appeared this was a prosperous day. Off to the side on a wrought-iron bench sat a solitary workman throwing crumbs to the birds from his lunch pail. He was a man in his thirties, of ordinary appearance except for his left hand which had lost the

111

last two fingers, probably the result of an industrial accident. But he made it seem like a small thing by using the hand with such dexterity that the handicap was hardly noticeable. What the body cannot heal, it adjusts to.

To the casual observer, he blended easily into the fabric of everyday life: an ordinary citizen taking a few moments to relax before going home to the evening meal. Perhaps he was working out his anger at an unfair rebuke from the foreman. Perhaps he was considering whether to tell his wife about the small bonus he had been given by the manager. Should he add it to the grocery money or use it for a good time at the neighborhood tavern?

From a few yards away, he belonged there. But if one were to study him closely it would have been apparent that he was not relaxed, that he was ignoring the pigeons except for the careless spreading of the crumbs. Try though he might, the man could not quite achieve the hunched-shoulder, languid ease of a loafing laborer. His presence here was not aimless; his attention was riveted on the inn and its two unknowing bargainers.

When Konrad finally left the inn and drove away in his Mercedes, the workman moved swiftly to a black Volkswagen parked nearby. He first studied the route taken by the Mercedes, then climbed in, threw the empty lunch pail into the backseat and took off in the same direction.

Konrad loved the *Autobahns* where German drivers threw off the constraints of their normally restricted and disciplined lives on the long, wide stretches of freeway and indulged in the most hair-raising, death-defying driving in the world. It was the sort of thing Konrad could get caught up in, especially now with enough money to rent a powerful, fast car.

Gripping the wheel of the Mercedes, he watched with a quiet excitement as the speedometer needle swept past 100 kilometers per hour, past 120, past 140 without hesitation, and settled on 160. Konrad calculated by dividing by ten and then multiplying by six that he was traveling 96 miles per hour. God, he thought, try this on the San Diego Freeway and every CHP smoky in two counties would be on your tail like white on ivory.

Konrad sped past the ancient city of Heidelburg and down the rolling plain another one hundred kilometers to the stately old spa city of Baden-Baden. He drove with curiosity through the old city, in which waters with curative magic had first been discovered by the Romans and eventually had become the "in" destination for the elite of the last century. He slowly moved past the stately, ornate monuments to Victorian opulence—past the *Trinkhall* where gothic columns stand noble guard to the god of Baden-Baden eminence, the mineral-water drinking fountains; past the gambling casino where ladies and gentlemen lose fortunes with a dignity and elan foreign to the boisterous ways of Las Vegas; past the state-owned baths which offer convincing granite evidence of what man is willing to pay to think something good is happening to him without any effort on his part. How appropriate that the man he had come to visit chose this city to look down upon from the heights he had ascended.

Konrad stopped at a tourist information booth, and after asking a few questions of an apple-cheeked young girl in peasant costume, turned the powerful car to the north and started the long climb out of the city and into the surrounding hills.

As he watched the familiar Mercedes hood ornament

113

point a steady uphill course on the gradually narrowing road, Konrad was reminded by the encroaching dark pines and dense brush that he had entered the Black Forest. As the sun gradually dipped, further deepening the dark woods, he thought of the ghosts that such scenes had birthed in the spirit of medieval Germany, and which had created a superstition that blossomed into the richest folklore in the world.

It's so indicative of these people, his ancestors, he thought, that rather than turn their minds from the foreboding mysteries around them and onto lighter subjects—whistling by the graveyard, we now call it—they made the supernatural the center of their lives. What does that say about the German mentality? he pondered.

He was tiring of his musing when the road started to flatten and he saw a narrow lane off to the left, just as the tourism girl's instructions had indicated. The gravel lane was barely wide enough to allow passage for the Mercedes, but a slow, careful drive of a few hundred meters saw the lane widen into a paved courtyard fronting a yellow brick chateau.

The house was two stories of about a dozen rooms. It was well constructed and maintained as were the two smaller outbuildings of similar appearance. Konrad guessed the age of the chateau at about one hundred years. It had obviously never known poverty, and the current resident was no exception.

Konrad parked the car and sat for a moment, taking in the scene before him. Off to the left in the distance was the ruin of an old Roman fort. To the right and far below lay the city of Baden-Baden, the first lights of dusk already twinkling. And all around and below him, as far

114

as he could see, were the thick, autumn-rich colors of the Black Forest, the reds and oranges deepening with the approaching twilight.

As his eyes swept the brooding, elegant scene, he thought of how it fitted the occupant of the large house, Walter Schell.

Walter Schell was a victim of nature and society in conflict with each other. Nature endowed him with a great talent, but society denied him discovery of it until it was too late to give him full benefit. Schell was born in rural northern Germany in the mid-twenties, a bad time to be born in Germany. The country was gripped by a terrible economic depression and had just lost a devastating war. He grew up on a farm where there was always too much work and too little to eat. Kindness was non-existent and education was minimal. Peasant families considered learning a luxury to be indulged in sparingly, and then only in the best of times.

His early years were an endless and blurred succession of labor and hunger, and his mind did not yearn for things it could not know existed. The only music that came into his life was the discordant strivings of the village brass band on the rare holiday. When he married at seventeen, he was only doing what was expected of a youth of his station. His bride was a sixteen-year-old farm girl of dull wit and round body, a person to whom it never occurred being anything other than what she was, which was exactly what her mother, and generations before her, had been.

The newlyweds lived in a cottage that was little more than a ramshackel small barn, and settled into the routine of a farm hired hand.

The young couple might have led a toilsome,

115

uneventful life, filled with children and debts, but untroubled by the problems of the outside world, were it not for the ambitions of Adolf Hitler.

One pleasant spring day in 1939, when Walter was preparing his landlord's horses for the season's plowing, a recruiter in the dress green of the *Wermacht* was driven up in the sidecar of a motorcycle. The purpose of his visit was to tell Walter the fatherland needed him.

So, leaving his plump and bewildered bride, Walter abandoned the plow for a weapon to be used against strangers against whom he had no quarrel, just as countless generations of peasant boys had done before him. Whether the implement is a rifle, halberd, sword or bow, the litany is usually the same: expendable fodder to shed blood on the battlefields of Europe to settle petty political quarrels the merits of which are forgotten before the blood is dried, or to serve the manic ambitions of greedy men.

For six years Walter slogged through the mud and snow of Russia, Poland and France. Some might consider this a broadening experience, a chance to see something of the world, but all Walter ever saw were the same kinds of fields he had left behind, peopled by the same kinds of farmers who were his neighbors. The only wisdom he was exposed to was that of sergeants.

At first, Walter was repulsed by the brutality and killing that seemed an everyday occurrence, and was approached with the same nonchalance. He questioned what advantage was to be gained for Germany by slaughtering innocent peasants long after the battle had forged ahead. But when everyone else seemed to take it for granted, and especially when those same peasants began trying to kill him, he simply accepted it as the way things were supposed to be.

Though he might not have thought so at the time, Walter was one of the lucky ones. In almost six years of war, he suffered only two minor wounds and was transferred from Russia to the Western Front toward the end of the war, the military equivalent of going from a coal mine to a sandy beach.

As Germany's defenses collapsed, Walter joined the hungry, frightened mob of what had once been a great army in its demoralized surge back to Germany.

One day in Karlsruhe he joined a shabby, frightened group of soldiers, children and housewives surrounding a civilian provisions wagon loaded down with canned meats and vegetables. The besieged driver had realized too late his mistake of not doing a better job of camouflaging the cargo. The angry mob was incensed that this abundance, obviously intended for government or army big shots, should be flaunted before their hungering eyes.

As the nasty mood of the crowd intensified, the driver and his helper became more aggressive in attempting to protect their responsibility. Shouting curses, stepping on hands that reached into the cargo area, they fought with the knowledge that if they lost the food they might also lose their lives when they reported it missing to their no-less-desperate commanders.

Suddenly a shot rang out and the crowd froze as the driver stared in astonishment at the spreading red stain across his tunic that his clutching fingers could not contain. At the same instant the driver toppled into the crowd, a small detachment of civilian police rounded the corner and bore down on the throng with clubs swinging and whistles blowing. Like cockroaches when a light is turned on, the crowd scattered. All except Walter whose fatigued brain couldn't comprehend all the fuss over just one man being shot.

Had Walter been apprehended by the hard-nosed military police, he would have been executed on the spot. As it was, a hasty civilian criminal trial gave him a sentence of twenty years. Not that it mattered, in those years all Germany was a prison. Being behind bars simply guaranteed eating regularly.

As the years passed, his early marriage slipped from his mind, and apparently from his wife's, too, since he never heard from her. He didn't mind the company of criminals; life in the trenches facing the Red Army had hardly been genteel.

But one day his life changed forever. He was mopping the prison chapel when he stopped for a few minutes' rest. Having nothing to occupy his attention, he strolled over to the piano and idly began running his fingers over the keys. On rare occasions he had seen and heard pianos played, but had never touched one before. As he began to have a sense of what each key represented, a song came into his head, a simple German folk melody. As he hummed the tune, he found that, magically, his fingers sought out the proper keys and reproduced the music on the piano. It was rough, but recognizable.

As Walter experimented with his new discovery, the chaplain, a kindly Lutheran named Dr. Hammer, stood silently listening at the doorway to his office. When Walter noticed him, he quickly moved away from the piano and continued his mopping.

"No, no, please don't stop. I didn't intend to interrupt. How many years have you been playing?"

"Uh, I haven't. I mean, I never played it before."

118

The chaplain thought he was hearing a convict's typical game of evading the truth with authorities, but a brief conversation convinced him Walter was being honest.

"How would you like to learn to really play?" he asked the wary, suspicious prisoner.

"How could I do that?"

"I could teach you."

The enthusiastic nod of Walter's head was followed by months of concentrated instruction. What the clergyman had intended as a friendly gesture gradually became his obsession. With every lesson he saw more and more the extent of Walter's genius. He realized that by bringing out Walter's talent, he could make a contribution to the music he loved far beyond what his own meager talent would allow.

A year passed, two, then five. With each day Walter became more accomplished. Finally, his sentence was commuted, mainly on the strength of recommendations from musicians and critics who had come to hear the late-blooming phenomenon, and had left marveling.

Walter Schell left prison in his thirty-fourth year, a man with a dream of the fame and fortune of the concert stage. But it was not to be. While he was as good as the best, he was not without his detractors, especially those most threatened by his skill. Genius, he found out, is not spared the pettiness of this world, and jealousy doesn't fight fair. There soon was no stage for Walter Schell.

Walter was stuck. He had developed an enormous talent, a lofty ambition, and a deep love for music that he could not satisfy. Thus he turned to the only people he really knew and trusted—his fellow criminals. Walter was widely known among the German underworld;

119

others with a criminal background had been proud of his accomplishments and angered along with him by the disappointments. That empathy, together with his congenial personality and reputation for trustworthiness, made him a natural for the business he went into.

Walter became an expert on criminal recruitment—the personnel business, as it were. If a certain operator needed the services of, say, a second-story man, or a pickpocket, or an explosives expert, he would let his needs be known to Walter, and with payment of a reasonable fee, the contact would be made. The business was novel and ingenious. The public thinks every criminal knows every other one, and that alliances for illicit purposes form almost on whim. The truth is, the difficulty of criminal recruitment is magnified a thousandfold over that of legitimate business. It is difficult enough for normal enterprises to find the right personnel, but add the scrutiny of police, the inability to advertise and the unreliability of the breed, and the staggering problems become apparent. Walter helped solve the problem, and thus filled a need.

The fees quickly became numerous, and Walter prospered considerably, even though he normally limited himself by refusing to get involved with murderers, terrorists and kidnappers.

German police had vague knowledge of his activities, but they could never prove anything. His pleasant personality and cultivated manner had its salutary effect on them, too, so no policeman had the personal motive to single him out for special attention. Instead, they concentrated on catching those he placed.

Konrad had done business with Walter Schell briefly during his black-market days in the Army. When he needed a driver for stolen trucks, and knew of no one else, a mutual friend had put him in contact with Schell. They had immediately become good friends.

He left the Mercedes and approached the big house in anticipation of renewing that friendship.

The heavy, polished oak door opened immediately to his ring, and he was invited inside by a servant with manners as smooth as a con man facing St. Peter. He was expected, so the servant led him directly through the antique-lined hallway toward an open, large room with stained-glass windows dominating one wall, and a huge fireplace crackling on the opposite. Chamber music burst from the room as he entered the double-width door.

Schell was sitting at a beautiful grand piano playing Schubert's "Piano Quintet in A." The four string parts had been recorded separately and were serving as accompaniment to Schell's piano out of an elaborate stereo system. Konrad watched and listened from the doorway. Schell had aged in the way expected of a man nearing sixty, but the lines of his face were softened by his contentment as he played the lilting music. Finally noticing his silent observer, he smiled in recognition and flicked off the stereo.

"Konrad! What a pleasure to see you after these past years," he said, rushing across the room to grab Konrad in a friendly bear hug. "Now, my friend, before we talk business, bring me up to date on what you've been up to."

For an hour the two men sat across from each other sipping Napoleon brandy while Schell clucked sympathetically at Konrad's bad fortune and marvelled at his stories of life in San Francisco.

Finally, Schell said, "So tell me, my friend, what can I

121

do for you?"

"This might be difficult for even you, Walter. My client is a large multinational corporation that wants to enter the German market. Their product line is, shall we say, volatile and very competitive. They want me to put together a security force willing to put the interests of the company above any squeamishness about the fine points of the law. In return for very handsome pay, I might add."

Schell knew that Konrad's story about his client was probably a ruse, and he appreciated it, having no desire to know the real purpose. In this business, to know too much was to be incriminated. "How many men will you need?"

"Forty."

Schell masked his surprise as he paused thoughtfully and pursed his lips. "Even if I could recruit such a number for you, understand that the quality might be a bit uneven."

"I understand that."

"What skills are you looking for?"

"I need people experienced in handling automatic weapons who can follow orders. That probably means a military background. Two of them should be experts with explosives. All will need valid passports."

Schell interrupted. "If any have to have passports 'created,' will you pay for that?"

"OK. Let me make it clear that I don't want any who are fast on the trigger or who like to hurt people. Sickos like that only complicate an operation."

"As you know, I try to avoid referring individuals with sadistic tendencies, but considering the business and the people we deal with, I can't make any guarantees."

After seeing Konrad's silent nod, he continued. "Now, a couple of other things: On a scale of one to ten, how would you rate the danger of prison if captured? I need this, you understand, to fit the job description to possible candidates, and also to be candid with the applicants themselves."

"I would rate that at about a five."

"Very well, how would you rate the danger of loss of life on the same scale?"

"Three."

"How long will you need them, and what will the pay be?"

"About two weeks. The pay is twenty-five thousand dollars plus expenses. Ten thousand will be paid on acceptance and the rest upon successful completion of the job. Five thousand extra for the explosives men."

Schell whistled softly. "That's a good pay check. You can get competent men for much less, you know."

"I'm deliberately overpaying. I want their attention, loyalty and enthusiasm."

"I see." Schell thought for a moment. "Considering what you're willing to pay, I believe I can fill this order, but it'll take some time. How much do I have?"

"One month."

Schell whistled softly. "That's not much time for a job this size. I'll have to relax my normal standards. Are you willing to risk that? It'll mean I won't be able to promise that every one of them is a Sunday School graduate."

Konrad laughed. "I guess I can live with that."

"OK, then, call me one month from now and I'll give you the names of the forty. Since I don't have a telephone here at home—for good reason, as you can understand—phone and have me paged in the public

123

room at the Hotel Badisher Hof in Baden-Baden at one o'clock in the afternoon. Sharp. Ask for Herr Wessels. My fee is one thousand dollars per man, payable now, of course."

Konrad was already reaching for the thick wallet. As he removed the roll of bills and began counting them into Schell's hand, he said, "Agreed. Just two other things: They should speak fluent German and I prefer their acquaintance with each other to be at a minimum."

"Very well. The second request complicates the job a little, but I'll do my best. What instructions should I give them?"

"Here's a list of ten hotels in Munich. I've already booked and paid for four rooms in each hotel in the name of Trans-Europe Oil Corporation. Send four of them, separately, to each hotel. When you give me the list you can indicate who is staying where. Tell them to check in on December tenth and to stay in their rooms, near a phone, ready to leave at a moment's notice.

"The only other thing I need from you, Walter, is a top-notch deputy; someone who can lead others, but follow orders himself; a man who's quick on his feet and fast thinking. Above all, someone I can trust. If you know of such a guy, it'll mean a pretty good payday for him."

Schell was grinning broadly even before Konrad had finished. "I know just such a man; that is, if you don't mind someone about my age."

In spite of himself, Konrad found himself looking at the older man critically. "Well, I don't know. This could get pretty rough, and you know better than I that he'd have to boss some pretty rough customers."

"Have no fears on that point, Konrad. This fellow has been praised by such men as Otto Skorzeny, the SS officer who rescued Mussolini."

"Don't forget, Walter, that was almost forty years ago."

"All I'm asking is that you talk to him. Have I ever steered you wrong before? His name is Otto Ender. Why not talk to him?"

"Out of respect for you, Walter, I'll see what he has to say. In the event he does work out, what'll be your fee for him?"

"For Otto, nothing. It's difficult to put a price on genuine artistry, especially when the artist is a friend."

"One thing more that might make your job a little easier, Walter; I don't mind if the forty 'men' you're going after aren't all men. I just want good people period."

"So, women's liberation comes even to our little industry. Do you think the feminists would be flattered?"

As though to formally end the business discussion, Schell rose and went to an antique walnut sideboard and poured two glasses of a deep red wine that had been decanting. He extended a glass to Konrad. "In case you're curious, it's a 1956 Chateau Lafite-Rothschild, a fine bordeaux made possible by pleasant business relationships with honorable gentlemen such as yourself." He lifted the glass in salute. "Success to you in your undertakings." He smiled coyly. "I know this, ah, large multinational corporation you represent will be pleased by its choice."

Schell and Konrad wandered slowly around the large room chatting about people they had both known, and whatever else came to mind. Konrad's eye was attracted to a cracked, full-length mirror off to the left of the main door. Schell noticed his interest and walked over.

"I see you're interested in the mirror. Any idea how it got cracked?" he asked pointlessly. "When the French army was overrunning this part of Germany in 1945, I'm told a single French soldier entered the house, very cautiously, as you might expect. When he came to this room, out of the corner of his eye he noticed movement off to his left. He whirled and instinctively fired. What he shot was his own image in this mirror."

Schell's finger traced the lines of the crack which disappeared into a blank, round hole in the center. "This is the bullet hole. Do you wonder why I don't remove it or have it fixed?" He studied the mirror for a moment. "Perhaps because its presence reminds me that many of the things we seek to destroy in life are merely images of ourselves."

When they came to the large grand piano that Schell had been playing when Konrad entered, Schell ran his hand over it and said, "This piano is more than one-hundred-fifty years old. Paderewski played Chopin on it. I love this and the other beautiful things you see here—and drink," he said, raising his glass.

He slowly, absently, played with the keys. "You know, Konrad, what we have done here today probably makes us guilty of conspiracy in the eyes of the law. Does that bother you?" Konrad shrugged and Schell continued. "I've done considerable thinking about my life, what has become of it, and how I live it. I've concluded that it's foolish to worry about things over which I have no control, one of which is how I make my living. Oh, I know silly romanticists spout foolishness about how you-are-what-you-make-yourself and crap like that. But that's because they're afraid to admit the truth—that no one has much command over the really meaningful things, the foundational events that start us down irreversible paths. Did I choose to grow up an ignorant peasant? Did I choose to spend my youth dodging Russian bullets? Was it my choice to be standing in the wrong place when someone else in a mob killed a truck driver defending his cargo? Was I to blame when small-minded, jealous bastards prevented me from having the musical career I earned?"

He answered his own questions with a firm, "No. So you see, to take control of my own life, I was forced to come to terms with negative factors not of my making. Thus, I became what I am because of a past that afforded no worthwhile alternatives. And I discovered a talent within myself—music—that demanded constant nourishment or the frustration would destroy me. So I pieced together the options available and became what you see before you.

"It has its drawbacks. Not too many of the people with whom I conduct business are masters of the social graces. Some are downright distasteful. But that type of person is exactly what you often find in the highest reaches of government and industry. And the things my clientele do are often matched or exceeded by those same holier-than-thou politicians and businessmen.

"You know, man the animal is often called a predator. Some are, Konrad, a very few are. The rest are scavengers. They hide in the shadows licking their chops greedily while the predator feasts on his kill. Then they slink up to tear at the offal when their better has eaten his fill. In this world where there is too little of the good things to go around, I choose to be a predator."

Schell paused, then a broad smile broke over his face.

"Actually, I think I'm a better musician."

Konrad's host glanced outside to see that night had completely closed in. "Well, enough of this heavy talk. Can you stay for dinner?"

Konrad looked at his watch. "Believe me, there's nothing I would prefer more, but I have to catch a plane."

Konrad left the chateau and pointed his car down the return route to Baden-Baden. The landscape was no longer the fairy-tale garden it had been when he arrived. The enshrouding night made it ominous and shadowy, justifying the name Black Forest. He could not have noticed a dark shape standing next to a black car pulled off the road and out of sight on a small path close to the chateau. It wasn't until Konrad's taillights disappeared around the first curve that the figure stirred. He took a deep drag from the cigarette he had kept cupped behind him. The glow briefly illuminated his face, and cast in eerie red illumination the strange outline of a hand missing two fingers.

There was no obvious sign of it, but the tension that permeates South Africa was a very real thing to Konrad as he walked from his British Airways flight through the Cape Town airport. He could sense it in the body language. The people didn't move with the casual, unthinking freedom of most people who think themselves alone in a crowd. Here, men and women were visibly aware of those around them, constantly casting glances like hunters entering dense undergrowth, trying to spot danger before it located them. From what he could see, Cape Town seemed more like a medievel city under siege than a modern, bustling center of commerce. It was not a happy place.

He finally came to the cocktail lounge which was to be his rendezvous. He peered through the smoky half-light until he saw a solitary figure sitting at a booth along the back wall. He recognized the man from photos he had seen in newspapers.

"Major Davis?" Konrad asked the distinguished-looking older man with the thin, gray British military moustache.

Despite small size, unimposing appearance and cultivated manner, Maj. Dirk Davis was a feared and revered living military legend in Africa. After serving twenty years in the British army as a commando leader during World War II and after the war in numerous colonial outpost skirmishes, Davis retired and came to South Africa where he quickly found wealth and celebrity status as leader of anti-guerrilla forces for the white South Africa government.

When independence was granted many of the former black colonies during the sixties and seventies, his talents were very much in demand as a mercenary leader. Time and again, Davis thrilled the world with his swashbuckling adventures where he always seemed to be leading a handful of mercenaries to the rescue of beleaguered colonists from hordes of barbaric black soldiers intent on mayhem, plunder and rape. Now he was considered the elder statesman of soldiers of fortune throughout southern Africa and had evolved into a sort of organizer and clearinghouse for mercenary activities and employment. He was what Errol Flynn would have been, had Errol Flynn been real.

The man flashed a smile and extended his hand. "Yes,

I'm Dirk Davis. You must be Mr. Konrad. Please join me," he said, patting the booth beside him. "What would you like to drink?" Konrad's polite refusal made him frown. "I have another coming. We'll be off, as soon as I finish that."

Davis had barely finished speaking when a waitress brought another tall glass of amber liquid and ice. With only the briefest pause between gulps, Davis finished the drink, threw a bill on the table and stood. "Shall we go out to the house where we can talk privately?" he asked Konrad, but making a reply pointless by rapidly walking toward the exit.

Leaning back in the plush comfort of the Jaguar, Konrad devoted his attention to the spectacular beauty of Cape Town, barely aware of Davis' best tourist-guide monologue.

A modern, bustling city of one million at the very tip of the African continent, Cape Town is the seat of South Africa's parliament with all the attendant activity of a capital city, especially one geared for war. Konrad stared at the massive majesty of Table Mountain which hovered protectively over the entire city. As the purring luxury car surged up into the foothills of the mountain's lower slopes, he swiveled his gaze toward the bedazzling yellow sands of the beaches reaching out the Cape of Good Hope as far as he could see, a yellow glimmer fading into the blur of the sparkling blue horizon of the south Atlantic. Palm trees everywhere gave erect witness to the balmy paradise he had entered. What, he wondered, must it have been like to live here before man imported hate and fear, when anything considered dangerous would have come from the wilds; threatening, maybe fatal, but at least natural and belonging?

130

Konrad noticed they were gradually entering the most luxurious part of the city. As they drove upward, the homes became larger and farther apart. So, too, did the security guards become more numerous and competent-looking.

They abruptly turned into a driveway shrouded by high shrubs and barred by a closed wire-mesh fence about eight feet high. As the car nosed up to the gate, a young man dressed in khaki battle fatigues and a light blue beret moved out of the shadows carrying an Israeli Uzi machine pistol. He approached the car and saluted Major Davis, then peered closely at Konrad and inspected the floor of the back seat. He politely requested the car keys from Davis and opened the trunk. Apparently satisfied, the young man politely returned the keys, saluted again, and opened the gate. At one corner of the gate, discreet but noticeable, Konrad saw a "for sale" sign; he was curious, but said nothing. As they drove into view of a large neo-Tudor house with manicured lawn dotted with iron ornamentry, Konrad commented, "Your own guard acted like he didn't trust you, Major."

"We're professional, Mr. Konrad. Being professional means being cautious and thorough to an extreme, or at least what amateurs would consider extreme. What if a terrorist had been lying on the back seat floor with a pistol aimed up my backsides, or if one had crept into the car boot? And don't think it couldn't happen. In my business, we learn to be ready for anything; especially, for God's sake, in our own back yard."

There were black servants everywhere: one to open the car door, another to park it, one to open the front door, another to take their coats. Another servant hovered nearby and acted as though his services would

131

also be needed.

Davis gestured to the expectant servant, then turned to Konrad. "Would you like a drink now? Good, what will it be?" Davis turned to the servant. "Stephan, our guest will have white wine. I'll have the usual." As soon as the servant brought the drinks on a silver tray, Davis told him, "My guest and I will be in the study. You can bring us more drinks in there."

The study was a large room behind double mahogany doors that opened to a display of the conflicting cultures that the white man had created for himself in Africa. Along one wall were bookcases filled with hundreds of volumes which Konrad noticed covered a wide range of topics from modern psychology to military tactics to medieval humanism. Unlike so many collections, these books looked well-thumbed.

Along the opposite wall were mounted trophies of most of the dangerous and prized game animals of the continent: lion, cape buffalo, leopard and rhino. Interspersed among the mounted heads were artifacts of the ancient weapons used by native warriors. Beneath each spear, blowgun or club was a neatly typed card explaining the instrument's derivation, how it was used and to what effect.

Davis gave Konrad a few minutes to study the displays, then approached with another drink for each of them. "The mutual friend who called me gave you the highest marks, Mr. Konrad. By the way, do you mind if I drop the mister? I understand you prefer just Konrad."

Assured the less formal name was acceptable, Davis continued, "Anyone who is a friend of that person is certainly welcome in my home, and welcome as a potential client, which leads me to ask, how can I be of service to you?"

"I need the temporary services of some people whom I believe are in your acquaintance."

"I have a lot of friends. Tell me what you need and I'll tell you if I can help."

Konrad had another fictitious story prepared for the occasion. "I have been retained by some men to ferry—"

Davis held up a hand to silence his guest. "Sorry, you misunderstood. I specifically don't want to know what you have planned, just the exact skills you require to accomplish it from any person I might be in a position to recommend. You see, I can't be accused of conspiring in something I know nothing about. I'm not a criminal, you know. The only thing I insist upon is that I not be asked to aid in any way the cause of communism or black nationalism. Some of my chaps—and I myself, for that matter—feel pretty strongly about that sort of thing. Now, just what do you need?"

"I need three men available on short notice who can expertly fly the DC-3 aircraft over mountainous terrain at very low levels: two main pilots and a backup."

Davis nodded in recognition. "Ah, the DC-3. In the British army we called it the Dakota. One of the truly great aeroplanes, reliable and versatile. It'll fly in almost any weather and land about anyplace. The DC-3 has been the workhorse of Africa—marvelous bush plane, even today."

"I'll also need the best radio man you've got."

Davis smiled reassuringly. "I know at least a dozen who can make a radio talk back to them."

Konrad continued. "All four need valid passports, the self-discipline to operate on a split-second schedule, willingness to follow orders instantly, and to be

133

completely reliable at all times. If they know German, that would be nice, too. Do you think I can find such men in South Africa, Major?"

"Konrad, if my men didn't have the qualities you refer to, they wouldn't be my men—they'd be long since dead. And by all odds, I probably wouldn't be here discussing the subject.

"Understand, Konrad, that my colleagues, whether you want to call them mercenaries, soldiers of fortune or what-have-you, are the most resourceful, well-trained and toughest fighting men in the world. They're also a bit crazy—not the pilots, of course. They're veterans of the most elite commando units of the best armies. In many cases, they were too good, too intense, even for those outfits. Konrad, if my men are not the very best, they don't remain my men."

"Does that mean we do business?"

"That depends. What are you willing to pay, and when would you need them?"

"The pay is thirty thousand dollars plus expenses, ten thousand in advance." Konrad noted Davis' encouraging nod and continued. "I would want them in Paris on December eighth. They'll find four reservations at the Paris Hiton in the name of Trans-Europe Oil Corporation. They're to take those rooms and wait to be contacted."

"Konrad, you don't strike me as a fool. You surely know you're paying far more than the market requires."

"Of course. Let me put it this way: I don't want any squabbles over money in the middle of the operation. And I want some real enthusiasm for our success."

"Very wise, if you can afford it." Davis gave Konrad a

long look, then said, "Konrad, what would you think if I told you I'm very interested for myself? Would you like me for one of your pilots?"

"You?" Konrad didn't conceal his surprise.

"Why not? My men follow me because I'm the best of the very best. But even a legend has to make a living, and you promise a very nice payday."

Konrad quickly evaluated the pros and cons, then said, "With all respect, Major, I can't afford your face. You're an international figure. Wherever you are is where the press would like to be. The attention you might draw to me would be ruinous. I'm sure you can understand."

Davis shrugged and then nodded. "A wise decision professionally, but personally I'm very disappointed. Oh well, I'll just have to be content with the fee, which I presume you're prepared to pay."

Konrad withdrew a pink piece of paper from his wallet. "I came prepared. Here's a cashier's check for twenty-eight thousand dollars. Is my calculation correct?"

"Very precise, sir." Davis quickly examined the check and then pocketed it. "Done. Rest assured the men you need will be where you want them. Now we can concentrate on a fine dinner and good conversation. And no more business."

As they stood and stretched their legs by walking around the room, Davis said, "You know, it seems a little strange to fly halfway around the world just to spend a few hours hiring four men."

"Well, I guess that proves good men are hard to find. By the way, I'm curious about something. You never asked me if the operation was dangerous."

"With us, that's never a big consideration."

"Major, would you satisfy my curiosity on something?"

"Certainly, if I can."

"How come you're still alive? You've survived so many tight scrapes against overwhelming odds that you should have died several times over. You've rolled the dice a lot of times, but they've always come up seven. How do you do it?"

Davis chuckled, but he was obviously pleased by the flattering question. "The secret, if you care to call it that, lies with small numbers. In guerrilla warfare, a small, disciplined strike force is the ideal instrument. All of the ingredients of victory spring from that—speed, surprise and execution. Always remember that when you know exactly what you want to do, how to do it, and when to quit, you have an almost insurmountable advantage against an undisciplined and unexpecting enemy.

"I guess we were romantically portrayed as the underdogs during our little adventures in the bush. The truth is, against us, those overmanned, untrained and ill-equipped black buggers had no chance. We didn't do it with dice, we just used sound military tactics and damned good men."

All during the discussion, Davis had been ordering drink after drink from the obliging servants. He finally instructed one to leave a full bottle of Johnnie Walker Red Scotch with them. Although Konrad had slowed his drinking to an occasional sip, the bottle was almost empty. And Davis showed no inclination to stop.

They watched as the servants proceeded to set a beautiful table in a corner of the study. Thinking to make small talk as they waited, Konrad asked, "Do you have a family?"

Davis snorted into his glass. "I've had two or three. Women like money, and they like fame, but they never ask how you got those things until after the ceremony and their right to alimony is secured. My wives all suffered from the same delusion. Each thought she was marrying a hero, and each found out she'd married a hired hand. You see, Konrad, the South African ruling class styles itself after the British model. To them, I'm a mascot, a lethal one, to be sure, but a mascot just the same. They'll praise me, pay me, in some cases almost pray to me, but they would never socialize with me. My dear wives learned, each in her turn, that to be married to Major Dirk Davis was no ticket to social standing. No, those fine gentry would have nothing to do with the spouses of a soldier with blood on his hands; no matter that the blood got there defending their lives and property. It's simply a matter that blood is unsightly and ungentlemanly. 'Thank you, Major Davis, you can collect your pay at the back door.' The poor ladies I married couldn't handle that, bless their tiny hearts. I hope they've since found the mousy bankers they were intended for."

"Does that make you bitter?" Konrad asked.

"Bitter? Why? I always knew the ground rules. Here, let me read you something." Davis went to a bookcase and rummaged around looking for a certain volume. "Here we go. Kipling. Should be required reading for any British soldier. Listen to this: 'For it's Tommy this, an' Tommy that, an' "chuck 'im out, the brute!" but it's "Saviour of 'is country" when the guns begin to shoot.'

"Any English soldier soon learns what Kipling meant by that. Unfortunately, his lady often does not."

When they sat down to dinner, Konrad was surprised to find the meal identical to the traditional English roast

137

beef dinner, complete with gravy and vegetables. No sign whatsoever of an African influence on the menu. Konrad asked why.

"It's enough to live in this bloody, godforsaken land; I don't have to eat like a savage, too. One of the few ways I can still feel like an Englishman is to eat properly like one."

Though he talked of food, Davis didn't touch it. Instead, he turned his attention to the nearest servant. "Where in hell is the wine? Don't you know to bring a good bordeaux with roast beef? At once, you bloody imbeciles."

Davis turned apologetically to Konrad. "Pardon me, old fellow, don't like to raise my voice, but it's the only way to communicate with these beggars."

The wine appeared instantly and Davis gave it his undivided attention while Konrad concentrated on the delicious meal. As he ate and Davis drank, Konrad noticed the tension between the master and his servants, a condition the servants tried to cover up and Davis ignored.

Konrad helped himself to more roast beef and commented, "Considering what you've done in the bush, I'm a little surprised you'd be so much at ease with blacks under your own roof."

Davis gave a short laugh. "You can't understand the answer to that unless you understand the black mind. These people are basically children. All the trouble we've had with them is because of do-gooder whites who've told them they're equal and should be independent. They don't tell them that starvation is one of the less desirable byproducts of independence. Anyway, my blacks feel secure and well cared for. I scold them as I would children, firmly but kindly, but they know it's for their own good."

Davis' words were beginning to slur slightly, but he didn't drift from the subject. "Of course, I can't guarantee one of those bloody soft-headed white liberals won't poison the mind of one of my boys, so I hire only servants from tribes out in the bush."

"How does that make a difference?"

"Very simple. In Africa, the tribe is still the basis for native society. I go to a tribal chieftain I know to be loyal to the government and let him recruit servants for me. If he offers one I find acceptable, I pay him fifty dollars on the spot. If the boy proves satisfactory and serves five years, the chief gets another hundred dollars. So, everyone prospers: I get my servants, the chief gets paid, and the boy learns a trade. Of course, just to make sure the system works, I pay two of the servants double wages to spy on the others."

"What happens to the servant if he's fired and the village doesn't get its final payment?"

"He's beaten or killed when he returns. If he doesn't go home, he becomes a beggar, a man without a tribe, that sort of thing."

Davis stood a bit unsteadily and poured each of them more wine. Konrad pushed the bottle back gently before his glass was entirely full, but Davis filled his own to the brim.

"You must understand, Konrad, the black is genetically incapable of handling his own affairs. If our ways seem harsh, it's because we understand what works best—for them and for ourselves."

"Well, I can only judge from my own experience in America, but I see no real difference between black and

139

white in any of the ways that count. They seem OK to me."

"That's because you Americans can afford to indulge your fantasies of equality. You've basically got your blacks domesticated, socially housebroken, as it were. Out here, they're still savages, and we're surrounded by millions of the filthy heathens. Being absolutely realistic about that is the price we pay for remaining alive."

Konrad suppressed a growing irritation at the conversation; he didn't want to jeopardize his deal over some philosophical nit-picking. He also noticed that Davis was becoming increasingly maudlin as he went deeper into his cups. Self-pity is one of the least tolerable forms of drunkenness, and Konrad braced himself to endure seeing Davis wallow in it.

Davis lurched to his feet and started to slowly wave his free arm. "See this damned big old barn? Keeps me broke just holding it together, but I have to do it. If you're going to be a mercenary, you have to live like a successful one. Just like a fucking shopkeeper. Well, I'm getting rid of it, going to retire. I've done my share of letting people try to shoot my ass off. It's time I became an English country gentleman and wrote my memoirs. No more chasing bloody savages all over the bush. I've done that enough, and seen too much."

Davis flopped into an overstuffed easy chair. His voice became softer. "I've got pictures in my mind an old man shouldn't have. The reason war is a young man's game is so the memories have time to fade before he grows old. Every time I close my eyes I see bayoneted babies, raped nuns, flies feeding on bloated bodies we were too late to save. You do your damnedest, drive yourself for days on end to reach a settlement, only to get there an hour too

140

late. Then you have to face the accusations in the eyes of a mother holding the remains of her baby whose brains had been bashed out against a tree. Goddamnit, they were told to get out. How could they blame me?"

All of a sudden, Davis exercised the drunk's prerogative and changed the subject. His red-rimmed eyes became filled with self-pity. "All of us who kill for a living—black, white, whatever—tell ourselves that life's cheap, and we go on killing. Then we learn one day that we're right, life *is* cheap, and the cheapest of all is our own. The killing game . . . a grand game when you're young and good at it. But when we get old, we learn it's the only game where winners lose."

Davis shook his head in amazement. "I'll tell you something: The real reason I'm bailing out is that it's over. It's just a matter of time before the white man is pushed off this continent. And do you know why? Not because we've lost, but because we have to keep winning, again, again and then again. Every time we rout the guerrillas, some other country comes along with fresh arms, the same old promises and lies, and off it starts again. It wears a man down, wears a country down, never being able to rest after victory. After so many battles, people have to rest."

Davis' head was gently rolling and his eyelids fluttered with the burden of their weight. The empty glass rolled slowly out of his hand. "That's what I need, a long rest . . . so tired."

Konrad stared sympathetically at the man, suddenly much older in his vulnerability, softly snoring with his mouth open. The wrinkles and flaccid skin of his sunburned face betrayed his deep weariness. He was playing out the string, and was very near the end of it.

141

Konrad was reminded of his feelings when Willie Mac went out, stumbling in the center field that once was a stage on which he performed his ballet, or of a fat and old Ali, plodding around the ring chasing one final payday.

Major Dirk Davis, Konrad realized sadly, was now a mopping-up exercise.

Early the next morning, Konrad was awakened by a black hand shaking him gently. He opened his eyes to the face of one of Davis' servants.

"Major Davis is not feeling well this morning, sir. He wonders if you would mind taking a taxi to the airport?"

Konrad didn't mind at all.

The phone rang persistently until the bartender finished pouring a margarita and cut it off in mid-jangle. "Manny's," he growled impatiently while signaling "just a minute" to a pair of clamoring customers down the bar. "I can't hear you, operator. What? Angus O'Callahan? Just a minute." The bartender cupped the receiver and called, "Hey, lardass. Angus. It's for you. You can take it here. Sounds like long distance."

"Haaalo." A pause, and then a look of delight crossed Angus' face. "Hey, Konrad! Where you been? Where you calling from? Sounds like the bottom of a well. You hiding from a bill collector or something? Germany? Well, some guys will do anything to get out of buying a round."

Konrad cradled the phone and strolled the length of the cord around the hotel room until a familiar big voice boomed out at him through the receiver and a grin crossed his face. "Hello, *gordo*," he used the Spanish insult for obesity and waited for the counterinsult from

142

San Francisco. "Greetings from—" he glanced out the window—"rainy Germany. Hey, listen, if you want to bullshit, you pay for the call. I've got a deal for you. How'd you like to work for me?"

Angus released a belly laugh. "Work for you? What the hell doing? You need someone to fix your writing? Buddy, you'd better get Shakespeare or somebody like that."

"Goddamnit, I'm serious. I've got a good deal going here, finally going to have a good payday, and I want you in on it."

"How the hell am I going to get over there, hitchhike? I left my Mastercard in some bar so I don't have any plastic to spend. I was going to pick it up, but I figured they were using it less than I was, so I thought to hell with it. Besides, I've already got a job."

"I'll pay your expenses."

"All my expenses?"

"All of them."

"Including Jack Daniel's?"

"I'll even buy your Jack Daniel's."

"All I can drink?"

"All you can drink. Listen, you big jerk, I'll wire you five thousand dollars—that convince you? I want you to hop on the first available plane to Munich. When you arrive, take a cab to the Hilton. There'll be a room reserved for you. Stay there until you hear from me. By the way, how's your German these days?"

"It was good enough to get me laid in Hamburg, last time I was over there."

Konrad feigned disgust. "Hamburg? A tongue-tied midget speaking Sanskrit would have to fight to keep from getting laid there. Listen, I want you to do two

143

things. First, call that two-bit radio station that's been fucking you so royally, and tell them to go fuck themselves for a change. Second, make sure your ticket is first class. I'm going to start showing you the right way to go. We're going to show the world how to operate with style—the whole fucking world."

Chapter Six

The big man with the unruly red hair scanned the assortment of black and white photographs strewn across the rumpled hotel-room bed and picked up a candid shot of a man who appeared to be in his mid-sixties. He braced the photo in his left hand, a feat of some dexterity, considering he was missing the last two fingers on that hand. He slowly raised his right hand, then cocking the thumb like a pistol, he pointed a finger at the grim elderly man in the picture and softly said, "Pow." He stared at the photo a moment longer, then threw it back on the bed.

Levi Riley turned to a younger man watching him from a chair in the corner and said, "If I were a betting man, Moshe, I would lay plenty of shekels that our friend, Herr Karl Kaltbrunner, formerly of Hitler's personal staff, late of the SS goon squads, is on his way to that big Nazi reunion in Valhalla where they can just party with each other at Odin's elbow all day. Bang, another superior being bites the dust."

The younger man shrugged. He was used to his

partner's attempts to clown around while preparing for a manhunt. I guess that's what happens when a good Jewish girl falls in love with an Irish sailor, he thought. But then, Moshe Pritzer, twenty-five years old and filled with Zionist zeal, found little amusement in the operation they were conducting. He felt he had no time to chase around the world tracking down senile old Nazis who passed from the world's center stage many years ago. He would much rather be lining up a PLO terrorist in his gunsights right now. But the old people who ran things in Israel couldn't seem to get the Nazis off their minds. Anytime they got the scent of some decrepit ex-concentration camp guard trying to live out his miserable last days in some German farm village or Paraguayan jungle settlement, they had to launch a crusade of vengeance against him, and thus sidetrack agents like Moshe who should have been doing things more essential to the survival of Israel.

Pritzer maintained his quiet, relaxed position and studied Riley, but in a thousand years of pondering he would never really understand this man who was so different from himself.

Although Levi Riley was known as one of the more effective agents in the Mossad, the Israeli intelligence agency, his birth had been as colorful as his life.

Levi's mother was a refugee in that period shortly after World War II when desperate Jewish survivors of the holocaust in Europe chartered any tramp ship that could float with owners willing to risk the British blockade of the Palestine coast. Having endured two thousand years of European persecution, the refugees were determined to make "Next year in Jerusalem" a reality.

It was on such a ship, the *Dublin Star*, that young

146

Hanna Mecklin, orphaned daughter of a Berlin physician, met Michael Riley, son of a Shannon hod-carrier. She was one of the passengers crammed into the ship's stinking hold; he was an able-bodied seaman.

They met on deck one night as she was exercising while the hold was being halfheartedly cleaned. They had nothing in common except a desire to better their current state: He wanted money, she wanted roots. But as sometimes happens, occasionally for the better, their hearts overruled reason, and the two young seekers fell in love. They were quickly married by the captain because there was no one to object to such a hasty and ill-suited match; no one cared.

The captain should have known better than to allow young Riley to be among the crew ferrying the refugees ashore on a dark Palestine night, frightened mice scurrying to avoid the British hawk's gaze. But then, the captain was not accustomed to giving much thought to the fate of his crew. So when the opportunity arose for the young sailor to slip off into the shadows of that foreboding coast with his refugee bride, he took it.

The search for fortune that young Michael Riley so intently pursued came to a quick, undramatic end on a night patrol against the Arab enemy a year later. A sniper, not knowing or caring about the dreams of the happy-go-lucky Irishman, put a round hole through his chest. The last thought Michael Riley had on this earth was that he shouldn't be so cold in the middle of the desert.

The young widow fared very nicely; death was something with which she had learned to cope very early and well. Hanna followed in her father's memory and became a physician. She devoted her life to healing the sick and raising her son, a half Irish, all Jewish leprechaun; a red-headed, Israeli-born *Sabra* with a gallic grin.

It would be nice to say that young Levi was studious and obedient, and excelled at all things. Unfortunately for his doting mother's peace of mind, he found a hundred ways each week to defy that description. If there were a way to get into trouble or tweak the nose of authority and he hadn't done it, it just meant he hadn't thought of it—yet.

Though his early years could hardly be called suspended animation, Levi really came to life when he reached the age of military service. His natural gifts found their purpose when he first climbed into his big Sherman tank.

He was a good tank commander and he knew it and gloried in it. Levi funneled all of his youthful exuberance and energy into making his tank crew a dashing embodiment of the new-found Israeli warrior spirit. War to him was not death, but life. The stench of burnt flesh which he first experienced in the tank battles of the Yom Kippur war of 1973 was but a nauseating reminder that even the best games have their drawbacks.

Levi Riley was not a cruel man, nor was he one who lusted for blood. He was simply a soldier who liked his work. Killing was one of the least appealing parts of his job—like rain to a bricklayer, or a hot stove to a chef.

Fearless and audacious as he was, the loss of his fingers became all the more ironic. He didn't lose them to a Syrian's bayonet thrust, or to Egyptian shrapnel. No, to his eternal chagrin, he lost the fingers during training maneuvers in the Negev Desert. A stupid driver-trainee accidentally pushed the gear lever forward as Riley was down on his hands and knees inspecting the tread. The tank shot forward just a few feet, but it was enough to grind his fingers into pulp under tons of crushing steel.

Riley had suffered two minor wounds in battle, and didn't even remember the moment of either. But he would never forget the white-hot flash of pain that shot through his body when that heavy metal crushed his hand. He had visions of killing the driver, but contented himself with hopping around holding his hand, cursing and howling.

It was in the hospital following that accident when the Mossad first approached him as a potential agent. They didn't have to explain to him that the Mossad was one of the four great intelligence services, rivaled only by the American CIA, the British M-1, and the Russian KGB. Every citizen took pride in their unbroken record of outfoxing the enemies of Israel.

As Riley talked with the two operatives sent to interview him, it quickly became apparent that he was the type of man they were seeking, and that what they offered fit his temperament and skills perfectly. He was intrigued by living (and possibly dying) by his wits. He was stirred by visions of danger and glory in the often man-against-man world of international intrigue. When he was reminded that a good agent was sometimes more valuable to Israel than a division on the battlefield, they almost had to restrain him from leaving the hospital with them.

After a thorough and exhausting period of training, Riley found himself assigned to the division responsible for tracking down remaining Nazi war criminals. Although his group had the official title of L-17, other agents quickly nicknamed it the Kraut Korps and invented all sorts of comical tales involving toothless octogenarian Nazis counterattacking in wheelchairs.

Riley chafed at the ridicule, but he enjoyed the rich and varied life of the capitals of Europe where his work took him, especially Vienna where he was stationed. For the first time, he experienced how enjoyable and relaxed life could be without the ominous, ever-present shadow of war. He wasn't growing soft, just mixing a little spice into his duty ration.

The Nazi hunters of L-17 normally did not operate with a great sense of urgency; the quarry they hunted were not going anywhere, except possibly carried to an old man's grave by heart disease or stroke. The agents didn't consider disease a competitor because it tended to impose the same sentence anyway.

The tempo for Riley and fellow agent Moshe Pritzer suddenly intensified one day when they were summoned to a meeting at the Israeli embassy in Vienna with Ira Levin, chief of operations for L-17 in Western Europe. The two agents noticed immediately that the normally placid, methodical Levin was much more animated than usual.

As soon as they were seated in the small conference room borrowed for the occasion, Levin said, "Well, boys, this isn't another minnow of a concentration camp guard. We've found a shark for you this time. The guy we're going to take a look at today was close to the old paper hanger himself."

As he talked, Levin fiddled with a slide projector on the table. They waited as he finished his preparations, flicked off the wall light switch and turned on the projector. The thin beam of light illuminated a neatly typed card on the screen, which read:

150

The data card was quickly followed by the image of an elderly man with a hard-looking face. "Gentlemen, meet Herr Gerhard Bruner. Not a very interesting man—retired successful merchant living quietly on an estate near Marburg, West Germany. Not the sort of man who attracts much attention. Probably very boring and predictable in everything."

Levin pressed the projector button and the image changed to an older sepia-tone photograph of a group of Nazi officers arrogantly posed in front of a burned building, the burnished lightning-bolt SS runes on their collars glittering against the charred background. The tattered scrolls held by two of the men were displayed like trophies won at a soccer match. The three men at the table knew at a glance that they were Torah scrolls. It wasn't difficult to figure out that the destroyed building was a synagogue.

"Look at the man second from left. See any resemblance between him and the man in the previous photo?"

Riley and Pritzer peered closely at the enlarged but faded image. Their training in recognizing facial characteristics helped them sort out the identifiable similarities between the two images, allowing for the differences in age and setting. The man in the second photo was definitely a younger version of the old man in the first picture, even allowing for attempts to disguise the features.

Levin said, "Would you believe that this also is

Gerhard Bruner? Well, not exactly. He was Karl Kaltbrunner back in 1942 when this photo was taken in Czechoslovakia. But I assure you, both dogs were birthed by the same bitch. What we have here, men, are two views of one of the very worst Nazi assholes still alive or at large. Young or old, Bruner or Kaltbrunner, he's still the same Aryan hero."

A click followed by a shifting of the lighted screen produced another old photo of a group of men standing on a railroad loading dock. Of the dozen or so men in the photo, two clearly dominated. Levin pointed to them, circling the pair with the long shadow of a wooden pointer. "Welcome to Treblinka, Poland. Need I describe what happened to your ancestors there, some of whom you can see milling about in front of our distinguished visitors? In the background, you can see some of the barracks, those low, wooden buildings. The execution chambers are those windowless brick buildings in the upper right-hand corner.

"Anyway, the two men I pointed out are the infamous Adolf Eichmann—he's the one gesturing—and our new-found friend, Karl Kaltbrunner. At this time, 1943, he was chief liaison officer between the department that ran the concentration camps, in which Eichmann was quite powerful, as you know, and the department that coordinated supplemental war resources.

"Now, neither of you has to guess what 'supplemental war resources' were. They consisted of whatever their captured Jews could contribute to the war effort—gold from teeth, human hair, clothing no longer needed by humans turned to ash, body fat for soap, and so on. A very resourceful man, our Colonel Kaltbrunner. Very proficient at getting the most out of what our people had to offer."

Levin flicked to another photo. This one was a newspaper clipping much deteriorated by time, but the faces were still clear. "Let's look at an earlier phase of Kaltbrunner's career. This was in 1938 when he was a *wunderkind* of the SS general staff, a real achiever, and as you know, that kind of favor wasn't attained by Boy Scout merit badges. This is a clipping from a Berlin newspaper of the period. Sitting next to the main man himself, Der Führer, is Crown Prince Frederick of Liechtenstein. Sitting directly behind Hitler is Kaltbrunner. Anyone allowed that close to Hitler was definitely the occupant of a very plush easy chair.

"The meeting between Hitler and the crown prince was requested by Frederick to convince Hitler that his tiny country should not be overrun by the Germans. Apparently, Hitler had all but decided to occupy Liechtenstein and install Kaltbrunner as military governor, probably in charge of looting.

"Our World War II archivists tell us that Frederick convinced Hitler that negative world opinion would outweigh any benefits gained by controlling Liechtenstein. I guess the prince was a pretty smooth talker, because Hitler backed off. Needless to say, Kaltbrunner was royally pissed off."

Levin turned off the projector and flicked on the light switch. He reached into his attache case and produced two thick Manila folders which he handed to the men. "Here's the file on Kaltbrunner, also known as Bruner, from 1930 to the present. Study it well before you leave the building today. Then come back tomorrow and study

153

it some more. Get to know this man like he was a favorite uncle—then get him."

Riley asked, "Would you prefer a prisoner or a corpse?"

Levin didn't hesitate. "Kill him. Quick and clean. The days of dramatic, drawn-out Nazi war-crimes trials are over. For one thing, no one gives a shit anymore. The world has a very brief attention span, and an even shorter conscience. For another, it would irritate our West German allies to know we're still carrying on clandestine operations within their borders. No, I want an execution."

Levin closed the conference room door and the three men started walking down the corridor toward Levin's office where he maintained his convenient front as a cultural attache. Walking between the two agents, he put a hand on the shoulder of each, and said, "I'm as familiar as either of you with all the jokes about the 'Kraut Korps.' I know all about the toothless old quartermaster sergeants we're supposed to be chasing, and all that. But don't take those stupid-ass jokes seriously, especially now. This guy Kaltbrunner is dangerous. He's involved in every neo-Nazi scheme we've been able to uncover. He's smart, too. We only found him by a fluke and a bit of luck. He came out of the war safely with a stolen fortune, and he knows how to spend it to protect himself. He may be old, but he'll be dangerous when he's one hundred, which, with your cooperation, he'll never reach."

They stopped at Levin's office door and briefly shook hands. Riley and Pritzer started walking away, and Levin turned toward his office. He hesitated, then said, "Hey, wait a minute."

The two agents stopped and turned quizzically.

"One last thing: Do it fast, but before he goes, make sure he knows who did it."

Riley picked up the photos spread on the bed and shuffled them into a neat stack. He turned to the quiet Pritzer and studied him for a moment. "You don't have much enthusiasm for this assignment, do you, Moshe?"

The younger man stirred. "Why should I? I live in the present, not the past. And to help Israel survive, we'd better worry about the present, not the past."

Pritzer left his chair and paced up and down the room, distressed at the thought of being sidetracked from the main theater of action. "I volunteered for Mossad because I wanted to help fight the PLO, not to take myself completely out of action from that battle by chasing a bunch of demented old war criminals. Sure, I feel as strongly as anybody about the holocaust and all that, but this is a different time and there are different battles to fight."

A bemused Riley watched his partner's agitated pacing for a few moments, then said, "Moshe, for a Jew to speak of the past as irrelevant is heresy. The thing that keeps us a distinct people is our unwillingness to forget or forsake the past. We live in the present, for the future, because we know and understand the past. And what every Jew should now comprehend better than anything else is that we must never again passively accept persecution. You think the Nazi barbarities are in the past. Hell, that was just a few decades ago. As our persecutions are measured, that's yesterday.

"We track Nazis, not because we feel the need to kill a bunch of old men, but because we're sending a message.

155

The message tells every would-be Jew-baiter that they risk their asses when they try to push Jews around, that however long it takes or wherever we have to go, we'll get them for it."

Pritzer resumed his seat and listened intently. "Moshe, what happened during Hitler's time could happen tomorrow. To be a smart Jew is to know that you're never really safe anywhere on this planet, that anti-Semitism is never dead, it only sleeps, and then fitfully. The mistake the old Jews made was not to fight back however they could; that's a mistake we have to remedy by evening the score. It's just something that has to be done."

Riley laughed. "God, what could be more maudlin than a Mick Jew? Enough of this, we've got work to do."

Riley shifted his attention to a sheaf of notes he had made and which would be destroyed before he left the room. "Now, let's see . . . I think we pretty much have the book completed on Kaltbrunner. Except for brief trips to meet the American and the blonde, he hasn't left his estate since we started surveillance two months ago. What we have to figure out is what was so important about meeting those two that he was willing to leave his well-protected lair? It just may be that they could lead us to neo-Nazi activities that Kaltbrunner has been involved in. Maybe the net can widen. What have you been able to find out about the woman, Moshe?"

"Not a lot. Her name is Honi Miller; seems to be her real name. She was born in Liechtenstein about thirty years ago, but hasn't been back for about ten. She's a high-priced hooker. Works the resorts where the big spenders congregate. Doesn't seem to have any close friends, and absolutely no previous political involvement. Kaltbrunner doesn't seem to be a customer, and he's never shown any interest in prostitution as a business, so I don't know what they'd have in common."

Riley interrupted. "There's no limit to the ways a good-looking whore can be used. The oldest profession is also the most versatile. An imaginative man like Kaltbrunner could think of a thousand ways to use her skills."

"I grant you that," Pritzer replied. "But Rothstein and Lassler trailed her to Zurich as soon as she left Frankfurt. She took a room at an out-of-the-way residential hotel, and proceeded to do nothing for two weeks, up to the present. Our guys bugged her room and telephone, and got nothing. All she does every day is shop, eat, sleep and visit museums and art galleries. They assume she's waiting for someone or something."

"Well, that doesn't help us much," Riley said. "Fortunately, we've had better luck with the American." Riley proceeded to read the astonishing amount of material Mossad agents had gathered on Konrad in a very short time. They had compiled a very accurate profile on him from his birth in Freiburg, through his army days, mercenary activities and frustrated writing career.

"An interesting character," Pritzer said. "What's he been doing since meeting Kaltbrunner?"

"Konrad's been a busy boy. I followed him to a rendezvous with a sleazy Frankfurt munitions black-marketeer who goes by the street name Owl. He then visited Walter Schell. Ever hear of him? Fascinating fellow. Supposedly recruits criminals to work for other criminals. Probably a handy fellow for us to get to know someday. Anyway, Konrad spent a couple of hours with him.

"After seeing Schell, he boarded a flight to Cape Town, South Africa. One of our agents picked up his trail at the airport there. He was met by Major Dirk Davis, the famous mercenary. They drove to Davis' house and spent the night there. Konrad returned to Europe the next day."

"What else did he do?" Pritzer asked.

"That was a little strange. He spent a lot of time at libraries and travel bureaus gathering information about Liechtenstein."

Both men remained silent for several moments to digest the information they had exchanged. Riley finally removed fingertips from pursed lips. "I have a test question from Elementary Spying 101: What ties the three of them together?"

"Liechtenstein, professor."

"Congratulations."

"But the big question, Riley, is what does it mean?"

"Whatever it is, I guarantee it won't be good for Liechtenstein. Let's look at it from Kaltbrunner's viewpoint, since you can bet he's the brains behind whatever they're doing. What would you need with the hooker? Possibly because she knows the country, but that's pretty tenuous. What would you need with a crooked ex-soldier? Kaltbrunner knows better crooks, but this guy was a very good soldier. Liechtenstein is a country that was neutral during World War II, which were Kaltbrunner's salad days; it borders Switzerland, where many big Nazis kept their stolen money; it's close to Germany and they speak the same language."

"I think I've got it," Pritzer broke in excitedly. "I'll bet Kaltbrunner has part of his World War II loot hidden in Liechtenstein and he's hired the American to put a gang together to get it out. The girl will serve as local contact."

Riley looked apprehensive. "Why would you need a gang to sneak out hidden treasure? I think it's more likely they plan to knock off a bank or something. And you never know, the Liechtenstein angle could be nothing more than a coincidence. My biggest worry is that since we have only a handful of agents to track this thing, they could pull off whatever they have planned and be long gone before we could catch up. We need to find out for certain what they're going to do before they do it. Who knows, we might not only bag a Nazi, but his loot as well."

"How do we find out what their plan is?" Pritzer asked.

"Simple. We kidnap the American and force him to tell us. Then we kill the Nazi and go pick up his loot, if that's what it is, and then turn it over to Mossad. Chances are, what they stole came from Jews, anyway. If that's not their scheme, but maybe some Nazi organizing plot, then we'll be prepared to deal with that, too. If we can't get it from the American, then we'll take the woman, the prostitute, if we have to."

"So then what happens to the American?"

Riley shrugged. "That's up to him and how deeply he's messed up in this. At best, he turns on the Nazi and joins us; at worst, he's the unfortunate victim of a nasty automobile accident. Happens every day."

"Wouldn't that bother you? He hasn't been proved guilty of anything."

"That's not the most pleasurable part of this job, at least not for me. But to respond to your statement, yes, he is guilty. He's guilty of keeping bad company. That can

159

be fatally bad judgment when the consort is a Jew-killing Nazi bastard." Riley slapped his leg in mild frustration. "What kind of person do you think would agree to do Kaltbrunner's dirty work? This guy Konrad is no virgin, you can bet. He's playing in a dirty game with some nasty playmates. Don't waste your pity on him."

"Well, I'm not comfortable with the idea."

"*C'est la guerre.*"

"What do you mean, 'that's war'? What war?"

"World War II. It's not over yet."

Chapter Seven

Konrad looked again at the address Walter Schell had given him, then glanced back at the small, ramshackle house in the poor section of Hamburg. If one had to live in poverty, it could at least be where the sun shone, not in this slate-gray industrial city of the cold north. One thing became obvious about Otto Ender, he didn't seem to have much of a bargaining position.

Konrad shrugged and pushed open the squeaky gate. He'd be the last to put down someone for living on the thin side.

Just as he raised his hand to knock on the paint-flecked door, it swung open and he was face to face with a man who, if this were Otto Ender, was the youngest-looking old man he had ever seen. He was about Konrad's height. His hair was wavy brown. His build was slim with no hint of a paunch. His face was deeply furrowed, but with lines of rugged exposure, not age. When he asked, "I assume you're Herr Konrad?" his voice was clear and resonant. The hand he extended in response to Konrad's, "Yes, I am," was firm and strong.

Konrad completed his survey and thought, if that's me in twenty-five years, I'll take it. Hell, maybe in ten.

Ender stood aside and ushered Konrad into the small parlor with a slow sweep of his hand. The room inside revealed that the outside was not a modest understatement. A glance at the three rooms—parlor, kitchen and bedroom—reflected a spartan simplicity and starkness. This man lived frugally, simply and very cleanly. If a woman lived here, too, she left no signs of her presence.

"The only thing I have to offer is schnapps," Ender said as they sat on straight-back wooden chairs. "It may not be the best, but you'll find the makers didn't cheat on the alcohol," he joked wryly as he poured the potent, clear liquid.

"*Probst*," they saluted each other. Ender spoke first. "I've looked forward to this visit ever since our mutual friend told me you might be coming. Man, all I want is to get back to work."

"What've you been doing for a living?" Konrad took an involuntary glance around the sparse quarters as he asked.

"Currently or altogether?"

"Both."

"I'm a janitor at an elementary school. Not exactly the type of work I'm trained for, but it's a living—sort of." Ender's eyes followed Konrad's across the meager room. "The last decent job I had was training officer for the Libyan army, about five years ago. I say 'decent' because it was at least in my line of work. But, shit, I'm not sure being a janitor isn't better than trying to teach those stupid-ass Arabs to be soldiers. Like watching a monkey try to fuck a football. They should stick to being camel drivers and lazy thieves, that's all they're suited for.

162

"Before that, it was the foreign legion, twenty-five years with mandatory retirement in 1972."

"How'd you like the legion?" Konrad asked.

"Compared to what? I went there straight from five years in a Russian prisoner of war camp. Believe me, I liked the legion fine. Before my vacation in Siberia, it was the German army, starting before the war. I guess you could say the fact that I carry a gun seems to be more important to me than the uniform I wear. I was a mercenary before it became fashionable—and profitable."

Konrad shifted restlessly, then decided not to waste time. "I'm going to put it to you straight, Ender. I came here because Walter Schell, a man I respect, suggested it. What I find is a janitor old enough to be my father, living just slightly better than a bum. You look OK for your age, but how do I know you could command the respect of my men?" Konrad shrugged. "Sorry, but that's the way I see it; that's the way it is."

When Ender finally spoke, it was between clenched teeth. "Herr Konrad, 'the way it is,' as you put it, is no mystery to me. Why do you think I'm a janitor? I'll tell you why. Because young punks like yourself who serve two years in some peacetime army, never firing at anything more dangerous than a paper target, never getting a more serious wound than the clap, think they really understand soldiering. Well, I'm not impressed. I don't consider a man a soldier because he wears a jaunty beret, or because he pigeon-shoots some primitive savage in Africa who hardly knows which end of a gun to point.

"Let me tell you, I've seen some soldiers in my time. I've seen them in places you can't even imagine, like the Eastern Front near the end. It was so cold the oil in

163

vehicles would freeze, and we were sleeping on the open ground in summer-issue clothing. We knew the situation was hopeless, that we would die either with a bayonet in our guts or doing slave labor in a Siberian prison." Ender's voice trailed off and he looked at Konrad with derision. "And you question me . . . shit."

Konrad started to respond, but Ender commanded, "Let me finish. I suppose you've been in the American army, probably Vietnam." Konrad's confirming nod encouraged Ender to continue. "Big fucking deal. In Vietnam, you went into battle with picnic lunches, cold beer, and then came back to air-conditioned barracks each night at quitting time. If you got wounded or surrounded, you called in the Air Force to level the countryside for ten miles around, or more likely, you called for helicopters to haul your asses the hell out of danger. Let me tell you something about Vietnam—"

"OK, OK," Konrad said in a conciliatory tone.

"OK nothing, damnit. You come in here, take one look, form a snap judgment and start degrading me. You're going to hear me out. I was in Vietnam, too, only we called it French Indochina. But it was the same place. I was with the legion at a place called Dien Bien Phu. Ever hear of it? Well, Ho Chi Mihn and Giap were there, too. They had fifty thousand troops, we had fifteen thousand. We didn't have hot lunches or cold beer. We didn't have helicopters to save our asses. When men were wounded, we tried to do what we could, but when our medicines ran out, they just lay there suffering, and bleeding, and stinking, and dying. The lice were so thick you could watch your clothes move. After a while we didn't give a damn. Our misery became so bad it was like a companion, not one we were fond of, but one we got

164

used to.

"Do you know how long we held out? Fifty-five days. Do you know why? I'll tell you: because we were soldiers. Most of us weren't even French. We didn't give a fuck for the whole French nation. No, we fought because we were soldiers, and to quit or fight poorly would be self-denial. The only things we had in the world were what we could cram into our knapsacks, and pride. Take away the pride and we were beggars. We fought to keep that pride. If we came out alive, we knew we could call ourselves soldiers. If we didn't come out, our comrades would call us soldiers, and that was almost as good.

"You look at me and see an old man, and you ask yourself, 'What can that old bastard do for me?' Well, let me tell you what I can do. I can run a marathon. Twenty-six miles, three-hundred-eighty-five yards. Can you?"

Ender walked over to the iron stove and selected a thick piece of kindling. He beckoned for Konrad to follow him and went into the kitchen. Ender placed one end of the wood on the window sill and the other on the edge of the sink. With a motion too fast for Konrad to follow, he brought the flat of his hand down on the board. The two ends flew into the air and fell with a clatter. Ender had neatly broken it in two with the flat of his hand. Ender looked at him challengingly. "Not bad for an old man, eh?"

Konrad's stare became a grin. He extended his hand. "You've convinced me. Man, did I guess wrong. But apparently that comes with being a young punk. Ender, do you want to go back to work?"

"If it isn't mopping floors and being called 'Old Otto' by a bunch of snot-nosed brats, I'm your man."

"Before I describe the job, answer this: Are you willing

165

to break the law and risk jail or maybe death?"

Ender looked at Konrad with amusement. "You make that sound like a big deal. Let me tell you something. I believe the world was created on August 21, 1942. That was the day we attacked Stalingrad. Before that, I actually believed there were such things as decency, happiness, laughter and even Christmas. But from that day to this, life has done a damn good job of educating me. What I gained from that hell on the banks of the Volga, and the five years of hopelessness in Siberia, and the misery of the Indochina jungles, is numbness. Pain doesn't exist for me, because I've felt it worse than I could ever feel it again. I don't give a damn about crime because I've seen people tortured and killed in the name of law and order. I've read books, trying to find out from the world's great thinkers and philosophers where my thinking has gone wrong. And do you know what? I think they're all full of shit. They sit in their libraries and cozy parlors next to a cheerful fireplace and write about what life is all about. Well, maybe their lives, but not mine. I've seen right and wrong so twisted during my time that I don't recognize the shape of either. To me, what counts is pride and loyalty to my outfit."

Konrad decided to plunge ahead. "What I have in mind is the armed takeover of Liechtenstein."

Ender didn't bat an eyelash. "How many men will you have, and how long do you intend to hold it?"

"Forty men; two days."

Ender was thinking hard. "There are things forty men can do that an entire army can't. Yeah, I'd say it's possible."

"If we do it, it'll be worth one hundred thousand dollars to you."

166

"And if we fail?"

"Nothing."

"Fair. When do we start?"

"Right now." Konrad removed a large topographical map of Liechtenstein from his briefcase and spread it out on the small kitchen table. The two men began studying it like a great painting. They rarely lifted their eyes as they pored over details of terrain and deployment. They chatted and argued amiably about how to seal off routes and how to stretch a thin force to make it appear larger. Konrad quickly noticed that Ender had an excellent grasp of tactics. In the space of a few hours, he made suggestions that considerably strengthened Konrad's basic plan. Far into the night and all the next day they argued, cajoled, and agreed with each other on the fine points of a plan that was quickly reflecting an increasing number of fine points.

Ender pointed on the map to a Swiss army base adjoining the southern border of Liechtenstein. "That makes me nervous. If the Swiss wanted, they could squash us like a worm on an *Autobahn*."

"That's why I've restricted our arms to only those necessary to control a civilian population. No way are we going to declare war on the Swiss army."

"What happens if they aren't taken in by our little scheme and come down on us?"

"We say, 'Legs, don't fail us now,' and get the hell out. Every man for himself. But if that's not possible, we've got a big ace we can still pull out of the deck."

"What do you mean?"

"Stop and think. What's the most important thing in a principality?"

A smile crossed Ender's face. "What a beautiful

167

hostage he'd make."

Both men were exhausted from hours of uninter-
rupted thinking, but they hammered out the details of a
plan that left them confident and eager. Finally, they
gathered up all of their notes and drawings and burned
most in Ender's ancient stove.

Konrad removed twenty thousand Swiss francs from
his wallet and gave the wad of bills to Ender. "Go directly
to Liechtenstein and get a hotel room, just like an
ordinary tourist, but familiarize yourself with all the
places we've discussed here. I'll be there in a few days.
We can talk again then."

Ender looked at the money lying in his open hand.
"You know," he said, "it's not so much the money that
matters, but the feeling of being worth something again."

Konrad clapped him on the back. "Well, you're now
my main man, my lieutenant."

"Not lieutenant, Konrad. Sergeant. A sergeant is all
I've ever been, and all I want to be. But I'm a damned
good one."

"I'll settle for a damned good sergeant."

Konrad was feeling pretty good. He had just completed
arrangements for the construction of twenty fifty-gallon
oil drums, very special oil drums. These would contain
oil only in the top and bottom twelve inches. Between the
removable false compartments was an area three-feet
deep. That space would be filled mostly with sand, but
buried in the sand, hidden from the prying searches of
Swiss border guards, would be the guns and ammunition
necessary to conquer Liechtenstein. The total weight
would be exactly that of a barrel of oil. The work would be

done in a Frankfurt metals shop known in the underground for their fine craftsmanship and lack of curiosity.

As he left the metals shop, Konrad was bundled against the evening chill of the early-winter wind that swept down the grimy back street of the city's industrial area. The factories and warehouses had closed for the day and Konrad could see his car parked along the deserted street just a few hundred feet beyond. The only person visible in either direction was a derelict in shabby clothing sprawled on the sidewalk just ahead of him.

Following the natural inclination to avoid encountering a messy drunk, Konrad started to circle him, but the man suddenly spoke in a pained voice. "Help me," he pleaded in English.

Startled, Konrad hesitated. "Please help me. I'm an American, and I'm hurt," the man again asked. "Here, see."

Konrad's attention was frozen. He moved closer at the man's urging. He had red hair and looked too alert for a common drunk. Konrad's senses started to bristle, but too late. The man's foot swung out, expertly kicking Konrad's legs from beneath him. Konrad felt his knee hit the pavement hard, and he struggled to regain his feet, but as he did, the iron vise of a strong forearm wrapped around his neck. He instinctively grabbed the arm with both hands to relieve the pressure. Things were happening too fast. The man behind him swiftly brought his other arm around and covered Konrad's face with a wide cloth.

Konrad felt the suffocating presence of the cloth and fought for breath. But every time he gasped, his lungs filled with a sweet, pungent odor that slowly made his

169

mind go numb and his legs slack. He fought for consciousness, but the iron arm wouldn't let go; it grew stronger as he weakened. His eyes lost focus and he felt the sensation of falling, but he couldn't stop. The falling accelerated, but he never hit bottom: Nothingness came first.

Konrad's assailant caught his limp form and easily held him erect, grabbing the waist and slipping his head under Konrad's arm. To anyone happening by, it would have appeared that one drunk was propping up another. Within seconds, a car screeched up to the curb and both men disappeared into the back seat.

Opening his eyes seemed to trigger the pain. A second after he first squinted into the blinding lights, Konrad's head exploded in triphammer pounding. He closed his eyes, but the pain remained. He wanted to caress his eyelids but his hands wouldn't move. Cautiously, he reopened his eyes. The lights were still there, but he slowly adjusted to the glare. He let out a low moan, his body's protest at how cruelly it had been treated.

The heads of the two men standing just beyond the bright lights simultaneously turned toward the groan. They looked at each other meaningfully and approached Konrad.

He was tied to a straight-back wooden chair. His legs were bound with heavy rope and his arms were secured tightly behind him. Despite being awake, Konrad's head continued to loll as he fought the lingering effects of the chloroform. He worked at focusing his eyes on the approaching blurs that he knew instinctively were the assailants who had put him in this condition.

The big, red-haired one spoke first. "Well, well. Good evening, Konrad. Have a pleasant nap? We're pleased you were able to accept our invitation. To make the evening memorable, we plan a lively little discussion. And to show you what good hosts we are, we're going to let you do most of the talking. In fact, we shall insist on it."

Konrad only half heard the man. He was trying to comprehend his situation and surroundings. The room was a small one with high ceilings. It was stripped of furniture, so he had no idea of what its normal function was, unless this was it. There was one door, a large stone fireplace and a pair of double windows ribbed with lead in the old style. His position was too low to see anything out of them. Konrad had no idea where he was, and he knew it would be pointless to ask.

The second man moved closer to him. He was smaller and darker than the first and seemed to be a subordinate. At first, Konrad was not so frightened as confused. Nothing in his experience had prepared him for being forcibly kidnapped and tied like a goose ready for market. If he had been aware of the possibility of this happening, or even knew the reason, at least he could have mentally prepared himself. But this way, his pain and apprehension were compounded by shock and confusion. But, even so, he remained silent. Obviously, these two had something in mind, and it would involve him sooner than he wanted. He had ruled out mistaken identity the moment they used his name. No, he was the one they wanted. He could only fervently hope that what they wanted was something he could furnish quickly and satisfactorily. At the moment, Konrad was not feeling heroic.

171

The big man broke the silence. This time there was no humor in his voice. "OK, Konrad, this can be simple and quick, or long and painful. If you want to live, you'll tell us what we need to know straight out. But you better know for damn certain that we'll find out one way or the other. And I promise you, the 'other' will not be pleasant."

The other man spoke. His words came faster and more demandingly. "What are you doing for Kaltbrunner?"

Konrad's confused silence was interrupted by a white-hot pain that started in his leg and seared its way to the brain, leaving a trail of quivering nerves along its path. Konrad moaned and tried to catch his breath. More than anything else he wanted to hold his right shin where Pritzer had kicked it with full force. At that moment, he would have given a year off his life to be able to massage away that pulsing ache.

"Why . . . why did you do that?" he gasped. "I don't know any Kaltbrunner. I swear I don't. For God's sake, don't you think I'd tell you?"

He was answered by another kick, this one by the other man, in the same spot with equal force. This time he cried out in anguish as the tortured shinbone sent its pain signal with double intensity to the brain. His whole body wiggled and arched against the ropes, trying desperately, futilely to get away from its tormentor. He was unaware he had urinated in his pants.

Riley gave a small motion to Pritzer to desist and leaned over toward Konrad. "Tell me now, or it'll happen again."

Konrad was desperate to make them understand. Why wouldn't they give him time to answer? "Wait, please wait. Describe him, this man you're talking about. Maybe

I'll know him that way, but I've never heard that name. I'll tell you anything you want to hear, I mean, know."

"The old Nazi you met in the Frankfurt Airport Hotel. What did you discuss? What are you doing for him?"

Konrad's mind started to clear. He knew his life might depend on what he said. He had to tell them enough to avoid being tortured, but not so much that his value would be ended. Above all, he had to think of a way to escape.

"Look, I know you two are going to get what you want; I know how this sort of thing works. But will you please loosen these ropes? I'm losing feeling in my legs. Please."

Riley looked doubtful for a moment, then said to Pritzer, "Loosen the ropes on his legs, but just a little."

Konrad sighed as he wiggled his feet trying to restore circulation despite the protests of his battered shin.

"Now, Konrad, you better sing like Caruso. Start from the beginning, we have time. We want to know how you met Kaltbrunner, what he wants you to do, and how you propose to do it. I warn you, we're experts at this—we'll know when you're lying."

Konrad started from the beginning, when he received the anonymous letter at his apartment, his first meeting with the old German, and his contacts with Schell, Owl and Davis. He told them enough to prevent more torturous kicks, but managed to conceal the purpose of the scheme.

As Konrad talked, he continuously worked his feet to restore circulation in his bound legs. By accident, he hooked one foot behind the other and noticed the shoe on his left foot was loose. He cautiously used the toe of the right shoe to work the heel of the loose one up and down, back and forth. He managed to slip his foot half out of the

173

shoe. Could he work the shoeless foot through the loosened ropes? His hopes leaped. Maybe there was a chance. He carefully maintained eye contact with the two men and kept talking so their eyes wouldn't drift downward to where his only chance was desperately being readied.

The questioning went on for hours. Riley and Pritzer alternated the constant haranguing under the hot lights. They slowly pulled detail after detail out of Konrad, but were unsuccessful at learning the real purpose of his alliance with Kaltbrunner.

"Once again, what were you going to do in Liechtenstein?"

"I told you before, we were going to rob a bank."

"Which one?"

"The National Bank of Liechtenstein."

"Why that one?"

"It has the most money."

"When was this to take place?"

"We hadn't decided yet."

"Why did you need twelve men and automatic weapons?"

"Ten men. I told you ten. We needed automatic rifles because of the local police; we didn't want to take chances."

"How long have you been a Nazi sympathizer, Konrad?"

"For the thousandth time, I'm not. I have no politics. I'm just interested in money."

"Why did Kaltbrunner choose you?"

"I told you, because of my background. He'd heard about me somewhere."

Riley suddenly stood up and motioned for Pritzer to

follow him to the opposite end of the room. They studied Konrad from that distance in thoughtful silence. Finally, Riley spoke. "He's lying about something, but I'm not certain what."

"I know. He's clever enough to give us most of the truth, but holds enough back so we can't know what to believe."

Riley pursed his lips, then spoke firmly, as though he had made a crucial decision. "I'll make him tell all the truth, and then wish he had more to give us." He went to a file cabinet in a corner of the room and located an envelope. He opened it and removed a small object. He walked over to Konrad.

"Konrad, we know your game. You're telling us enough to keep from being abused, but also concealing the most important facts. You aren't bad at it, but we're better at this sort of thing than you. We're out of patience, my friend, which means you're out of luck. But don't worry, we're not going to bruise our knuckles batting you around like a couple of thugs. I have something much more interesting for you." He held up the object for Konrad to see. It was a small glass tube, about three inches long. Riley held it between two fingers in front of Konrad's face.

"Do you know what this is, Konrad? It's a section of an old-fashioned glass catheter. This was a favorite toy of Ilse Koch. Do you know who Ilse Koch was?"

Konrad shook his head slowly, his eyes riveted to the innocent-looking glass tube.

"Well, considering that you enjoy befriending Nazi criminals, you really should know about Ilse Koch. She was better known as the Bitch of Buchenwald. Her husband was Karl Koch. He was the commandant of that

175

monstrous concentration camp. His position gave her carte blanche all over the camp. It provided her a chance to display her skill at arts and crafts, like designing the human lampshade. Oh yes, a very creative lady. She must have been particularly fond of this."

Riley rolled the tube between his fingers. "Our sweet, charming Ilse got her jollies by requiring prisoners to drink all the beer they could hold, and then she would have the guards insert these things in their penises."

Konrad reacted as though he had been slapped.

"You really should get to know more about your friends, Konrad, they're quite fascinating people. Ilse would then twist and hit those poor bastards' dicks until the glass was smashed to pieces. Then she would wait until they couldn't hold their bladders any longer— remember the beer? It really made her day to watch them try to piss through the broken glass. Most of them went to the ovens before they could die of gangrene."

Riley beckoned to Pritzer with his head. "Come on over here and give me a hand."

Konrad started squirming, trying to put distance between himself and the suddenly loathsome tube. "Don't," he pleaded. "I'll tell you everything, but please don't do that."

Pritzer came up to Riley as ordered, but he, too, was startled by the idea. "Riley, for God's sake."

Riley ignored the protest. "Open his pants," he ordered.

Pritzer hesitated, looked at Riley, then quickly unzipped Konrad's pants.

"OK, now take it out. Damnit, hold it right," Riley demanded.

Riley smeared the glass tube with petroleum jelly and

deftly slid the lubricated tube into the head of Konrad's penis and down the urethra until only the tip protruded.

"Now, Konrad, if you tell us everything—and I mean everything—we want to know, I'll remove the tube. If you don't, then by God, I swear I'll smash it into a million pieces."

He motioned the shaken Pritzer off to one side. "Let's give him a few minutes to sweat."

Pritzer asked disbelievingly, "You aren't really going to break that thing, are you?"

Riley regarded him with exasperation. "Moshe, what do I look like, some medieval torturer? Of course I'm not going to break the damned glass. But *he* doesn't know that. For all he knows, we're going to smash that thing and he'll be looking for his dick with a magnifying glass and tweezers."

"Then you won't kill him?"

"Only if I have to, and he forces the issue." Riley's voice softened. "Look, I've got to take a leak. You keep an eye on him. I'll be back in a few minutes."

Riley left the room and Pritzer paced up and down, trying to calm his nerves before Riley returned.

Konrad worked to free his feet with an intensified feverishness. Now he was not just fighting for his life, but to avoid a terrible disfigurement and then death. He felt his left foot slip out of its shoe. Gradually, he worked it past the abrasive ropes. The pain it caused made him grit his teeth, but in his desperation, he pulled the foot even harder. Slowly, very slowly, the foot worked free. The sock was almost pulled off, and he could feel the wetness of blood beneath it where the ropes had shredded skin, but he almost shouted with relief. He rolled his head back and forth to keep Pritzer's attention on his face, and

177

waited for the opportunity he desperately hoped would come before Riley returned.

Pritzer stopped pacing and sat down in the chair directly in front of Konrad. Maybe he could talk some reason into this stubborn man, he hoped. "Look, Konrad, why don't you use some good sense? Tell us what you know, the whole truth, and I promise you that I won't let him break that thing. Come on, man, I don't want to be a part of something like that."

Konrad glanced at the water pitcher on a nearby table. "Please, may I have a drink of water?"

Pritzer reached for the pitcher and a glass next to it. He filled the glass halfway and held it to Konrad's lips then watched his captive drink. Pritzer started to put the glass down, but watching Konrad drink reminded him of his own thirst. He filled another glass and started to drink.

Konrad knew this had to be it. But could he trust his cramped, abused body? He had to try. Konrad pulled his foot completely free. He tipped the chair back until he feared it would go over backwards. With a force born of desperation, he lunged forward with his left foot and drove the heel into Pritzer's face. The glass that Pritzer still held to his mouth disintegrated into a shower of jagged crystal. As blood spurted from the stunned man's face, Konrad kicked again, this time catching Pritzer in the nose, sending him reeling backward and into an unconscious, moaning heap against the wall.

The dilemma Konrad now faced was to find a way to get free of the chair he was tied to and make his escape before Riley returned or Pritzer regained his senses. He had to act fast. The method he settled on entailed extreme danger, but it seemed the only way.

He awkwardly hopped over to the stone fireplace, the

chair tied to his back making him look like a grotesque hunchback. Squaring his back to the round, mortared stones, he took two steps forward, then thrust himself backward with all his power. He knew that a splintered wooden chair could be dangerous as a spear, but that thought made him thrust all the harder, as though wanting to get it done, one way or the other.

A sharp pain hit him between the shoulders as the chair made a loud cracking noise and splintered. He gasped for breath and tried to ignore the pain. He stepped forward and again threw himself at the stones. This time, the chair collapsed, dropping in pieces and throwing the off-balance Konrad to the floor. His body hurt all over, so much that any individual pain could not be sorted out.

The tube! The unspoken phrase chilled his mind. What if the glass tube had broken? Oh, dear God, he fervently prayed, don't let the glass be broken. With heart in mouth, Konrad reached down and removed the slender, innocuous-looking tube. He almost fainted with relief when he inspected it. Along the length of the tube was a faint crack. Tiny, smaller cracks branched off like tendrils. He held the glass between his fingers and exerted the smallest pressure possible. The tube burst in a shower of glass mist. Konrad's bladder grew weak and his knees felt like water as he realized what had almost happened.

He stepped out of the ropes that now hung loosely around his neck and waist. He flexed his shoulders. They worked, although the protest that resulted from the movement made tears come to his eyes. He walked to the large double windows and faced a pitch-black wall. It was so dark outside he couldn't see the ground. Was it five feet or fifty? He had to jump, but was it to safety or death?

Konrad picked up the chair that was now slippery with Pritzer's blood. He slammed it against the windows time and time again in a frustrating contest with the lead ribs that gave a grudging inch at a time. The noise terrified him; surely it could be heard throughout the building. The fear drove him to frantic efforts and he smashed and smashed until the window had given way to a gaping black hole. He threw the chair aside and hesitated at the edge. His throat tightened as he thought of the possibility that he was far above the ground, perhaps even concrete. A fear of height suddenly invaded his mind, a place where it had never before been. His brain searched desperately for alternatives. Should he chance the corridors in hopes of stumbling on an outside door?

The sudden echo of approaching footsteps forced the doubts from his mind and galvanized him into action. He gripped the window sill and carefully lowered himself backward into the cold night air. When he was stretched full length, he took a deep breath and let go. The sense of falling lasted only a second, but it was climaxed by an excruciating pain in his left ankle as the shoeless foot twisted beneath him and his weight collapsed on it. The pain made him groan pitifully, but it was crowded from his thoughts by the sound of a door slamming above him and someone running into the room and then stopping.

Konrad looked up. He could see the luminescence of the room about ten feet directly above. In his panic, he tried to get up and run, but forgot the ankle and fell heavily when it refused to support his weight without being carefully favored. He heard the steps moving toward the window and wildly looked for a place to hide. Konrad knew that if he tried to stagger away on his bad

180

leg, probably stumbling and crashing into objects lying in the dark to entrap him, he would be easy prey for someone looking out the window for just such signs.

He noticed a dark ledge extending from the window sill about eighteen inches. He realized his only hope was to press himself against the wall of the building directly beneath the protective overhang. He quickly dragged himself into that position as the steps above stopped at the window. He held his breath and closed his eyes, trying to surrender to the silence and blend into the darkness. The time stretched interminably as the mute contest between pursued and pursuer dragged out.

Lying in the snow with his back pressed against the hard stones of the building, Konrad became aware of the numbing cold for the first time. He wanted to massage his shirt-sleeve arms and perspiring chest to find some relief, but dared not move.

After an eternity that must have been two minutes, Konrad heard the steps retreat back through the room and the door slam. He waited; it could be a trick. He counted to one hundred. Nothing. He painfully raised himself to his feet, carefully staying beneath the overhang. His eyes were now fully adjusted to the dark, and he could faintly see the outline of utility poles making an orderly march through the landscape a few hundred yards distant. That has to be a road, he promised himself, and started struggling slowly, carefully along the uneven and unknown ground toward it.

He knew instinctively that these people—whoever they were—would not give up easily and drew on will power to force his senses to full alert. Whatever they did, however they came at him, he had to see them first. That simple fact could determine whether he escaped safely, and whether he lived or died.

Every few faltering steps Konrad would pause and attune eyes and ears to the silent surrounding darkness. As he drew near the road, his caution was rewarded. He heard the slightest scrape of feet against the frozen ground. Konrad inched his neck in the direction of the sound as though the action of his muscles might betray his position. In the dim distance he could make out a shape moving his way, moving slowly, carefully examining the dark.

With panic welling up in his throat, Konrad looked for a place to hide. He picked out a low, square shape near the road and headed toward it even though he knew the anonymous pursuer behind him would also be drawn to it as the only possible hiding place in the area. When he reached it, Konrad discovered it to be a small, covered bench, the kind used as a shelter for those awaiting buses.

He slipped into a corner and, with the sudden inactivity turning his swelling foot into a throbbing mass of pain, waited for the approach of whatever danger was coming his way.

Within moments, he heard slow, careful footsteps. Then the shadow of a man; then the man. Konrad could see he was much smaller than his red-haired tormentor, but that made the man no less dangerous, no less a mortal enemy. He was within two feet of the crouching Konrad, peering right and left, ahead and behind. Extended before him was the unmistakable outline of a pistol. Konrad shifted his eyes, looking for a weapon. But he knew he had only one movement before he was spotted, and that movement had to destroy, or he himself would be destroyed.

The man was now directly to the left of Konrad and

concentrating straight ahead toward the road. The moment he looked to his right he would see Konrad crouched in the hut. It had to be now, quickly. Konrad decided on a punch to the man's neck. That was the only place where a single blow from a fist could be relied upon to incapacitate a man before he could raise a pistol and fire.

Despite the Hollywood stunt men who invariably show this type of attack to be sure, swift and always successful, Konrad knew it was a risky, and probably messy, business with a greater chance of failure than success. It would be doubtful even in the best of conditions, and as Konrad felt his cold, abused body resist the tightening of muscles as he prepared to spring, his heart sank with the burden of his handicap.

But it had to be done—and now.

Konrad pushed off on his good right leg. As he gritted his teeth and planted his injured left foot to deliver the blow, the man turned suddenly in the direction of the movement he picked up in his peripheral vision. Konrad swung and felt his fist impact solidly on flesh. But the slight movement of his enemy's head allowed the lower jaw to absorb some of the blow and convert what was intended to be a disabling punch into one that merely stunned. Konrad saw the man stagger but not collapse. Even as he reeled, the man raised his pistol in Konrad's direction. As he watched the pistol begin to align with his face, Konrad converted dismay into desperation and, ignoring the pain in his protesting foot, lunged for the still-stunned man. He felt the hot rush of air singe his scalp and then the stunning roar of the pistol as he clutched his adversary.

There was nothing scientific or pretty about it as

Konrad fought blindly and clumsily. He was trying to stay alive, and there is nothing calculated about the will to live.

The grappling men fell heavily against the wooden hut. Konrad landed on top, but he was beginning to feel the superior strength of his opponent asserting itself. Fear came into his throat like bile with the knowledge that his opponent was gaining the upper hand. He instinctively stopped trying to overpower him and sought another vulnerability. His fingers entwined in the man's hair and Konrad pulled forward and viciously slammed the head against the corner post of the hut. Again and again he slammed. With each hollow thud he felt the strength and will leave the strong arms that encircled him until they fell weakly at the man's side.

Konrad collapsed beside him, exhausted and panting, but was roused seconds later by the discomfort of the clammy sweat of effort and fear turned icy by the winter cold. He knew the shot would bring the man's companions on the run, but he delayed while he patted the ground looking for the dropped pistol. In growing panic he crabbed over the ground, searching for the weapon. In his whole life he had never wanted anything more than the feel of that cold steel with which he could stand up and confront these bastards and repay them for the agony they had inflicted on him.

Damn, damn, damn, where is the goddamn thing? He argued with his own judgment: I know I must hurry, but surely it has to be here somewhere; I know I can find it in a second. No! Go now. They're coming. Leave it. Run while you can.

Fear conquered the desire for vengeance, and Konrad reluctantly abandoned his search and hobbled off. When he reached the road, he realized he had no idea in which direction he should go, so he struck out blindly toward the right, down a lonely, dark road that would take him further into the unknown, except it would be away from that frightening house with its menace, dead body, and chilling memories of fear and pain.

Riley held himself responsible and felt sick with the guilt. Why had he left Moshe alone in the room? Why? Why? He assailed himself with recrminations, but all he could do now was try to recoup the situation.

Riley hurried to his car in the certain knowledge that Konrad would have to try for the road. He drove down the lane to where it intersected the farm road that Konrad had to be on—somewhere. Which way would Konrad have turned? Riley's fingers drummed impatiently on the steering wheel as he tried to figure out which way to go. He tried to put himself in Konrad's place. There were no lights in either direction to provide a beacon; neither way offered an easy downgrade; the fields bordering the road were equally flat and bare, offering no cover.

Wait a minute . . . something was tickling the edge of his memory. All things being even, a person will turn the way his body is directed. But was Konrad right- or left-handed? He didn't know, so Riley went with the odds.

Konrad, in silhouette along the moonless road, resembled a man pulling a heavy, ungainly burden. He would push his right foot forward, then drag the complaining, stiffening left leg even with it. He hobbled sideways, crab fashion. Only the sweat of his exertion kept the cold from benumbing the rest of his body and leaving him an exhausted, shivering heap in the road, to be collected by his tormentors like a dead animal struck by a speeding auto. But the adrenalin that fueled his desperate efforts was deserting him, and was being replaced by the slowly advancing paralysis of shock.

Konrad knew the big, red-haired man would be coming. His backward glances found no reassurance in the unbroken darkness. Where are you? Damn you, when are you coming?

Konrad was almost relieved when finally a look thrown over his shoulder revealed the pencillike beams of the car leaving the house. As he dragged his body along, Konrad followed its progress down the lane until it paused at the intersection with the road.

Konrad stopped. Which way the car turned would probably determine whether he lived or died. Eternity seemed to be a freeze-frame as Konrad's life hung suspended in that moment of decision.

The spell was broken with Konrad's spirit as he watched the headlights slowly turn and point mockingly toward him. He couldn't fight any longer. His shoulders sagged as he awaited the end.

In his concentration on his pursuer's car, Konrad hadn't noticed the lights coming from the other direction. But when he turned and saw them, hope became almost a physical thing, pulsing energy into his body. He was all but dead, now there was a chance he might live. The idea briefly occurred to him that perhaps this vehicle might also belong to the house he had escaped from; but no, fate wasn't so twisted to be that cruel to him. He pushed the idea aside. This car was his salvation, if only it would get to him before the red-haired man, and then only if it stopped.

Konrad measured with his eyes the distance of both cars; they looked about equal. He started dragging himself toward the oncoming car of his hopes, as though the few feet he could skitter would make a difference. Down the road he shuffled, throwing looks back and forth at both sets of headlights, waving his arms and trying to place himself in the car's direct path. If the driver didn't stop, he would have to run Konrad over.

With vast relief, Konrad saw that the car would arrive slightly ahead of his enemy. The driver seemed to brake hesitantly, as though frightened by the strange apparition that was dragging itself directly toward him. The car finally screeched to a stop practically atop the frantically waving Konrad who scrambled to the passenger door and opened it. He could see that the driver was startled and frightened and knew he had to get into the car before the driver surrendered to his fear and drove off. Out of the corner of his eye Konrad saw the other car pull up to the scene.

He heaved himself into the passenger's seat and slammed the door shut. He gasped for breath and turned to the driver. He saw an elderly man, a farmer, judging from his work clothes. The old man returned Konrad's look with mouth wide open. His hands tightened on the steering wheel as though that was his grip on reality amidst the craziness that had suddenly emerged from the dark, lonely road.

Konrad caught his breath and sought to reassure the driver. "Thank you for stopping." He fought to maintain a steady, normal voice. "God, I was afraid no one would ever come along. My car ran into a ditch a short way

187

down that side road just ahead, and I hurt my ankle. It seems like I've been walking all night, and it kept getting colder. Your arrival was a godsend. I couldn't afford the chance you'd not see me, that's why I was waving like a maniac." Konrad paused for breath. "I need desperately to get to Frankfurt. I'll pay you well for taking me there."

The old man relaxed visibly. "I can see you're hurt. Perhaps that other driver could take you to Frankfurt quicker, he's headed that way. Let me ask him." The farmer started to roll down the window and speak to Riley who by this time was stopped directly opposite and only a few feet away.

Konrad shouted. "No! I mean, I couldn't possibly leave this car and move again. The pain is too bad." He was pleading now. "Look, I'll pay you well. Please drive me. Now."

The farmer's eyes softened and he spoke gently. "Very well, my friend. It's my duty to help a stranded, hurt traveler. We'll go to Frankfurt."

Before the old man pulled ahead to turn the ancient Volkswagen around, Konrad looked directly at his enemy almost within touching distance. They stared at each other intently for a second. Konrad said to himself, it's up to you now, fellow. You can have me if you're willing to kill this old man, too. Your play.

The old man seemed to make a major production out of turning his car around in the narrow road; finally, he wrestled it around to face in the right direction. The other car was still sitting in the same position with motor running and lights on.

He's deciding, Konrad warned himself. If he decides one way, we both die; if it goes the other way, we live. Is he willing to kill an innocent person to get at me?

188

As they started to pass, Konrad saw its brake lights go off and the car move forward. He held his breath and waited for a bullet to crash through the glass and into his face. Suddenly, the brake lights went on again. As they passed, Konrad looked across the old man's shoulder and saw the red-haired man's face reflected in the lights. He smiled at Konrad in the momentary meeting of their eyes. But it was a smile that gave Konrad no comfort.

As the threatening headlights receded, Konrad's tension eased and he devoted his attention to the throbbing ankle. He rubbed it gingerly and groaned as the torn ligaments protested his attentions.

The old man looked over and started to say something. He hesitated, then changed his mind. They drove on in silence until reaching the outskirts of Frankfurt. Konrad guessed the trip to be about twenty kilometers. He assumed the big redhead and his friends would be anticipating a counterattack from Kaltbrunner's group now that Konrad knew the location of their headquarters. But the last thing Konrad wanted was revenge. Kaltbrunner's battles were not his; he just wanted out from the middle.

The old man broke the silence. "What doctor would you like to be taken to, or would you prefer the hospital?"

"Just take me to my hotel; it's not far from here."

The old man started to protest, then shrugged and turned in the direction requested by Konrad. When the old car pulled up to the front, he got out and went around to help his passenger.

"Thank you more than I can say," Konrad said and fumbled for his wallet. He took out several bills. "Here are two hundred marks; it's all I have with me. You've more than earned it."

The old man smiled and shook his head. "No, my friend, I don't accept money for trying to be a good neighbor. It seems we get too few opportunities, anyway."

The old farmer closed Konrad's door and started back around the front of the car, then stopped and turned again to Konrad. "By the way, I've lived in that area all my life, and there's no side road anywhere close to where I picked you up." He smiled gently. "Whatever your quarrel is with the man in that other car, I hope it ends peacefully."

Konrad limped into the exclusive hotel, aware that his presence would draw disapproving stares from all eyes. His disheveled appearance was an unpleasant reminder of the ungraceful world they paid well to keep outside. He made his way to the concierge's desk and squared himself before the frowning man in the smart uniform. He decided to take the offensive.

"Is this any example of how Germany treats its visitors?" he demanded. "Where are the police that I could be accosted on a public street? If I hadn't fought them off, they would have robbed me, and probably left me a corpse in some dirty alley. I should have stayed in a nicer hotel."

The concierge began fawning sympathetically. "My dear, sir, I'm terribly sorry. May I call the police? An ambulance?"

Konrad shook his head. "No point in that, I can take care of myself." He took the same two hundred marks rejected by the old farmer and thrust them toward the concierge. "Take this and buy me lots of bandages, tape and disinfectant, and also several packages of ice. Bring it

190

to my room as soon as possible. And another thing, a bottle of good Scotch."

The concierge did some fast arithmetic and realized his profit would be about half the sum. His enthusiasm soared. "Immediately, sir. Immediately."

A showered, patched-up, bone-weary Konrad relaxed in an easy chair in his room. He lifted his foot from the depths of a large bowl of ice water and examined the swollen flesh around the ankle. The swelling had made it a grotesque balloon of red, yellow and purple discoloration. Konrad flexed it gingerly. No bones broken, but a very bad sprain, he decided; a nuisance, but manageable. He returned the foot to the ice and took a long drink of straight Scotch. God, what a close call, he mused with relief. I could just as easily be dead—or worse. He thought of the glass tube and shuddered. The fearful recollection was overcome by weariness, and Konrad slipped into a coma-like sleep behind the double-lock security of the hotel room.

Konrad was awakened by the shrill demands of the telephone. He shook the sleep from his fatigued mind and stumbled over to answer it.

"Good evening, sir. This is the hotel operator. A gentleman called earlier today and left a message. He said he knew you were tired so not to disturb you until evening. Would you like me to read it?"

"Please do."

"It says, 'Sorry to have missed you. Perhaps we will meet again. In the meantime, tell your friend, Herr K, not to be impatient, the day of atonement nears.'"

Silence hung heavy on the line until the operator said, "Sir, are you there?"

"Uh, thank you, operator."

Konrad waited a moment for the line to clear and then impatiently dialed a number from memory.

"Yes?" a curt voice answered.

"Owl, this is Konrad."

"It sounds like Konrad, but how can I be sure?"

Konrad gave a prearranged code word that turned Owl's suspicions into syrupy concern. "What can I do for you, my friend?"

"I need to add to that order I placed."

"What else would you like?"

"A snub-nose .357 magnum, and I want it tonight."

Chapter Eight

Konrad felt tense as he searched Zurich's side streets for Honi's hotel. He was nervous the way a man is when he anticipates a rendezvous with a beautiful woman, wondering what to say and how to make the best impression. Even though they were business partners, in a manner of speaking, he was still a man and she was still a woman—very much a woman, as one glance would quickly affirm. As a practical man who knew his masculine inclinations, Konrad was glad he'd already had sex with her, otherwise his very active male urgings would be in overdrive right now, keeping him from the more important, if less enjoyable, duties of planning the takeover. As it was, his curiosity was nicely satisfied.

He saw Honi and the hotel at the same time. She was in front of the entrance sitting on her luggage, expertly ignoring the doorman's gaze at her long, slim legs and his feeble attempts at enamoring small talk.

She bounced into the car, either happy to see him or eager to escape the doorman, maybe both. "Hello! Hey, am I glad to see you," she said, settling back in the plush upholstery of the Mercedes and sighing with pleasure. She felt comfortable with this man, far beyond what their brief prior encounter would normally justify, and certainly more than her compulsive distrust of men should allow. "I never thought I'd get tired of doing nothing. All I've done these past weeks is eat and buy clothes. Look at me! I've gained eight pounds."

Konrad glanced appreciatively. "A few more pounds on you is like the chrome on this Mercedes—it's not necessary, but it sure doesn't hurt."

"That kind of flattery has been known to destroy diets." She looked at him appraisingly. "You look a bit chewed up. What happened?"

As they drove east from Zurich along the long, narrow, shimmering expanse of Lake Zurich with its shoreline dotted by evergreens, pines and weekend cottages, Konrad told her of the munitions and men he had arranged. He described Otto Ender, and finally he told her of the encounter with his almost-assassins.

"Are you going to get word to Kaltbrunner, or whatever his name is?"

"Do you think I should?" Konrad was deliberately vague because he wanted to see how her mind worked.

"No, of course not."

"Why not? He may be in danger."

Honi flashed on the needless humiliation she was forced to endure during her abduction. "So, who cares? I'm not going to waste sympathy on the likes of him."

Konrad laughed good-naturedly. "You're just too sentimental."

"I've learned to read men and to figure out how they're trying to use me, that's all. People like him leave a long string of unpaid debts behind them, and it sounds to me like someone wants to collect. You said one of them was called Moshe; that's a Jewish name. I think they were a Jewish revenge squad, like you read about. Anyway, it's no business of ours. The best way to keep them on your tail is to get in the middle of the mess by trying to warn him. Let's stay out of it. Kaltbrunner will probably deserve whatever he gets; I'm sure not going to worry about him."

"But what if they kill him before this operation is completed?"

"The war has been over for two generations and they haven't caught him yet. People like him tend to be good survivors. Besides, if you notified him, he might call this operation off, then where would we be? No, let's hope that if we mind our own business, they'll leave us out of it."

"They sure as hell didn't leave me out of it when they almost killed me."

"Maybe they were only trying to find out what you knew about Kaltbrunner, like they said. Just hope they're satisfied that we're not involved in the Nazi thing."

Konrad alternated quick looks between her and the road. "OK, but consider the possibility that you're one hundred percent wrong and it's not like that at all. Then what?"

Honi shrugged. "Then I'm wrong, that's all. But you tell me, what else can we do? Right or wrong, we've got to play it out."

Konrad nodded. "I guess you're right." He smiled. "You're a sentimental little sweetheart, aren't you?"

"I've learned to be sentimental about one thing only."

"What's that?"

195

"Me."

Konrad reached into his pocket and handed her a small automatic pistol. "In that case, you'll understand why I'm giving you this. Carry it, be ready to use it, and be suspicious of everyone."

She pushed it back at him. "No, thanks. I don't know anything about those things. Having it would only give me a false sense of security. I'll just be damned careful."

Absorbed with their discussion, Konrad and Honi hardly noticed the terrain of the Swiss countryside change from rolling farmland to steeper hills and then to rocky mountainsides pierced frequently by long tunnels carved through granite barriers. But as they emerged from a tunnel, a sign snapped them back to where they were, and where they were headed.

Furstentum Liechtenstein, 20 km. Konrad read the sign aloud. "Principality of Liechtenstein, twelve miles. We're almost there. How does it feel to be going home?"

Honi's voice became tense. "I'm not going home. I'm returning to the place where I was born."

"I still don't know why you left in the first place."

She exhaled with impatience. "Well, if you really have to know, I had an abortion, and it wasn't appreciated by some people who were in a position to make things uncomfortable for me."

Konrad shook his head in amazement. "Just an abortion? Is that all?"

"It seemed important at the time."

"Do you have parents, relatives, friends, anyone still there?"

"My parents are dead, and the ones I considered friends might as well be."

"You mentioned a house for us to live in. Where's

it at?"

"In Planken. That's a small farming village above the valley."

"Have you seen the house?"

"I was born in it. When my parents died, they left their farm to me—I was the only heir." Honi said it as though there had to be a plausible reason for her parents to bequeath her anything. "I sold the land but kept the house. I've been renting it out until now."

"Why didn't you sell the house, too?"

Honi's answer was a shrug.

Konrad suddenly braked hard to avoid a police car and ambulance that straddled the middle of the road with emergency lights flashing while paramedics removed the body of a young man from a crushed sports car that had rammed a concrete abutment. As the bloodied corpse was placed on a gurney and covered by a sheet that immediately began to stain red, Konrad caught a glimpse of Honi crossing herself in quick, almost-hidden movements.

He grinned as a policeman waved their car past the scene. "Think that voodoo will help?"

Honi blushed with embarrassment. "Carryover from childhood, I suppose; I can't stand the sight of blood." She looked at him with mild curiosity. "Religion doesn't do much for you, it seems."

He smiled sardonically. "You might say that. Funny, but at one time I was shooting for sainthood, a real world-class defender of the faith."

"When was that?"

"A million years ago."

"What changed your mind?"

Honi noticed a slight tightening of his jaw. "Life."

197

"Meaning?"

"Let's leave it at that." Konrad looked straight ahead at the mountain road.

They drove in silence for a few minutes, and then the road took them around a blind, sweeping curve that gradually unfolded on a vista of startling beauty. Konrad silently pulled off to the roadside and got out of the car. After a very long pause, he heard Honi's door slam and the crunch of gravel as she came up beside him. In front of them lay the nation of Liechtenstein.

They stood together in silence, high above a breathtaking scenic tapestry. At the bottom was the sparkling silver ribbon of the Rhine, glinting in the sun. Above that, the farm lands rested in the winter dun. The symmetry of the fields was broken by clusters of villages, each one proclaiming its character and individuality by church and school spires that asserted the uniqueness of those who, through the generations, tried to make their village an expression of something they saw, or hoped to see, in themselves.

Higher on the tableau, the meadows and forests gradually assumed a mantle of white as they grew steeper. At the very top were the awesome gray peaks of the Alps, their spiny peaks puncturing the clouds that hovered around their shoulders.

The scene overpowered Honi's determination to remain uncaring. One by one, she pointed out landmarks and sites that had meaning to her and in which she took obvious pride. Honi, unknown to herself, once again luxuriated in a feeling of belonging.

"Off to the right, on that hill, is the Gutenburg Castle at Balzars. See it?" She pointed and Konrad sighted down her arm. "That dates from the twelfth century. See how similar it is to the prince's castle? There it is, just above Vaduz."

She was pointing out, as casually as she would factory buildings or farm houses, two of the world's finest standing examples of medieval architecture; each was a splendid hodgepodge of round turrets and peaked roofs as succeeding centuries tried to tack on to fit their needs. It took little for Konrad to imagine flags flying on battlements and mounted knights riding forth. That was the way it had been once, and standing here five hundred years ago, he would have seen it.

Honi interrupted his fantasy. "Down there in Vaduz, see that white building? No, over that way a little. That's the *Realschule*. I graduated from there," she said, not quite disguising her pride.

"Now look up and to the left. See that cluster of houses? That's Planken. That's my ho—I was born there."

Honi's voice suddenly turned cold. "We'd better go. It gets dark early now." Without another word or look she turned back to the car.

The Rhine was crossed in silence. Konrad knew this was not the time to disturb his sullen companion. The river was faster and narrower here, due to being near its source and the momentum of rushing out of the mountains. How different, Konrad thought, from the broad, gentle Rhine of Germany. Konrad had a sudden hunch he would discover many different things about this place before he left it.

He was all attention as they drove the few miles from the border to Vaduz.

The sense communicated by the Liechtenstein landscape was one of order and cleanliness. Homes and farms were arranged in a manner that spoke of planning, of being in control of the environment, but sensitive to its needs. Factories were small, clean and could pass as hospitals.

People tend to shape their surroundings after themselves, and Konrad guessed the people of Liechtenstein would be as orderly as their grape arbors.

If the valleys and villages presented Konrad with a sense of man-made organization, the forests above were a dramatic contrast. Their wildness was a defiant assertion of nature that the Alps were beyond any human attempt to tame them. The mountainsides at the lower and midway levels were covered with thick clusters of sycamores, Norway maples, beeches and elms. In the summer, he knew the mountain meadows would be brightly daubed with splashes of edelweiss, iris, larkspur and wolf's bane.

After ten minutes of leisurely driving, they entered Vaduz, capital of Liechtenstein. In another country, Vaduz would be just another bustling village. Here, it exuded the importance of being the center of things: the seat of government, of worship, of art—of wealth.

As they drove slowly through the center of town, Konrad had a strange sense of *déjà vu* as he saw for the first time buildings which he had been studying in photos and books. The broad street carried them past the stately pink-granite presence of Government Building, the Stamp Museum, the National Museum, the National Bank of Liechtenstein, the details of which he already knew far better than most citizens. He felt like a Caribbean pirate visiting a port city he was planning to loot. He smiled tightly at the comparison.

Konrad noticed that while he had been looking at

buildings, Honi had silently been scrutinizing the people. When she would see a familiar face, she would avert her gaze or try to scrunch down in the seat.

Konrad broke the silence. "Hungry?"

She nodded.

"Any ideas? There must be some good restaurants here."

Her lack of response created an awkward moment, but then Konrad noticed the Hotel Real directly in front of them, and said, "Let's try this."

Honi seemed to relax when they were seated in the near-empty dining room, but whenever the door opened, her eyes immediately turned to search the face of whomever entered.

"Why don't you order for us," Konrad suggested.

Honi studied the menu for a few minutes, then ordered *wiener backhuhn*, Viennese fried chicken, with a bottle of sylvaner riesling from the winery of the Prince of Liechtenstein.

As they ate the delicious entree, an old woman approached from the side and surprised Honi who jerked her head back nervously when the old woman asked, "Aren't you Ernst Miller's girl?"

Honi whispered, "Yes, ma'am," and the woman forged ahead in the meandering way of the very old. "I'm Frau Reich. You probably don't remember me, but when you were a young girl you came to my home in Schaan to study my embroidery. I guess most of the women of Liechtenstein have copied my patterns. It's a nuisance, but I don't mind doing it for the children. Your parents both died, didn't they?" Without waiting for Honi to respond, the old woman rambled on. "Heard you were living out of the country. Married? Any children?" The

201

woman pressed her information attacks over the nervous attempts of Honi to answer. "I liked your parents, good, God-fearing people."

Honi struggled to gain control of the conversation. "Frau Reich, this is my husband, Herr Konrad, he's a writer."

Konrad rose for the introduction, but the old woman had lost interest in them. "Well, welcome home. Too many young people leave for no good reason."

After she wandered away, Konrad noticed Honi's shoulders slump slightly in relief. "See, that wasn't too bad. Always remember that people have short memories. They're too busy worrying about what everyone else thinks of *them*."

Konrad and Honi spent the afternoon touring the countryside, visiting every village and driving the roads. Konrad engrossed himself in analyzing and memorizing details and locations that he knew would either aid or hinder his plan, but either way would have to be dealt with.

At the end of their long afternoon, when dusk was beginning to absorb the weakened sun of winter, Honi directed Konrad to the outskirts of Planken. About a half mile from the village she indicated a driveway partially hidden by tall shrubs. Konrad pulled in and stopped. They sat for a long moment, both looking at a modest farmhouse with a steep roof. It was made of field stone with the front wall plastered smooth and covered with a colorful mural of a stag leaping over a fallen log. Konrad wondered how a small farmer trying to scratch a livelihood out of a rocky hillside farm would find the money or inclination to hire an artist to decorate the outside of his home.

Honi noticed his interest in the mural. "It's an Alpine tradition. It's expensive, and not all the paintings are good, but it shows that a house and those who live in it are in harmony with the forests and mountains. Maybe if factories were required to wear such murals, fewer rivers would be polluted." Honi opened the car door. "Well, this is where we're going to live; might as well go inside."

Konrad sensed her need to be alone in the house of her childhood. "You go on in; I'll be there in a little while. I want to walk around and familiarize myself with the area."

Honi approached the house slowly, as though she were both afraid of it, and afraid it would go away. She turned the key in the lock and stepped inside. The interior was much as she remembered. Renters had made minor changes, but it was very plainly the home of her youth. She wandered from room to room, absorbing the memories that thrust themselves at her from every direction, from every shelf and every piece of furniture on which she had cavorted as a child: the large, overstuffed chair on which her father would read his newspaper in the evening, grouchy if disturbed needlessly; the old-fashioned sewing machine that her mother pedaled tirelessly to produce magically frilly dresses for her little blond daughter.

Honi searched for the photo albums that her mother had maintained so conscientiously, always making certain that each snapshot was accurately encoded with date and circumstances. Her search was disappointingly fruitless. They were gone, either carelessly thrown out by a tenant trying to find more room for his own memorabilia, or maybe packed away carefully but stored in an anonymous place, of value only as a resting place

203

for dust.

As Honi approached the closed door of her bedroom, the emotions roiled within her like boiling water. Should she open this door to her painful past? Should she deny herself the opportunity to hear again the echoes of laughter, of pain, of wonder, of joy that the walls of this small room must yet contain?

The doorknob turned slowly under her hesitant hand. It swung open, and she stepped inside. She turned first to the bed. It was still there, and she involuntarily, irrationally sighed in relief to see that the bloodstains were gone. Honi looked around—the curtains and bed quilt were different, of course, and the walls had been painted, but it was still the same room in many other ways, certainly enough to reach down into the hidden emotions deep in her mind and stir a response of sadness and joy: Sadness for what could be no more, joy at what had been.

Honi reached up on the wall and removed a small wooden heart. She ran her fingers over its rough surface and smiled wanly at its crude form. It was no masterpiece, but when her father had carved it for her years ago, it had seemed perfect. She had placed it around the neck of Gertrude, the lead cow of their small herd, and then tied a small milk stool upside down on the animal's horns. Thus adorned, the cow was ready to lead the herd back to the farm from summer high pasture in the mountains. Honi brushed away a tear as she thought of that silly annual ceremony that the children looked forward to at the beginning of autumn. But right now, she didn't feel silly, only empty, and very lonely.

Konrad made it a point to enter the house noisily, not wanting to embarrass Honi in her private moment. She met him in the hallway, composed and tight-lipped. She gave him a quick tour of the house, matter-of-factly indicating each room as though she were showing a stranger's house to a prospective buyer. When they came to her bedroom, Konrad asked, "Is this where we'll be sleeping?"

Honi led the way out of the room, closing the door firmly behind them. "This is my room. You'll sleep in the guest bedroom."

Honi fixed a light dinner with the groceries they had bought on the way while Konrad relaxed by reading some German magazines on animal husbandry he found in the house. Although he had no interest in Holsteins, letting his eyes roam aimlessly over the pages provided relaxing diversion.

The pages soon started to blur and his eyelids gained insupportable weight. His head nodded and collapsed on his chest in surrender to sleep.

Being alone in the house with a beautiful woman, relaxing in an easy chair with the smells of dinner on the air had reminded Konrad of another time, another woman. It was an issue with which his conscious mind would not deal, so the memory punched through the fabric of his sleep. . . .

Konrad slipped the key quietly into the lock because he didn't want to disturb his wife in mid-afternoon. He knew she usually took a nap at this time, and since he was home early, he didn't want to awaken her. Maybe they could go out to dinner tonight, visit a pleasant little German inn. Something was needed to break the ice and bring them back together. The marriage was hurting, and

Konrad didn't know how to heal it. Saving a marriage, he had found out, wasn't easy, especially for the people who screwed it up to begin with.

He eased silently into the hall and tiptoed toward the bedroom. If she were napping and he woke her prematurely, he could look forward to a crabby welcome.

Konrad pushed the bedroom door slightly ajar. Stunned, he pushed it farther until his body filled the doorway and he stood watching, not knowing how to stop watching.

The couple lay entwined, thrashing on the bed in the heat of their passion. The sight of their heaving, sweating bodies etched into Konrad's mind, forcing him to accept the truth of what lay before him.

The lovers saw him in the door and recoiled from each other as though stung. They stared at him; Konrad stared back, and for a moment it was an impasse in shock. Then Konrad said to the man with the quiet of death, "Get out. Now."

The words galvanized the frustrated lover and he grabbed the pile of khaki clothes with the sergeant's chevrons flashing on a trailing sleeve, and dashed past Konrad into the living room, as far from the husband and as near the front door as possible.

Konrad sat heavily on his wife's dressing bench. They stared wordlessly at each other until he broke the spell. "Get some clothes on," he ordered in an ominous whisper.

She came out of the closet wearing a dressing gown just as the front door slammed. She sat on the bed and confronted him with defiance. "I suppose you want me to start blubbering and begging your forgiveness? Well, I don't feel the least bit sorry, at least not for that."

206

Konrad started to protest indignantly. "That man is in my outfit. He's *under* me. Don't you care about embarrassing me?"

She stood up and pointed at him. "There! It's not, 'What have you done to our marriage?' or 'What have I done to deserve this?' but only concern about being embarrassed in front of your precious, goddamn soldiers. That type of selfish non-caring is what brought us to this sorry state. The reason, Lieutenant, that you saw me screwing some poor, witless sergeant is that I can't get any affection from my husband."

Konrad shook his head defensively. "I give you what you want. What are you lacking?"

She lifted her arms and beseeched the heavens in frustration. "What am I lacking? What am I lacking? I'm lacking *you*." She came over and stood in front of him. "You give me what it pleases you to give me. What you don't give me, and never have, is yourself. You can't share that with anyone."

She burst into tears. "I'm not like this. I was married to a good man for five years and never thought of cheating on him. Why did he have to die?" She dabbed at her tears. "Konrad, how do you think I feel when you're out fooling around with those hoodlum German friends of yours and their slutty girlfriends? Don't you think that makes me question my own womanhood? For the last three years, the only love I've known is what I've been able to sneak."

She confronted his dismay. "That's right, husband. He wasn't the first, and as long as this marriage continues the way it's been going, he won't be the last."

Her composure regained, she paced the room, the robe only partly concealing her lovely body. "You don't care

207

about anybody, including yourself. I'm not sure I didn't invite that dope here today just hoping this showdown would happen. I'm not proud of what I've become, but I didn't make it alone. I had help from a husband who just doesn't give a damn about anyone.". She leaned forward as though her intensity might get through to him. "I've tried to get close to you, tried to pry open your mind and find out what you're hiding, or hiding from, but I can't. Mister, whatever is bugging you, you're welcome to keep it all to yourself."

Konrad closed his eyes trying to make it all go away. But as he shut out his wife's voice, that of Willie Mac's cut in like an overpowering radio signal. "Shit," the new voice said derisively, drawing out the word so it sounded like a dozen E's. "Can't you even keep your old lady from fuckin' every stud who comes along? In my old neighborhood we had a word for fools like you. Face it, Lieutenant, you're so bad, your own bitch won't even screw you."

Not true, not true, Konrad argued with himself, stung by Willie Mac's charges. Spurred on, as though challenged, he watched her soft breast as the robe parted, the swing of her hips as she walked defiantly around the room. He suddenly reached for her.

Surprised, she pushed him away. "For God's sake, stop it. How disgusting. Can't you even have the decency to be outraged? Why don't you have the courtesy to beat me when you find me in bed with another man? Konrad, don't you realize what a humiliation it is for a woman when her husband wants to have sex after finding her with another man? It's sick. It's insulting."

She sat down on the bed again and looked at him squarely. "There's something missing in you, Konrad.

Something I can't put in place. Maybe it was Vietnam, or your childhood, or maybe you were just born that way, but you don't seem capable of making a commitment to anyone or anything."

"What do you want?"

"I want out. I want a divorce."

He was trying to answer his wife, trying to say, "No, I'll try harder. I don't want to fail; please give me another chance," when another voice intruded.

"Konrad, dinner is ready."

He opened his eyes and saw Honi bending over him, blond hair falling into his face and making his nose itch.

After dinner, Konrad struggled to start a fire in the stone fireplace while Honi poured wine and scanned the radio dial looking for mood music. They settled down in the comfortable parlor and drank chilled riesling before the shadows of the dancing fire and listened to the ponderous tones of Wagner's *Tristan und Isolde* on a Zurich station.

As the mellowness settled over them like a mist, Konrad asked quietly, "How does it feel to return?"

"I don't think it's possible to give a simple answer. In some ways, it's as though I never left. In other ways, it's as though I'm a total stranger. Most of the good things, good feelings I ever experienced happened right here. So also have sadness and bitterness. If I understood exactly how I feel, then I would understand myself. I suspect the only place that can happen is in heaven, not by returning to a farmhouse."

"You've made it pretty obvious that you've been a prostitute. Mind telling me what that's like?"

209

Honi was not surprised by the question. She had learned very early of the fascination men have for the life of a prostitute. Instead of brushing it off, she tried to answer, perhaps as much for herself as for Konrad. The past few years had given her much to think about, but no opportunity to share the thoughts.

"I think it's something you go into when you have no pride and no options. Like when you ask yourself, 'So what?' and the answer is silence. You hear of young girls being lured or tricked into prostitution by pimps. That's not the way it is. The pimp just provides know-how and an excuse. The real decision has already been made by the girl herself, even if she's unaware of it."

"You don't seem very high on the life," Konrad said.

She shrugged her shoulders. "I'm a realist, but when you look at other people and see how they prostitute their own lives in so many ways, you begin to realize that turning tricks is only the most obvious and literal way of whoring. People say whores are cynical. Perhaps we get that way because we have a unique vantage point for a close-up of how other people fuck themselves."

"What are most customers like?"

Honi laughed at the question but there was no humor in her voice. "Pretty pathetic; men who can't find a woman who wants to share with them, so they're forced to buy one to use, and 'use' is exactly what I mean. Most men go to a prostitute because they can't get laid anywhere else. And with every young secretary out on the prowl trying to see how much she can give away, the only guys who can't score are real losers."

"Losers in what sense?" Konrad was listening attentively, but with compassion, not sarcasm or macho humor.

"Real animals—fat, stupid, ugly. Anyone who makes you shudder at the thought of going to bed with him. How would you like to make your living by sharing your body with someone whose touch makes you cringe? The clean, good-looking ones are worse, though. They're the ones who come to you for a purpose, either kinky or cruel. I won't shock you by describing some of the things I've done just to pay the rent. You know, people speak of hookers becoming hard and faded. Well, let me tell you, that isn't because of the work itself, most of that is easy, at least physically. It comes from having your face six inches away from some slobbering, mumbling pig who thinks you're nothing but a piece of ass with no higher purpose in life than making him feel like a man for a few minutes. It's pretty tough to be high on yourself or the human race when your working day is full of assholes, jerks, sadists and creeps. Pretty difficult to maintain a lofty set of ideals."

Konrad reached over and gently took her hand in his. "How long do you plan to continue?"

Honi stared into the dying coals of the fire. "I need to find something. The profession doesn't have a good retirement plan, you know. But I haven't exactly been swamped with offers. I guess that's why I'm here with you, trying to find a way out—at least part of the reason." Honi turned to face Konrad. "How about you, what are you trying to find a way out of?"

Konrad got to his feet and jabbed at the fire with a long poker. He watched in satisfaction as the aroused flames flared into life, then refilled their wine glasses. Handing Honi's to her, he sat down next to her on the couch, conscious of the nearness of those long legs that teased by their mere presence.

"The last few years, everything I've tried started out with high hopes and ended with a big bust . . . no, not a big bust, more like a tiny poof. I haven't even succeeded in making my busts big. Marriage—we seemed perfectly suited; suited for something, I guess, but not each other. I took up the black market and she took up sergeants, or at least two of them that I know of; I can only guess at the other ranks. I have no reason to think she was just turned on by chevrons. The marriage ended in a nasty, name-calling little mess. The only good thing that came out of it was no children."

"Was it the Army that drove you apart?"

"Naw, that wasn't it. We both liked the Army, especially me, at first. Closest I ever came to a real profession. I guess we tend to gravitate to those things we do best. Well, I was a damned good officer. On maneuvers, I would do naturally what other fellows would hesitate on or stumble over. I loved the feeling of being one step ahead, just a little quicker than the others."

Konrad reached for the wine bottle and emptied it evenly into their glasses. He leaned back against the soft cushions and stared into the fire. "But there's a quality a soldier must possess that I hadn't counted on. A soldier also has to survive the boredom of the peacetime army, spending endless days in barracks inspecting lockers, checking on things fifty times a day that don't need checking once a month. But, of course, all the silly routines have a purpose—to keep idle men busy. I learned the goal of military life is for smart people—the brass—to figure out ways to keep dumb people—the troops—busy and in line. Unfortunately, the ones chosen to administer this bullshit are the junior officers.

212

That was me, Lieutenant Busywork.

"Well, I discovered that a smart operator can find more creative ways to spend his time, especially on an American base in Europe. In short order I had a thriving little black-market business going in Germany where I was stationed. Anything that Uncle Sam could ship over, I could ship out. Being able to speak fluent German was a help, but basically I was one damned talented operator, and proud of it."

Honi watched him stop and reach for his wine glass, a slightly defensive look on his face. "That sounds too pat to me. I have a hunch there was more to it than that. The ideal soldier doesn't overnight become a criminal just because he's bored. Now, come on, fill in the blank spaces."

He glared at her. "What do you mean?"

Honi was unfazed by his sudden anger. She had seen too many men embarrassed to be bothered by it. She curled her legs underneath her and leaned back on her arm. "Just forget it," she said in a conciliatory voice. "Did it bother you to be doing something dishonest against your country?"

"Well, I suppose anytime you do something dishonest you're doing it against your country, if you believe the Fourth of July speeches. But you have to understand America. We make a big deal out of repeating such things as, 'Ask not what your country can do for you; ask what you can do for your country.' Jack Kennedy said that, or something like it. But political horseshit aside, what it comes down to is that most Americans believe that the best thing they can do for their country is to make a lot of bucks, any way they can. If you somehow fail to make your mark, as we call it, then you haven't taken

213

advantage of the Land of Opportunity, you've failed the American Dream. In the States we don't punish white-collar crime, we reward it by giving respectability to those who get away with it. You're only punished when your victim is a bigger practitioner of the American Way than you are."

Honi's brow furrowed in puzzlemenet. "But for a soldier, aren't pride and duty the most important things?"

Konrad snorted. "Those are luxury items for success-ful people, just like Cadillacs. Who gives a shit about the pride or sense of duty of a failure?

"Anyway, after the Army booted me out, I tried being a mercenary for a while, like I told you, but that was a bummer. Man, you can't believe the psychos and crazies you run into.

"After that, I decided to give writing a whirl. Wow, was that a disaster. It would have been funny, except all the laughs were on me." Konrad tried to laugh, but it came out as a choking sound, quickly stifled. He looked away in embarrassment. He was telling her things he didn't even want to admit to himself, but for some reason, he continued.

"Did you ever try to do something you really wanted? Try your guts out? I tried and tried and got nothing except rejections and ridicule from my friends." He stopped and took a deep breath. "I was going to write the song of the human spirit, find myself through my own words. I was going to be a 'message writer,' but I couldn't match words to my feelings. I sweated blood over that typewriter, but every time I got close, my emotions and thoughts just dried up. It was like looking in a mirror and seeing the image go foggy."

Konrad's voice had changed from conversational to brittle as the too-fresh memories of his failures corroded the mellowness of the evening. Honi scooted closer so their thighs were touching. She gently stroked his hair with her long fingers. "Hey, this is a relaxing evening, remember?"

Konrad pushed on, caught up in the reminiscence of disappointment. "I guess that if my appetite for self-punishment were for food, I'd weight about three hundred pounds. Maybe I should consider myself a failure, but the problem is, I'm not ready to be one. Something makes me keep trying. I guess that's why I'm here, the only thing I'm any good with is a gun."

Honi watched him wilt under the heat of his memories, and said to herself: Poor guy, you've tied yourself up in a psychological package wrapped with self-pity. But I sense something's been left out, a great hurt, too painful to include. You're giving me results, not reasons. You haven't told me why this pleasant, good-looking man named Konrad must be punished. What terrible thing did he do?

For the first time in a very long time, Honi felt the stirring of genuine passion. She had used sex as a tool for too long not to realize that it is usually the end result of deeper psychological drives, but she really didn't care why she felt this way, it was enough that she did. She told herself she didn't love this man, but she was undeniable drawn to him, or something he represented.

Under Konrad's silent, searching look, Honi slowly started to undo the buttons of his shirt, being careful to gently rake her fingernails across the hair on his chest. His arousal, as she expected, was immediate.

He reached for her and they kissed long and fiercely,

their tongues performing a nimble dance of exploration. Konrad slipped his hand under her blouse and reached behind and fumbled with the clasp of her bra. They both laughed at his clumsy failure to open the maddening device.

Honi stood up and straightened her clothes. "Let's go someplace more comfortable." She took his hand and led him down the hall. She hesitated a moment at the door of her childhood room, then went straight to the guest bedroom.

Konrad reached for her, but she slipped away. "Whoa, let's not rush. There are some things that are best done lazily and slowly. You slip into bed and I'll be there in a minute."

Honi closed the bathroom door behind her and leaned weakly against it. She was scared. She knew how to give sex, but she had forgotten how to give herself, and for a moment her fears almost made her back down. She took several deep breaths and struggled to recapture the feeling she had known only moments before when they had kissed. It was worth fighting to keep. She would make it good for both of them, and she would force her doubts back into the depths of her mind.

A tense and impatient Konrad lay quietly between the crisp, clean sheets listening to her shower. Time seemed the cruelest of companions until the bathroom door slowly swung open. Konrad caught his breath as he looked at her. She was steamy wet and naked and standing proudly in front of him. She smiled as he swallowed hard. He had seen attractive women before, but there was something in her manner that made Honi different and more desirable. What was it? Perhaps pride in her beauty, pride without arrogance. Maybe her obvious display of desire magnified his own. Whatever it was, it would take some time to study, and at that moment, he could think of nothing on which he would rather spend a very long time.

She walked to the side of the bed and stood very close to him, the glistening reddish-blond triangle just inches from his reclined face. He tenderly reached for her, his hand coming to rest on her smooth, round buttock. He felt the muscles harden at his touch. He slowly reached his lips toward her. They came to rest at the top of the mound, just where it begins to part to form the soft folds that would later open for him. He breathed deeply and the heady female musk flooded his senses. He wanted to stay there forever, not moving, only absorbing the scent of delight.

Konrad felt frustrated, frustrated in the nicest possible way, that his senses could contain no more. In mock despair, he threw himself back on the bed and cried, "I think I'm going to die."

Honi chuckled. "In that case, let me show you how."

She took command of his body, of both their bodies, and molded them into one. His penis seemed the center of her existence. She expressed her feeling for the hardness of his body with hand, mouth and tongue, alternating at exactly the right moment to take him up one more step on the staircase of ecstasy that she had created in his mind and nerves. She was driving him crazy, teasing him to within a breath of a bursting climax and then dropping it, only to start again as soon as he recovered.

He was reaching the point where even her knowing touch could not forestall the inevitable. He ached for the release that grand and final moment promised. Then she was atop him, guiding him into her. Her hips thrust rhythmically against him, her soft, warm thighs hugged his own. He reached up with both hands to touch the extended pink nipples on her small, firm breasts. He saw her sweating, her lips compressed, her eyes squeezed shut, her breathing deep and frantic.

He felt it first in his toes, then the pulsing sensation moved slowly up his legs until it seized his whole body. His shoulders shuddered, his head thrashed back and forth. He caught a glimpse of her. Honi's mouth was wide open and she was moaning and trembling. Together they reached for the stars that appeared before them, saw them flash to a brilliant hue, and then gradually subside to a pleasant memory of warm color.

Honi and Konrad collapsed into each other's arms, breathing hard and feeling the slipperiness of their sweat-soaked bodies. Neither had the strength to move. Finally, Honi raised her head and smiled languidly at Konrad. "I hope you know, this is never for sale."

He reached for her, but with a kiss blown in his direction, she gathered up her clothes and padded softly into her own room, leaving him alone and too exhausted to ask why.

Honi walked up the steps to the big door with the sign that said: *Polezei*. She had had to leave her car parked in a prohibited zone for three hours before she was given the citation she now clutched in her hand. It's never taken me more than five minutes to get a ticket before, she thought, and now when I want one, it takes three hours.

Approaching the public counter, she scanned the small station house looking for the reason she wasted an entire morning creating the pretext for coming here. She finally

218

spotted the communications center in the corner of the squad room, but the operator was sitting in front of the radio, blocking her view of the information she sought. As the officer at the counter wrote out her receipt, she remarked, "Oh, what a lovely old print! I just love them. Do you mind terribly if I take a closer look?"

The policeman followed her gesture and looked back at a faded, nondescript old lithograph of a farm scene hanging just above the head of the radio operator. With a bemused little smile, he opened the swinging door and invited Honi in. She spent a couple of minutes examining the picture from every possible angle and apologizing to the radio operator for getting in his way. When she left, the policeman who had invited her in strolled back to the picture, studied it carefully, then shrugged and returned to work.

Honi decided to lunch at a small cafe in Vaduz. Gradually, as the days passed, she was beginning to feel more comfortable, so she looked forward to eating in a place she had known for many years. She even exchanged greetings with familiar faces she passed on the street. She still wore the large dark glasses to preserve a feeling of anonymity, but she knew that all the back yard gossips had learned she had returned, and that meant soon everyone would know. Such was the inevitability of living in Liechtenstein.

She was seated at a small table in the corner of the cafe waiting for her food when she happened to glance up at the large window that faced the street. She froze. Hans was ten years older, but her recognition was instantaneous. He stood just a few feet from where she sat, oblivious to her presence and idly reading the notices that were taped to the window. His appearance was that of a farmer: workman's clothes, sunburned face, a casual slouch that made his big, raw-boned body seem less imposing than she knew it to be.

He seemed at peace with himself and the world, but she saw deeper. The eyes reflected the lifelessness of someone staring into unhappy memories. Her face softened as she stared at her first lover. He might also have been her betrayer, but he was a sad man, and she found it difficult to hate a sad man with the same intensity as a proud one.

His attention was caught by something else, and he moved on down the street. Honi had lost her appetite, but she did not leave the table. She sat for an hour twirling the stem of a wine glass between her fingers, gazing thoughtfully into the untouched amber liquid as the cafe gradually emptied around her.

Chapter Nine

Hans slouched deeper in the easy chair, shielded his eyes with his free hand and tried to concentrate on the newspaper. His tormentor was not discouraged. Moving her bulk across the room, she stood above him, huge stomach hovering like a menacing boulder over his crossed legs. Hands on hips, she glared at him. "What kind of husband are you? I told you I wanted that closet cleaned out and you just sit there reading that damned paper. What kind of example do you set for your child? Do you want her to grow up shiftless, too?"

Hans didn't take his eyes from the page. "Hester, I said I would clean the closet, but I've had a hard day. Just give me a chance to relax. I'll do it in a few minutes."

She mocked his words, shaking her head back and forth in derision. "'In a few minutes, in a few minutes.' If I added up all the times you've dodged work around this house by promising, 'In a few minutes,' it would take hours just to count them. I'm sick and tired of your laziness. I work like a slave every day to keep up this miserable hut." She waved her huge arm to encompass their small, cluttered five-room cottage. "And what help do I get from you? I don't know why I didn't take my mother's advice and marry a man with some ambition. You'll never be anything more than a dumb, lazy farmer."

There was a time when Hans would have responded angrily to that, her favorite insult. But after almost ten years of marriage and an equal time spent listening to her abuse, he had built up an immunity that allowed him to block it out. Now, he just buried his head farther into the pages of whatever he was attempting to read at the moment and ignored the belittling nagging.

Hans had seldom noticed Hester Stouffer until shortly after Honi disappeared from the hospital. Hester had always been one of those mousy, plump girls usually thought of as just being there, part of the peoplescape that dot the surroundings. She and her mother lived alone in the back of a small dress shop Frau Stouffer ran. The father-husband had long since departed; for America, he said, where once settled he would send for his wife and daughter. However, once gone, no one ever heard from him again.

The mother's manner and appearance were forerunners for the daughter: large, loud and insufferable. The kind who become themselves only after the man they have selected as quarry is safely bound by matrimony.

Hans couldn't remember why he turned to Hester when Honi left. In his despair he had reached out blindly in a desperate search for comfort and reassurance, and she was just there, positioning herself to fall into his life.

The three-month courtship was listless, and the marriage ceremony joyless. Even the alcoholic guests seemed to attack the schnapps out of a sense of duty.

222

Maybe that was the way Hans remembered it, because that was the way he felt. He had had ten years to nurse regret into misery, misery into depression. Every night when he came home from his fields, he had the living evidence of his stupid mistake ready to assault him at the door. She not only irritated him, she permeated his existence. She got under his skin, she stifled his attempts to breathe, she choked off what laughter he had left.

As Hester expanded in girth, she likewise grew in her domination. She laid siege daily to those areas of life he might have found enjoyable: She belittled his work; she scorned him as a provider; whenever he sought relaxation she accused him of laziness. Steadily, remorselessly, her assault on his spirit sealed off and destroyed all parts of his life until the whole was a joyless, shapeless lump of routine.

The situation might have been tolerable had there been children from whom he could take pleasure, but the only offspring had been a daughter who rapidly was becoming the miniaturized duplicate of her mother and grandmother. Hans knew the child was his also, and he felt guilty for the lack of joy he took in the girl, but damnit, she *was* just like them.

The idea of having more children was repulsive to Hans; not because he disliked children, but because on those rare nights when Hester made herself available, it was invariably an occasion to which he did not rise.

Hester's eyes glinted in anticipation as she watched her husband pretend to concentrate on his newspaper. A cold smile twisted her lips. "By the way, I heard today that your old girlfriend has returned. You remember Honi Miller, don't you?"

The words struck Hans like a slap, but he auto-

223

matically braced himself to conceal a reaction. "Is that right?" he asked nonchalantly, fighting to keep the excitement from his voice. He wanted to ask more: Is she married? How does she look? Is she planning to live here? and many other questions, but he remained impassive, knowing Hester was watching him carefully.

Hester lost the waiting game. "They say she's living in her parents' old place outside Planken. Got herself a man, supposed to be a writer or something. Hah. Hard telling what sort of man her kind could get. You know the stories they used to tell about her. Once a whore, always a whore. This country would be better off if people like her—Hans, where are you going?"

"To bed. I'm very tired."

In ten years he hadn't seemed to age a day. He was just as Honi remembered—erect of carriage, but not stiff; gray, but not old; kindly, but not familiar; and above all, dignified. She stood in the front of the crowd as the crown prince took the microphone from the master of ceremonies. "Good afternoon, friends and countrymen. I am honored to be present today on the dedication of this building that so many have worked . . ."

Honi quickly removed the small tape recorder from her purse that Konrad had given her and flicked the switch to "record," holding the machine in front of her as several in the crowd were doing. But Honi didn't do so with the pleasure so evident in the others. She felt like an eavesdropper, knowing that her purpose lacked the innocence of the others.

As the prince completed his comments, Honi switched off her recorder and headed for the back of the crowd.

Suddenly, she felt a firm grip on her arm.

"Just a moment," a brusque voice commanded.

Honi whirled in surprise. The tall, red-haired man holding her arm quickly released his grip with a look of chagrin on his face. "Oh, no, fräulein, I'm terribly sorry. I mistook you for an acquaintance. Please forgive me for startling you."

The tension of her assignment plus the shock of the man grabbing her was almost too much. Her knees felt weak and she fought for composure.

The man looked at her with concern and guilt. "I feel terrible about this. It seems every time I try to do something clever, it turns out stupid. Fräulein, I wish you'd let me buy you a brandy. It'd calm your nerves and help me atone for my rudeness."

Honi hesitated. She, of all people, had no fear of unfamiliar men, but she knew it was wise to avoid encounters with strangers during this stage of the operation, as Konrad had warned. But the man looked so apologetic, and she could certainly use the drink.

"Very well, but only one and then I have to go."

They settled into a booth at a nearby small inn where he ordered brandy for both, then raised his glass toward her. "Here's to beautiful women being charitable to bumbling oafs." They each took a long sip. "Allow me to introduce myself. I'm Lewis O'Grady, from the United States, Arizona actually. I'm in computer sales."

"Your German is excellent, Herr O'Grady."

"Afraid it has to be. The computer business is so competitive it's tough enough to sell to Germans in their own language, let alone trying it in English."

They chatted easily about little things, the way people do who take an immediate liking to each other. Honi

225

thought about asking how he lost two fingers of his left hand as she watched him lift the brandy glass with three fingers as gracefully as another person could with five, but she decided that would be pushing a conversation between strangers. Instead, she settled on, "What brings you to Liechtenstein?"

He shrugged in the casual American manner he had perfected, mainly because it came so naturally to him. "I was close—had a sales call in Zurich—so I thought I'd take a couple of days off and come see the little country." He glanced out the window at the towering Alps in the distance, then at Honi. "Sure glad I did. This is a beautiful place, all right." His voice leaned heavily on the word beautiful.

Honi couldn't resist a slight smirk that didn't go unnoticed by her companion. "Don't you agree?" he asked.

"Well, it's pretty enough, the part you can see, but I have no love for it. A den of snakes may be in a scenic place, but it's still a den of snakes. Would you believe it if, for example, I told you women don't even have the vote here yet?"

"Really?" he shook his head in amazement. "I'd have to agree that doesn't sound very progressive, but the women don't seem too upset about it. I haven't seen any bra burnings since I got here."

She shrugged. "The women here are too well trained for that. Contented cows." Honi stopped; she had let her natural candor carry her beyond discretion. She had to remember who she was and what she was doing, and keep her mouth shut until it was over.

Riley smiled sympathetically. "Where I live is beautiful, too. The desert in spring and the hills anytime

226

are like lovely music to me; Brahms for the eyes and Mozart for the soul." As he spoke, his mind's eye was focused not on Arizona, but his similar-looking homeland of Israel. "I suppose any place one loves is beautiful to that person, but I don't think how a place looks has much to do with how one feels about it."

Riley spoke more softly now, and with the feel of an Irish poet, for he really believed this deeply. "The beauty of what I guess we could call patriotism is not in meadows and mountains, but in knowing that you belong, belong to something bigger and more important than what you can ever be. Those sentiments can be twisted and become evil—look at Nazi Germany—but if your homeland stands for things that are good and decent, then your patriotism will be a thing of warmth, no matter how cold the rest of your life becomes."

Honi shrugged. "Great, just great, if it weren't for the people. When you get stung by enough bees, you tend to lose your desire for honey."

"Hey," he cautioned with a broad smile, "no one's perfect, at least none that I've met. People have to be people, which means their personalities are usually covered with warts. But you can't let who *you* are be determined by how others treat you. That's surrendering control of your life." He paused and studied her discreetly. His purpose was to get her to open up, to trust him, so he was willing to talk about whatever she wished, but this subject was one that aroused deep feelings in him. "All people are natural pain-inflictors; that's just part of the baggage we have to carry around. But the salve for that pain is not to run away from our roots. Patriotism, on the personal level, is reaching out and touching—touching ourselves."

Honi looked at the stranger for a long moment. "You're sure different, but I suspect you're really a good person." She laughed. "You drop troublesome thoughts like confetti."

Smiling, she took a final sip of brandy and gathered her things. "It's been nice, but I really have to be going."

Riley jumped to his feet and assisted her with the heavy coat. They walked out of the inn together and toward a cluster of parked cars in a nearby lot. "Looks like we parked in the same lot," he said offhandedly. When they got to the lot they gave a final goodbye and headed for their cars.

Honi turned the ignition key and listened with growing dismay to the lifeless grinding of the engine. With exasperation, she tried again and again until a sluggish growl was all that came from the motor.

A familiar voice interrupted her fuming. "Having trouble?" Riley tapped on her window and she promptly rolled it down.

"This stupid car won't start," she complained unnecessarily. "I just had it tuned, too. Of all the rotten luck."

Riley looked up at the darkened sky. "I'd say it's going to snow pretty soon. Could I give you a lift?"

Honi hesitated. Konrad's warnings rustled in her memory, but she looked again at the friendly redhead and, with a snap judgment, relied on her self-confidence in evaluating men. "Sure, if it's no trouble."

Riley's car headed up the deserted mountain road in the descending gloom of late afternoon. It was too easy. He had expected to have to take her by force, but here she was, voluntarily in his car on a lonely road. Not far away, in a secluded villa in Switzerland, his men waited to take this beautiful woman and pry, twist, beat and kick information out of her, then drop her dead body like a sack of garbage into the middle of a deep Alpine lake. She was in his hands, ready to deliver.

"Right over there, the farmhouse," she said, pointing.

Riley hesitated, then slowed and stopped the car, but left it in gear, arguing with himself. He gunned the motor once, ready to let the car spring forward in the direction of his waiting men. He sat staring ahead grimly, his hands squeezing the steering wheel while Honi gave him a perplexed look. Finally, he turned to her and grinned broadly. "If I'm lucky, we'll meet again."

Honi returned his smile and swung the car door open and walked quickly down the path as he watched silently from the car.

Riley returned to the same inn and sat quietly for a long time in the same booth sipping more brandy. Jerk, fool, idiot, he swore at himself in recrimination for letting his liking for the woman lead him to such an unforgivable breach of professionalism. Damn my stupid Irish sentimentality, he thought angrily.

But he knew he would never be sorry he let her go. Riley believed he possessed special insight into the makeup of women, and there was something about this one that left him with a very good feeling.

Despite that feeling, Riley knew he had failed professionally since he had come to Liechtenstein to learn why Konrad and this young woman were involved with a snake like Kaltbrunner, and why this tiny country was the target of their conspiracy. All of their investigations, incuding the interrogation of Konrad, had left them with the same uncertainty they had when they started. As the theories collapsed, so did the

229

patience of Ira Levin. "I don't give a damn about Liechtenstein," he had fumed, "our job is to kill Kaltbrunner, not meddle in the affairs of another country. We want him for what he did forty years ago, not what he's doing today. Anyway, if you kill him, any project he's involved in will die with him."

Despite those misgivings, Levin had reluctantly given Riley a few days to try and abduct the woman to learn what Konrad had not told them. Then, after all the preparations and having actually had the woman in his car, he had let her go. All he had to show for the effort was a pleasant glass of brandy with her. And all that would be left him after he reported the lies he would have to manufacture would be an I-told-you-so look from Levin.

Riley grunted disgustedly, picked up his coat, paid the bill and left the inn. He couldn't tolerate thinking of the lovely Honi Miller being tortured and neither could he stand by and allow this tiny country to be ravaged with no warning.

He walked straight to the police station, up the wide steps and into the lobby of the ornate building. He asked to see the chief of police and then sat patiently on a bench along the wall until an officer asked him to follow.

The chief's office made it clear that the occupant placed great importance on ceremony. The room was spacious, richly furnished with diplomas, certificates and photographs lining paneled walls, each one featuring a grinning image of the man who stood expectantly in front of Riley behind an expensive, clean desk.

Chief Franz Houser greeted him with the manner of someone obligated to be polite and helpful, but with a minimum of enthusiasm. "I was told only I could help

230

you, Herr . . . O'Grady," he said with a glance at the note given him by the ushering officer. "What can I do for you?"

"Thank you, Chief. I have some information I believe is of considerable importance."

"Oh? Then please continue. We're always grateful for assistance."

"Chief, a couple has just moved to this country whom I believe pose a threat to the security of Liechtenstein."

"Just who might these people be, Herr O'Grady?"

"Their names are Herr and Frau Konrad. The woman is a Liechtenstein native, maiden name Honi Miller."

The chief fingered through a stack of papers and came up with a slim file which he read through quickly. "Our records indicate that everything is in order with their residential status. The woman is a native and citizen, daughter of a very respected couple, now dead. She has a right to live here with her husband who apparently is a writer with a means of support. Neither has a criminal record. You can see why I'm a bit perplexed by your accusation."

Riley had known this would be a long shot, but he had to give it a try. "All I can tell you is that I know they're a threat to your security. I can't even tell you how I know all this. Look, I probably wouldn't believe me, either, if I were you, but please take my advice and watch them. Maybe if they're aware of your surveillance, nothing will happen."

Houser's lips compressed in irritation. "Herr O'Grady, may I see your passport?" He studied the false document expertly prepared by the Mossad and returned it. "May I ask your occupation?"

"Computer sales."

"Computer sales . . . hmmm." The pause told what he thought of computer salesmen playing detective. "Let's be frank. I resent your attempt to slander a citizen of this country. If you have evidence to support these—these bizarre charges, you are obligated to give it to me. But you refuse. What am I to make of that?" The chief walked to the door and opened it wide. "I have no idea what your motives are, disappointed lover, uncollected debt, or what, but you've brought your wild charges to the wrong place." The chief crumpled the note with Riley's false name on it. "Good day, sir."

Riley walked slowly to his car and stood alongside it for a few moments gazing mutely at the Alps in the distance, then got in and drove toward the border.

Konrad sat next to a large window so he could watch the black, spidery spans shooting into the air just a few hundred yards from where he sat in the Paris Hilton. He never tired of the Eiffel Tower. It was massive, but so are many uninteresting things. He decided his fascination was due to it being so absolutely useless. Here was something grand, but without a purpose in the world other than to sit there generation after generation just being grand and stared at. He didn't know why that should turn him on, but he figured if that tower could fascinate him without his knowing why, then any reason would be redundant.

Konrad snapped to when he heard the voice. It came from an average-looking man of medium size in his early thirties with sun-bleached hair and the ruddy look of the outdoors. He wore his suit awkwardly, in a way that made it obvious he would prefer other clothing. The three men

232

standing right behind him were copies of his look and style.

"I assume you're Mr. Konrad?" Taking Konrad's nod as an invitation, the four sat down at the table and the leader extended his hand. "My name is Mike Dawson. These two are Peter Gross and Ray Casey. We're the pilots you wanted. This is Ray Mallen, he's radio."

Konrad reached across and shook hands with each. "You fellows are right on time."

Dawson grinned. "When you're visiting Paris, the tendency is to arrive early."

These were not the kind of men inclined to waste time on formalities or small talk. Konrad went right to the point. "I assume you've been told that this mission will be dangerous and illegal, that you could get jailed or killed?"

"The major fully briefed us."

"Any misgivings, doubts, hesitations?"

"We're here, aren't we? Look, we're already outlaws to most of the civilized world, and all the uncivilized world. As far as it being dangerous, well, I guess we'll just have to let our reputations speak for us. You don't work for Major Davis if slippers and a pipe by the fireplace are your goal."

Konrad nodded. "OK, I'll buy that. I just wanted to make sure. How much experience have you three pilots had with the DC-3, or Dakota?"

Dawson continued to speak with the obvious approval of his silent companions. "In the bush that baby's the standard workhorse. Even though most are older than us, the Dakota's still the best damned plane ever made. Takes off on a penny and lands in a mud puddle, can be held together by baling wire. Yes, sir, we rate that old girl just slightly ahead of our mothers."

Konrad turned to the one named Peter Gross and asked, "Give me the specs on the plane."

The man's words leaped in reply. "Wing span, 28.96 meters; standard engines, 1,450-horsepower Pratt and Whitney R-2000s; cruising speed, 274 kilomet—"

"OK, I'm convinced, but I'll still want you to take my associate on a test ride. If I seem overly suspicious, it's because the role you men fill is going to be vital. Now, the radio man, you said your name was Ray—"

"Mallen, Mr. Konrad. Ray Mallen. Have no concerns. There isn't a radio made that I can't operate, repair, or make burp if it has indigestion. I'll be happy to demonstrate if you happen to have one."

Konrad handed him a sheet of paper on which had been written the information gathered by Honi in the Vaduz police station. Mallen studied it briefly, then smiled. "Whoever wrote this knew nothing about radios, but it obviously describes a standard radio of Swiss make. A rather good one, actually. If you're wondering if I can operate this equipment, you might as well ask a baby if he can shit his pants."

Konrad nodded. He took four envelopes from his pocket and handed them around the table. "Here's the advance pay you were promised. There are airline tickets in these for you three pilots. You'll be met in Augsburg by my associate, Otto Ender. I've leased two DC-3s in the name of Trans-Europe Oil Corporation. You'll pick them up at the charter company and fly to Munich where hangar space has been reserved. You'll maintain a state of high readiness and keep your mouths shut until you're contacted. You'll be told your destination only when I

234

think the time is right." He turned to Mallen. "You'll come with me; we have to buy a radio."

Honi was clearing the breakfast dishes when she happened to glance out the front window and saw him walking up the drive. She froze, gripped by fear and anger. Her fingertips turned white as she squeezed the plate in her hand. She waited an eternity for the doorbell to ring. When it did, the effect was like an electric shock, causing her to drop the plate. For a moment she was bewildered, looking first at the door, then at the shattered plate, then back to the door. Finally, she walked tentatively across the room and opened it.

She had often thought of such a moment, savored it in her dreams of revenge. He would start to say something and she would then slam the door in his face. Now, faced with the reality, she just stood numbly. He was older, of course, and heavier, but the lines in his face were deeper than a mere ten years should have caused. There was something about him that bespoke self-doubt and the gentleness that comes from soul-searching and trial.

They stared at each other. Finally, Father Hammer-schmidt asked, "May I come in, Honi?"

She hesitated. All she had to do was slam the door and her vengeance would become real. Instead, she word-lessly walked away toward the parlor, leaving him to follow.

They sat facing each other across the room in uncomfortable silence. The small talk that would normally begin a priest's visit had no place here. Finally, the priest spoke: "Thank you for allowing me in; I would have understood if you hadn't." He cleared his throat and shifted uncomfortably, stiff with formality. "Let me get right to the point. I'm here to ask your forgiveness. Ten years ago, when you were lying in that hospital, trying to find the love and understanding that might have healed you, it was in my power to give it to you. Instead, I made you the victim of my own littleness. Rather than serve your needs, I served my own self-righteousness. But that's not the worst of it."

Honi eyed him coldly. "It's apparent you spent a lot of time preparing that little speech, but your apology doesn't mean a thing, it comes a bit late. Come back and apologize when it will wipe away the painful memories, the nightmares, the years of loneliness and heartache. When you can do that, then I'll listen to your apology."

The priest sadly shook his head and gazed sympathetically at her. "You have good reason to be bitter, but even so, you must realize that bitterness doesn't heal, it just keeps the wound open."

Honi glared defiantly at him, the stored-up resentment seeping out in low, angry words. "Frankly, you're wasting your time. If you've come here to ease your conscience, you'll get no help from me." Honi stood up. "Before you go, tell me what you meant when you said, 'That's not the worst of it.'"

The priest turned his eyes to the floor and spoke in a halting, choked voice. "When your parents asked my advice on how to react to your . . . to your . . ."

"The word is abortion," Honi interrupted sarcastically.

"Yes, well, when they asked me, I told them to send you away. I had never faced anything like that before, and I . . . anyway, they trusted me and didn't know what else to do, so they did. Later, after they had a chance to listen to their hearts, they begged me to find you and bring you home. From that moment until they died, not a day passed that they didn't mourn your absence and do everything possible to find you. They died heartbroken and before their time because they listened to me that day. However much you've suffered, my child, they suffered more, because they knew they had failed you. But the one who deserves to suffer most is me, because I failed all three of you."

Honi abruptly sat back down, her defiance replaced by streaming tears.

The priest reached for his coat and swiftly walked to the door, then turned to face her. She hadn't moved except to bury her shaking head in her hands. "I don't know why you finally came home, Honi, but I hope you know it *is* home."

Chapter Ten

Konrad absently scribbled a series of crude stars and then examined his handiwork while he cradled the phone and waited until the smooth voice of Walter Schell flowed through the receiver. "Hello, Konrad. You're right on time. I found forty bodies for you."

"Terrific."

"I hope terrific is the right word. I've screened them as much as time allowed, but I can't swear by all of them. You don't get my usual guarantees."

"I understand. I'll just have to take my chances."

For better than an hour Konrad wrote names and data about his recruits. He occasionally asked a question, but spent most of the time scribbling to keep up with the information dictated by the criminal recruiter.

Konrad finally put down his pen and flexed tired fingers. He looked at his watch and saw he was running an hour late to keep an appointment with a special recruit. "Well, Walter, you've done it again."

"I wish I had more time so I could give you stronger assurances about the people you're getting, but all I can do now is wish you good luck."

"So far, so good, but I'm afraid 'so far' is just starting."

Konrad heard the booming voice as he rushed into the lobby. As he neared the lounge, it became more distinct. "Innkeeper! More wine, my good man. How can I give my blessing to the vintages of Germany without tasting them all? My reputation's at stake here. This is serious business."

From the entryway Konrad saw the unmistakable figure of Angus O'Callahan sitting at the bar with several half-empty wine bottles lined up in front of him. The bartender was staring at the huge man pensively, not certain if he should stop serving the bombastic American and risk losing the fat tip that seemed assured from the mounting pile of bills and coins in front of him.

Angus turned and saw Konrad approaching. "Ah, hah! My sugar daddy approacheth; late, but even now approachething. Konrad, my good man, welcome to our little wine tasting. What would you like?" Angus fumbled with the bottles. "White, red, pink, gold—we have a wine color for every taste." He squinted at a champagne bottle. "Bubbles are optional."

Konrad poured himself a glass of *gewurztraminer*. "Angus, you ass. How the hell long have you been guzzling this junk?"

Angus jerked his head back in mock insult. "Junk? The very essence of the vintner's art, and you call it junk. Ugly American! You should be lashed with a Chardonnay vine, sir. I'll have you know that this fine gentleman—" he gestured to the bartender who was polishing a glass and watching them out of the corner of his eye—

239

"advised me of the high quality of this hostelry's wine cellar. I did him the courtesy of sampling some. And as you know, I'm a careful researcher. I don't shoot from the hip on something as important as this. You can call me the Pasteur of the vine."

"You drink too damned much," Konrad grumbled.

"Drink too much? Drink too much?" Angus' eyes opened wide with shock. "I'll have you know I once had a friend who for five years didn't know I touched a drop."

Konrad bit. "What happened then?"

"He saw me sober."

Angus' expression turned to one of hurt. "You didn't have the courtesy to compliment my new suit."

Konrad sipped his wine and evaluated the clothing. "You look like an unmade bed—king size."

"Well, fuck you, too. I paid eighty bucks of your money for this suit, and you insult me."

"How long have you had it on?"

"Three days. When you have a good thing, you go with it."

Angus reached for one of the bottles and filled his glass. Konrad pointed to the glass. "Do you know what you just did, jerk? You filled that glass with red wine."

"So what?"

"The glass was already half full of white."

Angus knitted his brow and studied the pinkish mixture, and then announced with satisfaction, "Well, for your information, that is how we make rosé." Pleased with his logic, he tipped his head back and drained the glass.

Angus rested his chin disconsolately in the palm of his hand. "Konrad, old friend, don't let the brave mask of jollity fool you. I'm hiding a broken heart."

"Huh?"

"It's Herschel. He's gone."

"Who's Herschel?"

"My cat, stupid."

"What happened to your cat?"

"It's a long story. A long, sad story. I found Herschel in the streets, homeless, hungry, held in scorn by his peers for his mixed ancestry. I befriended him and gave him a home, thinking an act of Christian charity would put him on his feet and make him the cat I knew he was capable of being. We got along just fine until a certain female acquaintance of ours—Imogene, the bitch—who claimed she was an expert on cats, said if Herschel was going to live in a small apartment, I should have him declawed and castrated. And for the first—and last—time, I listened to that dumb broad."

"What happened?"

"Well, I took poor old trusting Hersh to the vet and shot the works. Cut his balls clean off. What happened then is a classic example of what assholes cats can be. There was this old tomcat across the street—torn-up fur, one eye missing, that old cat was a mess. Anyway, the son of a bitch made life miserable for Hersh. Every time Hersh would go outside to smell flowers, bury a dump, or just get some sun, that old cat would sit on the curb, trying to look cool, and just stare at him. You could almost hear him telling some little cat he was trying to make points with, 'Look at the dude from across the street; he's got no balls and no claws. What the hell's he doing down here among real toms? Think I'll kick me some cat ass.'

"That old cat would just tear into Hersh. And since old Hersh didn't have any claws, he'd get nailed every time.

Sort of like fighting with pillows on your hands. Since he wasn't hunting pussy anymore, Hersh didn't even know what pissed the old tom off. I think the old cat just figured there weren't too many asses he could still kick, so no point in letting an easy one get away. Pretty good reasoning, even if it was Hersh's ass getting kicked. Anyway, I had to give him away. Gave him to the same bitch who said I should get his nuts cut off in the first place."

"Why didn't you get a dog?"

Angus topped his "rosé" with champagne and took a long swig. "A dog? Fuck dogs. Hate 'em. One time I was banging this chick and her fucking little dog attacked me. Yeah! There I was humpin' away and this little cur tries to bite me. Probably figured I was trying to hurt his old lady; although I got to tell you she was doing some pretty heavy-duty groaning. Never thought I'd be more worried about rabies than the clap. Haven't been able to stand dogs since."

Konrad gestured toward the accumulated wine bottles. "Wonder what the record is for drinking German wine in one sitting?"

"Record? Listen, I've got a record I'm going to send in to the Guinness people. I'll bet I'm the only guy who ever got busted for drunk driving twice in one morning."

"Not one day, one *morning*?"

"Right. Cop got me just after midnight on the Bay Bridge. Ran my ass in right there."

"What sobriety test did you flunk?"

"Standing. They let me out about four a.m. so I figured I'd celebrate my release a little. The same cop got me on the same bridge about an hour later."

"The same cop? What did you say to him?"

242

"The only thing I could. I said, 'Officer, I was just on my way down to turn myself in.'"

Konrad's laughter was drowned out by a roar of surprise from Angus. He had thrown his head back to laugh with Konrad, but his alcohol-confused reflexes didn't cooperate, and his whole body decided to take the trip. For one desperate moment, the issue was undecided. He teetered at the apex, flailing arms trying to restore balance, but slowly, surely, gravity prevailed and, like a great tree, his huge body toppled backward off the bar stool, seeming to gather momentum as it fell. It happened too fast for Konrad to catch him, and when he saw the feet rise above the level of the bar, Konrad knew a mighty crash was about to occur.

Angus landed square. The concussion rattled glasses at nearby tables and left customers gaping in shell-shocked astonishment. The prone Angus lay like a beached whale, groaning, gasping and twitching.

Bartenders and assistant managers converged on the scene like ants on a picnic, wringing their hands, apologizing to other customers and to each other, and wondering what could be done, everything but dealing with the problem at hand, namely a supine body in the middle of their floor that gave no indication of moving.

"What an embarrassment," a distraught assistant manager wailed to Konrad while wagging his finger in Angus' direction.

"Don't blame him," Konrad countered, pointing to the bartender who suddenly became very busy. "Your man furnished the wine. He just obliged by trying to drink it all."

"Is he hurt?" another finally asked.

Konrad knelt down and studied Angus for a moment.

243

"He's just drunk, and probably figured that since he was already lying down, this was as good a time as any to pass out. All we have to do is get him on his feet and up to his room."

Four of them took Angus by the arms and shoulders and tried to hoist him to his feet, but they might as well have been trying to stabilize a three-hundred-pound noodle. Even worse. A noodle doesn't have a rolling head and limp arms and legs flopping around. In dismay, they returned the snoring hulk to the floor and looked around in desperation.

Konrad took charge. Shortly, two men returned from the hotel's first-aid room carrying a stretcher. At Konrad's direction they placed it next to Angus and rolled his body onto it. Konrad went to the bar and removed every last coin of Angus' change, ominously eyeing the bartender as he did so, then took his place at the head of the procession that was forming up. As surprised guests made way and clucked sympathetically, the retinue of tuxedoed men paraded after the stretcher, through the main lobby and into an elevator.

Otto Ender's hands sweated as he gripped the wheel of the rented truck and inched it forward in the line awaiting clearance at the Swiss border inspection station. He glanced again at the manifest to make certain everything was in order. It showed he carried twenty fifty-gallon barrels of machine oil from Meyer Oil Products Company of Munich to Zeissig Tool Foundry of Zurich. The only thing known about either firm by Otto or Konrad was their listing in telephone directories of those cities. Otherwise, the connection was as bogus as the oil drums in the back of the truck.

Resting between false tops and bottoms of oil, in a mixture of sand and dirt providing the approximate weight of oil, were the guns and equipment intended for the capture of Liechtenstein. Despite the pains they had taken to make this truck and its cargo appear authentic, there was always the possibility of chance discovery. It was that "chance" rather than the precautions that Otto dwelled on while waiting.

"May I see your bill of lading and passport, please?" The Swiss customs officer was polite but watchful. Otto hoped his efforts to appear nonchalant didn't have the opposite effect.

The inspector was a woman, pretty and serious-looking in her mid-thirties with dark blond hair pulled severely back in a bun just below her cap. The bronze tag on her jacket said Hanna Moltke. She studied the documents intently. "Herr Ender, are you aware these papers aren't in order?"

"Huh?" Otto's knees started to turn weak. "What— what's wrong?"

"This bill of lading is not signed by the shipper, down here in the corner. Regulations say we must hold the truck until German authorities can contact your employer, the owner of the cargo. A phone call to Meyer Oil Products should do it."

Otto saw the world falling apart before his eyes. "Look, if they're called it'll be my job. I'm supposed to recheck the papers before leaving. This shipment is overdue already and any delay would mean my neck. You don't want to see a man fired for something like this, do you? Can't you give a poor working guy a break?"

Hanna Moltke eyed him narrowly and carefuly walked

around the truck, checking every part of it. She motioned to Otto to open the cargo area. Once inside, she walked among the strapped-down barrels, tapping one occasionally and listening intently for the sound. She motioned Otto to climb up. "Open this one," she said, pointing to a barrel.

Otto adjusted a wrench to fit the plug and removed it to allow the inspector to peer into the dark, smelly interior. She carefully poked a finger down until she felt the wetness, rubbed the black liquid between two fingers and then motioned for Otto to replug the barrel.

They walked back to the cab in silence. The inspector studied Otto for a moment, then said, "You ought to be more careful. You can go this time because I don't like to make a working man pay for one of his boss' mistakes. But if your papers are not in order the next time, you won't like the result."

Otto tried to mask his profound relief. "I appreciate that, Inspector. You can bet it won't happen again."

Hardly able to control his shaking, Otto slowly pulled away from the border and drove into Switzerland. He could handle being shot at but his close call at Swiss customs was a type of tension he had not experienced. He was unnerved by his narrow escape and at how such a simple thing as a carelessly omitted signature almost cost them the game and his freedom. He was disgusted with himself for the panic he barely controlled under stress. Otto's self-image was centered on a belief that he was fearless. It was beyond his comprehension that what he had encountered was not fear, at least not in the accepted sense of fear of dying or of being hurt, but a sense of helplessness, of powerlessness. For those few minutes at the customs station, he was at the mercy of the situation and unable to change it; he had no control. At least in a battle, even if you're surrounded and outnumbered, you can fight your way out or die with honor trying. Otto was more comfortable in attacking the center in daylight than sneaking around the flank at night.

Otto drove through Zurich and headed east into the mountains, cursing himself all the way. Late that night he entered St. Gallen, the nearest large city to the Liechtenstein border. Following memorized instructions he drove the streets of the industrial section until he found the address he was looking for. It was a nondescript garage tucked into a row of warehouses. He opened the door with the key Konrad had provided and parked the truck inside then checked both doors and the barred, grimy window to make certain the garage was secure. Satisfied, he walked to a busier thoroughfare and hailed a taxi. As he rode to the airport and a flight back to Germany, his thoughts were in conflict: The mission was accomplished, but was he still the man he once was? He didn't want to end as a shaky old man frightened by shadows. God, he didn't want that.

Otto checked into the Munich Hilton, took a hot shower and wandered down to the lobby. He sat there for a few minutes reading a newspaper, but the more he glanced around and saw the crowds of scurrying businessmen dressed in different styles, of different sizes, colors and appearances, but all somehow looking alike, the more uncomfortable he became.

He suddenly threw aside the paper and walked briskly through the main exit and down the street, putting distance between himself and a strange new world he couldn't embrace and which, in turn, did not welcome him.

Otto walked for more than an hour accompanied only by troubled thoughts. As though guided by subconscious forces from a less confusing past, he gradually made his way deep into an older, working class neighborhood that had survived decades of war and modernization and looked like a reincarnation of the 1930s. As though in response, his pace slowed and he discovered a ravenous hunger. He walked into a nearby rathskeller and sat down at a table with a frayed, but clean, checkered tablecloth and hard wooden chairs with wire backs. The place was almost empty so he was barely seated when the waitress appeared at his elbow. The menu was posted on the wall and was limited to three items, so Otto ordered ham, boiled cabbage and potatoes plus a schooner of dark beer.

The dinner was robust and filling, if not exactly gourmet fare. Otto was content with a full belly, strong beer, and surroundings that made him feel at home. His attention idly wandered to the waitress sitting alone at a table near the kitchen, chin in hand, waiting for the closing hour. On an impulse, Otto spoke across the room, "Ma'am, would you like to have a beer with me?"

She looked up and gazed directly at him for a long moment, then brought herself heavily to her feet, drew two beers and walked over and sat down. Otto smiled and looked more closely. She was a plain woman, plainness accentuated by a heavy weariness to give her a tired look that surpassed the effects of mere labor. The years pressed down on her. Although she was about Otto's age, time had been more demanding on her and she wore it like threadbare clothing.

"Thank you, Herr . . ."

"Otto, and you are?"

"Gerta."

"That was a nice meal, Gerta. My compliments to the chef."

She laughed hoarsely. "That's no chef, just old Herman the cook. I could give him your compliment, but he wouldn't care. Besides, the meal wasn't nice, it was filling. There's a difference."

Taken back by her sarcasm, Otto fumbled for an opening. "Where are you from, Gerta?"

"Nuremburg, at least originally."

"Really? I was stationed there once, in the army."

"When?"

Otto looked at the ceiling studiously, counting the years backward. "Let's see . . . 1941. I spent three months there. It was between France and the Eastern Front."

Her eyes showed a flash of life. "I was there then. Who knows, maybe we saw each other someplace. Of course, I was a young girl then." She gave a short laugh. "You might not recognize me today."

He gave the required, awkward compliment. "Oh, I don't know about that. Anyway, I remember Nuremburg as a beautiful city."

She sighed. "Once; it was once, but that's all in the past. I haven't been there in years. No reason to go anymore, everyone's dead."

It was not a desire he could have pinpointed, but Otto very much wanted to know about prewar Nuremburg from this woman who had been there when, like him, she was a cheerful youth eager to join life. "Tell me, what was it like there back before the war? I remember newsreels of the giant rallies. It sure looked exciting."

Gerta's face came alive, and her hands joined in drawing word pictures from vivid memories. "Oh, it was, there were thousands and thousands of people—soldiers, sweethearts, children, old people. Everyone was marching and cheering. It was like a carnival and party all in one. It was like everyone was celebrating the coming of spring—a German spring.

"That new spirit came just at the right time for us. You remember how it was: no money, no pride, no hope. Well, the politicians gave us those things in their speeches. They told us to be proud of being German, that we were destined to lead the world. They also told us a lot of things we didn't want to hear, about Jews and Slavs and other people we had no quarrel with. But we only heard the nice things, and pretended the others weren't said. We learned later that the world heard, though, and didn't forget."

Otto reflected the typical soldier's scorn for politicians. "Ah, no one listens to those pompous asses."

"No, we listened, and turned a deaf ear to the ugly things. But our generation can never say we didn't hear them. We listened to vultures and called them eagles, telling each other that their coarse cackles were really the cries of proud birds. No, Otto, I was there. We heard."

Otto had little patience for exorcising ghosts, especially those forty years old. "Did you have a lover during those days?"

"Yes." She paused, then spoke words he understood. "France, 1944."

She surged to her feet. "I have to close now." She hesitated, silently weighing this stranger on her scale of human values, then deciding. "Would you like to come to my room? We can talk more there."

He stood beside her. "I'd like that very much. I'll buy some wine on the way."

Gerta's room was on the third floor, facing an alley through one small window. The furniture was non-descript and indestructible, the kind bought by cheap landlords who expect the worst from tenants. It was neat and clean; the institutional appearance was broken up rather pathetically by a few small figurines and ornaments that must have meant something to her since they were cheap and had no esthetic reason to exist.

Gerta stood at the entry with him and let her hands fall to her side in resignation. "Well, this is where I ended up."

"You haven't *ended* yet."

"Thanks for the try, but I know better. Did I tell you I was almost through training as a teacher when the war closed the school? Literature was my specialty. From Goethe and Schiller to serving beer in a low-class tavern." The irony made her shake her head. "And you say it's not the end. Oh, well, let's have some wine."

Otto sat in the only chair, an old wing model, lumpy where the stuffing had been pushed back. She sat on the edge of the bed. Facing each other, they raised glasses and drank. "It was funny," she said, "that you mentioned the old Nazi rallies. People never talk about that anymore. But when I have happy dreams, and it's not too often, they seem to be of those days. God knows there aren't too many happy things to remember after that."

She stood and began pacing the small room, not in anxiety, but with the measured walk of the person searching for an elusive thought. "For years after the war they drummed into our heads that our generation of Germans was evil, that we were barbarians, sadists and killers. But we weren't, at least we didn't think we were. God, Otto, I'm talking about people like you and me. Are we monsters? No, we're just ordinary people. The only thing we ever wanted was a little time in the sun.

"We're called evil for what we did, but others were just as bad. I was in Berlin when the Russians entered—" the memory made her pause and shudder—"and despite what they did to us, they were the good guys. Sometimes I think it was like a cowboy movie and all of us had black hats crammed down on our heads. I think about it a lot, and no matter what they say, I still can't think of us as evil."

Otto answered with the smugness of one who has dealt with a question to his own satisfaction. "The hell with it. It's not for us to say. Winners decide who was right and who was wrong. It's part of what you win. Don't strain your head over it."

Her thoughts kept tumbling. "When I remember those terrible war years with the starvation, the bombings, the endless death, and then see the kids of today with their designer jeans and new cars, I don't know whether to envy or feel sorry for them." She paused, then gave a grudging little laugh. "I envy them."

"Don't; their time is coming," Otto said. "No country can stand prosperity for very long. If things are going too well, the goddamn politicians will find a way to screw it up."

They both knew how the evening would end; each had traveled this route before. Otto finished the wine in his glass in one final gulp, and as she watched him, he rose, walked over and took her in his arms. They kissed gently, exploringly. She pulled back, not out of his arms, but enough so she could look into his face. "I don't want to be old and have all my dreams behind me. I still want a chance to feel young."

"We can try, Gerta, we can try."

They made love in an unhurried, almost sad way. The act was not without passion, but seemed more to be a uniting of kindred seekers, the joining of two drifting souls who can take comfort in each other since each understands the loneliness of the other.

According to popular standards, or myths, their coupling was a disappointing episode. But disappointment should be measured by expectation, and neither was looking for orgiastic fireworks. The silent quest of each was for the quiet reassurance that someone was still willing to care, to hold them, to find pleasure in them, to seek the sharing of smiles, to say, "I love you" in a breathless moment, even if it's sincere only for that moment.

Otto leaned back on his pillow and lit a cigarette, the ceremonial act that signaled the end. Discreetly, out of the corner of his eye, he examined her. Not much to look at: sagging breasts; wrinkled, pearl-white skin that hadn't seen the sun in years; lumpy deposits of fat in places that should have been smooth and trim; bony leanness where soft roundness would have pleased. What the hell, he thought, a soldier's woman grows old, just like the soldier. He liked this woman.

She leaned against him and ran her hand randomly over the gray hair on his chest. Her fingers dropped into a recess in his shoulder, the lasting reminder of an incompetent surgeon removing a bullet under impossible conditions. "Oh, that must have been painful," she said, running her finger over the contour of the scar. "Does it still bother you?"

He pulled in his chin so he could look down his nose at the scar, as though he had forgotten it was still there.

"When you let yourself start worrying about old wounds, that's when you get new ones."

Otto glanced at his watch out of the corner of his eye, hoping she wouldn't notice, but, of course, she did. He had to meet Konrad for breakfast early and he wanted to be fresh. It was two in the morning. It was time.

"Uh, I'm supposed to meet—"

"It's OK. You don't have to explain."

This was what he dreaded. The act of dressing afterward seemed to underscore the pointlessness of a night like this. He did it hurriedly and in silence, eager now to escape the disappointment that his quick glances read in her face.

Otto sat on the edge of the bed and laced up his shoes. Then, that done, there was no longer a reason not to leave. He reached over and ran his finger lightly over her forehead, gently pushing a gray strand of hair back into place. He lifted her rough, wrinkled hand and softly touched it with his lips. "May I come back?"

"No."

"Why not?"

"Because tonight was a dream; the next time would be reality."

Otto was waiting patiently over coffee in the hotel dining room when Konrad and Honi joined him. "Sorry to be late," Konrad apologized, "but the airport traffic was rough this morning." He gestured toward the waiting man as he pulled out Honi's chair for her. "This is Otto; Otto, meet Honi. You each know of the other, so I won't waste time on formalities because we've got a lot to do and not much time left. Otto, did you have a good trip?"

254

"Good enough. The truck is hidden in St. Gallen."

"Did you meet the pilots?"

"Right. Pretty good boys; I flew with each. I'll tell you, they really know how to handle those old planes. You'd think they were Piper Cubs, the way they play with them."

"Do you think they're reliable?"

"Which? Planes or men?"

"Men."

"I'm satisfied. Tried to get them drunk the first night; couldn't do it, at least not to the point where any of them became loose-tongued. They're strictly military. They also know they won't get paid unless this comes off without a hitch."

"How much do they know?"

"Only what you told me to tell them. They each have flown the route, and I gave them the code, but they don't know what we're going to be doing in Liechtenstein."

"Good. How about fog? Do you think they could fly through it if we got socked in?"

"I'd bet on them."

"I've got news for you, Otto, you are, we all are."

Otto gave an obligatory short laugh that didn't sound very amused. "How about the radios?"

"We're all set. Our South African picked out a short-wave and the walkie-talkies just like he was shopping for handkerchiefs and underwear."

The conversation came to a halt as the waiter placed in front of them orange juice, dark bread and soft-boiled eggs in their quaint little European-style pedestal holders.

Otto cracked the top off his egg and started to spoon out the soft yolk. "Are you sticking to Christmas Eve for zero hour?"

"I can't think of a more ideal time."

"That doesn't leave much time. There are ten thousand details to take care of first. It'll be tough."

"Stick with those details, Otto, that's your job. But the big picture has to come first and that tells me Christmas Eve is perfect. Everyone we're concerned about—inside or outside of Liechtenstein—will have their guard down on that night. Second, I don't want whatever animals we manage to recruit to spend more than two days in the country before we strike. If we wait longer than that with forty bored men lying around, about ten things can happen, and nine of them are bad."

"I understand that, but we won't have much time to familiarize the men with the lay of the ground."

"We'll just have to train them with maps and descriptions. But what the hell, that's the way it's done when you plan an invasion. Not too many countries invite you in for a holiday look-see before you take them over."

Otto traced patterns in the tablecloth with bread crumbs. "I'm still a little bothered by the lack of heavy weapons."

"You're not going back to the Russian Front. Remember, we're not going there to start the battle of the Rhine, but to steal their treasure. We're a band of thieves, not a Panzer division."

Honi picked without interest at her breakfast as she listened to the two men talk about casualty ratios, strike-impact capabilities, acceptable withdrawal losses, and terror-intimidation factors. My God, she thought with astonishment, the matter-of-fact way they're talking, you'd think they were discussing opening an appliance store or auto repair shop instead of taking people's lives.

She looked closely at Konrad and Otto and was chilled by the transformation the subject of conquest had made. Their faces were flushed with excitement as they fought to keep their voices low, and their eyes darted impatiently from each other to the notes they were quickly scribbling. It was as though they were seeing things not visible to her, exciting things that made their blood rush. Honi suddenly understood why there were wars and how men could be found to fight them. It was a game, like football, where victory was sought regardless of cost. But unlike football, the cost of this game wouldn't be shattered egos and disappointment, but shattered lives and death.

She wasn't squeamish, but Honi couldn't understand how the prospect of taking human life could be so incidental. She had never seen men act like this, and the experience unnerved her. She had an impulse to squeeze Konrad's hand and rub it softly against her cheek to cool the fever that possessed him, then lead him far away from here where she could make him into the good man instinct told her was hidden beneath that unnerving drive to dominate. But she quickly chided herself for such thoughts. Konrad was only a business partner, she reminded herself, little more than a stranger who meant nothing to her.

She reached for a piece of bread she wasn't hungry for.

After breakfast, Konrad signed his name to the bottom of the check, and said, "Let's go upstairs, I want you two to meet Angus, the one I've been telling you about." He chuckled. "If he's still alive. He had a pretty rough day yesterday."

Almost as an afterthought, Konrad turned to Honi.

"Do you have any questions about what we've been talking about?"

She stared at him wide-eyed for a long moment, then slowly shook her head.

Konrad knocked on the door several times. When there was no answer, he turned the knob and entered the darkened room. From a corner he heard a voice in obvious pain: "Go away and let a man die in peace."

Konrad flicked on the light. "Good morning, bright eyes. Have you decided yet which is the best German wine?"

Angus looked up with bleary, bloodshot eyes. His bathrobe flopped open to reveal a sagging midsection that would have made Falstaff suck in his gut. "This morning, they're all tied for last place. I feel like death with a toothache. How in hell did I get in this room?"

Konrad chuckled at the memory of the stretcher-borne Angus. "You're better off not knowing. By the way, this is the man I told you about, Otto Ender. Otto, this is Angus O'Callahan, the biggest disc jockey in California— by at least thirty pounds."

The ramrod-straight Otto stepped forward to shake hands with the disheveled Angus. "You look like you survived a war, my friend."

"I feel like I didn't, but I'll recover to fight again."

Honi's presence in the room was hidden by the poor light and the bodies of her two companions. As she stepped into the center of the room, Angus' eyes seemed to clear and widen as he stared. "God," he sighed. "I'm feeling better already. Nurse, take my temperature, please."

Konrad laughed as he steered Honi by the arm until she was standing before Angus. "This is my, ah, my wife, Honi. Honi, this example of depravity you see in the flesh—a whole lot of flesh—is Angus O'Callahan. All you have to know about him is don't loan him money and don't turn your back on him."

Angus winked lewdly. "It's OK to turn your back as long as you remember to bend over." He turned to Konrad. "Damn, you didn't tell me you were married. But I can understand wanting to hide this beautiful creature from me; you know we'll probably run off together."

The comic encounter with Angus was what Honi needed to take her mind off the ominous conversation at breakfast. "I'm sure I'll find you irresistible," she teased.

"Ok, let's get down to business." Konrad sat on the edge of the bed and motioned for Honi and Otto to take the remaining chairs. "Angus, the party's over. It's time you knew why you've been brought here." Konrad snapped his fingers at Angus who was still staring at Honi. "Come on, I'm only going to give this spiel one time." Konrad went over the plan with Angus, sparing few details but knowing much would be incomprehensible to this man who had never entertained a warlike thought in his life.

At the end, Angus sat staring in disbelief. "Jeeesus!" he said with a long, low whistle. "You're serious, aren't you?" Without awaiting a reply, he continued, "What do you want me to do? I've never raided anything except a women's dorm in college." He slapped his palm against his broad forehead. "I knew I should have stayed in neurosurgery. This is the scariest thing I've heard of since visiting Rotary Club."

"OK, knock off the bullshit and get serious," Konrad said. "Your usefulness will be your voice, especially your talent as a mimic. But you'll also have to carry a gun."

Angus leered at the group. "I've only handled one gun in my life, and that's not big enough to hurt anyone."

"We'll show you enough so you don't shoot it off. The important thing is, until you get the feel of the operation, stick close to Otto and me, but don't be obvious about it."

"Don't worry, I'll stick closer than stink to shit."

Honi made a face. "Where did you learn such beautiful language?"

Angus struck a haughty pose. "Education. Education, and moving only in the finest circles."

Konrad handed Angus a small tape cassette and recorder. "I want you to listen to this tape and practice imitating the voice. Maybe you can finally use your voice skills for something other than bad jokes."

Honi and Otto followed Konrad to the door. "One more thing: Think of a phony name for yourself. Then we'll get a passport made for you. Now get some sleep, stay out of the bar, and we'll see you tomorrow."

Early the next morning Konrad and Honi knocked on Angus' door, and entered at the sound of his booming, "Who goes there? Advance and be recognized." Standing in the middle of the room in a defiant Che Guevara pose was Angus. He was dressed in camouflage fatigues, webbed belt, combat boots and a red beret carefully arranged at a rakish angle.

Honi broke into peals of laughter and Konrad wailed, "Where in hell did you find that Hollywood outfit?"

Angus' look turned from Napoleonic pride to a pout. "After we talked yesterday I went shopping. I think it looks neat."

260

"Angus, you look ready to storm a machine gun nest. The only problem is, we don't want people to think we're on our way to storm machine gun nests. Now please, please get into some normal-people clothes. That won't make you normal, but it may fool people for a little while."

Angus grudgingly selected a change of clothing and started for the bathroom. He stopped in the middle of the room and turned around, his arms full of clothes. "By the way, I've thought of my new name."

Konrad was on guard. "What's that?"

"Thaddeus Bruzinski, American-born son of an exiled Polish count."

"Oh, no."

"'Oh, no' nothing, asshole. What do you take me for, a . . . a Richard Wilson, or something like that? Do I look like a Richard Wilson? I'm gonna be me, and right now 'me' is Thaddeus Bruzinski. That's my style."

"Oh, what the hell. OK then, Thaddeus."

"Thad. Call me Thad. For royalty, I'm a regular guy."

"You're a royal pain in the ass," Konrad said affectionately. "Now get out of that clown costume and let's go."

When they reached the street and Angus saw the bus Otto had leased, he gave an appreciative whistle. It was long and luxurious, the kind usually stuffed full of geriatric tourists and seen wending its way from scheduled restroom stop to restroom stop with an occasional castle thrown in. "God, that's big enough for a rock star. You could fit an army into that thing."

Konrad pushed the bus door open. "Just hop aboard and we'll begin collecting our army."

Chapter Eleven

The big bus snaked slowly through the streets of Munich, making stops at all the major hotels. At each, Konrad would disappear inside and reappear a few minutes later with three or four men in tow. Except for following Konrad, they appeared to have little in common. Some were well-dressed, with the self-assurance and smart, leather luggage that are the constant companions of the successful and prosperous. Others had the scruffy look of the down and dispossessed.

Their luggage, too, was often leather, but it was old, cracked and faded, with contents presumably matching. Some were dressed in mod silks, others in business suits, still others in functional workman gray. Most were young, mid-twenties, but a few walked with the heavier step of approaching middle age. One was a brawny, hard-looking woman dressed in men's blue jeans with flannel shirt, heavy work shoes and with hair close-cropped above the ears.

They were a wide variety with but one significant

similarity: an alertness, a tension that stated they were not tourists relaxing in the crisp German winter air, but businessmen intent on the task ahead.

The bus slowly filled, each stop adding its few until the seats were occupied with men who sat in guarded ease, acutely aware of their surroundings, but ignoring each other except for the barest of nods.

With its cargo gathered, the bus left the city and lumbered north across the Danube River and through the hills and farmlands of northern Bavaria and Franconia, then into the low, green mountains of the Thuringian Forest. As the solitude of the forest gradually swallowed them, a sense of destination permeated the bus. They didn't know where they were going, or what would happen once there, but they knew it would at least have to start in secret, and the loneliness of the area meant they were getting close. These men carried stealth with the unconscious ease of another worker carrying a tool box.

Just as the narrow road seemed to disappear into the snow-burdened evergreens, the bus cut sharply into a gravel lane. After one hundred meters of bumpy maneuvering, it stopped in front of a low log building that blended so well into the surrounding trees it wasn't visible until the bus stopped almost at the front door. The massive, rustic hunting lodge was the most remote Konrad could find. He felt doubly secure because a handsomely overpaid landlord promised absolute privacy for what he had been led to believe was to be the location for shooting pornographic movies.

"All right," Konrad shouted above the idling engine, "grab your bags and assemble inside."

Konrad stood on a chair at the front of the big room

263

and looked over the crew while he waited for them to settle down. They were about what he expected, which is to say, they defied categorization. He knew no consistency could be expected in a gang of mercenaries, there being no university offering a degree in the subject, no trade union requiring an apprenticeship, and certainly no father-son tradition (few mercenaries have the inclination of lifespan to raise families). No, a mercenary force is an amalgam of the refuse and the elite of the world's armies, which in themselves represent infinite variety. As Konrad's eyes swept the room, that reality was unmistakable.

"All right, men, listen up." Konrad semi-deliberately lapsed into military jargon. He wanted to instill a sense of military discipline, but it was also a vocabulary he loved and could fall into with little prompting.

He couldn't resist a quip. Looking at the butch-appearing female, he said, "I use the term 'men' in the broad sense. I don't mean to exclude anyone."

She jutted her chin out. "Don't worry about me. Men don't bother me at all." Her inflection leaned heavily on the "at all."

A mock falsetto voice in the rear shot back: "You don't bother us either, sweetheart."

Over the roar of laughter, the woman shouted, "Fuck you."

The mocking voice: "That's what I call an empty threat."

Konrad motioned them into silence. He had accomplished two things: defusing the possible issue of having a woman in the group, and relaxing the men on the common ground of laughter. "My name is Konrad, and you can spell that G-O-D for the rest of this operation. Now, each of you should have a passport, a business suit and fatigues. Everyone have those?"

The silence of assent lasted only a moment before Konrad continued. "We're going to pass out name tags which I want each of you to wear at all times while we're here. That may seem silly, but remember, we've got to become acquainted in damn short order. Plus," he joked, "it might help some of you learn your new names while you're here."

Konrad waited while Otto and Honi passed out the tags. He wanted no distractions for what he would say next. "There has to be only one question on each of your minds: What's the action? I'm going to tell you shortly, but first get this straight. You've all been told that this is going to be dangerous and highly illegal. You accepted under those conditions, and everyone is in, for better or worse. The only way to leave now is with your pockets full of cash or in a body bag. Now, if we all understand each other, here's the plan—we're going to take over a country."

As if on cue, his statement gave way to a buzz of whispered questions and exclamations. "Take it easy, relax, it's only a little nation. It's Liechtenstein, a plump jewel of a country just lying there, fat and helpless. It's what in wartime we might call a target of opportunity. Well, boys, we're going to give Liechtenstein a little socialist revolution for a very capitalistic reason—all the loot we can carry."

A hand raised in the back. "No, no questions right now, time enough for that later. In the next few days, we're going to get to know each other a lot better, and in that time you can ask your questions. I might even answer some of them if I feel inclined."

Konrad paused for emphasis. When he had the group looking up at him in silent anticipation, he continued. "Now hear me on this, and hear me well. This is no game. We're going to conduct this operation under strict military rules of discipline: absolute obedience at all times, no hassling or mistreating civilians, and no independent looting. Any violations of these rules will be dealt with harshly. What that means is this: We'll kill any son of a bitch who's dumb enough to cross me on this—point-blank and without ceremony.

"Several of you will be appointed guards and will be authorized to shoot anyone foolish enough to try to leave the group from this moment forward."

Konrad motioned for Otto to come forward. "You'll be under my direct orders, and my second-in-command is this man right here." Konrad rested his hand on Otto's shoulder. "His name is Sergeant Ender. He's been around and he's tough. I doubt if you can teach him any new tricks; in fact, it might not be a good idea to try."

Konrad sauntered toward a small bar in the corner. "One last thing: After tonight no drinking will be allowed until we sew this thing up." He raised his voice for emphasis. "Now get this straight—no booze. Period." He gave that a moment to sink in, then smiled broadly. "However, tonight we happen to have a couple of cases of damned good French champagne on hand to toast our success in advance."

Konrad had brought the champagne for a stronger purpose than just to have a good time. He knew that men are more their true selves when relaxed and holding a glass, and he wanted—needed—the measure of these strange humans on whom he was relying for so much.

For the next few minutes the sound of pulling corks

was like a barrage of popguns. The mood of concern and concentration lifted as if by magic, and the men stood around in circles, laughing and relaxed. Konrad wandered among them, chatting in the peculiar manner of men who have little to say and much to hide. Any casual phrase that strayed too close to the personal would be shied away from like a growling dog. But Konrad knew that men of action rarely communicate best by words, anyway. There's a body language common to the breed that each of them understand and speak. The way a man holds himself, the look he gives in answering a question or not answering it, can tell more about him than a rehearsed speech.

As the men milled about drinking, Konrad found himself overhearing a tall, amazingly thin black man standing a few feet away whose German bore unmistakable traces of a deep-South accent. He smiled at the thought of hillbilly German. The black man interpreted the smile as an invitation and ambled over.

"Hey, man, how ya doin'?"

Konrad looked at the name tag. "Jesse James Jones; very colorful, but doesn't exactly sound like it came from a German phone book."

"Man, this is my *own* name. My grandmomma used to say if you lost your name, you lost your soul."

"How many countries your grandmother try to take over?"

"None that I know of, but she was a pretty good dictator in her own way. All the same, I figure a man should have the last word on what he's called."

"I'll grant you that, but if certain authorities learn it, you might find the name something of a nuisance later."

"In that case, I'll become Reinhold von Furstenburg,

267

or something like that, but not until I have to."

"Anyway, Jesse, where *did* the name come from?"

"My daddy thought it up. Said Jesse James was the only white man he ever admired 'cause he stole from other white men and got away with it, at least for a while. Got shot in the back, too, so my daddy figured old Jesse was part blood to get hisself screwed all over by white men like that."

They were suddenly joined by a burly man with a blind eye that was so ugly it made Konrad's eyes start to water just by looking at it. It had a way of seeming to stare at a person through the faded, milky film that covered the pupil and turned the white of the eye into a sickening, washed-out blue. Konrad remembered Schell's description of this man: "Emil Damser. Convicted rapist and murderer. Watch him. If I've given you a bad one, he's it."

Konrad cursed the lack of time that forced Schell to send him scum like this. He would have to keep a close eye on this maniac.

Damser looked at Jones and grinned. "Well, blackie, this job should beat picking cotton, eh?"

Jones stared at his antagonist. "Am I bothering you, man? I left one country already to get away from shit like that. I'm not going to leave another one. I'm going to stay and fight." The intensity of his words left no doubt as to the person he was thinking of fighting. Konrad thought for a moment of playing the peacemaker, but quickly changed his mind. These men were not the types to whom you try to teach the social graces. They would just have to learn to tolerate each other's prejudices and bad manners. That was part of the shakedown that would take place over the next few days.

Konrad wandered away and started talking to a pipe-smoking man in his forties with a North German accent about the tactics of the Vietnam War. As he listened to the man's knowledgeable comments, he saw in the corner of his eye a person edge up to his right side.

"Herr Konrad."

He turned to see a slight, smooth-cheeked boy. A little startled, by one so young and innocent-looking in the group. His name was Tony Tenelli. Konrad didn't get a close look at the youth when he boarded the bus and didn't realize Schell had sent one so virginal among the rest of these hard cases.

"Just Konrad will be fine." He smiled.

The boy quietly, without taking eyes from Konrad's, reached up to his own face and ripped off false eyebrows, one after the other. In the next motion, he pulled off his cloth cap and shook out the hair piled underneath. It was reddish-brown with highlights that glinted as it tumbled to shoulder-length. She—that was now obvious—quickly slipped out of her bulky wool sweater and stood challengingly before Konrad with full breasts pushing prominently against the thin jersey she wore.

The room hushed. Attention had been gradually turning toward the activity around Konrad, but now as they saw what was unfolding, mouths fell open and tongues stopped. The woman stood glaring at Konrad, as though to say, Well, what are you going to do about it?

Konrad sensed he was expected to say something. He didn't do it well. "Uh . . . I thought you were Tony Tenelli."

"I *am* Toni Tenelli. You spell it your way, and I'll spell it mine. I prefer the feminine form."

"Well, why?"

"Now, really, Konrad, would you have taken me if you had known?"

He started to recover. "It wasn't necessary to stage this little masquerade. I have no problem at all with you being here, as long as you're not excess baggage."

"You see," she snapped back in triumph. "Have you mentioned 'excess baggage' to anyone else? No, of course not. Well, don't worry about me, I'll more than carry my own weight."

"Well, you're here, but please, no more theatrics. Now I have to find a place for you to sleep."

"How about with me?" a small, gap-toothed man asked with a leer.

The woman whirled and shouted at him, but it was really intended for the entire room. "Keep your filthy mind away from me. Anyone who sneaks into my bedroll will find a knife waiting for him instead of what he expects."

Konrad decided this had gone far enough. "OK, everybody settle down." Turning to Toni, he said loudly enough for all to hear, "You can have the small private room Honi and I were going to use. We'll sleep in the kitchen. You'll be left alone—you'd better be."

With perfect timing, Otto sensed the need for diversion. "OK, men, let's get this place organized. Move it."

The group started to break up and go about the business of setting up a bivouac in the large, barren lodge. Bedrolls and food were brought in from the bus, and Otto designated several volunteers to begin the evening meal.

As the lodge gradually settled down for the night like a

large, restless barnyard, and while Honi slept quietly alongside, Konrad huddled in a corner of the kitchen with a small flashlight reviewing the notes from his conversation with Walter Schell. Except for her sex, Walter had apparently gathered a complete dossier on Toni Tenelli. She had once been a member of a Red Brigade terrorist unit. She and her compatriots were the scourge of Italy, determined to impose their own ideals of justice on a population that had its own ideal—to be left alone in peace. For reasons known only to her, she had suddenly fled from the gang several years ago. In his mind's eye, Konrad could see her at the time: an embittered, frightened girl in her early twenties who knew only how to kill and how to run. She made the simple conversion from criminal-for-ideology to criminal-for-profit, similar occupations requiring the same skills. How she had fooled Schell on such a basic thing as her sex baffled Konrad, but he grinned at the recent memory, it *was* a pleasant surprise.

The little, gap-toothed man named Brandhorst pretended to sleep while he waited for the silence and snores to tell him it was safe to move. He closed his eyes and thought of the feisty bitch's tight body. He imagined that naked flesh in his hands. He caressed the small, firm breasts and cupped his hands around the hard buttocks. Her long, lean legs wrapped themselves around him. Damn. He felt himself grow hard in anticipation. Sure, she warned the men to stay away from her, but she had to do that publicly. What she really wanted was another matter. No woman who ran with men like these could

271

pretend to be a vestal virgin. She was there for the taking, and Brandhorst needed it. He really needed it. If the bitch gave him trouble . . . well, he could handle women.

The room had quieted and Brandhorst carefully peered around to see if anyone was still awake. No one was. The little man slid out of his sleeping bag and crept across the floor toward the door that hid what he needed. With a final glance at the humps lying around the big room, he carefully unlatched the door and pushed it open silently and eased inside.

Brandhorst studied he sleeping form in the far corner of the room for several long seconds. Satisfied, he eased himself slowly across the room until he was next to her motionless back. Carefully, he removed his clothes until he was naked. Very gently, he lifted the top of the unzipped sleeping bag until she was uncovered. She lay there in the warm room unaware of his greedy stare. The sight of her stretched out in only bra and panties fueled his desire to the frenzy level. He threw himself on top of her and tried to tear the bra off with one hand. He clamped her mouth tightly shut with the other.

She awoke instantly upon feeling the weight of his assault. She instinctively tried to cry out but the rough hand pressing down on her mouth allowed only a muffled moan to escape. She struggled wildly against his ripping and fumbling, but the effort only seemed to assist his attempt to subdue her.

He sought desperately to calm her, but at the same time maintained the ferocity of his attack. "Shhh," he whispered breathlessly, "I don't want to hurt you. It'll be good for you, too. You'll like me. Just give me a chance. Stop fighting, damn it. Please stop. It'll be good, I promise."

He was winning. Even though he was a small man, his weight, coupled with her own desperate struggling, quickly exhausted Toni. She realized this was not the way to fight him, and suddenly relaxed.

Thinking she was responding to his pleas, Brandhorst stopped his tearing at her but didn't relax his grip. He slowly removed his hand from her mouth, ready in an instant to reclamp it. He studied her cautiously, then started to pry her legs apart with his knee, and at the same time, fumbled with the elastic band of her panties.

The thought of screaming didn't even occur to her; this had become a personal matter to be settled between the two of them. As she felt his hardness against her thigh, her free left hand was searching the inside of the sleeping bag. At the moment he slid between her forced-apart legs, she found it. Her fingers tightened around the handle.

He thought she was trying to help him enter her when she suddenly slid an arm around his back and pulled herself closer. Then he felt it. The pain was so intense it overflowed his nervous system. At first it felt like a burn, then the full shock of the sharp blade hit his system as it entered his body just below the ribs and sliced upward into his lungs. Pain flooded his brain and became a red and black splotch before his eyes. His penis, which had been rock hard and conquering just moments before, instantly became a comical miniature hose spurting urine in all directions. The scream was a tortured but useless protest.

He had already started a slow, anguished slide toward death when she leaped to her feet, wiped his urine from

273

her legs and started to adjust her own underclothing. She ignored the writhing figure at her feet; it was beneath contempt.

Konrad felt his eyelids drooping. Yawning, he turned off his light, arranged his sleeping bag and tried to settle into a comfortable position on the kitchen floor. He quickly dozed, lulled by the discordant yet oddly soothing snores and coughs of forty other humans. He was sinking into a deep sleep when he was jerked awake by a shrill scream followed by a deep groan. Everyone in the lodge was instantly awake and alert to danger in the way of men trained to respond to the unexpected. The next groan turned everyone's heads toward the small room occupied by Toni.

"Everyone stay put," Konrad commanded and sprinted across the room to the closed door. He pushed inside and flicked on the light switch. Toni stood before him like a hissing cat ready to spring. Her eyes were wild and her bare skin streaked with blood from bra to panties. In her hand she held a thin, wickedly curved linoleum knife dripping blood. At her feet lay the small, curled-up body of the gap-toothed man who had leered at her earlier. Blood spurted from his side like a tiny fountain, the surges corresponding to the beat of his heart which continued in a lost cause. Red bubbles formed on his lips and then ran down his chin in thin streams. He gasped for breath with a loud sucking noise.

"What the hell happened in here?" Konrad bellowed with the exasperation of a man who suddenly sees holes appear in plans carefully laid.

"I warned him—I warned all of you," Toni shouted at

274

the group flowing into the room in Konrad's wake. She menacingly waved the knife at them as she spoke, providing unneeded emphasis for her words. "He tried to rape me, the slimy little bastard." She looked down at her victim with scorn.

Konrad leaned down to Brandhorst. "Get me the first-aid kit, quickly." But as he spoke Konrad saw the futility of trying to treat such a grave wound; the man needed a surgeon, not a Band-Aid. "This man's in bad shape," he said unnecessarily. Turning to Toni, he asked savagely, "Why did you have to do this? Couldn't you have called for help?"

"Call for help? Like a damsel in distress?" She spat out the words in mockery. "I don't need a bunch of smirking men rushing in here to save me from one of their buddies just out for a 'little piece of tail.' I don't have to apologize to you for defending myself."

Konrad's anger at her drained because he knew she was right. If she weren't that kind of woman, she wouldn't belong here. "Well, if he doesn't get some help pretty soon, he'll die." He stood up and looked at the circle of men around him as though one of them might have the answer.

The roar of the gun behind him shocked Konrad into momentary numbness. In truth, it scared hell out of him. Konrad whirled and found himself looking into the grinning face of Damser; the grotesque dead eye seemed to return the stare. Konrad's eyes dropped to a tiny derringer in Damser's right hand. Before his eyes dropped farther, he knew what he would see.

The wounded man was no longer trying to breathe. He had gone limp and his wound was now only seeping blood. The pump that had made it spurt seconds before

275

had been stilled. The small, blue-edged hole in his forehead gave an almost comical third-eye look to the sallow face as it joined the unfocused, half-closed eyes directly below.

"Your problem just went away," Damser joked as he started to pocket the pistol.

Konrad hit him from the blind side, the blow glancing off the forehead, making Damser stumble backward into the frantically scattering crowd. Before Damser had a chance to recover, Konrad followed with a kick to the kneecap. Damser shrieked and fell into a heap where he lay rubbing his knee and cursing.

Konrad picked up the pistol, cocked it and jammed the muzzle into Damser's mouth. The front sight cut his lip and blood flowed down his chin. "You dirty, sick bastard. If there's any killing to be done around here, it'll be done by me—and I'll start with you." Konrad jerked the pistol out of the man's mouth and put it in his pocket. Even in anger, Konrad knew Damser had done the sensible thing. Brandhorst had no chance for anything but a slow, agonizing death. But, nevertheless, Konrad could not let the initiative for that type of decision pass to any of his men. He didn't hit Damser because he shot Brandhorst, but for the way he did it, and also because he seemed to enjoy it.

Konrad leaned back against the soft headrest, closed his eyes and let himself be massaged by the gentle rocking of the bus. He felt guardedly at ease as he reviewed the progress shown by his crew during their stay at the lodge.

Though no stranger to command, Konrad was still amazed by the skills his thrown-together squad brought to their task. In just a few days, under the relentless prodding of Otto, they had mastered the logistics of Liechtenstein. Even with only maps and photographs to work with, familiarity with military planning gave them a working knowledge that few native Liechtensteiners could match.

He had instructed Honi and Angus in the use of the M-16 rifle in a deep glen far from the others—both to protect their identities as novices, and to protect the world in general from their wild aim. But the "training" of the others with the weapons and explosives had made him feel a little foolish. The squad, without fail, had displayed the skill and deadliness not normally found outside crack commando units.

As the kilometers clicked off and Liechtenstein drew closer, Konrad re-examined the many parts of his plan and the ways each might go wrong. He was realist enough to know this scheme could go either way, but if it failed, how would it happen? Would it be a screw-up in his planning? Unexpected opposition from the natives? Foreign intervention? The weather? The possibilities were depressingly numerous, and all he could do at this point was to stay loose, alert and prepared for anything.

Honi reached over and softly shook his arm. "We're almost to the border."

Konrad stirred, straightened his tie and coat and looked around him. Otto was dressed in a bus driver's uniform and concentrating on guiding them through the increased traffic near the border crossing. The bus was filled with what could have passed for a chamber of commerce. Everyone was dressed in sober business suits, carried attache cases, business magazines or newspapers. In some cases, men with perfect eyesight who could put a two-inch grouping into a target at three hundred meters wore thick, horn-rimmed spectacles of plain glass to achieve the proper appearance of age and seriousness. The women were outfitted, despite their loud and long protests, in conservative secretarial clothing that suggested the only thing they could terrorize would be a typing pool.

Konrad stood and faced the length of the bus, swaying with its motion. "OK, we're almost to the border. Have your passports ready. Remember, you're salesmen for the Trans-Europe Oil Corporation, and we're headed for Liechtenstein to attend a sales conference." Konrad studied their quiet concentration. "C'mon, show some life. Act like you're happy to get away from the office and the wife and kids."

The bus pulled up to the German border station; Konrad knew this would be the easy one. Since these men were Germans, as their passports showed, the scrutiny would be minimal.

The green-uniformed German guard made a quick pass down the aisle casually inspecting passports, then hopped off and waved them through.

A few hundred meters farther they stopped before a wooden barricade. Flying from a nearby flagpole was the thick white cross of Switzerland on its field of bright red.

The border inspector tapped on the closed door of the bus and quickly ascended the steps when it swung open. She stood beside Otto momentarily and studied him as he set the air brakes. "Are your papers in order this time?"

Otto turned to the woman in the gray uniform; her face looked vaguely familiar. Then he glanced at her name tag—Hanna Moltke—and froze. It was the same person who had stopped him two weeks before. "Huh? I think so," was all he could think to say.

"I guess you don't remember me. You were through here a couple of weeks ago with incorrect papers. The reason I remember, you were the first driver I've let through like that in almost ten years. You spoiled my record. What'd you do, change jobs?"

"Oh . . . oh, yes. Driving this bus is a much better job."

The inspector held out her hand. "Well, I hope your papers are in order this time." She studied the bus rental agreement as Otto and Konrad, watching from his nearby seat, held their breath. Finally, the inspector folded the papers and softly cleared her throat. "I see you're driving for a Trans-Europe Oil Corporation. You seem to have a fondness for oil. What's your destination?"

Konrad stepped next to the inspector. "Excuse me, Madam Inspector, I'm in charge of this group. Here's my passport. As you can see, I'm an American."

"What is your business in Switzerland, Herr Konrad?"

"I'm with the Trans-Europe Oil Corporation. These people are our sales staff for Germany. We're headed for Liechtenstein for a sales meeting and a little relaxation."

"Where will you be staying in Liechtenstein?"

"At the Wagoner Hof. Here's the reservation confirmation."

The inspector beckoned Otto and Konrad to follow her outside the bus. "I'd like to take a look at the baggage compartment."

The inspector randomly opened a few bags, thoughtfully shifting the contents, then turned to Konrad. "Your men must be planning some vigorous relaxation. I see a lot of heavy-duty clothing and boots."

Konrad thought quickly, then laughed. "I know. Several of our group belong to a hiking club. It makes me tired just to listen to them. I guess things like that are catching, just happy it missed me."

The inspector continued her rummaging. "Tourists who go to Liechtenstein this time of year usually plan on doing some skiing, but I see no ski equipment. Why is that?"

Konrad silently cursed his forgetfulness. "The ones who want to ski decided they'd rent equipment. There wasn't that much room on the bus, and besides, the company is picking up the tab."

Hanna Moltke gave no visible reaction. Was she convinced, or did she suspect something? Konrad waited pensively while she thoughtfully looked at the luggage. Finally, she said, "Let's go back inside. I'd like to see everyone's passport."

She slowly made her way down the aisle, checking passports first on one side and then the other. She was within two rows of finishing when she seemed to pause longer while studying the papers of a tall, blond man who called himself Schultz and who displayed a vivid red scar along the left side of his face that emerged from the sideburn, and then ran along the edge of the ear to the bottom of the jaw.

Hanna reached into her jacket pocket for a pen, fumbled for it, and then dropped a pack of cigarettes into Schultz' lap with several of the cigarettes spilling out. Obligingly, Schultz picked up the scattered cigarettes, slipped them back into the pack and handed it to the inspector.

"Thank you, and please pardon my clumsiness," she said as she returned the pack to her pocket and turned her attention to the next man. Shortly, she said to Otto, "You're all clear. Enjoy your trip through Switzerland and drive carefully."

Hanna Moltke watched from the station office as the bus slowly pulled away from the barricade. She called an aide over and handed him the pack of cigarettes. "Have the lab in Bern test the first few cigarettes in this pack for fingerprints. Ask them to rush; I saw something on that bus that bothered me."

"What do you expect them to find, Inspector?"

"I can't be certain, but I saw a face—and a scar—on that bus that I could swear I've seen before."

The young aide shook his head. "I'll do my best to get this expedited, but it's tough to get anyone to hurry this close to Christmas."

Chapter Twelve

As the bus pulled away from the border crossing, the release of tension in Konrad was a visible thing. He sighed and relaxed his head against the seat in relief. After long moments of breathing deeply, his muscles unknotted and the beads of sweat on his forehead evaporated.

He turned to Honi with a wide grin and in a voice barely lifting above the loud hum of the engines, asked, "Have you figured out how to spend your share?"

Honi, equally shaken by the close call, didn't hide her irritation. "We don't have it yet. Your cockiness is a bit premature."

"Maybe, but that was a big hurdle, and we got over it. We're getting closer, lady, we're getting closer."

Honi's voice became apologetic, and she reached for his hand and clasped it in both of hers. "I'm sorry I snapped at you, but I'm just not used to this sort of thing. I'm scared; I don't want to get hurt, and I don't want to hurt anyone else."

Konrad's eyes narrowed. "You're not getting cold feet, are you? You're not thinking of backing out?"

"And if I were?"

"I don't think our German friend would take kindly to that. If you do back out, please don't stand too close to me."

Honi looked at him squarely. "What would you do if I did?"

Konrad shrugged. "I wouldn't hurt you, if that's what you mean. Actually, you're no longer that essential to the operation." He gave her the flash of a smile. "And I've grown to kind of like you. But make no mistake: Our sponsor would have you killed, I'm sure of that. My advice is to see it through. Look, it's not unusual for a beginner to get cold feet. Just give it time."

Honi gazed at a passing Swiss village. "Am I the only one who has doubts? Are you that sure of this thing? The risk to yourself . . . the danger of hurting others."

Konrad snorted. "Do I look worried? Hurting's part of the game, and getting your share usually depends on who you're willing to hurt, and being smart enough to make the other guy hurt first."

As Konrad's bitter words poured over her mind, Honi caught a glimpse of herself, of her own attitudes, but she quickly turned away from that reflection with an inward shudder. "I think we both need to feel better about ourselves," she said, "but I don't know how to do it."

He laughed hollowly. "A million bucks might help, for starters."

"We'll see," she whispered to herself. She had a sudden desire to take him in her arms and caress the hurt out of his life, but her subconscious warned her away and instead she picked up a magazine and stared unseeing at its pages.

*　　*　　*

The big bus crawled into the small hotel parking lot with a roar and a final puff of diesel smoke. As Konrad's crew clattered off one by one and stretched their legs in the slush of churned-up snow, the manager and several aides rushed out a front door festooned with colorful Christmas decorations and approached the group with loud greetings, their professional-host manner reinforced by a genuine delight to see such a large group arriving in the mid-winter slow time.

"Herr Konrad," the manager gushed as he greeted the man he knew as a writer living locally who was earning some extra money setting up this sales conference. He threw out his arms to make his greeting embrace the whole group. "Welcome to Liechtenstein. Welcome to the Wagoner Hof. Merry Christmas." He signaled imperiously for nearby porters to handle the mounting pile of luggage. "I trust you had a pleasant trip?" Without waiting for a reply, he rushed on. "Everything is ready, including your own dining room. Just as we agreed, your privacy will be assured."

"Thank you," Konrad said. "Now, Frau Konrad and I will be going to our own home for the evening. Herr Ender, the tall man right over there, will be in charge if you have any questions."

Forty people milled nervously in the dining room. After two days in this small hotel, interrupted only by brief scouting trips around the countryside, and with no liquor or chance to do any woman chasing, they were on edge and ill-tempered. Angus, as usual, was the center of a group which was being amused by his staccato one-liners. They were not accustomed in their world of violence and danger to a man whose only weapon was humor.

Angus' attention was captured by the approach of the brutish Emil Damser dressed in red slacks and red turtleneck. Topped by his florid face and knob of a sunburned bald skull, the image was monochromatic red.

Angus eyed Damser, who was obviously proud of his appearance, from head to toe. "I like your outfit," Angus said. Damser preened and looked around to see who had heard the compliment. Then Angus dropped the punch line. "You look like a constipated strawberry."

Damser stared at Angus with bewilderment. He didn't have a sharp wit to begin with, and he was unaccustomed to being the butt of jokes, but the snickers he heard around the room told him he was being toyed with.

He glared at Angus, then, seeking to regain control of the situation, loudly declared, "I need a piece of ass. I'm used to having it every day." He wheezed a rolling laugh. "It's not fair to the ladies, either."

Angus seemed to play it straight. "How many times you been laid?"

Damser grinned, enjoying the attention. "I lost track a long time ago, but I gave four broads the clap in one weekend once."

Angus knitted his brow as though he were mentally calculating. "Hmm, that comes to forty-four."

Damser looked at him blankly. "Forty-four what?"

"Well, if each of those whores had ten customers after you that weekend, that makes a tot—"

With a roar, Damser had Angus by the throat and the two tumbled over a chair and fell to the floor. The room immediately surrendered to pandemonium with the bellowing of Damser, the choking protests of Angus, and the shouts of a group grateful for an interlude to their boredom.

Finally, a score of grasping hands got them separated and standing. With the wiliness of a bully, Damser sensed that violence was an art form Angus didn't understand, and it gave him a big advantage, one that could help him dominate the group. As the others started to lose interest, assuming the confrontation had passed, Damser suddenly flicked open a switchblade knife and held it high in front of him, pointed menacingly at Angus. "Now, you fat fucker, you'll see what happens when you jive with Emil Damser."

The others scurried out of the way. They were too familiar with this sort of trouble to want to be too close.

As he stood facing the threatening figure in red, Angus seemed perplexed; he couldn't fathom someone actually wanting to hurt him just because he told a joke.

Knowing he was in no danger, a sly smile crossed Damser's piggish face and he advanced slowly, waving the gleaming knife. "Die, you fat fucker," he said softly.

Angus' eyes bulged as he watched the knife swing closer, mesmerized by the glittering blade.

Damser chuckled. It was rare to have such a chance to show off his knife-fighting prowess without the risk of being cut in return. "Get ready to die," he cooed, trying to build drama into a no-contest fight. He slashed the air lazily, but Angus still had difficulty stumbling out of the way.

Damser slashed again, this time with more speed and aim. As the arc of the knife passed before Angus, he reflexively threw up a forearm to ward off the knife.

Instantly, a thin, red line appeared on his arm. The line slowly widened until the forearm was dripping blood. Damser grinned in glee and moved menacingly, ready to strike again.

The room was deathly still and waiting. Suddenly, the silence was broken by the loud shattering of glass. All eyes turned to see Otto Ender standing a few feet away with a dripping bottle in his hand, the jagged edges forming long, irregular daggers.

Otto slowly raised the broken bottle and pointed it meaningfully at Damser's knife hand. "You've got a choice, bastard. Use it and die, or put it away and live. If you ruin this operation for the rest of us, you're gonna pay. Now, do one or the other."

"You threatening me, old man?"

"You're goddamn right. Now make up your mind, Damser. Don't make us wait."

Damser glared at Otto, then glanced around at the suddenly hostile room where Otto's words had just reminded them that the whole job—including their money—was in jeopardy if Damser killed Angus and the police were called.

With a face-saving laugh, Damser slowly closed and pocketed the switchblade. "I wasn't hungry for pork anyway," he tried to joke. When no one laughed, he shouldered his way out of the room.

After Damser disappeared, Otto took a towel and wrapped Angus' arm. "It's not as bad as it looks, you won't even need stitches."

Angus shook his head in mock disgust. "And just when I had him where I wanted him. Let me tell you, if I'm ever in charge of improving the human race, I'm gonna start by sterilizing him."

287

Otto turned on him in fury. "Listen, you dumb son of a bitch, your wisecracking will get you killed around these guys. They don't have a sense of humor, and they don't like being laughed at, so just shut the fuck up."

Otto stalked out of the room. While all eyes followed the old sergeant, no one noticed another observer watching from the slit of a barely opened door leading to the kitchen. As the slam of Otto's closing door echoed through the room, that door closed also, but more gently.

Like any career hotel man, Eric Winstert had seen a little of everything, and learned to turn his head at most, but he was frightened by what he had witnessed through the kitchen door. The big, ugly man in red actually seemed intent on killing the fat one while the entire group watched with no particular emotion. Even when the old one stopped it with the broken bottle, he, too, seemed unmoved by the idea of violent death. Something was wrong, frighteningly wrong with this group of oil salesmen he had invited into his hotel.

Winstert looked nervously over his shoulder toward the dining room as he impatiently waited for the ringing phone to be answered. When a voice finally spoke on the other end, he asked in relief to speak to the chief of police. After another wait, an officious voice said, "Chief Houser here. What can I do for you?"

"Chief, this is Eric Winstert at the Wagoner Hof. I thought I'd better let you know about some of our guests."

"Well, what about them?"

"Two of them just had a fight in the dining room, and—"

"Was anyone badly hurt?"

"No, not badly, but I don't like their looks. They—"

"Slow down, Herr Winstert. We don't arrest people for their looks, so why don't you just tell me who they are and exactly what it is they've done wrong."

"They're a group of oil salesmen from Germany who rented the hotel for a sales conference. They've been here two days and seem to spend most of their time going off in small groups and touring the countryside in rental cars. They don't even drink."

"Are their wives with them?"

"They say their wives are supposed to arrive tomorrow, Christmas Eve. A strange way to spend Christmas. The whole thing is odd."

The chief's voice was coated with reassurance. "Don't worry about it, Winstert. Everyone knows Germans are strange, ill-mannered swine. But they also spend a lot of money, and I shouldn't have to tell you that we can use the tourist business. They're pigs—feed them like that and let them behave like that, and make sure they pay their bill."

The chief hung up and shook his head with resignation in the direction of the desk sergeant. "No one told me that the chief of police has to hold the hand of innkeepers scared of their own guests. I should have become something more interesting—like a file clerk."

The sergeant was barely interested enough to ask, "What did the guests do?"

"Nothing, really. Just acting like tourists." Then, to himself, he muttered, "Germans that don't drink. Amazing."

Honi was bored and restless. Since their return, Konrad seemed constantly busy with Otto holding planning sessions far into the night, driving the back roads with the men, and when he wasn't doing anything else, sitting and staring into the distance. And though she wasn't really a wife, she chafed at being tied to a workaholic. Relations between the two of them had become strained, anyway, since she refused to have sex with him after the first night they arrived. She just wasn't comfortable with the thought of going to bed with him; she didn't understand it, and he certainly didn't.

Konrad had asked her to stay near the house to monitor the telephone, but it never rang, so she impatiently paced the rooms, gnawed at her fingernails and tried to ignore what was bothering her in the recesses of her conscience.

After two days, she could stand it no longer. She opened a window and let the bracing December chill wash over her face. The gray skies seemed to be resting on the white shoulders of the Alps and the scent of pine was in the air. This was the way winter was supposed to be, the way it was when she was a girl and at peace with life. She reached for her coat.

Honi walked for hours along the rutted country lanes of her childhood. Trees and houses that a few days ago would have gone unnoticed as part of a blurred landscape, now began to represent memories, and be associated with people and events of days past. Good times, good memories.

Honi climbed, putting her frustrations and uneasiness to work laboring up the steep hillsides. She didn't know where she was headed, didn't really care. It was enough to be draining herself climbing these hills again.

Finally, her aching legs and heaving lungs surrendered to gravity and she let herself down slowly on a log and relaxed with deep breaths. Down the mountain, she could see the twinkling lights of Vaduz peeking through the mists of twilight. Around her, the towering, silent pines framed the little hillside clearing and made her feel safe, removed from the confusion and turmoil far below.

Her musings of quiet childhood winter evenings were suddenly shattered by the rustle of nearby branches. Honi tensed and was instantly alert; her years of defensive caution in the cities snapped her back. Like all women who live alone among men, she was always aware of her vulnerability. She got up and headed warily toward the sound. "Who's there?" she asked timorously.

Honi could make out a figure with the bulk of a large man half hidden by a pine tree. With shaky voice and pounding heart, she said, "Who are you? Why are you hiding?"

The shadowy form hesitantly stepped forward and approached slowly out of the gloom. She was frozen by apprehension. As he came within touching distance, a ray of the fading light filtered through the trees and illuminated his face faintly.

Honi gasped. "Hans?" she asked, unwilling to trust what she saw.

"Hello, Honi."

Honi nervously swept her hair back with both hands. Despite rehearsing it bitterly in her imagination for years, this was a confrontation she was not prepared for. "What are you doing here?" she asked.

"I come here whenever I'm lonely, which is very often. Is that why you're here?"

Honi was perplexed. "What do you mean?"

"Don't you know where we're standing?"

Confused, she looked around the small clearing, then

she began to recognize small landmarks and realized they were standing in the place that long ago they had claimed as theirs. This was where so many good memories—and bad—were rooted.

"I didn't realize. . . ."

"I'd prefer not to believe that," Hans said.

Honi regained her composure and managed a cold edge to her voice. "Believe what you like." She backed away. "Anyway, I have to be going."

Hans moved quickly to her side, but carefully avoided touching her. "Please don't leave. We need to talk. This may be the only chance we have; please don't take it away."

"I can't think of anything we have to discuss," she said, but stopped backing away. "What was between us is over. Long over."

He was pleading. "Please, I want to explain what happened back—"

"I *know* what happened," she said bitterly, but allowed him to gently guide her to a seat on a nearby log. "All I want is to forget it." Despite her words, Honi was beginning to realize that something needed to get settled for both their sakes.

"Forget?" His voice twisted in pain. "How can I forget how we ruined our lives when they had barely started?"

"How did *we* ruin our lives, Hans? What did *we* do? I was the one who was pushed out of my home and country, not you. You've still got your precious farm, and I hear you have a wife and child. Would you like to know what I've had for the past ten years? Would you like to know what my life's been like? I've been a whore, Hans. A *whore*. How does that sound? Would you like to know what that life is like?" She was shouting, releasing

292

the pent-up pain accumulated over the years. "That was your baby, too, Hans, but you abandoned me. So don't ask me to feel sorry for you."

"We both made mistakes, Honi, but we were young and scared."

Honi's voice lowered and she hissed the words: "You said the baby wasn't yours. You *denied* it." Saying it made the ghosts stir. The despair of being alone and abandoned in that hospital room years ago revived in her mind causing a deep shudder. She pushed the images out of her mind and back into the mists of pain grown dull where she had struggled for so long to contain them. Those thoughts just made her tired, a weariness grown of pointless repetition.

Hans knelt beside her. "I've rehearsed in my mind a thousand times what I'd say to you so you'd understand that I was confused, that I never wanted to hurt you. And in those daydreams, you always understood and forgave." His voice broke. "And in the end, you always took me in your arms and held me and said it was all right."

In a swift movement, Hans reached up and encircled her with his arms. With desperate passion, he smothered her with kisses and pleas for another chance to love her.

Honi didn't react. She felt a strange sense of detachment and found herself coolly analyzing the behavior of this man she had once cared for so deeply. Her anger was gone, replaced by a sorrow for lives gone wrong, for dreams ended in such desperation. She tiredly pushed him back. "Let's just forget it, Hans. Go home to your family and your farm."

"Go home," he repeated bitterly, "do you think that will make me feel better? The only time I have peace is when I come up here and relive what we once had." With a choking, halting voice, Hans told Honi of his quick, unhappy marriage and the misery that had become his daily companion. As he ended, a silence fell between them.

Honi realized that she, not Hans, was the one fighting for life. He had surrendered to self-pity, a man whose only hope for the future depended on somehow recapturing the past. "I'm sorry, Hans, but there's nothing I can do for you."

He took her hands and squeezed them so hard that Honi winced. "Don't you think . . . don't you think we could pick up where we left off? We could meet up here and be together, and maybe it would be like before. No one else would have to know."

Honi studied him sadly. She couldn't avoid a comparison with Konrad. Each suffered from a sense of rejection and defeat, but this man was a whiner, while Konrad forced a smile on his face and took another crack at life. Although she was having deep misgivings about their purpose here in Liechtenstein, when she compared Konrad with this man before her, she recognized a strength in him that she had never really defined before. He was not only a fun man to whom she could talk and reveal many of her feelings, he was in his own way a good man. "Good" to Honi had deep personal meanings. She had long since dismissed as irrelevant the posturing definition of good that society framed to keep people in line; she applied the standards of the code she learned from the streets. Good to her meant fighting the odds, clawing upward, spitting in their eye and not begging for pity. Honi recognized some of herself in Konrad. He wouldn't quit, and he didn't cry, at least not aloud. He was gentle when he felt he could afford to be.

Honi's feelings came into focus: the times she laughed at Konrad's jokes, admired his intelligence, sympathized with his hurts, shared his passion. These things suddenly took on meaning with combined emotional impact far greater than their individual parts had seemed to have as they accumulated over the past weeks. Sitting on a hard log in a cold twilight forest listening with compassion to a beaten man, it struck her like a star shell in the night sky that she wanted Konrad, wanted to be with him and share all things. With that realization came the warmth and fullness of a sense of belonging, of purpose intertwined with another person.

Hans broke the silence. "It could be just the same again, you'd see. I still love you."

She turned and studied him for a moment. He was still a young boy in his feelings and commitments. She didn't want to witness his pain and thrashings anymore. "I'm sorry, but that's not possible."

"Why not, for God's sake?"

"Because I'm in love with someone else."

Silently, he got up from the log and walked with shoulders slumped and head bowed into the darkness. Honi thought of calling after him, a last attempt to comfort the man she thought for so many years that she hated. But she didn't, she just watched him disappear.

It was completely dark when Honi arrived at the driveway to her home. There were lights burning in the kitchen and she noticed the rental truck which Otto had brought over from its St. Gallen hiding place was parked in a secluded spot near the rear of the house. As she entered the kitchen, Konrad was sitting at the table

295

hunched over a large, detailed map. Dirty coffee cups and overflowing ash trays testified to a number of earlier visitors.

Konrad looked up as she entered. "In wartime, you'd be shot for abandoning your post," he said absently.

"I'm sorry. I just had to get out of the house for a while." She looked at the messy table. "It doesn't look like you've been lonesome."

"Otto and some of the boys were over to unload the truck and iron out a few last-minute details." Konrad folded the map and pushed back from the table, stretching to ease his cramped muscles. He reached down to the floor. "Let me show you something." He produced a black, gleaming automatic rifle and hefted it for balance then took mock aim out the window. "Isn't she beautiful?"

Honi declined to handle the gun when Konrad extended it to her. "To me, it's a *he*, not a *she*. But whatever the thing's sex, I think it's ugly. How could anyone love a thing like that?"

Konrad shrugged his shoulders. "Why would anyone love a violin or a fast automobile? Because you understand it and know how to coax perfection out of it."

"There's no perfection in killing."

Konrad had given up trying to explain military ways and thoughts to her, so he changed the subject. "All the equipment is unloaded and assembled, ready to go. We move tomorrow, Christmas Eve."

"Christmas Eve," Honi echoed hollowly.

Konrad studied her closely. "What's the matter, you getting cold feet again? I thought you said you were ready."

Honi busied herself with fixing soup. "I'll be there."

296

"But you won't like it, huh?"

"That's right, I won't like it."

"What's made you change? The woman I met a few weeks ago was gung-ho, ready to come back here and stick it in their ear."

Honi put the soup in the pan she was holding and turned to face him. "I've learned a few things since then. I learned that the people I thought had turned on me were just as dumb and scared as I was. I learned that my hatred was really just self-pity."

Konrad leaned his elbows on the table and stared at her. "Then why are you going ahead?"

Despite her efforts at self-control, Honi had sudden difficulty holding the pan and it clattered into the sink. Her lower lip trembled as she stared at the spilled soup. She couldn't believe it could be so difficult to say something so simple. She tried to be calm and steady her voice so it wouldn't sound silly. Then she said it. "Because I fell in love."

"What does falling in love have to do with this job?"

Honi took a deep breath and let it rush out with the words. "You're the man I fell in love with."

Konrad shot to his feet with a stunned look and started pacing. "Hey, hold on. That's not part of the deal. That's very unprofessional. I mean . . ."

Honi laughed. Watching him befuddled gave her an extra tug of affection for him. "I know what you mean, and believe me, I didn't plan it that way. It just happened. Only today, in fact, did I face the truth of it myself."

"Well, why? Why me, for God's sake?"

Honi walked over and took both his hands in hers. She looked in his face. "Why you? To understand that, you'd have to see yourself as I see you. Oh, I know you're arrogant and cynical, but I think those are just fronts to disguise loneliness, confusion and disillusionment. Beneath the facade, I think you're a great guy, really. You stick by your friends, you don't deliberately try to screw up people's lives, and you turn me on something awful."

Konrad stared at her with open mouth. "Turn you on? Why would you, of all people, feel that . . ." He suddenly realized what he was about to say and decided to shut up, but the meaning was not lost on Honi.

"Why would a hooker have an urge for only one man? That's what you were about to ask, I know. Well, let me tell you something about hookers: They're ordinary people, trying to survive the best way they can, just like anybody else. They feel a lot of things people never ask about, like love."

Konrad walked away, shaking his head. "I didn't intend . . ."

Honi interrupted, "Of course you did, but I don't mind because we've got to deal honestly with both our lives. That's part of it, part of being in love. Let me tell you something else; you may have wondered why I haven't made love to you since that first night we were in this house. I wondered, too, but I just assumed I didn't have the desire. But now I know different. It was because my love for you was growing deeper, and something inside of me wouldn't let me share myself with you until you could share with me in the same way. The strange ways of a woman, I suppose. All of a sudden it meant more than just screwing."

Konrad held up his hand as though to ward her off. "This is really going too far. Don't let this fake marriage business go to your head. It takes two to dance to your little tune, and I don't hear the music. I'm not about to fall in love with anyone."

His words stung Honi and she stood looking at him with tears forming in her eyes. "Please don't be mean about it; there are worse things people can say to you than, 'I love you.'"

By way of apologizing for his harshness, Konrad took her by the hand and guided her into the parlor where he sat next to her on the sofa. He spoke more softly. "I didn't mean to sound nasty, it's just that I had no idea this was coming. Is this why you said you'd go ahead with the job even though you don't want to, just for me?"

Honi nodded. "I'll do it to be doing it with you. I want to be your woman, and to prove it, I'll go all the way. It's that simple, but I do wish you'd change your mind."

"I can't. This is my one chance to make it big. I can't handle being a nobody. Maybe you can't understand it, but the only way to protect yourself in this life is to be so high others can't reach you, and that takes money."

"But people could be hurt, even killed."

"That's the chance we have to take, but if it goes smoothly, no one should get a scratch."

Konrad's face changed to a deep frown, and Honi could see he was bothered by something else. "What is it?" she asked.

"Let's just forget what you said about falling in love. Of all people, I'm not the man you want, trust me on that."

Honi loaded her voice with determination. "Of all people, you *are* the man I want."

Konrad closed his eyes for a long moment and took a deep breath before speaking. "You don't know what you'd be getting. Let me tell you something: I'm a loser.

Everything I touch turns to shit. I let people down who rely on me; the only ones I'm comfortable with are the types you see in this outfit. They're so damned calloused and crooked themselves, there's no way I could hurt them. Anything that happens to them, they deserve anyway."

Honi shook her head resolutely. "I can't believe that. I've seen you with Angus; you're good to him and he's not crooked, at least not like the others."

"I should never have brought Angus over here. He doesn't belong, but I figured he'd never have another chance to make it big, so . . ."

Honi pressed the point. "I'm relying on you in this too, and I'm not afraid, at least not afraid for myself."

Konrad became very still, his body became stiff and awkward with tension, as though he had suddenly become an old man. "I'm going to tell you something I've never told anyone. After that, we'll see if you can still say you love me."

Konrad slowly, haltingly told her the story of Willie Mac Russell and how Konrad left him to die at the hands of the enemy while he ran away into the jungle. It took several minutes because Konrad had to stop several times to get control of his emotions. Even so, when he finished, his eyes were red-rimmed and watery. "So you see what happens to people who put their trust in me," he said.

Honi's reply was defiant. "I see no such thing. That man knew the chance he was taking when he volunteered to go with you. Besides, your first duty was to reach help. You had to think of your men."

"That's fine for you to say, but you weren't there. You didn't hear the pleading and the screams. And in my heart I know I wasn't thinking of the other men, I was only trying to save myself. Look," he almost pleaded, "there were only four Viet Cong. I could have taken them all by surprise."

"Since when is it so easy to kill four armed men?"

Konrad shook his head sadly. "You can rationalize all you want, but I know what a coward I was, and it left blood on my hands."

Honi acted disgusted. "Oh, for God's sake, stop it. What kind of romantic bullshit is this? You must see yourself as some sort of medieval knight. Do you think you're the first person to ever question your own courage? The point is, you did the only thing you could have done, you did what you had to do. The Army even acknowledged that by giving you a medal."

"That fat-ass colonel just wanted a hero in his outfit; he didn't care about some dead nigger soldier."

Honi softly rubbed her hand across his shoulders. "Did you go to anyone for help, maybe just to talk it out, like a psychiatrist?"

Konrad snorted derisively. "A psychiatrist? You've got to be kidding. Do you think I'm going to let one of those jokers play games with my emotions? What the hell would some shrink know about combat? He'd just stare at me like a bug, then prescribe a tranquilizer."

"How about talking with another combat officer?"

"I'd die first," he said through clenched teeth.

Honi was dogged. "No matter what you tell yourself, you did what you had to do."

Konrad looked away and mumbled, "You weren't there."

She moved closer. "That's right, I wasn't there. But I'm here. And what I see is a helluva good man eating himself up inside for doing the right thing, the smart thing, the only thing, in a situation that most people couldn't even imagine, let alone cope with." Honi's voice became more urgent and she started to plead. "For Christ's sake, let's pack up and get out of here tonight; go some place where no one will ever find us. Then we can put all of this behind us, all your bad memories and all of mine."

For a moment, she thought he might do it. But then Konrad pulled away and got to his feet. "Go to bed; you need sleep. We won't get much for the next couple of days."

Honi reached out for his hand. "Not without you. Let me take you into my room."

Konrad looked at her hand as though it were a rare gift, offered to him in surprise. She could see the desire spread across his face and the sudden tension in his body.

Without waiting for a response, Honi started undressing, slowly, casually, to heighten the anticipation that was already working in his eyes. She was out of everything except her black bikini panties and matching low-cut bra. She walked slowly to him, a teasing smile on her face and a suggestion in her walk. She kissed him long and hard, not passionately, but slowly, gently, as though to say, this is just the beginning, let the pulse quicken at its own speed.

Honi felt the hardness of his erection against her as she began to undress him, slowly, slowly. Then he was standing just as she, with nothing on except underwear. Honi lowered herself to one knee so her face was level with and almost touching his distended penis. She hooked her thumbs in his shorts and slowly pulled them down until he stood before her naked. She allowed her silky hair to brush against his penis, and felt him grow

302

even more tense in response. No more teasing, she thought, and led him into the bedroom of her childhood, a room from which all bad memories had fled.

It wasn't like the last time, it was better. The thrill of discovery was gone, but it was amply replaced by the new-found feelings they shared. Even though Konrad's detail-packed mind was preoccupied with the mission just ahead, just knowing she cared deeply made his passion soar to such heights that he dizzied from the effect.

Tonight was her night to serve him. Although she desired him inside her, Honi responded to some instinctive urge that told her to sacrifice her needs for a display of devotion that would leave him no doubt of her love.

She gently pushed him back on the bed and ran her fingernails slowly, softly down to his lower belly. She followed with her mouth, kissing and licking his body along the length of his hard chest. His shallow breathing and drumming heartbeat told her of the effect she was having. That excited her greatly as she continued along her purposeful course to the goal both knew she would inevitably attain.

He reached for her, tried to turn her around so he could do for her what he knew she was about to do to him. But she wouldn't. This was for him, a pleasure she wanted to watch consume him. This time, she would share in that way.

His penis ached for release. His desire pleaded to please hurry. He could feel her breath against him; that alone almost made him come. Then her fingernails ran lightly along his scrotum. Oh, God, he thought, don't let the pleasure kill me! Then he felt her mouth, and her tongue. Gently nibbling, kissing, a serendipitous course along the edges of eroticism. But then it took on direct purpose—the hand pumped the shaft in unison with the mouth on the head. His legs stiffened and his back arched. He felt it coming, back in that faraway, unknown place where begins that first tentative trickle that turns into a roaring flood. But she slowed, changing her rhythm, losing the climax's momentum.

Goddamn it, his emotions raged, didn't she know what was happening? She knew. Three times she did that, bringing him to the brink then letting him slide back, each time feeling the frustration in his confused loins intensify until, finally, she relented to his moans and knotted muscles and let it come all the way. As Konrad groaned and clutched at her, and the warm, viscous fluid spurted into her mouth and down her throat, the pleasure sought her out, too; nothing like this, not that kind, but a feeling of closeness, a primordial sense of having been a woman to her man.

He finally gasped and sagged back against the sheets, spent and sweating. She lay her head against his stomach and felt his breathless body slowly settle down into relaxed exhaustion. She turned her face toward his and looked up the length of his limp body. "I really do love you. Now let me hold you while you sleep."

Honi's embrace comforted Konrad like the sun on a spring day, and he gently surrendered to the soft, reassuring rest of a man who knows he is loved.

As he slept, a crack developed in the massive wall of suspicion and guilt he had built in his mind over the years; not a big crack, but enough to let a small hope slide through where it developed into a dream so pleasant that the trace of a smile played on his lips as he slept. . . .

Running hand in hand from danger, Honi and Konrad

escaped together into a small garden. It was surrounded by a high brick wall that separated it from the barren, seared desert inhabited by snakes and scorpions they had just fled across. As they passed through the gate, they collapsed with relief onto the soft, green grass and luxuriated in the spray of a gentle waterfall and tropical breezes rustling through the trees. Konrad turned to Honi and, in that setting, promised this would be their lifelong refuge and they never again would have to face the dangers of the desert. In elation, they danced around trees draped heavily with ripe, shiny fruit. On an impulse, Konrad reached up and plucked a firm, green pear which he showed to Honi in glee, then closed his eyes in blissful anticipation and took a bite.

He gagged at the foul taste and spat out the fruit. Konrad stared at the pear and saw that it had become rotten and filled with maggots. In the center was a fat worm that moved in a strangely hypnotic motion that froze his attention. He looked closer, then shrieked with horror. The face of the worm was that of Willie Mac Russell, laughing at the terror it had caused. The worm spoke in the voice of Willie Mac: "You don't belong here, my man, this be a garden, not a graveyard."

Terrified, Konrad tried to throw the rotten pear away, but it stuck to his hand, and as he frantically tried to get rid of it, the maggots slowly climbed up his arm, eating his body as they crept. . . .

Konrad awoke in panic. After long moments spent blinking away the sweat from his eyes and the nightmare from his brain, he carefully crept out from Honi's sleeping embrace. Standing naked next to her bed, he looked regretfully and longingly at the woman, then slowly gathered up his clothes and silently left the room.

Awakened by the sense of loss that comes with being left unexpectedly alone, Honi lay in bed watching the yellow glow of the kitchen light that spilled under her door and listened to the rustle of maps far into the night. She reached for an additional blanket, but the chill wouldn't leave her.

Chapter Thirteen

A light snow was falling from an overcast sky on the deserted streets of Vaduz completing the permeation of gray which obscured the heavy stone buildings near the government house, a two-story polished granite structure with ornate, rococo iron trim that bespoke the pride of its builders in order, form and durability.

The only relief from the pall of approaching twilight were the Christmas lights in the shop windows, and they were disappearing as the shopkeepers closed early to be home for Christmas Eve.

There was no one around to notice the strange caravan of cars led by a rental truck which moved slowly down the main street and into a parking lot across from the police station. Bulky figures sat stolidly in the fully loaded autos while four men from the lead car moved quickly toward the station and disappeared inside.

Sergeant Bruner was on the telephone trying to explain to his two young children why he couldn't be home on Christmas Eve with them like other fathers, when he heard the main entrance door open and close.

"Goodbye, Kurt," he said. "You be a good boy and go to bed early. I'll see you in the morning. Merry Christmas, son."

Bruner turned to see four men slowly approaching his desk. They were dressed in what appeared to be military fatigues. The man in front kept his hands in the pockets of a bulky green parka. The others carried brown paper grocery bags.

Bruner felt an undefined wariness, but asked pleasantly, "Can I help you gentlemen?"

Konrad said, "Yes, uh, I believe you can," but his eyes were at the back of the large squad room where the radio operator was engrossed in a magazine and two policemen were laughing together with their backs turned. Bruner watched blankly as Konrad's eyes swept all parts of the station and felt the slow creep of irritation. "I can't help you unless you tell me how."

Konrad removed his hand from the parka to reveal a gleaming automatic pistol and pointed it straight at Bruner. "What I need, officer, is your complete cooperation."

Instantly, Otto and the two others reached into their bags and removed automatic rifles which they pointed threateningly at the policemen in back. "Hands up, right now," Otto shouted as they rushed toward the startled officers who hesitantly threw up their arms and stared in wide-eyed shock at their sudden assailants.

The radio operator was slow to react and lurched to his feet in surprise. Not taking any chances, and also wanting to drive home a point, Otto clipped him in the face with his rifle butt. The radio man slumped to the floor, groaning and trying to stem the gush of blood from his broken nose.

The other policemen stared aghast at the crumpled figure. "You bastards," one muttered.

Otto shot back, "Would you rather I'd shot him? That's what'll happen to the next one who doesn't move fast enough."

Konrad came over, prodding the sergeant ahead of him with the pistol muzzle. "OK," he said to two of his men, "lock them in the cells in back." To his captives, he said, "Just do what you're told and you won't get hurt. But get one fucking step out of line and we'll shoot."

As the prisoners were led back to the cells, Konrad told the sergeant to return to his desk where he offered Bruner a cigarette which was accepted with a shaky hand. Konrad gave him a moment to relax and calm his abused nerves. "OK, here's what I want you to do: Call Chief Houser at home and ask him to come down here on the double."

The sergeant stared incredulously, for the moment more afraid of disturbing his superior than of the pistol still pointed at him. "I can't do that. He'd kill me. This is Christmas Eve."

Konrad glanced meaningfully at the pistol. "I don't think your boss is your main worry in that regard." Then his voice hardened. "Look, I'm not here to play games; get on that damned phone and tell him he's needed here right now. When he asks why, say it's too touchy to talk about over the phone. Put some anxiety in your voice." As he said it, Konrad knew that would be no problem for the sergeant.

While one of the intruders rushed over to the abandoned radio and started examining it, Otto and the remaining guard ushered their captives into the cell area. A solitary prisoner watched in bewilderment as the policemen were told to shed their uniforms and fold them into separate piles, then were pushed into the biggest cell where they stood shivering in their underwear, more from a sense of nakedness than from the cold. They watched glumly as their captors sorted through the clothing looking for a proper fit.

Konrad kept his finger on the receiver button, ready to break the connection should the sergeant try to warn the chief. But Bruner did as he was told. The apprehension in his voice was no problem since that was the way Houser's men often addressed him, especially when they disturbed him with after-hours calls. Judging from the growls coming from the phone, the chief responded as expected, but finally said he would come right down.

Konrad moved quickly to the front door, opened it, looked carefully in both directions, then gave a signal to the waiting cars. Eight more men ran toward the station; once inside, Konrad instructed them to search for weapons and stay out of sight.

Returning to Bruner, Konrad asked, "How many men do you have on duty right now?"

Bruner was still shaken, but had recovered from the first shock of capture. He answered defiantly. "Six, in three patrols, plus the men who were in here."

"Why so few?"

"It's Christmas Eve, man. Most self-respecting criminals are at home with their families. All except you."

"Don't waste your breath with insults. I don't give a shit what you think. What I want you to do is get on that radio and call them in, two at a time. And you'd better not let on that anything's wrong."

"What's going to happen to them—and us? Why should I cooperate with you to maybe get these men killed?"

Konrad tried to reassure him. "Look, we'll kill if we have to, but only if you try to get in our way. We won't hurt anyone if we can avoid it, you have my word on that."

Bruner gave a look to show what he thought of Konrad's word, but moved toward the radio.

Two by two, the on-duty policemen sauntered into the station in response to Bruner's "routine" call. As they stepped through the door, Konrad's men seized their weapons and herded them back to the cells where they joined their stripped comrades.

The process of disarming the Liechtenstein police force went smoothly and very quietly until a commotion erupted at the back entrance. Within seconds, an angry middle-age man came bursting into the squad room and stood panting, sharp eyes embedded in a fleshy, red face snapping with rage as he glared around the room. He quickly singled out Konrad as the leader and marched up and put his face directly into the younger man's. The guard who had been mostly amused at the initial outburst, now moved with concern toward the irate man.

Konrad held up his hand. "It's OK. I assume this is Chief Houser; he looks like he wants to say something."

Houser sputtered with indignation. "You're damned right I do. What's the meaning of this? Who in hell do you think you are, coming into *my* station with guns and trying to take it over?"

Konrad let him continue, sensing that his rage would run down with his wind. When the chief was finally gasping for breath, Konrad reached for the telephone and extended it toward the chief. "Before we start discussing details, I suggest you call home."

Houser looked at him blankly, then with alarm. Frantically, he dialed his home number. It was answered by a woman wailing with panic. "Franz, there's a man here with a gun threatening the children and me. Tell him to stop, Franz, tell him to go away."

He tried to comfort her, but in a voice that lacked conviction. "Now calm down, Frieda, it'll be OK, you won't be harmed. I'm going to take care of everything."

"Come home, Franz, come home, please," she pleaded.

Houser knew he was beaten. Sadly, he handed the phone back to Konrad, and said, "What do you want from me?"

Konrad replaced the phone in its cradle. Now that he had the chief in his control, he sought to console him. "Let us take what we want and no one will be hurt, I promise you that."

Houser glared and snapped, "Is the word of a hoodlum supposed to make me feel better?"

Konrad shrugged, then sat the chief at a nearby desk with instructions to call the remaining members of the police force and order them to report immediately in full uniform. Because it was Christmas Eve, some of the men grumbled slightly, but none dared disobey the chief's summons.

As the off-duty officers arrived, they were met just inside the door by armed men who escorted them roughly into the cell block, forced them to strip, then shoved them into cells. Within an hour, the cells were jammed with more than forty grumbling men milling about in their underwear, required to watch their laughing captors putting on the uniforms of Liechtenstein police.

Horst Ullman had reason to be satisfied with himself. At age fifty, life was treating him like a favored son. By

312

hard work and careful manipulation, he had risen to prime minister of Liechtenstein. His friends said he had a gift for politics, his enemies described it as a duplicitous nature skilled at twisting facts out of shape and relationships even further. Ullman thought the truth was somewhere in between, but he accepted all that as the price of successful public life. He saw himself as a man of the world, skilled in the social graces as befitted a head of state. It occurred only to others that the social graces he mastered mainly carried a great many calories, most of which seemed to go straight to his ever-expanding girth.

Thus the prime minister had every reason to be content this Christmas Eve: power, position, pleasant home, doting family, the best foods on the table, and a ringing doorbell that probably meant a visit from admirers.

The visitor, who wore the uniform of a Liechtenstein police officer, was a stranger, which struck Ullman as odd because he was acquainted with every member of the force. He stared expectantly at the man on the landing. "Yes, what is it?" he asked, and then followed with a yell of surprise as the man roughly pushed him back with a strong shoulder and jumped inside, slamming the door behind him.

When Ullman recovered from the shock, he demanded in great indignation, "How dare you. Don't you know who I am?"

Otto ignored the question and pulled out a pistol which he pointed casually at Ullman's chest. "Get your coat, tubby, you're coming with me."

Ullman looked appealingly at his family huddled together in horror in a far corner of the room. Finding no help there, he sucked in his stomach and assumed his

313

most magisterial tone. "I'll have you know I'm the prime minister. As such, I demand—"

Otto cocked his pistol and pointed it at Ullman's brains, so close that the cold, hard barrel could be felt against the sweating temple. "I don't give a shit if you're the pimp of paradise, you're going to do as I say."

Ullman rolled his eyes upward to stare at the ugly, black gun. He hardly breathed and his voice quavered. "I—I'll get my c-coat."

Before Otto left with the prime minister, he went to all three telephones in the house and ripped them out of the wall. Then without a word to the terrified family, he pushed Ullman through the door and into a squad car. Christmas ended early for the prime minister.

Konrad hovered impatiently as Ray Mallen unpacked the radio equipment in the police station. Konrad paced up and down as Mallen lovingly removed, assembled and fondled each piece of the complicated gear. "Are you going to fuck that stuff or put it together? I don't know if it'll even work."

Mallen looked up from his task. "No problem at all. This little sweetheart is powered by one hundred watts with a one-thousand-watt amplifier. It'll reach the moon if you like."

Konrad knew little of radios and his nervousness reflected his concern over anything in the operation he had no direct control over. He looked over Mallen's shoulder. "How do you know they'll be listening?"

The radio expert turned toward Konrad with a smug smile. "Broadcasting a message by radio is not quite like picking up a telephone and starting to talk. You have to

314

know what frequencies are being monitored by which governments and at what times. For example, I know that the Soviet foreign ministry constantly monitors the frequency on 14.296 megaHurtz. I have the complete list of all reserved government frequencies for the major powers which the South African government gave me. Pretty valuable bit of information, don't you think?"

The radio started to hum and the methodical operator listened carefully as he turned knobs to get the exact adjustment he wanted. After what seemed an interminable time, he turned to Konrad with a self-satisfied smile, and said, "Anytime you're ready, boss."

Konrad motioned for Angus who had been standing in silent, wide-eyed awe of what had been happening in the police station. As he came over, Konrad handed him a sheath of typewritten papers. "Here's your script. Get on that radio and read, baby. And so help me, don't you add or delete one single word."

Angus rehearsed the script twice then sat down before the radio, adjusted his chair, cleared his throat and waited for Mallen to give him the go-ahead.

"This is radio liberated Liechtenstein informing the world that a new era has emerged in this nation. The people's revolutionary soldiers have freed us from the yoke of the capitalist-monarchist oppressors. Freedom-loving comrades have been victorious in the bloodless liberation of our people. We declare our country to be the People's Socialist Republic of Liechtenstein and renounce all former alliances and treaties made against the people's will and interests by the former despotic rulers of this land.

"We appeal for the recognition, support and protection of our socialist brothers and comrades of the

315

German Democratic Republic and the Union of Soviet Socialist Republics. We fear that the capitalist oppressors of Switzerland and the United States may attempt to overthrow the people's will and reimpose by force of arms their brutal tyranny.

"We warn those who would enslave the Liechtenstein nation that we will resist with all our power their attempts to overthrow the new, lawful government of our nation.

"We are hereby cancelling all treaties with Switzerland. From this day forward, Liechtenstein will not rely on duplicitous, greedy capitalists to conduct our foreign affairs. I repeat, we are dissolving our relationship with Switzerland. Their border guards are no longer welcome on our soil.

"In very short order, all citizens of other nations will be free to leave Liechtenstein unharmed. I give total reassurance that absolutely no harm will come to citizens of other countries. Therefore, the Swiss cannot claim the protection of their citizens if they invade our country. If they do so, it will be recognized for what it is: brutal, naked imperialist aggression.

"Again, we appeal for the succor and support of our socialist brothers. Protect us from the forces that lie in wait to smother the will of the working classes. Help us."

Angus repeated the message several times on frequencies given him by Mallen. Finally, he turned off the radio and leaned back in his chair to ponder the strange, frightening situation his friendship with Konrad had gotten him into.

* * *

The Swiss border guard watched the men climb out of the police patrol car and head toward his small guardhouse. It was an unexpected visit, but anything was welcome to break up the monotony of his shift. It was his duty to guard the Liechtenstein border with Austria as part of the Swiss customs contingent assigned to Liechtenstein. They were there as a result of a unique treaty between the two countries which gave Switzerland responsibility for the customs and foreign affairs of Liechtenstein, thus reason for protecting its borders. It was a lonely, boring job because no one ever tried to sneak anything in or out of Liechtenstein.

As the group from the patrol car approached, the guard recognized the man in civilian clothes from newspaper photos as Horst Ullman, the prime minister. He appeared to be sick or very troubled. The three policemen with him were strangers and, oddly, carried automatic rifles.

The guard gave a friendly salute. "Good evening. What are you gentlemen doing out on Christmas Eve?"

The prime minister ignored the greeting and strode directly up to the guard, the policemen close behind. "I must ask you to pack up and go back to Switzerland. Right now," Ullman said.

The guard stared open-mouthed. He didn't comprehend what was being said. "My relief isn't here yet."

The prime minister raised his voice, not in anger, but in agitation. "Look, this is Liechtenstein, not Switzerland. Clear out. Get across that damned border."

"I'm sorry, sir. I can't do that without an order from my superior."

The policemen moved off to the side threateningly. The prime minister lowered his voice, but the agitation

317

remained. "Our country has had a change of government. The old treaty with Switzerland is no longer in effect. You are no longer wanted here. You won't get in any trouble with your superiors. Now go."

Confused, the guard hesitantly gathered up his gear and mounted his motorcycle to return to Swiss territory. He took one backward glance and saw the policemen erecting a barricade across the road with a stop sign placed in front of it. He twisted the throttle and the motorcycle roared away.

At every crossing into Austria, the scene was repeated as bewildered Swiss customs guards were asked politely, but firmly, by either the prime minister or the chief of police to leave the country. In each instance, their presence was promptly replaced by barricades and uniformed policemen carrying automatic rifles. The bridges across the Rhine into Switzerland, customarily unguarded, also bristled with guards and barricades. Liechtenstein had suddenly become very inhospitable.

Pierre Dumas was angered when the maid told him the telephone call was from his office. It not only interrupted his Christmas Eve cocktail party, it made him look bad in front of his guests. A deputy minister of foreign intelligence should not be bothered by office affairs at such an awkward time, it gave the impression his assistants weren't competent or didn't have the proper respect. It just wasn't good form. "Yes, what is it?" he growled.

"Andre Wittenburg, sir."

"Yes, I know you're there, but what in blazes do you want?"

"Sorry to disturb you, sir, but we received a strange radio message on one of the reserved frequencies that's very confusing. Thought I'd better give you a call."

Wittenburg irritated Dumas with his unflappable manner. A junior member of the staff should be more flustered when talking to an angry senior. It was almost impertinent to be so calm. "Get on with it, man, what did the message say?"

"It said there's been a revolution in Liechtenstein—a socialist one—and the new government is ending the treaty with us. Also, it seems they're kicking our customs guards out of their country."

Dumas was shocked. "What? They can't do that."

"Afraid they've already done it, sir. It happened right after we received the radio communication. Not only that, but they've erected border barricades manned by armed guards."

"Now listen, Wittenburg, I want you—"

"Pierre!" His wife was at the door with a look on her face that superseded any affairs of state. "You have guests, very important guests, in case you've forgotten. Your absence is embarrassing and rude. Get back to your party. Sneaking away to conduct business like this, one would think you're nothing but an insignificant bureaucrat."

Dumas cupped his hand over the phone. "Yes, dear." He cleared his throat and returned to the conversation. "Now, look, Wittenburg. It's Christmas Eve, so there's not much we can do now, is there? I want you to continue monitoring the situation and give me a briefing in the morning."

Wittenburg responded in an irritatingly calm voice. "May I suggest, sir, that we should act on this

319

immediately. It could be serious."

The anger poured out of Dumas. It was mixed with some subconscious guilt, but what the hell, he had to live with the woman. "Now look, fellow, don't forget you're junior, *very* junior. I suggest you start acting the part and do what I say without impertinent questions. Goodnight."

"There's more, sir."

"Tomorrow. Goodnight!"

Yuri Terishnikov fidgeted with excitement as the powerful, chauffeured car roared out of the guarded underground garage of the austere, half-moon-shaped KGB foreign directorate building on Moscow's outlying Ring Road. As it entered the sparse traffic, he nagged the driver to push the car faster along the snow-packed streets. The big ZIL 114 responded with a roar and gravity pushed his head back against the luxurious cushions of the limousine. Releasing himself to the sensation, Terishnikov realized again how lucky he was to be conveying the valuable data he possessed in this style instead of on the circuitous subways of Moscow. He fondly caressed the brown attache case cradled in his lap because he knew it could be the ticket to what ambitious public servants dream about: the chance to help shape affairs of state, to be a respected voice speaking for the welfare of his country, not to mention the good fortune that would come to the possessor of such a voice.

Terishnikov rehearsed in his mind the presentation he would make to his superior, Serghi Yonolokev, a man whose power was represented by this car which he had sent for Yuri. As Yonolokev's protege, Terishnikov had learned how his tutor's mind worked, the sort of things that would spark interest. Like a good subordinate, he knew how to stimulate his superior. This skill worked to the advantage of both: Terishnikov had a patron, and Yonolokev had a bright follower who would tell him what he thought, and, equally important, what others who would never have the nerve to do so were thinking, too.

Terishnikov was well aware of his good fortune in having access to such an important man as Yonolokev, European section chief in the KGB foreign intelligence unit. A less connected person would have to fight through endless barricades erected by jealous bureaucrats whose time-consuming resistance would erode the importance of the information he carried. One of the most shocking realizations Terishnikov had made upon entering KGB service was how vital government decisions could be delayed and sidetracked by minor officialdom. And that was in an outfit stripped for decisive action like the KGB; how much worse was it in regular government service? Sometimes he wondered if the KGB wasn't almost as bumbling as the CIA, the boners of which provided most of the jokes at parties of the KGB staff.

The fact that Terishnikov was approaching the private residence of so important a figure as Yonolokev was due to the happy circumstance that Yonolokev and Terishnikov's father had served together during the Korean War when both had been advisors to the Chinese army. They were such good friends that when Yuri's father had been mortally wounded during a surprise American attack, Yonolokev had vowed to the dying man that his infant son would never lack for someone to look after him. And true to his word, as Yonolokev rose through the ranks of the KGB and the Communist Party, he never forgot his promise. Although the term godfather was out of style in the Societ Union, that was the role Yonolokev had played in the upbringing, education and good connections of young Yuri.

The car braked in front of a stylish apartment house in a section of Moscow favored by high party and military officials. As the driver waited deferentially, Yuri tried to brush the wrinkles out of his suit. It had been bought in one of the better shops in the city, but was still baggy and of poor material. He wished he were wearing his three-piece English wool suit, but the old-timers of the KGB considered it disloyal to wear foreign clothes on duty. "How can we send men into space but not make a decent suit?" he grumbled. Yonolokev may have been his patron, but he was still a section chief and therefore one did not go lightly into his presence.

Yonolokev met him in work clothes covered with sawdust which he was brushing onto his wife's freshly cleaned carpet, an expensive Oriental. Yuri smiled as he thought how those who feared the name KGB and especially the scowling, inscrutable Yonolokev, would react to see this pleasant-looking, almost old man absently soiling his wife's clean carpet for which he would undoubtedly catch hell later.

"Good afternoon, Yuri. You caught me in my workshop. I sometimes like to take my frustrations out on a few boards. Maybe I should become a carpenter. I'd gladly trade a few sore fingers to be able to sleep better at night." Then, as though reminding himself to curb such loose talk, even in front of Yuri, he asked, "Tell me, what is this strange radio transmission that has you acting like a horny dog?"

"How much do you know about Liechtenstein, sir?" Except on public occasions, Yuri ignored the official "comrade" in favor of the more respectful form of address.

"About as much as I need to know." He held two fingers inches apart in front of Yuri. "But come now, don't play games. What do you have?"

Terishnikov unzipped the attache case, growing even more excited with the possibilities of the material within, now that he was about to show it. He handed two typed sheets to Yonolokev and waited impatiently while they were read.

Yonolokev put the papers aside and looked expectantly at Yuri. Although he had instantly formed his own opinion, he wanted first to hear the subordinate's viewpoint before it was colored by the influence of his own. "What do you make of this?"

"Well, sir, it's really quite simple."

"Nothing's simple, except to simpletons," Yonolokev interrupted professorially.

Yuri coughed uncomfortably, but his enthusiasm drove him back to the subject. "Yes, well, just a figure of speech, sir. Getting right to the point, this is an opportunity for us to get the stronghold in Western Europe we've always needed. I think we should recognize this new government in Liechtenstein quickly, before the West has a chance to throw them out of power."

Yonolokev was now the exacting schoolmaster, challenging every conclusion, every argument of his pupil. "How do we know they're not a bunch of crackpots?"

Yuri knew Yonolokev's methods and had tried to prepare his responses accordingly. "Crackpots have their uses, too. All the easier to control them."

"What if the Western powers don't want us in their European back yard?"

"The past has shown that the side that makes the first move is usually left holding that position when the diplomatic mumbo-jumbo takes over."

"What about the Swiss? Won't they be expected to protect their own back yard?"

Yuri gained increased confidence with every response. His was the sharp wit of the excellent student fresh enough from the snobbish, but demanding, Institute of International Relations, and he had not lost his zeal for the exhilaration of debate. "The Swiss are interested in one thing—making money. And Liechtenstein is too tiny to represent very much of that. They're cold-blooded bastards who've kept their skins intact through two world wars by being careful not to piss off either side, while making money off both. They're not about to jeopardize their precious, profitable neutrality over a little asshole of a country."

"Yuri, swearing is an ill-mannered American habit; try to remember that. Now, back to the subject, would you risk world war over this?"

"No, and neither would anybody else. That's why the country that acts fast and first is going to end up with this little gem."

Yonolokev gazed steadily at him. "Who else heard the transmission?"

Terishnikov knew what he was referring to: the GRU, the intelligence arm of the Red Army and the KGB's arch competitor in the continual wrestling for power that took place in the heights of the Communist Party ranks. "The GRU hasn't communicated anything regarding this that

I'mi aware of. Normally, we keep in pretty close touch with what they're working on. It's probably fair to assume they keep equally close tabs on us, too. That's why I said nothing to anyone about this."

Terishnikov's euphemisms weren't lost on Yonolokev, he was talking about interagency spying, a practice so widespread among Soviet government agencies it was almost spoken of openly. He frowned and paced up and down for a few moments with his hands clasped behind his back. He had learned through the years that sometimes the most sure-thing situations hide the greatest dangers. Khrushchev had learned that sad fact over the Cuban missiles. Caution is always called for, but sometimes being timid in the face of opportunity is even more treacherous when that opportunity is lost and a scapegoat is sought. Yonolokev's instinct for survival, honed to sharpness through the Stalin purges and lifelong party infighting, had always served him well. Assess . . . analyze . . . look twice, ten times . . . then, if it's right—act!

His mind made up, Yonolokev strode briskly over to Terishnikov. "Yuri, you're right. I'm going to push for quick action; that's the only way we can gain the initiative. I want you to gather all the information you have, including lots of data on Liechtenstein, its history, industry, population, everything. We have to remember, the Old Bear isn't exactly a schol—"

Yuri gasped. "The Old Bear?" He repeated the nickname almost reverently. "You mean you're going to the chairman himself?"

"No, lad, *we're* going to the chairman. What'd you think I'd do with something like this, write a letter to the editor of *Pravda*?" Yonolokev laughed suddenly. "Think of the look on the face of that fat fool, General Malinchuk of the GRU, when he has to sit there and listen to the pretty tune we'll be singing." He clapped Terishnikov on the back. "You understand that normally this takes about three months to push through channels—meetings like the one I have in mind aren't easy to arrange—but this calls for speed." He gazed at Yuri affectionately. "We make quite a team, don't we? The old-dog spy with the contacts and the eager young puppy who's found a very valuable bone. I wish your father could be here to see this."

Terishnikov sat deeply in the plush armchair and looked at his reflection in the polished mahogany table. He gazed out the window at the snow-capped head and shoulders of Felix Dzerzhinsky, the first chief of the secret police whose solemn statue fronted the ornate, mustard-colored KGB headquarters near the Kremlin where they were meeting. He reviewed his surroundings again and marveled at how quickly governments can push aside red tape and move into action when powerful, purposeful men push the right buttons.

The silence was slightly broken as the chairman muttered something to an elderly man seated at his right while each of the remaining eight men in the room finished reading the transcript of the radio communiqué and the briefing material hastily finished by Yuri only two hours earlier.

Yuri studied the men around the table. Except for Yonolokev, he knew them only from their television images; gaunt, gray men who were boys when the revolution was born and who had grown old with it.

As the chairman nodded to each in turn, the men proceeded to give their analyses of the situation as they saw it according to their specialties. A couple were experts only in the fine art of political survival, but that in itself represented a valuable expertise, the wiliness of men who live and prosper by mastering the pursuit of self-interest and who develop a sixth sense against the threat of danger.

Yuri was dismayed by some of the asinine objections he heard against going ahead with a quick recognition of the People's Republic of Liechtenstein. God, he thought, couldn't someone come up with a more original name? He wished he could have included his own opinions in the briefing, but Yonolokev had wisely said that when the chairman and his council needed a junior official's opinion, they would certainly make a request for it.

His heart sank as the nos mounted around the table. The Red Army, surprisingly, urged caution in fear of upsetting arms limitation talks then underway and which appeared to be going the way they wanted.

General Malinchuk of the GRU, bearing the expression of a sore loser, wanted to delay until he could move agents based in East Germany into Liechtenstein for a first-hand look. Yuri wanted to shout that that would be exactly what other countries would be doing, and in a few days there would be so many agents in Liechtenstein, they would have to share hotel rooms.

The agriculture minister worried that the grain trade with the United States might be disrupted. The foreign minister argued that valuable trade concessions recently gained from the European Common Market could be lost.

Yuri's fears, although unknown to him, were unfounded. The chairman was politely listening to members

327

of his council, because that is what a council is for, but his own mind had been made up at the end of an earlier secret briefing by Yonolokev. The council meeting was a formality, a tipping of the hat to the ponderous structure of government. Most of those around the table knew that, but as long as they kept their seats and their *dachas* on the Black Sea, they didn't care too much.

The chairman cleared his throat and peered over his glasses. Silence enveloped the room. He looked at Terishnikov. "First, let me thank this young comrade for his diligence in promptly reporting this development." Then he turned from Yuri as though he no longer existed.

"Comrades," the chairman addressed the entire room. "Thank you for your thoughtful opinions. Now, let me give mine." He paused to let that sink in, to make certain everyone knew that what they were about to hear was not just another opinion. He slipped on thick bifocals and leaned forward to his notes. "I believe it is our solemn duty to the memory of Comrade Lenin and all the other fighters for revolution who have gone before us, to reach out and clasp hands with these valiant revolutionaries who have begged for our strong grip."

Yuri was astonished. Why the bullshit? He didn't realize that the chairman wasn't talking to the men in the room, he was talking to a recording machine, he was talking to history, and he was talking to those who might come to the tapes looking for someone to blame if it all went wrong.

The chairman droned on with the rhetoric of revolution for a while, then finally said, "As your chairman, I rcommend we proceed with an immediate and forceful recognition of the new government in

Liechtenstein. However, we must be aware of the dangers of the situation and be prepared to modify our position depending on the responses of other interested nations. In short, comrades, we want to take advantage of this chance to establish a beachhead, if we may call it that, in Western Europe, but we also want to keep the risk manageable. Let's keep one eye on opportunity and the other on the trigger-happy hawks, as they call themselves, currently in control of the United States government. Let's not commit ourselves so far that we can't strategically retreat if such a course proves to be the wisest."

The chairman surveyed the table carefully. "Does anyone object to this proposal or care to offer a differing one?" After deciding the stony silence wasn't going to change, he smiled slightly and said, "Good. I'm going to appoint Comrade Yonolokev to implement this program, with daily updates to every member of this committee. Thank you, comrades."

As they walked out together, Yonolokev whispered to Terishnikov, "Well, it went exactly the way you recommended, but if my experience means anything, that may be the easiest part of the whole thing. It's easier to release a bear from a cage than to return him to it—even an old one."

329

Chapter Fourteen

The lesbian Lisel Hendrick went first, pushing the heavy oak doors inward with the butt of her M-16. Honi followed, past the familiar vestibule with its bulletin board of announcements that reflected the simple life of those who worshipped here. Honi knew the announcements; they had once touched her own life and helped set the clock by which it functioned. She had even been here as the singing families were here now, joining in the carols and old hymns at early Christmas Eve vespers.

Honi closed her eyes and listened to the hymn that was being sung in the chapel just behind the doors in front of her. At a different time she might have hummed along.

She was painfully jabbed back to reality by Hendrick who flicked the rifle butt lightly at her arm. "Hey, look alive, goddamnit. Cut out the dreaming." She looked at her watch. "Ten minutes to eight. You ready?"

Honi nodded reluctantly.

Hendrick stood back and swung the bottom of her boot at the twin polished doors. They parted with a crash and the organ music suspended in mid-verse as though to protest the loud interruption.

As the two women in their rugged fatigues and menacing automatic rifles stood in back of the sanctuary, one hundred pairs of eyes swung around. For long seconds it was a standoff; intruders stared at worshippers, worshippers stared at intruders. Finally, Father Hammerschmidt stood and, seemingly swollen with the power his vestments implied, demanded of the pair who were only vaguely visible to him in the shadows, "Who is that? Why have you interrupted the service? If you care to join us, please do so, but more quietly please."

Hendrick sauntered down the aisle, appearing, as she intended, very manlike. She stood directly in front of the altar, slowly raised her M-16 and flicked it to full automatic. The staccato crash of the rifle reverberated through the auditorium, underscored by the screams of startled children. The shots sounded even louder because of the silence they interrupted and the fine acoustics of the room which was built to amplify more harmonious sounds.

Hendrick stood grinning and gestured toward the ripped-apart stained-glass image of the Virgin. "Pretty good shooting, eh?" she asked no one in particular.

"Sacrilege," a shocked Father Hammerschmidt protested hoarsely in the silence.

"Shit," Hendrick spat back. "Tell you what you'd better do, priest, you'd better start praying none of your flock here disobeys my orders or that'll be them." She gestured toward the gaping hole in the window that had been the head of the destroyed figure.

At that moment, Hammerschmidt noticed Honi. He stared at the rifle she carried and his eyes widened, then seemed to close in a deep, profound sorrow that was known only to the two of them. Then he turned back to Hendrick and asked, "What do you want?"

Hendrick moved to the platform, faced the congregation and pushed the priest down among them. "Now listen," she shouted. "No one here is going to get hurt if you obey orders. Just stay right where you are, keep quiet, and get comfortable. You're going to be here a couple of nights."

An immediate chorus of wails and protests rose from the huddled group. Riding the crest of a loud, general moan were cries about the welfare of infants, of meals needing preparation, and a variety of other problems that suddenly seemed very pressing.

Hendrick pointed the rifle at the ceiling and squeezed off a single shot. It was evident she enjoyed using the gun. "Shut the fuck up, for chrissakes. Be glad you're going to stay alive—maybe," she threatened. She turned to Honi and gestured with her head to the back of the room. "You get back there and watch 'em."

All eyes followed Honi, many of them recognized her and their whispers followed her as she walked slowly to her station. She felt no shame, only a foggy sense of unreality. The rifle she carried felt like a dead, useless arm.

Father Hammerschmidt stood among the parishioners without his vestments. Hendrick looked at him and chuckled. "Where'd your holy clothes go, priest?"

"I won't allow the symbols of God to be profaned in the face of your blasphemy." His voice softened. "*Fräulein*, I don't know what you want, but please tell us. If we're captives, we at least have a right to know why."

Hendrick couldn't resist a little gloating despite Konrad's warning not to reveal their purpose. "This is a pretty rich little country, and as your fat sorcerer there can tell you—" she pointed at the priest and laughed— "it ain't Christian to hoard riches. We're going to do something good for your souls. Now that's all you're going to be told, so shut up."

Hammerschmidt persisted. "Sister, don't you know that what you're doing is an abomination in the eyes of God, especially on this night?"

Hendrick glared at him. "Fuck your God."

The congregation gasped in unison. She turned on them, raising her voice shrilly. "That's right, fuck Him. If He doesn't like it, let Him do something about it." She looked upward and gave the finger to the ceiling. "You simple, weak peasants might be taken in by all this superstitious crap, but not me. I don't like priests, and they don't like me; said I was unnatural . . . unnatural and impure. Well, there's nothing unnatural or impure about this baby—" she patted the rifle—"and it just about makes me god around here. And your new god says for everyone to shut up and stay shut up."

Christmas Eve descended on the peaceful villages and countryside of Liechtenstein like a soft lullaby. The empty streets seemed to provide barriers of tranquility between the brightly lit houses where families gathered in happy circles before roaring fireplaces to greet the most traditional observance of their old culture.

While Liechtensteiners laughed, ate, worshipped, and, in a few discreet cases, made love, others were moving among them, others who would turn this holiest of times into a period of terror.

Silently, a fleet of squad cars snaked out of the police

station parking lot and fanned onto the roads connecting Vaduz to the rest of the principality. The dark procession headed toward Schaan, Ruggell, Eschen, Malbun, Triesenberg, Balzars and the other hamlets spread through the little land: innocent prey vulnerable to the stealthy approach of the predator.

Each of the cars held two of Konrad's men armed with M-16s and dressed in the confiscated uniforms of Liechtenstein police. Each was equipped with a loudspeaker which at a given time would boom out recorded tapes designed to both frighten and reassure the bewildered populace.

One car glided quietly to a stop in front of the castle standing on a hill high above Vaduz. When the guard standing in front sauntered over, he was greeted by a black muzzle protruding from the car window. Shocked, the guard raised his hands. What was happening was beyond his comprehension, even though his job was to guard against any possible threat to the prince and his family. But he had long ago accepted the tranqility of the principality as the natural and perpetual order of things, and had come to think of himself as more of a night watchman, lazily making his rounds, and as a sort of uniformed ornamentation.

"How dare you," he stammered, as much from confusion as fright. "Don't you know this is the royal residence?"

"Well, I'll be a son of a bitch, we didn't know that," the man holding the rifle drawled. The man quickly disarmed the guard, shoved him into the back seat, and as the car drove away, a new guard, armed with an automatic rifle, took his position in front of the castle.

The cars were given fifteen minutes to reach their

positions, then, in a coordinated movement at precisely eight p.m., both power stations were shut down and the telephone system knocked out. In an instant, those happy, glowing homes were plunged into ominous darkness. Out of force of habit, residents tried to phone the utilities authority only to discover the phone lines dead. They were caught by twin tentacles of fear— darkness and isolation.

Shortly after the lights and telephones went out, the confused citizens held fingers to lips so they could hear the booming voice coming from the street. It sounded familiar . . . wait a minute . . . it was! The crown prince was speaking. As the cars with loudspeakers slowly wound their way through village streets, people would rush to doors and windows to listen for the message. People suddenly sealed off from others instantly become psychologically dependent on any information, any contact available to them. So when the soothing voice of the crown prince was heard, the tendency was to relax, at least temporarily, to grab any relief and reassurance available following the frightening onset of darkness.

The recording of the crown prince's voice was the finest imitation Angus had ever done. The accent was perfect, down to the minor mispronunciations he had picked up from Honi's tape. He even made his voice sound years older, the slightly gravelly voice of a man in later middle-age.

Standing outside the police station, he marveled at his own work of art as a sound truck slowly moved by, repeating the message over and over:

"Fellow citizens of Liechtenstein, this is your prince speaking: let me beg your cooperation and patience. You have nothing to fear if you simply do as you are told. Stay

335

inside your homes. I repeat, stay inside your homes. We are in the midst of a national emergency, but out of which will rise a better Liechtenstein. You will be safe if you obey the police and stay inside your homes. Your power and telephones will be restored very soon, provided you cooperate. Everything will be fine if you will obey me and the police. I repeat, stay indoors. Let me also wish you a merry Christmas."

Toni Tenelli was in the driver's seat and her partner didn't like it. He was a nondescript, short, dull man named Kunst who had spent most of his youth in prison being an equally uninspired burglar. Getting caught, it seemed, was the only dependable thing about the man. Although Konrad stated clearly that Tenelli was in charge of their patrol, it still bothered Kunst who suffered in pained silence at being subordinate to a woman.

Tenelli's combination of amusement and contempt wasn't content to let it rest at that. "Hey, Kunst," she asked, "what's it like to take orders from a woman? What are all the girls at the ski resort going to think when they see you huddled in the passenger seat like a little boy being driven to school?" She laughed merrily. "I guess Konrad knows the better *man*, eh? Maybe if you were a little taller, Kunst . . ."

He felt like slapping some respect into the bitch, but he'd seen the carved up body of the would-be rapist Brandhorst back at the training lodge, and decided in favor of prudence. He wasn't too clever, but he tried. "I'll bet you fucked Konrad so he'd put you in charge. That's the only way he'd do it."

336

Tenelli winked at him. "I offered to, but he said you'd just given him a blow-job, so he wasn't in the mood."

Enraged, he pulled back his hand to strike her, but in an instant he was staring at the same wicked knife that had done the job on Brandhorst. Not knowing what else to do with his upraised hand, he used it to smooth his hair. Tenelli decided to end the games before even this halfwit became really dangerous. She knew their destination was only five minutes away, and Kunst would need all of that to reassemble the pieces of his shattered masculine ego.

They drove in silence up the twisting, narrow road with the hood emblem of the car pointed consistently at the peaks of the Alps. They soon came to a large, filled parking lot beyond which was a brightly lit A-frame building. As they drove cautiously up to the lodge, Toni could see that the Christmas Eve partying was in full swing. These were not the quiet-evening-at-home or Midnight Mass celebrants, but the beautiful people and expense-account playboys who had chosen to observe the season at Liechtenstein's famed Malbun ski resort. Judging from the cars, Toni guessed there were about one hundred of them, mostly foreigners.

After parking the car, Toni slipped unnoticed through the front door with Kunst right behind her, their M-16s held low along their legs. She elbowed her way through the milling, dancing, drinking revelers and walked a half-dozen steps up a landing so she and Kunst were higher than anyone else in the large room. She knew she couldn't gain attention by shouting, the band would easily overwhelm any sound she could muster. Instead, she pointed the M-16 at several chandeliers hanging above the dance floor and sprayed bullets into them.

The crashing noise of the M-16 and the falling shattered glass transformed the room into screams and indignant protests. The music abruptly stopped and all eyes swung to the pretty woman menacingly pointing the ugly black mouth of an automatic rifle directly into their midst.

After allowing a few moments of silence to let the shock pass, Toni shouted in a tense voice, "OK, I want everyone to sit down on the floor, back to back. Do it now!"

There was a rustle of slow compliance. A man in a whining, nasal voice complained, "I'm a French citizen; you can't do this to me."

"I don't care if you're Charles De Gaulle, sit down!"

A woman protested, "But there's glass on the floor."

Toni raised the muzzle and shot out another chandelier and the people ducked reflexively with arms held over heads in self-protection.

"Sit, goddamnit, glass slivers are better than bullet holes."

No one else complained as everyone hurried to find a glass-free seat.

No sooner had the people in the lodge settled down in positions that gave them meager degrees of comfort on the cold, hard, glass-strewn floor, than a steady series of single rifle shots gave rise to panic-edged murmuring among them.

Tenelli spoke loudly above the buzz. "Don't worry, nobody's shooting at you. The only victims of those shots are the front tires of every car in the parking lot. My partner never misses a tire from two feet."

An anonymous, angry voice rose from the back of the room. "You have no right. How'll we get them repaired?"

338

"No right? You want to see my *right* again?" She brandished the rifle. "At least this way, we won't have to shoot some idiot who thinks he can escape. Would you rather lose your lives or your tires? We've already destroyed the tires, and we'll accommodate you on the other if you like. Think of it this way: Some tire-repair man is going to come up here after we've gone and have himself a very nice Christmas."

An elderly voice called out, "How long are you going to keep us here?"

"Until I say you can leave," she snapped. "Don't worry, I couldn't stand it very long. Behave yourselves and you'll survive."

At that instant the remaining chandeliers blinked off and the room was enveloped in solid blackness. Again, the screams and excited babbling caused Tenelli to raise her voice. "It's only the goddamned lights. Just stay put and you'll be OK. We won't let the bogeyman get you."

The room soon settled down to the makeshift business of trying to find some comfort. It was gradually becoming colder with the power shut off, so lodge clerks were accompanied by Kunst to get piles of blankets and pillows. Toni allowed the liquor bottles to be passed freely among the captives. She knew there was a slight chance of a brandy-fortified fool making trouble that a sober man wouldn't dare, but she decided it was better to chance facing one ill-coordinated drunk than perhaps a coolly designed plot hatched in the darkness by desperate, sober people. She knew that for every hero created by liquor, it created a lot more drunk, sleepy ones.

The only movement was the periodic escorting of small groups to the toilets as the liquor had its inevitable consequences. Tenelli escorted the men and Kunst the women. She figured there would be less inclination to tarry with the leering Kunst standing in the women's toilet doorway, or with her pointing a powerful flashlight in an indelicate direction. To one dignified old man seemingly bent on an interminable dripping conclusion, she said, "Come on, old timer, shake off that little devil and get back out there." His response was a loud harrumph followed by a quick zipping noise and a hasty retreat.

Toni and Kunst maintained a careful vigil on their captives with flashlights constantly scouring the room until she called him over and told him to get a few hours' sleep while she stood guard. Soon, it was only her light that probed the slumbering room.

As Tenelli scanned the sleeping prisoners, her light suddenly interrupted its methodical swing to freeze on a man who was slowly getting to his feet, arms raised high above his head.

"Get down," she whispered fiercely, as though not to awaken the others.

"Please," he whispered in reply, "may I come forward? I want to talk."

She hesitated. What if it were a trap? But she was also curious. She tightened her grip on the M-16 and pointed it directly at the man with her free hand. "All right, but be slow; keep your arms up and stay in the light."

The man walked carefully into the full beam of her light and stopped about three feet short of the menacing gun barrel.

"Now, what do you want?" she demanded.

He smiled. "Hello, Toni. Is it still Toni? I hope so, that was such a pretty name."

340

She studied the man carefully. He was a typical member of the disgusting bourgeoise class that strutted their affluence and infuriating arrogance at such places as this. Her flashlight quickly panned the soft Gucci loafers, the skin-tight pants and silk shirt open almost to the navel with gold chains softly tinkling against the mat of chest hair. She shined the light directly into the face framed by a long razor-cut and a tiny, manicured mustache. "OK, what do you want, and how do you know my name, pimp?"

"Toni, it's me, Lorenzo."

Startled, she looked again. This time she mentally superimposed a beard on the face and long, brown hair tied in a ponytail. Her imagination put rough workman's clothes on his body, and slowly the stranger in front of her dissolved into Lorenzo Belotto, fierce socialist revolutionary, member of the Red Brigade, comrade in arms, and not least in her memory, tender lover and soulmate in countless whispering sessions of idealistic dreams and mutual resolve to right social injustices.

"Lorenzo," she breathed in wide-eyed surprise. "What are you doing here? Like this?" She played the flashlight over his *nouveau riche* clothes. "I thought you were captured in the police raid on the Milano safe house?"

"I was. Captured and sentenced to life."

"But, but," she hesitated as though trying to comprehend how a man could be given a life sentence three years ago and yet be standing here resplendent in expensive clothing. Then she figured it out, the only way it could be possible. "Bastard," she spat at him. "You turned informer. You sold out the movement."

He sighed. "I did what I had to do. But I only

341

confirmed to them what they already knew about comrades already in prison. I didn't help them take anyone else. Spending one's youth in a cold, stone cell isn't very romantic when one is locked inside it." He took a small step forward, but stopped when she tensed. "But let's not point fingers at one another, pretty one. Joining the *banditti* as you seem to have done, is not exactly being a handmaiden in the house of Marx."

She listened until he finished, then hissed, "What I do, I do to raise money so the cause can go forward. Your smart mouth doesn't work on me anymore. Look at you in that faggot clothing. It makes me sick to think I once looked up to you, thought you were committed to our cause."

"What cause, Toni? What cause was it that told us to kidnap frightened accountants? To shoot fat, stupid policemen in the kneecap? To rob working men of their savings so we could buy the guns to 'liberate' them? No, I didn't lose my ideals, I just grew up. If I'm going to be a thief, I'd just as soon have a multinational corporation give me a paycheck for it instead of posting a reward on my head."

Toni's head was swimming; she remembered the sweet caresses from this handsome, tender man, but he wasn't the same man. He was just another lie from the past. She ached for her world to stand still so she could understand it.

Toni made a quick motion with the gun barrel and tried to make her voice sound fierce. "Get back there with your faggot friends." She watched him turn and go, but the memories remained.

*   *   *

342

When the lights in the church abruptly went out, Hendrick and Honi were ready, instantly flicking on strong flashlights that created bright paths of light. But it was of no consolation to the many small children huddled in the hard pews next to worried parents. One child started a muffled but persistent whimpering that proved contagious among the others. Soon, most of the children were wailing and sobbing beyond the ability of anyone to quiet them.

Hendrick ran up to one woman who was frantically imploring her small son to be quiet and poked her rifle butt in the direction of the mother. "Shut that fucking kid up," she screamed.

Out of fatigue and frustration, the mother shouted back, "I can't, they're hungry. When children are hungry and frightened, they cry, and that gun you keep pointing at us won't make them stop." The mother broke down in sobs while Hendrick stared at her blankly.

Trying to head off a confrontation, Father Hammerschmidt moved hastily to the scene. "There's a grocery just two doors away. Why don't we send someone to break in for food? Given the circumstances, I'm sure the owner will forgive us."

Hendrick thought for a moment. "Like hell, no one leaves here. Those are my orders."

The priest persisted. "Do your orders require small children to cry all night out of hunger? Why don't you or—" he paused and looked in the direction of Honi's flashlight—"your partner take some of the larger children and bring food so these kids can eat and go to sleep?"

Hendrick thought for a moment, listened to the irritating, shrill cries of the children and then decided

343

that a slight deviation from orders was better than tolerating such nerve-wracking noise all night. She walked over to Honi and said in a stage whisper intended for all ears, "We'll be right back. Shoot anyone who even breathes wrong." Hendrick then ordered six of the largest children to follow her.

Honi had never felt so alone as in this crowded church. She shined her light along the rows of families waiting in terror for whatever their captors decided to do with them next. Honi was one of those captors and she now felt the guilt for what she was doing like a heavy stone on her chest. Why, oh, why did her life go from sorrow to misery to terror? she lamented. She didn't want this, but here she was. How could she be such a fool as to believe that one could justify this in the name of love?

Honi heard soft steps approaching to her left and moved the light in that direction with the awkward gun following in the swing of her arm. Two men stood directly in front of her staring grimly into the bright light. The lead man was Hans, the same man who begged for her love just one day before, but this time his lips were set tight in a white line slashed across his face and his eyes blazed in her direction, though she was invisible behind the beam. At his shoulder was Father Hammerschmidt, looking old and sad.

Hans started forward and Honi tensed, hugging the gun more tightly, without realizing how threatening the move looked to someone not knowing she had no idea of using it. Father Hammerschmidt put his hand on Hans' shoulder. "Everyone's nervous," he said. "Don't do anything that might suddenly become a tragedy."

Hans stopped, but his defiance raged. "You dirty bitch," he said, the words coming as though they were a foul taste. "Is this why you came back, to terrorize your own people? You really are a whore, in every sense."

Honi opened her mouth, but nothing came out. What could be said? Hans continued his angry assault. "Whatever you and these other bastards intend to do, I'll fight you all the way. You'd better use that gun now if you're going to, because I'm leaving here—right now."

Honi said nothing. Father Hammerschmidt took a step forward. "I'm going, too. Sister Mary Theresa can watch after these people. This is probably the safest place for them all to be, anyway." He looked into the beam. "Will you try to stop me, Honi?"

Confronted with her continued silence, Hans and the priest started to leave, but Father Hammerschmidt hesitated and turned back. "There's no one to blame for *this* except yourself, my child." Then, they were both gone.

Hendrick shortly returned, escorting at gunpoint her troupe of children each loaded with cans of food, bread, milk and disposable diapers. After leaving the children, she stomped over to Honi. "Where's the priest? That stupid nun over there won't tell me a thing. Did he sneak out of here?" She looked more closely at Honi. "Why are you crying? Stupid, blubbering cunt. You probably let the priest escape from under your sniffling nose. Oh, well, what harm can a fat priest do?"

Richard Graff was trying to think, but it wasn't made any easier by his wife's unceasing, nervous chatter. "Oh, Richard, what are we going to do? The children want to see the Christmas lights. They're getting cold. Do you think the power will go back on soon? Why is Prince

345

Frederick telling us to stay inside?"

"Quiet, Elsa." Graff spoke sharply, mainly because he had nothing else to say. This business made no sense, especially to a twenty-five-year-old plumber. What "national emergency" had caused the prince to order them to remain behind closed doors? Why had the power and telephones been turned off? Graff had none of the answers and it troubled him. Sitting in the cold and dark was perturbing enough, but to do so in total ignorance of the cause was frightening. All Richard could do was fall back on what had always worked in the past—reliance on an orderly society following the directions of a rational, predictable government looking after the welfare of law-abiding people. Whatever the emergency the prince referred to, it was out of character for Liechtensteiners to do other than what the authorities said. The best protection, as always, lay in being organized and obedient.

These were not things that Richard Graff thought, but in the absence of a clear understanding of the situation, he instinctively became what it had always made sense to be—a good Liechtensteiner, a follower of authority.

"Elsa," he commanded with a voice meant to convey reassurance. "It'll be OK if we just follow instructions. Tell the children they can go see the Christmas lights as soon as the power returns and the prince says it's all right."

With that resolved, the family sat down to enjoy what they could of Christmas in the dark and tried to eliminate from their minds the specter of the strange events that were happening beyond their door.

Elsa had just gotten the children started on a halfhearted a cappella version of "Silent Night" when a strange noise caused their voices to trail away to discordant murmurings. As the children sat in a mute, frightened huddle, the pecking at a kitchen window grew more pronounced. Richard suspiciously got to his feet, and with jaw muscles working nervously, went to the window and rubbed the condensation away. He peered through the clear spot briefly then ran to the kitchen door, threw it open, and disappeared outside. Moments later, he reappeared leading a shivering, sweating Hans Haas. His heavy coat was wide open leaving a thin shirt as the only protection from the biting December wind. His eyes were white with fear and exhaustion. He threw himself into a nearby chair, closed his eyes and took huge gulps of air.

Elsa ran over and knelt by the chair. "Hans, Hans, what is it?" The smaller children sensed trouble and began to wail. Richard put his arm on Elsa's shoulder. "You put the kids to bed, I'll take care of Hans." He poured Hans a double schnapps and watched in silence as Elsa nervously rounded up the children and shooed them off to bed. Then, as Hans emptied the glass in one gulp and let his arm fall limply to his side, Richard asked, "Now tell me just what the hell is going on."

"We've been invaded, Richard."

"What the hell are you talking about, invaded? We just heard a loudspeaker broadcast a message from Prince Frederick that everything is OK."

Hans struggled to a full sitting position and motioned for more schnapps. "It's a lie, it has to be. They either forced him to make the recording or are faking it."

Richard handed him the bottle. "Who the hell are *they*? Damnit, man, make sense."

"They're a bunch of criminals who've taken over the

347

country. Two of them took over the church at gunpoint while I was there. After I escaped and on the way here, I saw that they've closed all the bridges and are riding around the country in Liechtenstein police cars, all armed with military weapons. It seems like they're everywhere."

Richard put the schnapps bottle to his own lips and took a long drink. "That means they've captured some real police." He pondered that unpleasant thought for a moment, then asked, "What do they want?"

"I'm not sure, but whatever it is, you can bet it doesn't belong to them, and it's something we don't want them to have."

"We need to let Chief Houser know about this."

"I stopped by his house before I came over here. I saw a strange car parked in front so I looked in the window. There was a man with a flashlight, and in the glare of the light I could see a pistol pointed at Frau Houser. I'm afraid we can't count on the chief or the prime minister, his house was in the hands of those people, too."

Richard's voice became tense. "Then what can we do?"

"I've been thinking about that ever since I escaped. We've got to do something; we can't just let them rape our country, regardless of what they want. We've got to fight back."

"But how? They've shut off the power and phones, they've captured the police, they've got automatic rifles. . . ."

"I don't know exactly; we'll have to try to surprise them some way. Do you still have your shotgun?"

Richard nodded.

"OK, you and I'll have to spread the word, if you're

348

game. I'm sure most people believe that phony tape recording of the prince. We'll just have to go to the homes of men we think would be willing to help. I'll go north and you go south. Hit every village; ask others to spread the word and help recruit. Tell them to grab every gun they can lay their hands on, and pass the word to meet in the old chapel outside Triesenberg tomorrow night after dark, we'll be safe there. Be sure to tell them not to be seen—no cars, the enemy will be looking for those."

Richard examined the phrase, "the enemy" in his mind and realized how foreign it was to his own experience. "What happens when we meet at the chapel?" he asked.

Hans shook his head. "I don't know, Richard, I really don't know. I guess I'll have to think of something." Hans used the personal pronoun easily and naturally, making it clear he had decided who would lead.

Richard didn't question it. "You can count on me," he said.

Hans stood up to signal the end of the conversation, but all of a sudden Elsa burst into the room from the darkened doorway where she had been listening. "No, you're not, Hans Haas. You're not going to take my husband out of here and get him killed. You may not care about what happens to you, but Richard has a *happy* family, and we need him here to take care of us. Go away and leave us alone."

The way she said "happy" made Hans wince but he said nothing. Richard had to handle his own house.

Richard walked over and put his arm protectively around the now-sobbing Elsa. "It's OK, baby," he soothed. "Please settle down." He rocked her gently

349

until the sobs were only sniffles, then he held her at arm's length, to make sure she heard him out. "Elsa, I'm no hero, I don't know anything about guns, and I sure don't want to go sneaking all over the countryside on a cold winter night like this. What I really want is to stay here with you and the kids. But Hans is right. We have to do something, or at least find out what we can't do. I'll be careful, I'm too scared not to. I promise, no heroics. I'll just try to help if I can and stay out of the way if I can't."

Despite the calm reassurances to his wife, Richard had never felt such excitement, and could hardly force himself to appear reluctant while he took down his shotgun and slipped out the rear door with Hans.

Christmas Eve had eased down on Liechtenstein like sleep on an untroubled conscience. The empty, snow-carpeted asphalt reflected the twinkling street lights and the neon flowers of the shop windows.

Konrad watched from his command post in the police station. He glanced at his watch and knew that something was about to happen; he counted the seconds down—then the lights went out in a blink and blackness took over the land with the boding presence of the unwelcome. Liechtenstein was changed forever.

Konrad had mixed feelings on cutting the power. On one hand, he knew it gave him a stronger grip on the populace; a man huddled with his frightened family in a cold, dark house is less of a threat than one plotting revenge in a warm, well-lit kitchen. Discomfort tends to turn thoughts inward, toward self-protection, or self-pity, and that's just where Konrad wanted them. On the other hand, losing electricity meant that he couldn't begin to loot the museums or banks until daylight. The job was too meticulous to attempt with flashlights.

The delay was just as well, he thought, since the wait gave him time to make certain that all was secure. He and Otto took turns monitoring the radios, listening for any reports of difficulty from the patrolling cars. There was none. Tenelli controlled the ski resort and each of the border barricades was quiet and unchallenged. Shortly after midnight, Konrad turned command over to Otto and settled down on the couch in the chief's office to nap for a few hours. He needed to be fresh the next day, and besides, everything was going perfectly.

"It's going to work, it's going to work," Konrad sang to himself with a mixture of glee and relief, and dropped off into an easy sleep knowing he was in control.

Chapter Fifteen

The shrill, angry ring of the telephone was like sandpaper rubbing on his brain, and Pierre Dumas struggled to clear the hangover fuzziness so he could somehow make it stop. After a couple of fumbling tries, he managed to lift the receiver and gasp a shaky, "Hello," before falling back on the pillow. He peered at the bedside clock—4:20 a.m.—and realized his party had ended only two hours earlier, and felt even worse.

Dumas winced at the power and anger in the voice that boomed out at him. "Dumas? This is Foreign Minister Gluck speaking. What the hell is going on in Liechtenstein? We've gotten reports that some sort of left-wing coup has occurred. Why didn't I get an immediate report from your section on this?"

Dumas fought frantically to clear his mind. His career was at stake here. "Well, sir, one of my subordinates did tell me something about a minor disturbance in Liechtenstein last night. But he made it sound unimportant and vague so I just told him to continue monitoring and inform me the instant anything serious

352

happened. The incompetent—"

"Damnit, man," Gluck was sputtering in his fury, "the Russians have already declared recognition for some wild-ass People's Republic of Liechtenstein. BBC's early news this morning carried the text of the Russian statement. Dumas, why the hell did I have to hear this on the radio? What kind of a department are you running? What am I going to tell the president?"

Dumas forced his brain into action. His worry was not about Liechtenstein, Russia, or even the foreign minister's anger, but of how to save himself. "Sir, I'll have a report from my subordinate today on just why he didn't inform me of the seriousness—"

"I don't give a goddamn about your subordinate or your attempts to hang your incompetence on him. Do you think I'm such a fool that I don't know when a bureaucrat is trying to save his own ass? All I want is for you and that subordinate to be in my office in one hour. Do you understand that?" Dumas opened his mouth to reply but the loud click of the telephone left him holding a dead instrument.

It was still the full darkness of night when a sleepy secretary ushered Pierre Dumas and Andre Wittenburg into the ornate inner office of the foreign minister. The minister was still angry as he brusquely motioned for them to be seated along a long table. Customarily a courtly man and one educated in the diplomatic skills, the foreign minister confronted the two like a foundry foreman. "The others will be here in a minute, but," turning to Wittenburg, he demanded, "I want to know why you didn't see fit to inform Dumas of the importance of this Liechtenstein thing so we wouldn't have to be playing catch-up like this."

Wittenburg wasn't hearing anything he didn't expect. Dumas was passing the buck on down the line in the expected manner of the small-minded duty-shirker Andre knew him to be. But even if it meant taking unfair blame, Wittenburg knew he had to play along. To be vindicated here would prove a Pyrrhic victory that would haunt his career as one who didn't understand how the game was played. Wittenburg managed a faint smile in Dumas' direction, and replied matter-of-factly, "I used my best judgment, Minister."

Gluck's caustic reply was cut off before it reached his lips by the entry of a file of officialdom who padded across the plush carpet to the table where the three already there rose to greet them. Even with the stress of the unknown situation facing them, the ingrained practices of career diplomacy were dutifully observed before they took seats and turned to Gluck who began to share his own scant knowledge of the situation.

A sudden shifting of chairs and murmuring interrupted the foreign minister who, unaccustomed to being interrupted, looked up in irritation. But his vexed look vanished in favor of a broad, surprised smile as he sprang to his feet to greet the president of Switzerland unexpectedly marching into the room followed by a coterie of solemn, self-important aides.

"Sorry to interrupt your meeting, Minister," President Franz said, taking the chair at the table's head that Gluck had hastily vacated. "I read your message on Liechtenstein and thought I'd drop by to hear more." He looked at the still unsettled audience. "Merry Christmas, gentlemen; sorry we have to spend it here. Now, please tell me what we have facing us."

Still unsettled by the surprise visit, Gluck stammered,

"Uh, well, sir, we don't yet know how serious the situation is."

Franz' eyes swept the table making everyone sit up straighter as he established contact along the line. "Anything that affects the borders of Switzerland and our relations with the superpowers is important, I don't have to tell you. Our country has avoided war for hundreds of years because we take all threats seriously. Now, Minister, would you kindly read the entire text of the Soviet statement on Liechtenstein?"

Gluck, in turn, motioned to a secretary sitting nearby who nervously shuffled some papers, cleared his throat, and started reading: "The people of the Union of Soviet Socialist Republics wish to congratulate the comrades of the People's Republic of Liechtenstein on their liberation and welcome them into the fraternity of socialist brotherhood. To those who would seek to reinstate a yoke of capitalist oppression on this brave little nation, we express our most profound concern about the consequences of such action. Any attempt to thwart the will of the people of Liechtenstein as expressed by their recent revolution will be regarded as an act of aggression against world peace by the Soviet Union. We urge the immediate recognition by all nations of the new democratic government of the People's Republic of Liechtenstein."

The foreign minister shook his head in concern. "Pretty strong language."

The president held up a finger of caution. "But you'll notice the communique stopped short of specifics regarding what they might do. Gentlemen, it's possible the Russians are just as much in the dark as we. In fact, Minister, have we learned anything new since we got the first radio message from Vaduz?" He looked expectantly at Gluck who could only shake his head. "I'm afraid we don't know very much yet. Everything seems quiet, at least there is no report of gunfire or other violence. The whole country is blacked out, telephone lines dead, too. It's pretty clear that whoever is running things over there is clamping down on the public to discourage resistance. Actually, pretty standard stuff for a coup."

"Any response by the Americans to the Russian declaration?" the president asked.

Gluck gave a short laugh. "I think the only ones on duty in Washington are the janitors. I think they're stalling so they can get down their encyclopedias and read up on Liechtenstein. I don't expect any response from the U.S. State Department for a day or two at least. Look at it from their standpoint: skeleton crew on duty, completely unexpected development from an unknown source and a strong Russian warning. Not the sort of circumstances to make one start shooting from the hip."

Franz turned back to the rest of the group. "Very well, then, looks like we're in this alone, at least for the time being. Let me recap the situation: Last evening we received a radio transmission stating Liechtenstein had undergone a bloodless leftist revolution, a *fait accompli*. We are assured of the safety of foreign persons, as though whoever perpetrated this business wanted to make certain we had no pretext for a protective invasion, so to speak. Then, in a matter of just a few hours, the Soviets release a diplomatic statement recognizing the new government and giving it an umbrella of protection. Pretty fast action, which makes me wonder if the Russians weren't somehow involved in the takeover to begin with. But that's something we have no way of knowing at this point."

Franz surveyed the twin rows of faces who, in turn, looked expectantly back at him. "Does anyone have an opinion on what we should do?"

An army general sitting near the end in full dress uniform raised his arm slightly to speak. Upon the president's nod, he said, "Sir, our forces at Fort Sargans could move into Liechtenstein from their position directly on the border and easily overwhelm them."

The president frowned and removed his horn-rimmed glasses for added effect. "General, the last war we had was in the year 1515. You seem to want to make up for lost time by tackling the Russians. Another thing, you mention 'recapturing' Liechtenstein. Let me remind you that it isn't ours to recapture. Liechtenstein is an independent country, bound to us only by a treaty of convenience. As such, it's entitled to whatever government it chooses." Franz paused, then added decisively, "The course of this government is going to be one of watchful waiting. We will do nothing for the present. I don't relish any more than you the idea of having a Soviet satellite peeking over our shoulder from the other side of the Rhine, but please remember that Swiss neutrality is one of our most valuable national assets, and I'm not going to permit it to be jeopardized by rash actions."

Franz gathered up his papers. "Now, if no one else has anything to add, we'll go about our business." He turned to Gluck and shook hands. "Sorry to barge into your meeting; please let me know immediately of any developments on this."

Father Hammerschmidt pawed at his eyes to wipe away

the stinging, blinding sweat rolling profusely down his flushed face. His legs and arms shook with unaccustomed exertion; his muscles screamed protests to his brain and his breath came in rasping gulps, pumping large amounts of steam into the cold air. Despite the agonies his pampered and overfed body was enduring, the determined priest continued to push the bicycle on its wobbly journey down the gravel lane. Several times since his escape from the church, he had had to hide in ditches or behind buildings to escape the patrols of the strangers who had captured his country. He hadn't been on a bicycle in years, in fact, hard exercise was as foreign to his body as sex, but he gave no thought to quitting. Someone had to get through to tell the world that Liechtenstein had fallen into the hands of evil people who intended great harm. The priest's destination was Fort Sargans, a distance of fifteen kilometers from where he had started, a mere warm-up for an experienced cyclist, but for him it was an ordeal attended by the agonies of a martyr.

After what seemed like a lifetime of pedaling, Father Hammerschmidt topped a small hill and could see the border in the distance. He flopped into a ditch and rested as his body gradually relaxed from its unaccustomed abuse. What a beautiful Christmas morning, he thought as he looked at the covering of glistening snow on the fields that led into tree-studded hills. He longed to be spending this Christmas morning as he had for years, visiting the hospital to bring the joy of the sacred day to the sick. Why had God put him to such a test on this day of all days? Letting the unanswerable question float away, he concentrated on the task at hand.

The border was a familiar sight to the priest, but he had

358

never before viewed it as hostile territory. However, the sight of the two men standing at the barricade with menacing rifles held at the ready reminded him of the danger he faced. He looked again at the expanse lying before him. Running along the border a few hundred meters from him and scarring the horizon was an ugly line of rusted barbed wire strung along eight-foot-high X-shaped posts. The entanglement had been implanted by Switzerland during World War II just in case the Germans seized Liechtenstein. The work had been done so well no one had bothered to remove it, and there it lay year after year, the spiny, rotting reminder of yesterday's war. On the other side of the wire lay Fort Sargans, his destination. The priest hoped the Swiss military there would come to Liechtenstein's aid, but first he had to get there, and it couldn't be along the road where the men with the guns waited.

Father Hammerschmidt abandoned the bicycle and started on foot across a field at an angle intended to increase the distance between himself and the guards in order to cross the barbed wire about three hundred meters from them. He had no concept of using terrain for concealment or stealth, his only concern was just getting there so he could seek help and rest his tortured body.

He stumbled across the field like a crippled mannequin, his outline clear against the skyline. In the distance he could hear shouting, but he blocked it out; all of his concentration was needed to finish this terrible journey. It was a contest between the will of an exhausted man far out of his element and implacable, merciless forces—gravity, cold, exhaustion, and skilled men determined to stop him. And he was losing. He dragged himself through the fields and up to the barbed wire. It seemed an

359

impossible obstacle. His muscles defied orders from his benumbed brain, but slowly he forced his body to spread the rusted strands apart and put one leg through, then the other. He was struggling like a cripple; avoiding getting hung up on the sharp points required all his concentration. He was halfway through now; Switzerland was just a few feet away—Switzerland, warmth and rest. Again he parted the wire. Again he bent rheumatically to squeeze the strands. He could almost touch the other side, but he couldn't relax for an instant or he would collapse in exhaustion. The closeness was all that kept him going. So total was his concentration he didn't hear the angry shouts drawing nearer. Just a couple of steps more and he would be free.

He didn't hear the shots, either. The rapid popping noises of the warning shots swirled around him unheeded. A pause, then something hammered his chest and knocked the wind out of him. His body turned numb. He felt even more tired. His arms wouldn't work. He was dimly aware of the wet blood seeping through his heavy coat but he couldn't think clearly enough to understand what it meant. Then a heavy red veil descended over his eyes. He tried to remember something important, a prayer, but then that, too, faded, and he fell back into the barbed wire, heavily, because he could no longer feel the barbs.

Capt. Jacques Carpentier of the Swiss army heard the brief flurry of rifle fire, which wasn't unusual on an army post, except this came from the north, the opposite direction from the rifle range. He swore angrily. If any soldiers had rigged an impromptu target away from the authorized shooting areas, he would have their asses. But it didn't make sense, horseplay was one thing, but before breakfast? He hailed a passing Jeep and pointed generally toward the sound. The driver, who had heard it also, turned and headed that way.

Carpentier headed north until he reached the border, but he heard nothing more and the snow-covered pines seemed quietly at peace. He was about to tell the driver to turn around when he noticed a large object caught in the barbed wire. He casually motioned the driver closer, but the closer they approached, the more he tensed. Without conscious thought he automatically made the association between the gunfire and the shape in the wire that, disturbingly, was beginning to assume the proportions of a human.

Carpentier hopped from the Jeep and threaded his way through the wire to the body, but by the way it was contorted and unmoving, he knew there was no hurry. Even though the eyes had the unfocused glaze of the dead, he gently removed the body from the wire so as not to let the barbs do any more damage. With the help of the driver he carried the heavy dead weight to the open ground beyond the wire and stretched it out on the ground. It had been a middle-aged man, obviously on the plus side of the good life. Carpentier opened the coat in search of identification. What he saw made him gasp and hurriedly make the sign of the cross.

The man had been a priest.

In fury, he looked around for the gunmen. Then, for the first time, he noticed the armed men standing at the border crossing about three hundred meters away. Carpentier and the driver gently placed the body in the rear of the Jeep, then Carpentier pointed roughly at the men and the Jeep headed toward them.

Carpentier was too angry to think of danger to himself,

but as the Jeep approached, he noticed that the two men who stood watching him carried M-16s, and in the casual manner of familiarity.

Carpentier jumped from the Jeep before it had completely stopped and his momentum carried him right up to the two armed men at a half-run. He could see them tense and shift their rifles to a more ready position. He pointed to the body in the Jeep. "Are you the men responsible for this?" he demanded.

The two men glanced at each other, then one of them seemed to decide to be the spokesman. "He was a fugitive trying to run away. We warned him to stop."

Carpentier spoke in disbelief and frustration. "For God's sake, man, he was a priest." His voice rose sharply. "A *priest*!"

The other man shrugged. "We don't know that, anyone can wear a turned-around collar. Besides, what business is it of yours?"

Carpentier was speechless. This border had always been open, and now these men seemed to have taken it upon themselves to close it. "What's going on here? Who the hell are you two? Why is this barricade across the road?"

The men relaxed a bit, knowing that when men are talking the danger is minimal. "Maybe you haven't heard; Liechtenstein had a little revolution last night. We've got a new government now, and the border is closed." He paused and looked defiantly at Carpentier. "To everyone."

Carpentier was dumbfounded. "For chrissakes, Liechtenstein? I don't believe you. People don't start revolutions on Christmas Eve."

"Well, let me tell you something, soldier boy, I don't

much give a shit whether you believe me or not. But I'll tell you this, you keep fucking around this border crossing and cause an international incident, and I'll just bet you won't be very popular with the Swiss army. So why don't you just get the hell away from the territory of the People's Republic of Liechtenstein?"

Jacques' frustration welled in his throat like bile. He knew this situation was beyond his depth, even when he reported it to the general, the matter would be kicked back to Bern where the politicians would gnaw on it like a dog on a bone and the dead priest would be forgotten in the "larger issues." He pointed at the dead man. "What about this priest you killed?"

The man shrugged. "You found him, he's yours."

Jacques leveled a long look at the man, anger giving way to steely determination. "This doesn't end here."

The man laughed derisively. "Go play soldier."

In the hours before first light, Konrad busied himself with the many details of being a captor: feeding the grumbling, restless policemen held in the cells; making radio contact with all blockade positions and patrol cars; and preparing the equipment for the day's work.

The six men selected for the most vital detail dozed and fidgeted on a bench along a wall, practicing the age-old soldier's axiom that the best way to wait for action is to not think about it.

The dawn rose out of the east like a pearl-gray river, flowing around the mountain peaks and pooling in the valleys and villages. Christmas day was making its annual appearance, but no celebration greeted it this year in Liechtenstein. The people huddled together wrapped in heavy coats and blankets around cold, ashen fireplaces, kept awake by their fear of the unknown and the loudspeakers on the police cars that regularly drove by and proclaimed an ominous message that reminded the pensive audience that strange, frightening things were happening in their land, things they could do nothing about, even if they had understood them. All they could hope for was daylight, and as it slowly appeared, their spirits lifted to meet the dawn. But there was no joy in it and even the small children sensed that Christmas had ended before it began.

The heel of the invader seemed firmly planted on the neck of Liechtenstein, but among the thousands of bewildered citizens who passively awaited their fate in confused fright, there were a few—Hans Haas, Richard Graff and those they had recruited—who had other ideas. Maneuvering stealthily among the houses and farms they knew so well, carefully avoiding the patrols, they spread the word of what had really befallen their country and sought more recruits to help them fight. They used that strange word, fight, as though they had some idea of what it meant, or how to go about it. These were farmers, carpenters, bookkeepers, the yeomanry of the land; fighting was foreign to their nature and as altogether absent from their experience as beauty to a blind man.

But they listened silently and grimly as Hans or Richard or one of the others told them of the strangers who had appeared the night before with rifles and threats and meant to steal what belonged to the people of Liechtenstein. No, they had to fight; how, they didn't know, but they were told to grab shotguns, hunting rifles, old pistols, anything that might serve as a weapon, and come quietly and carefully after nightfall to the old chapel at Triesenberg. None of the recruits knew how many would heed the appeal, but slowly word spread throughout the principality that day—come.

Master burglar Frank Horn examined the main door of the plain-looking art museum while Konrad and the others stood by awaiting the expert verdict. Horn backed away from the door and laughed cynically. "This is about as safe as a dog in a famine. It's like breaking into a whore's bedroom." He reached for his tools. "Somebody time me, I bet I'll be inside within three minutes."

The door crashed open with thirty seconds to spare, and the men whooped and slapped Horn on the back, then danced through the broken door like conspirators in a schoolboy prank. Once inside, however, the laughter drifted off as though they had stepped into a funeral parlor. The sudden beauty all around them had the impact of a deaf man first hearing Beethoven. Since classical art isn't taught in the slums of Hamburg, it was like a fairy tale to a child, wondrous and a little scary. Despite their ignorance, they felt the power of beauty and the awe of a world suddenly grown larger. They padded quietly on the plush maroon carpeting through the three floors as meekly as a man asking a banker for more time. They gazed at the ornately framed, brilliantly colored paintings depicting worlds they never knew existed—elegant ladies with high coiffures and pearled bodices staring imperiously back at them; ancient warriors with pleated skirts covering heavily muscled thighs and holding bloodied short swords raised toward nameless, long-dead gods.

Although the men felt lost in such grandiose surroundings, they were fascinated by the unique genius of Rubens' art: the rich colors, the free and forceful sweep of the brush, the sense of fierce and exuberant energy, the quiet insight into the human spirit, the superhuman presence of Herculean figures defiantly glaring back at them.

These were men who thought reality belonged to them, that nothing in life was so large it wouldn't cower when confronted by a pointed rifle; yet here was reality of another, greater kind, a reality they couldn't threaten. Looking up at a Roman battle scene, they saw the rush of the Roman army falling upon its enemy, they sensed the fear, smelled the blood, heard the cymbal-sound of the clash of steel, quailed before the rearing of panicked horses, cringed before death more vivid and dark than even they knew. And the scene said to them: There is far more to life than you know, and in your ignorance, you are weak.

They were fascinated, but also ill at ease, and finally broke the spell, pushing discomforting impressions from their minds as they walked away.

Jesse James Jones moved away and stood in front of Rubens' *The Artist's Sons*. He was studying it with a perplexed look when he hailed the nearby Konrad. "Say, boss, who was this guy?"

"Who, Rubens?"

"Yeah, that guy."

"A Flemish master of about three-hundred-fifty years ago." Konrad checked himself, Jones knew no more of Flanders than the planet Mars. "He was one hell of a painter."

Jones studied the painting more closely. "How much

you figure this is worth?"

Konrad shrugged. "Maybe ten million dollars."

Jones whistled softly. "Just looks like two little dudes dressed like fags to me. My grandmother bought a picture at an auction once that was prettier than this, and she only paid two bucks for it." He shook his head at the mystery of it all.

Konrad chuckled. "I don't pretend to be an expert, all I know is what some people are willing to pay for stuff like this." He glanced at his watch and frowned. Crating all these art objects was no easy task, especially since some were fifteen feet in diameter and had to have frames removed to fit into the airplane. A lot of work lay ahead of them. "All right, Jesse, let's round up the men and get started."

Konrad assembled his men and was about to send some out to the truck for crating materials and tools when a single shot rang out. Everyone stood stunned; no matter how inured one grows to gunfire, it's always a shock when it erupts unexpectedly. But the reaction was swift. With a spontaneous roar that sounded like it came from one angry throat, three men turned in the direction of the shot and opened fire with M-16s on full automatic. Konrad caught a glimpse of an elderly man dodging behind a pillar.

"Stop firing," Konrad shouted, imagining as he spoke seeing bullets tearing gaping holes in priceless canvas.

The ear-shattering burst of gunfire stopped immediately, and except for the moaning of Frank Horn slumped against a wall holding his shoulder, the room was still. Only the stench of cordite gave evidence to what had just happened.

Konrad forced the ringing out of his ears and trained

his rifle on the pillar. "Come on out of there, you. Throw out your gun and then follow it nice and slow with your arms high. This is the only chance you get, then you're a dead man."

Seven rifles trained on the pillar and waited in silence. Konrad spoke threateningly. "Better decide if you want to live or die."

The man extended his arm from behind the pillar and let his pistol clatter to the floor. He edged his body out into the open room a short, slow shuffle at a time. He stood there, looking old, tired and frightened, his bushy gray mustache quivered as the men gathered around to stare curiously, a little abashed that such a harmless-looking old man could make them scurry for cover like rodents seeking their holes. The old man drew himself up to his full height, as much as his stooped body would allow, and stared defiantly straight ahead.

Konrad shook his head in exasperation at the old man, but yet there was also respect for a brave man. "What the hell you trying to do, old-timer, get yourself killed?"

The old man looked him squarely in the eye, the weathered head framed proudly between his upraised hands. "Doing my job; I'm the watchman here." He gestured toward the wounded man. "He looks like he wishes I hadn't tried."

Konrad walked over to Frank Horn who was groaning and clutching his shoulder. "How bad is it?"

"He got me right in the middle of the shoulder; hurts like hell, but doesn't seem to be bleeding much."

"That's good, means it missed the artery."

Horn gestured to the old man with his good arm. "That old son of a bitch did this to me? I'll kill him."

"No, you won't," Konrad said. "That old man was just

doing his job. He's my prisoner and no one'll touch him."
He flicked on his walkie-talkie and spoke into it; soon,
Otto's voice answered. "Otto, grab one of the local
doctors and bring him over here to the museum, we've
got a wounded man." Konrad listened for a moment.
"Not too bad, just a shoulder. Everything's quiet now."
That accomplished, Otto had something to tell Konrad
that made him grip the walkie-talkie until his knuckles
were white. When he spoke there was tension and
sadness in his voice. "A priest? Why did they have to do
it? Well, it's done. Keep me posted."

Konrad turned the walkie-talkie off and murmured
softly, "So the killing game begins."

"Say what?" Jesse James Jones standing nearby asked.

"Nothing, just remembering what an old drunk once
told me." Shaking his head slowly, he gathered the men
and spoke shortly through compressed lips, "Tie the old
man up; hurry, we're short a man and we've got a lot to
do here."

Andre Wittenburg felt disoriented as he watched the
sun emerge and transform a lifeless winter dawn into the
fiery opal of a sunny Christmas morning. He had been
awake and thinking for many hours, and at this stage, it
seemed, the sun should be going down instead of rising.
Across the room, slouched behind his expensive desk,
Pierre Dumas was yawning, the adrenalin that had raised
him from his hangover stupor to attend the foreign
minister's meeting on the Liechtenstein affair was fast
deserting him.

Dumas' eyes started to droop and he fought to keep
them open. "Wittenburg," he yawned, "I think we

369

should just wait and see what happens. I don't see this Liechtenstein thing as that important. Far as I'm concerned, they can have the goddamn little country. What's the big—"

The telephone jangled next to Wittenburg's chair. "I'll get it," he said with no protest from Dumas.

"Hello, Wittenburg here."

"Sir, this is Flufelder, I'm a clerk in data processing."

"Yes, I know who you are, Flufelder, what is it?"

"Well, sir, a phone call just came in on a public line from a man who said he wants to talk to someone about a Liechtenstein takeover. I told him I didn't know anything about any Liechtenstein takeover, but he insisted on talking to Herr Dumas."

Wittenburg glanced at his somnolent superior and made an instant decision. "Uh, Herr Dumas is unavailable. Keep the call on hold and I'll take it in my office in a moment."

As he hung up, Dumas asked sleepily, "What is it, Wittenburg?"

Wittenburg stood up and moved toward the door. "Nothing to bother you with, just some routine business I can take care of. Why don't you go home and spend Christmas day with your family?"

Dumas needed little coaxing and pushed himself to his feet. He was scheduled for another party that night and badly needed sleep. "OK, if you think you can handle it. But I suppose you better let me know if anything important comes up."

"I'll do my best. Merry Christmas, sir."

Wittenburg rushed to his own office and picked up the telephone. "Hello, Flufelder? Is he still there? Good, put him on this line." Andre took a deep breath to push the excitement out of his voice, then when he heard the line connect, said, "Herr Dumas is unavailable; this is Deputy Director Wittenburg, how can I help you?"

The voice that responded spoke fluent German but with an accent Andre couldn't identify. "I can't give you my name, but I'm a fellow professional from a friendly nation. I have some information you might like on the Liechtenstein situation. I don't think it's possible your people could have picked up yet the intelligence I can give you."

Wittenburg replied testily, "We don't get our information from the newspapers, you know."

Riley chuckled. "Touchy intelligence officers are usually those who don't know what they're paid to know."

Andre said in tired exasperation, "Look, I've had a long night and it's Christmas. What do you want to tell me?"

Riley became serious. "The socialist revolution that's supposedly taking place there, and has the Russians so lathered up, is nothing of the kind. It's a power grab by a Nazi element with an American mercenary as a front."

"Do you mean Nazis are behind it?"

"Not as a political movement as such. The head man is a war criminal; he hired the American to do the dirty work for him. I don't know their exact purpose, but you can bet it has nothing to do with social reform. People like that are interested in only one thing—getting rich at someone else's expense."

Wittenburg cut him short. "Look, whatever-your-name-is, this is all very interesting, but you could also be some nut. Give me something more solid to go on."

"OK, the American's name is Konrad. If you have

good contacts in the West German police, have them question a man in Baden-Baden named Walter Schell about a gang of approximately fifty men he recruited for Konrad. You could also talk to a black-market dealer named Owl in Frankfurt about some weapons Konrad bought from him. That should be enough to convince you and your superiors that you're dealing with thugs, not revolutionaries."

Andre wrote down the information then turned back to the phone. "One more thing, friend, why are you doing this?"

"I don't like Nazis."

Bert Kofler watched the kilometers glide by as the powerful BMW smoothly covered the distance between Stuttgart and Baden-Baden and headed into the Black Forest. He had long since become used to the crazy hours of a policeman, but being called out on Christmas day was something he hoped he would never have to become used to. If the request had come from anyone but Andre Wittenburg, he would have really been pissed off, but coming from his old college chum, he could handle it. And judging from Andre's urgent tone, it had to be today, and it had to be done by Kofler; no one but the regional director of the German national police would do.

Before leaving Stuttgart, he had quickly reviewed the file on Walter Schell which didn't take long because it was pretty thin. Schell was a man skilled at slipping through cracks. The police knew he was engaged in criminal recruitment, but since the activity was so unique, they had never quite gotten a handle on how to investigate. Consequently, their attitude toward Schell was one of benign sufferance. He didn't cause waves and they had other things to do. Police are like anyone else: What they don't understand they tend to put on the back burner.

Following directions from the Baden-Baden police, Kofler had no difficulty finding the handsome chateau in the hills above the city. He had more difficulty getting inside. The butler pointed out rather testily that the director was calling on Christmas day. In turn, the director pointed out that the significance of the day was not lost on him, and was one of the reasons standing on a cold doorstep arguing tended to make him unpleasant, and that perhaps Herr Schell should be informed there was a police director standing outside his home waiting to see him and growing more irritable by the moment.

His insistence eventually paid off and Kofler found himself standing in a wide hallway gazing absently at the dark, richly grained panels decorated with art that Kofler supposed must be very expensive, but the whole effect to him was that of a high-class funeral parlor.

The man who approached could have been the undertaker: black coat, perfectly knotted silk tie, striped pants and an inscrutable smile, proper but cold. "Good morning, Director Kofler, welcome to my home," he said as though Kofler were a long-awaited friend. He took the policeman by the elbow and led the way into a lighter room which featured a huge grand piano in one corner and an elegant bar in another. Schell gestured to a nearby easy chair, an invitation Kofler ignored. "Would you like a glass of wine, Herr Director?"

Kofler leveled a steady stare at Schell. "Let's skip the amenities, you know I didn't come here for Christmas cheer. In fact, being here today makes me pissed off, and when I'm pissed off, I'm not very nice to be around. I'm here on police business, in case you've forgotten who I am."

Schell lost his smile and put down the wine bottle. "I haven't forgotten. What can I do for you?"

"You know a man named Konrad, I believe."

Schell pursed his lips and squinted at the ceiling in deep thought. "The name doesn't sound familiar."

Kofler took a card from his pocket and waved it at Schell. "Would you like me to recite the date he visited you and the license number of his rental car?"

Schell spoke carefully. "Tell me, what do you suspect this Konrad fellow of doing?"

Kofler sighed in resignation. "Look, I'm going to leave in about one minute because I don't feel like playing games with you. But first, you should know that the interest in this business comes from very high places and they're in a hurry. If you don't play ball, just let me tell you what to expect. There'll be a lot of interest from now on in the affairs of Walter Schell. Your underworld friends will know of that interest, which may cause them to think twice before doing business with a man standing under such a spotlight. You may find business falling off a bit. And if you slip, even just a little, you'll be heading to jail as fast as a flea on a greyhound's ass. When that happens, don't say I didn't try to talk to you. It could happen anyway, but if you don't cooperate with me right here and now, it's the next thing to certain. So make up your mind; I want to get home while it's still Christmas."

Schell gave the beautiful room a look of deep sadness, recognizing that he had to choose between betraying a friend and losing the treasures he had surrounded himself with and that had become a part of him. He sat down at the piano and started to pick out Chopin's "Etude in E." "Konrad had a very unusual request. He wanted to recruit forty men for some unusual assignment; he said it had to do with protecting some oil company's interests. It was all very legitimate sounding. I wouldn't have anything to do with it otherwise, you understand," he said guardedly. "Believe me, that's all I know. I don't even have a record of the names of the men I recruited." He looked at Kofler apprehensively. "Is there anything else?"

Kofler headed for the door. "Yeah, retire, if you're smart."

While Walter Schell was telling all he knew to Bert Kofler, the Owl was squirming in a basement interrogation room in Frankfurt police headquarters. He was sweating heavily, but not so much from the heat and bright lights as the presence of three burly detectives hovering above the uncomfortable little stool on which he had been perched. "Why did you have to make such a big show out of picking me up?" he whined. "I would have come in if you'd just phoned."

"We wanted to make a good impression on the neighborhood, let 'em know what an important man you are," one of the detectives said.

Another detective picked up the theme. "Yeah, and everyone's gonna want to know why we brought you in. They'll be really pissed when we let the word out that you squealed on the craps game in the basement of your building—especially after we raid it. Do you know what they'll do to you, you ugly little asshole?"

"I didn't squeal on them," he protested pitifully.

"Oh," the third detective taunted, "in that case, just explain it to them. They'll certainly believe you. Everyone knows you do more squealing than a castrated pig."

"What do you want? I'll tell you anything," he pleaded.

"We want to know about a man named Konrad and the guns he bought from you."

Owl relaxed visibly and said, "Is that all? I'll tell you everything I know about that fucker. I never had any use for him. But first promise me you won't raid the craps game."

"We won't, not today, anyway. Now, about Konrad and those guns, we don't have much time."

Chapter Sixteen

The first light of Christmas day crept down the mountainsides and through the windows of the ski lodge which Tenelli and Kunst had guarded through the night.

The lodge was filled with groans and coughs as their captives stirred themselves awake in response to the morning's arrival. It had been a long night on a cold, hard floor for people unaccustomed to hardship, and the moans and curses that filled the air gave bold underscore to their resentment.

Lorenzo Belotto wasn't thinking about the cold or his sore muscles, he was too engrossed in watching and planning. Of their two guards, he quickly had seen that Toni was the cool one, the clever one. Except for trips outside to use the car radio which he had overheard her explaining to Kunst, and had timed at precisely every two hours, she didn't miss a movement.

The occasional eye contact between Toni and Lorenzo told him that she hadn't entirely forgotten the old days, either. When she looked at him, there was a barely perceptible softening, but strong enough to stir warm memories in him. And to his surprise, considering the circumstances, the thought gave him an erection. Toni could affect a man that way.

Kunst, on the other hand, was the careless one. Lorenzo could see him daydreaming and yawning when he should have been watching captives like Lorenzo as carefully as they were watching him. The last time Toni left the lodge, Lorenzo had carefully whispered to his partner, Georgio Valenti, a tall, dark, bemused man of thirty-three sitting next to him. He and Georgio were boyhood best friends and later became partners in the olive oil exporting business after Lorenzo's release from prison. Georgio was a paratrooper in the Italian army at the time Lorenzo was spreading terror in the Red Brigades, so neither was a stranger to action, nor was either reluctant to initiate it. They had come to this ski resort looking for women, but had now found something even more interesting.

In their hurried whisperings, they had devised a plan that was almost childishly simple, but considering the inept Kunst, had a good chance of working.

Promptly at ten a.m., Toni made a motion to Kunst to take over and went out the lodge door. The moment the door closed, Lorenzo slowly worked his way the few feet to the interior wall of the lodge where several pairs of skis were stacked. When he was positioned against the wall, he arched his eyebrows to Georgio who removed a cigarette lighter from his pocket and in quick, furtive gestures told those nearby to scoot out of the way and stay down.

Kunst was standing near a staircase at the edge of the room thinking how he'd like to fuck the bitch who had the nerve to boss him around and humiliate him in front

378

of all these people, even though they were rich, soft assholes. It was the principle of the thing: No woman was going to do that to him. Let her have a few inches of stiff Kunst cock and she might change her tune. He let his mind construct and relish the details of such an encounter, and smiled in satisfaction as he thought of her thrashing beneath the unmerciful thrusts of the mighty Kunst. Hah! No one ever told him he was a bad lay.

His fantasy was interrupted by a shout from the other side of the room. A fire had broken out among a pile of blankets. Already, thick, acrid smoke was coming from the pile and people were scrambling to get away from the small fire. Goddamnit, Kunst thought, why didn't someone just stomp it out? Suppose he'd have to do it. . . .

Kunst walked over to the fire and started stamping out the flames muttering to himself about good-for-nothing, lazy, rich bastards.

That was what Lorenzo had been waiting for. The moment Kunst gave his attention to the flames, Lorenzo grabbed a long downhill ski by the bindings and sprang. Everyone had obeyed Georgio and stayed down, giving Lorenzo a full swing at the erect Kunst. The long, slim ski whistled through the air, building momentum as the vicious cycle of its arc sped toward Kunst.

The ski hit him in the back of the neck, crushing the spinal cord and rendering the brain that had served him so badly during life totally void when he hit the floor. Kunst died a painless death.

Lorenzo scrambled to pick up the M-16 that had fallen from Kunst's hands, briefly checked the clip and safety, and headed for the back door. Georgio grabbed his arm. "Need some help?"

Lorenzo shook his head. "I want to meet her outside. The last thing we want is shooting in this crowded room. It's better if I go to intercept her."

Lorenzo slipped out the rear door and made his way around the lodge to the parking lot. It wasn't difficult to find Toni's car since the engine was running and condensation was pouring out the tailpipe as a cloud of white steam.

He knew she was about through with her radio message, so Lorenzo looked for a hiding place. He crouched behind a Volkswagen van after visually calculating that her shortest path back to the lodge went right along the opposite side of it. He glanced over his shoulder and squinted at the bright morning sun. It would be right in her eyes. He positioned himself so the front tires would block his legs from being seen at ground level. He waited, the inactivity reminding him that a flimsy silk shirt was his only protection from the biting wind.

Lorenzo didn't have long to wait. He tensed as her engine shut off and the car door slammed with a heavy thud. He gripped the M-16 as the crunch of Toni's footsteps drew closer. Then she was beyond him, carrying her rifle loosely in one hand by its top handle.

That's a mistake, Toni, didn't I teach you better than that? he thought. Lorenzo took several quick steps and was behind her; she started to turn at the sound and raise her rifle, but he was too fast. Lorenzo brought his rifle barrel down against the stock of her rifle in a quick, stinging swipe that knocked the gun from her hand. He curled one foot around her legs and gave a hard push that sent Toni sprawling in the snow. He picked up her rifle and pointed his own at her head. "Bang," he said with a sardonic smile, "you're dead, pretty girl."

Bitter tears filled Toni's eyes at the humiliation of being taken so easily. Lorenzo motioned for her to get up. "Come on, it's too cold out here to stand and listen to you blubber."

Instead of returning to the lodge, Lorenzo marched her to a small ski equipment shop and had her stand aside while he broke the door to gain entrance. Once inside, he motioned for her to sit. Impatient and still defiant, she said, "Well, why don't you get it over with?"

He looked at her blankly. "Get what over with?"

"Are you going to shoot me or rape me?"

Lorenzo broke into laughter. "Rape you? Good God, Toni, you used to give it to me without a fight. And why on earth should I shoot you? I didn't even have to break into a sweat to capture your gorgeous ass." He continued laughing as he had her stand up and surveyed her frame with a critical eye. He took a ski suit from the rack and threw it over to her. "Here, see if this fits." While Toni tried on the suit over her clothes, he grabbed a day-pack from a nearby rack, filled it with fruit bars from a container on the counter and threw in a filled water bottle. Then he went to a ski display and selected a pair of cross-country skis that appeared proper for her size. He motioned for her to try them on. "I assume you still ski as well as ever?" he asked, accepting her silence as affirmation.

In a moment, Toni, bedecked in ski outfit and skis, stood expectantly, but still defiantly, in front of him. "Now what?" she asked.

He took her by the arm and led her to a window facing east, making sure he stayed between her and the rifles. Squinting against the sun's glare, he pointed toward a low

381

break in the mountains. "See that pass? That'll take you to Austria. If you leave now, you should get there by nightfall."

Toni gaped at him. "You mean you're just letting me go?"

He laughed. "Why shouldn't I? I'm still the same old Lorenzo, Toni."

The fire in her rekindled and her eyes blazed. "No, you're not, you're the son of a bitch who betrayed the movement. I'll never forget that. I don't want any favors from you."

He sighed. "Why the hell don't you grow up? The only ones I've betrayed, as you call it, are the sadists and assholes who double-crossed what the movement stood for. Let's face it, the movement is dying a slow death from neglect and the disillusionment of so many of us romantic idealists who believed we could reform the world with a bomb."

He chuckled at the memory of his naivete, but the laugh trailed off when he saw the fury still in her face. "Enough chatter, you'd better be going or those people inside the lodge will be out here to see what happened. Let's just leave it like this: You've been lucky, and it'll buy you some time; use it to do a little serious thinking. If you ever get things straightened out, you're going to make someone a hell of a woman, unless some cop shoots you first."

Toni was almost out the door when he stopped her again and reached into his wallet and removed a business card and held it out toward her. "Here, if you ever get back to Italy, look me up."

They held the pose for a long instant, him with arm extended, she staring at the card. Just as he was about to

382

drop his arm, she suddenly reached out and took the card and stuffed it into her jacket. He opened his mouth to say something, but she was gone. All that remained was a swishing sound on the snow, then silence.

Back inside the lodge, the grateful guests crowded around Lorenzo with back-slaps and hoots of praise. Only Georgio, it seemed, remembered the young woman he had gone outside to capture. Georgio looked at him and asked the question with his eyes and a quizzical smile.

"She got away," Lorenzo answered with a shrug.

Konrad glanced at his watch with a frown. It had taken longer than he anticipated to crate the cumbersome paintings. His men were not accustomed to working with their hands, and a simple task for a couple of apprentice carpenters quickly degenerated for his men into something like an Iranian debating society. Konrad had just barley stopped one frustrated workman from trying to force a Raphael sculpture into a tight carton with a hammer. Another had almost put a nail through a Rubens tapestry.

As the last of the art was loaded onto the truck, he decided to break for lunch, which consisted of kicking in the door of a nearby delicatessen and helping themselves to the sausages and salads that lay ripe and unattended at their mercy.

While his men ate, Konrad radioed Otto who within two minutes drove up in his commandeered squad car. They stood side by side on the empty street and surveyed what for the time being belonged solely to them. Otto, anticipating his boss, said, "It's quiet. Except for the priest shot at the Sargans border crossing, not a peep out

383

of anyone."

"Why in hell did they have to shoot him?" Konrad asked again.

"The report I got, he was trying to sneak across the old barbed wire that's still there from the war. A Swiss army officer found him, but our men say he didn't cause any real trouble. I checked with the bull dyke we've got in charge of the church, and she said he sneaked out last night."

"Any other problems?"

"Some of our patrols say they've seen villagers sneaking around, but they run when our people get near; nothing to worry about."

Konrad knew the danger of complacency. "Well, let's just hope what we don't know won't hurt us."

Otto glanced curiously inside the truck. "How's it going here?"

"Slow, but we'll get there. We hit the stamp museum next, then split up for the banks. I'll need your help there. I don't want these monkeys left alone in those bank vaults."

Otto grinned. "How do you know you can trust me?"

Konrad laughed. "Because I know you're in this for the love of it, not for the money."

The stamp museum offered no more resistance than its art counterpart. One crowbar in the hands of an expert made short work of the heavy plate glass door. As the door snapped open, the man with the crowbar grunted and said, "Looks like they ran an honor society here. This is easy as breaking into an Irish bar on St. Patrick's Day."

The inside of the museum was filled with rows of glass-covered cases, each containing hundreds of postage

384

stamps. There were stamps yellowed with age, stamps of bright flowers, stamps of fierce warriors, stamps of long-dead princes. These were not stamps that routinely send letters through the mails, they were symbols of the enormous wealth that great scarcity creates. Each stamp represented a small, gummed, serrated testament to the need of some people to possess what others cannot. That greed had made Liechtenstein into a Mecca for stamp collectors, that beleaguered class of hoarders doomed to frustration because their collecting is never done—as soon as it all comes within their grasp, the printing presses in some tiny nation like Liechtenstein once again are turned on, and something new to lust for is created.

Jesse James Jones looked in open mystification at the display cases. "What's the big deal with this stuff? Looks like plain old stamps to me."

Konrad gave a short, preoccupied laugh. "They're plain old stamps about like the Hope diamond is a plain old rock." His concern with time gave Jesse only that brief moment. He watched impatiently as Max Brenner, an explosives expert with at least a half-dozen banks across Europe to his credit, took charge of blowing the vault door.

Brenner took the puttylike plastique and placed it under the time lock on the heavy steel door. He quickly rigged a detonator and signaled for the others to take cover. The blast reverberated through the big room, broke glass on the display cases and left a ringing in their ears, but when the smoke cleared, the heavy door stood ajar.

Konrad led the men into the interior of the vault where they found rows and rows of neatly arranged large flats of stamps, each flat containing dozens of the precious bits of paper. While the men stood around waiting, Konrad consulted a list and keyed it to the stacks of cardboard sheets. Slowly, carefully, he directed the men to search out and remove certain sheets located by number codes. As the men became familiar with the filing system the work went faster and in a short time they had selected a pile of the cardboard flats that contained about two thousand stamps.

As the men carefully wrapped and loaded the stamps on the truck, Konrad searched the vault looking for a specific drawer. Finally, by process of elimination, he stopped before an unmarked metal drawer. He tried it; locked, of course. He jammed the edge of a crowbar into the drawer's tight-fitting crease and gave a heave. Nothing. But after several attempts, his leverage battered and gradually forced open the thin steel of the drawer. He pried the metal aside and removed a slim, blue velvet box. As he lifted the lid, a single stamp on a bed of white satin came into view. From the one-inch square of paper, a bewhiskered Victorian wearing a tunic lined with medals glared imperiously out at him from a background of royal maroon. At the top was written "Fuerstentum" and at the bottom "Liechtenstein." Off to the side was the figure "1 fr." Konrad was staring at The Baron, one of the first stamps created by Liechtenstein in 1912 when they started making their own. By a typesetter's error, it had been given the wrong value, and the printing presses had been quickly stopped and the entire run destroyed— except for a few, of which this was the sole survivor. Thus, in a strange world of stamp collecting, a printer's goof-up created a useless stamp that couldn't even mail a letter, but which by virtue of its rarity, became one of the most famous and coveted stamps in the world and worth more than a million dollars.

Konrad closed the box and slipped it into his pocket which he patted tenderly and muttered, "A cool, fucking million dollars."

Then, as the men returned and with Konrad barking orders, they stacked the remaining boards of stamps in high piles in the middle of the floor. Konrad sent two men to the engraving department in the museum's basement, from where, after a few minutes, they emerged carefully carrying a heavy metal container. As Konrad directed their very cautious, arm's-length moves, they poured smoking sulphuric acid on each of the piles, taking great pains to avoid splattering. As the acid fumes rose to sting their noses and eyes, the men hastily withdrew from the vault and slammed the heavy door shut.

"Why did we have to do that?" one of the men asked between coughs.

Konrad said nothing, but one of the other men nearby gave an answer for him. "When there are only two of a kind of something and you own one of them, the smart thing to do is get rid of the other one."

Otto was waiting, right on time, outside the stamp museum when Konrad emerged. "How's it going?" he asked.

"As easy as licking a stamp," Konrad said. "Everything quiet?" he asked in return.

"It's like we figured. These people are so used to living the life of the fat burgher, they don't know anything else but to follow orders. It's as quiet as—Christmas." He laughed. "This is a pretty easy way to make a living."

Konrad looked up at the fading light of mid-afternoon.

"We'd better get busy while the light holds." He gestured toward a nearby group. "Otto, you take those three men and hit the private bank." He pointed to an imposing granite building down the street. "And I'll take care of the national bank," he said, pointing out another, more impressive stone building. "You take Kinder, he's good with explosives. I'll keep Brenner with me."

Konrad called over one of his men, a bookish-looking, quiet fellow. "Kruger, you know your way around a lawyer's office, I'm told," he said, alluding to the man's past as a promising attorney in West Berlin before an embezzling charge ended his practice. He handed him a folded piece of paper and pointed out a modern office building. "Go to this lawyer's office, over there in that building, and grab the files of the companies listed here. Bring them back to headquarters and wait for me there."

Kruger looked at the list and smiled. "I suspect there are things in those files that might prove embarrassing. I further suspect the profit potential in possessing those files is very promising."

Konrad cut him short. "Don't suspect anything, Kruger, just do it. And don't get any ideas." As Kruger jogged down the street, Konrad turned and faced the massive stone front of the National Bank of Liechtenstein. "Open up for Poppa," he whispered.

Konrad and his men stood in the cathedrallike main lobby of the bank and stared in 360-degree awe, not believing that they could stand in broad daylight with larcenous intent in the middle of an incredibly rich bank and be in no greater danger than a clerk among his files.

While two of his men stood by holding large plastic bags, ready to fill from the vault, Konrad and Brenner examined the huge safe door. Brenner laid down his

388

acetylene torch and ran both hands over the smooth, gleaming metal and frowned. "It'd take a whole day to cut through this steel. This baby was built to be tamper-proof, and by God, it is. I'll need a lot of time, and even then it'll be iffy."

Konrad looked at the door and snorted with the impatience of the non-expert who doesn't appreciate the beauty of a difficult challenge. "Goddamnit, Brenner, you're supposed to be the expert. Can you find another way? We don't have much time."

Brenner looked at him uncomprehendingly. Like so many experts, he had long since stopped looking for ways other than the ones they had perfected.

Seeing no help there, Konrad turned back to the safe. "If the door's too strong, then let's go for the wall. Let's blow the damned door right out of the building."

Brenner blinked. "Why that'd take *pounds* of explosives!"

Konrad swept his arm to show the deserted bank. "Well, why not? We've got the stuff, and there's no one here to object. A man has to adapt to the situation, Brenner, and right now, the situation belongs to us."

Konrad watched as Brenner carefully planted several pounds of plastique at the juncture of the safe door and the wall. He inserted the detonator, and he and Konrad, followed by the other men, left the bank, crossed the street and stood behind the corner of a building. Brenner lifted the detonation device and pushed the button. Instantly, there was a deep, muffled roar that shook the earth beneath their feet and filled the air with a cloud of granite dust that mushroomed out of the bank's doors and windows and settled like sand on their shoulders and invaded their lungs.

389

Coughing and brushing off their clothes, they re-entered the bank which now canted crazily and resembled the leavings of a nasty-tempered earthquake. The safe door was still proudly intact in its frame, but the wall it protected was gone, and now provided the vault all the protection of chicken wire against mosquitoes. Konrad led the way into what remained of the vault which now looked like King Midas had thrown a fit. Franc notes littered the floor like maple leaves in autumn. Gold bars lay at random like logs on a sawmill floor and glittered in the late-afternoon gloom.

The men subconsciously sought to memorize the sight, knowing they would never again see its equal. Konrad broke the trance by clapping his hands and joking, "All right, let's clean up this mess."

As they loaded the truck, a muffled boom in the direction of the private bank caused Konrad and Brenner to grin at each other. Otto, too, had discovered the easy way.

By outward appearances, it was another beautiful Christmas day in Liechtenstein. The snow lay on sidewalks and streets like it had been strewn by a stagehand trying to achieve the proper effect. The decorations in shop and home windows proclaimed their untiring message. The empty streets bespoke a day of putting aside the monotony of survival living. It was a scene of peace.

So much for peace. Inside those tranquil homes, the people huddled in cold and fear. The ubiquitous sound cars with their message of royal reassurance had assumed an ominousness that made their unwilling audience shudder each time they slowly drove by.

The home of Karl Beckhower was one. The middle-aged schoolteacher, his wife, Anna, and their teen-age son, Kurt, had tried to discuss the situation intelligently when the lights first went out in their modest clapboard home and the taped messages boomed into the house. Perhaps a gas main has broken, one surmised. Maybe a bad winter storm is on the way, another thought. Or perhaps a railroad car filled with chemicals has overturned. Then they were out of guesses, and the doubts began and soon invited fear. The ugly thing about fear is that it has little to say, and as Christmas Eve became gray dawn and then a bright new day, it just sat there silently on their shoulders, its heavy weight more and more difficult to support.

The Beckhowers ate, and then they drank; it was something to do. Then, when they weren't hungry or thirsty anymore, they turned on each other as available targets. Little irritations that would ordinarily go unnoticed became intolerable insults to be redressed with a snarl or angry complaint. Finally, they lapsed into silence and sat glumly in the parlor wrapped in blankets and staring into nothingness.

The back door opened and closed quickly and quietly, but it intruded on the Beckhowers' silence like shattered crystal. Before the family could move, Richard Graff slipped into the room and motioned for them to relax. Karl heaved a sigh of relief when he saw Richard, a former student and a good, steady man. He struggled to his feet. "Richard, what are you doing here?" he asked with more confusion than surprise, nervously adjusting his thick, horn-rimmed glasses as he spoke, glancing alternately at Richard's strained face and the shotgun he carried.

Graff leaned against the wall, closed his eyes and took several deep breaths seeking to rest and settle his jangled nerves. He waved away the offer of brandy and faced the shaken family. "Herr Beckhower, Frau Beckhower," he said with deference to his former teacher, "I need help— the country needs help. Those men out there—" he motioned toward the street—"are here to rob the country. We've got to stop them."

What Graff was trying to say swept by the peaceful, reflective Beckhower like a strong wind through the branches of a tree. "How?" he asked in wide-eyed wonder.

Graff had recovered his breath and was becoming more businesslike. He could grow to like this, the stealth, danger and romance of being hunted and becoming the hunter appealed to something in his nature that had never before been revealed, had never been given a reason to come forth. He exhilarated in having Herr Beckhower, someone who had been his teacher, a figure of respect and authority, look to him with utter dependence and respect. "The only thing we can do, the only patriotic thing, is to stop them," Richard answered self-importantly. "Hans Haas, myself and a few other men are going around visiting good men and asking them to help." He glanced through the curtain at the street. "We've had to be damned careful; those patrols seem to be everywhere. They know what they're doing."

"Who are *they*?" Beckhower asked.

"We don't know yet, but they sure as hell don't belong here, and we mean to make sure they don't leave with anything." Graff gave the stock of his gun a determined slap.

Beckhower looked at the gun. "But what can I do? I don't know anything about guns."

"Not many of us, do, Karl," Richard slipped effortlessly into the familiar address. "But we figure we've got to try. A man like yourself who's respected and trusted could be helpful in a lot of ways. Do you have a gun?"

Beckhower thought for a moment. "Just a small-bore, single-shot shotgun I bought to kill rats in the cellar. I haven't used it in years."

"Well, bring it."

"Bring it where?"

"We're asking volunteers to come to the old Triesenberg chapel right after nightfall." Richard squared his shoulders and lifted his chin in his own conception of command presence. "Can we count on you?"

Karl wanted to shout, Are you crazy? I'd be so clumsy and frightened you'd have to carry me. Not in a million years would I go with you.

Instead, he looked inquiringly at his wife, Anna. She ran the household, and though the question seemed vague, he supposed this fell under her jurisdiction.

Anna jutted her stern chin toward Richard and then back to her husband. "Karl will do his duty, won't you, Karl?"

Karl straightened his glasses, braced his thin shoulders as he had seen Richard do, sucked in his soft paunch, and smiled obediently at his wife.

Anna looked triumphantly at Richard. "What time should he start?"

Richard watched the interplay between husband and wife with no recognition. His marriage was yet of too short duration for him to appreciate the nuances of domination. "Don't leave until dark, and then walk or

393

ride a bicycle, and stay away from those patrols."

Richard crept out the door in the same manner as he entered, leaving Anna relishing her contribution to such a heroic effort, and her benumbed husband silently dreading his fate.

As winter's night descended on the Liechtenstein countryside like the closing of a shade, the beams of the full moon illuminated a dreary scene. For the second night, the bewildered, frightened people huddled in their cold, blacked-out homes and feared for the worst. The second night promised to be worse than the first because now they had an idea of what they faced. Hans Haas and his messengers had spread the word that what the people heard was not the reassuring voice of the prince, but the ruse of a ruthless gang intent on plundering this country which lay defenseless before them.

While Konrad and Otto returned to police headquarters with their plunder in the dim light of dusk, other men were moving, too. They moved quietly, carefully, flitting from house to house, slinking into ditches at the sight of a patrol, constantly moving toward the Triesenberg chapel. Hans and his men had done a thorough job of covering most of the countryside during the previous night and day. Although most of the men they talked to had begged off from the confrontation, citing ill health, lack of weapons, family concerns, or in a few honest cases, just plain fright, enough had volunteered so that as the roads and paths converged on the isolated, thousand-year-old chapel standing as a murky, dark outline against the hillside, a careful and expectant eye could make out many shadowy figures moving steadily toward the rendezvous. Even though the men could barely see the chapel, they knew it like their own homes: thick, white stone walls with an octagonal wooden upper story and a circular, peaked apse standing alongside like an immovable sentinel.

At this elevation, where an approaching patrol car could be seen from a great distance, the men hurried along, intent on reaching the chapel and learning what was to be asked of them.

They felt the blood-rush of excitement of a new and challenging adventure, and like all men never compelled to shed blood defending it, idealism raged strong within them. But they were also old and sensible enough to know that invulnerability is the myth of youth and that experience counts and guns kill. The general sentiment was that if any heroism was required, the next fellow should be given first chance to contribute it.

Inside the heavy stone walls of the chapel, Hans waited, his tired face making him look like an ancient Druid priest in the faint illumination of flickering candles once again burning in their age-old wall sockets. As the men slowly drifted in, they silently sat in the ancient pews or along the walls beneath the windows that had been shrouded to block the dim light from escaping.

An hour passed, two, then three; still they sat, saying little, occasionlly rustling for a more comfortable position, maybe scraping a gunstock on the stone floor or whispering a greeting as a friend or neighbor came in, but with stoical patience they awaited whatever was to come.

Finally, when about two hundred man jammed the small sanctuary, and the closeness of their bodies started to make them all sweat, even in the unheated stone dampness, Hans rose and signaled for silence, a needless act in that atmosphere of whispers and expectation. He stood in front of the altar, an eerie figure back-lit by ghostly candles. The effect was to deepen the hush and tighten nerves.

Hans cleared his throat, trying to exhale his own tension. He began in a low voice, but one that sounded like an Old Testament prophet in the stone acoustics of the chapel. "You probably want to know what you're doing here. Well, I don't know. I don't even know what I'm doing here. All anyone knows for sure is that criminals are trying to rob our country, and I'm damned mad enough to try and stop them. I don't know who they are, and it doesn't make any difference. All that counts at this point is that they have automatic rifles and seem to be pretty good at their work. Now, we're workmen, not soldiers, and it seems to me that trying to make war on experienced fighters is like trying to outplow a farmer—you're likely to be buried in a furrow. But, hell, men, we just can't let 'em come in and walk all over us. We've got to try and protect what's ours."

An anonymous voice from the back called out, "I've seen guns like that on TV. Boy, we can't stand up to that."

Hans ignored the comment, and there was silence until another voice said, "Since they haven't hurt anyone, why not just let them take what they want and leave quietly?"

Hans shook his head sadly. "I wish that was true." He searched out a familiar face. "Martin, tell them what you told me."

A big, red-faced farmer rose stiffly. "I'm Martin Bach, most of you know me, I have a farm south of Balzars, on the border. Early this morning I was watching the men who closed the border. All of a sudden they started shooting at a man trying to cross into Switzerland. They hit him and he collapsed into the old wire. Then, a Swiss officer came along and put him into the back of a Jeep. The Swiss started to argue with the men who shot him, but then he drove away taking the body with him."

A man demanded impatiently, "Who did they shoot?"

Bach continued in a faltering voice as though he didn't want to hear his own words. "As soon as it started I got my binoculars, so when the Swiss officer lifted him up, I saw who it was."

"Who?" three voices demanded in ragged unison.

"Father Hammerschmidt."

The crowd erupted in gasps and protests. One man asked, "How do you know he was dead?"

Bach shook his head with certainty. "You can tell."

Hans put his hand on the shaken Bach's shoulder who gave the appearance of feeling guilt just for reporting what he saw. "Father Hammerschmidt and I escaped together from these people when they took over the church in Vaduz last night. He told me he was going to try to reach Switzerland. Unfortunately, I believe what we just heard is true."

A worried voice interrupted him. "My wife and daughter attended that church service and they haven't been home since. Did you see them? Are they OK?"

Hans nodded. "They both were fine when I left, Walter."

Someone else asked, "How do you know they want to rob us?"

"You're from up north, Ernst, so you wouldn't have heard the explosions—a few hours ago they blew up both banks. Earlier, they were seen carrying large crates out of the art museum. It's not a question of whether they're going to rob, but how much they're going to rob."

"Have you talked to the prince?" another asked.

"The castle is guarded by more of these same people. It doesn't appear that they've gone inside, so we can consider the prince safe, but the same as a hostage."

An expectant hush fell over the worried men when one asked, "Tell us what to do, Hans."

Faced with the need for an immediate course of action, Hans seemed lost for words. Finally, he shrugged and said, "I'd be lying if I told you I knew. We're all new to this sort of thing, so let's hear some ideas."

There was a brief silence as everyone waited for the next man to speak. Finally, a short, stammering shopkeeper from Triesenberg rose to his feet, looking alternately at Hans and the crowd. "I say we send a delegation to the Swiss army at Sargans and ask them to help."

A lawyer seated nearby shook his head ruefully. "I'm afraid that wouldn't work. We don't have a defense treaty with Switzerland, and the army wouldn't move without orders from its government in Bern. That would take days at the very least. Obviously, we don't have days."

The next speaker was a rich manufacturer who stood as one accustomed to being heard and obeyed, his expensive hunting rifle held loosely in his left hand. "I say we negotiate. They've got to be reasonable people, maybe we can buy them off. Let's form a comm—"

"Herr Bruner," Hans interrupted, surprised at himself for cutting short a man he would normally pay great deference to. "These are criminals who are getting everything they want now, why should they negotiate with us? What could we give them in place of the prince's art collection and the contents of our bank vaults? All we'd be doing is alerting them to the fact that we're organized."

An old man with leathery skin and gnarled hands stood silently, waiting to be recognized. His patience testified that he was used to being ignored and wasn't too enamored of the attention of others, anyway. Finally, Hans asked, "You have something to say, old-timer?"

The old man spoke to the group with the shyness of a recluse, not afraid, but unsure of how to do it. His battered hat turned ceaselessly in his rough hands in front of him. "You men mostly don't know me. I'm Gruber, I cut wood in the mountains, don't get down much. Don't know much, either, but I seen this before."

Someone in the back stage-whispered that he should sit down and shut up, but the old men turned defiantly on his detractor. "I may be an ignorant woodcutter, but I know a hundred times more about this sort of thing than all of you put together. When I was young, I got trapped in Germany when the war broke out. Since my parents were German by birth, I got drafted and sent to Russia. Four years I spent in that Godforsaken country. Seen just about everything that concerns war. Seen the partisans. Toughest, most scary bunch of folks ever lived. The German army was more scared of the partisans than the whole Russian army.

"What I'm gettin' at is that's what you men are talkin' about being—partisans. Oh, I know, the other fellows got all the guns and experience and all that, but invaders always do. But what we've got is surprise and knowin' the lay of the land. Those are two of the three things you need to be good partisans."

A nearby voice asked, "What's the third thing?"

The old man wheeled to face his questioner. "Being ready to die." He turned back to Haas. "We can do it; we can take their guns from them, learn to use 'em, then kill 'em with their own guns. I seen it done. But plenty of us'll die tryin'. But we can win if we're ready to do that. I guess what I'm sayin' is something no one can understand without livin' it. You can't describe hell to a man, he's got to see it for himself."

Hans interrupted, "The big question, Gruber, is whether we would have a chance. Can we stand up to them?"

The old man stared silently for a long moment. "Like I said, I've seen it done, but that was by pretty determined folks. And until a man tries, he never knows. No man can say for sure he's willin' to die for something until the time comes for the dyin'. And make no mistake, that's what we're talkin' about, a lot of dyin'."

A disturbed silence fell over the room punctuated only by nervous coughing and shifting of bodies as many of the men turned to take wistful looks at the exit. The meeting was in jeopardy of breaking up when the door burst open and a boy of about ten stumbled into the chapel. He fell into the arms of a nearby man and lay there sobbing and shivering from fright and exhaustion. His clothes were ripped from running through the brush and his hands and face were an angry red from the cold. Someone said to no one in particular, "That's little Wally Diedrich, his mother runs a bakery in Vaduz."

Hans went over and gripped the boy by the shoulders. "What is it, Wally?"

The youth struggled to a sitting position and took a long moment to overcome the convulsive sobs. He finally said in a heartbroken voice, "They—they raped my sister, my mom told me to tell you that."

"Who did, Wally?"

"One of *them*. My mom told me to say that your daughters could be next. Poor Gretel won't stop crying; she doesn't say anything, she just cries."

As the word passed through the crowd, the murmurs grew angrier. One man raged, "The bastards, she's only twelve years old."

Hans and the men sat stunned. Their quiet lives had not inured them to the shock and pain of such bestiality so close to home. Their rage fed upon itself until it smothered every thought of moderation and caution and burned white-hot into every mind. The only word they would hear until this was settled: revenge. Revenge.

The child's rape had the effect of pulling from Hans' mind the final chock of restraint and released a landslide of bitterness against all the things that had conspired to make his life a day-to-day hell on earth. Now he would fight back. He raised his hand for silence and waited for the angry threats and swearing to subside. "Men, these bastards invade our country, steal our national treasures, kill our priests and rape our children. I say let's stop them."

"Tell us how," an angry voice demanded.

"How? We'll kill them, that's how," he said with an ugly snarl distorting his face. "We'll hunt them down: alone, in pairs, in groups, it doesn't matter. They have the fancy guns, but now we're going to see if they can use them."

"What are our tactics, Hans?"

"Tactics? I don't know any tactics. We'll just kill them, that'll be our tactics." He turned to the altar sitting in the shadows behind him. "I swear to almighty God that we'll get revenge."

A calm voice said from the back, "We'll fight, Hans, but don't blaspheme. Revenge belongs to God."

Knowing nothing else to do, Hans divided the men into groups of five and gave each a different destination. He checked his watch and instructed no group to act for two hours in order to allow them all to get into place. "At eleven p.m. the only order will be to kill, and keep killing until they turn and run and never come back."

Hans led his group into the darkness of night, followed by clusters of grim, silent men.

By their dress, armament, and unmartial mannerisms, the men of Liechtenstein perhaps looked a bit comical, but if Konrad and his gang could have seen them at that moment, they wouldn't have laughed.

Chapter Seventeen

Konrad had reason to be pleased with himself on this Christmas day evening. He was sitting in the police chief's chair with the chief and all his officers locked up in their own cells down the hall; he had keys in his pocket to a truck parked under triple guard just outside with a cargo consisting of inestimable millions of dollars of loot; the weather forecast for the next day was fair and sunny, perfect flying weather; all in all, a pretty nice Christmas.

He was a man almost without worries; the "almost" was the radio silence from the crew up at the ski resort. Tenelli hadn't checked in for several hours and that worried him. Maybe he should have sent more than two up there, he mulled; he certainly should have given her more than that dunce Kunst to help her. If she didn't report shortly, he'd send a patrol up to check. He was also still bothered by the killing of the priest. It was the sort of thing that superstitious people are quick to call a bad omen. But beyond that, it was the kind of act that reminds the soldier of the brutality of his chosen work and that success often depends on brutalizing weaker people. No one likes to think of himself as a bully.

Konrad forced himself to stir; sitting around worrying wouldn't solve any problems. He called Otto who was supervising the feeding of the prisoners which consisted of throwing boxes of candy bars in among the grumbling policemen, and instructed him to have a crew break into a hardware store, steal chain saws, and begin clearing telephone poles and trees along a stretch of straight highway outside Vaduz as a landing strip for the airplanes which would be landing tomorrow morning and flying them out. As usual, Otto quickly and silently absorbed his instructions and set off to make sure they were efficiently accomplished. Nodding with satisfaction, Konrad watched Otto gather four men and head out the station door. It was all going his way, but somewhere in the back of his mind a nagging doubt kept him from feeling at ease, a doubt that was threatening to grow into a premonition. It was now just a matter of waiting, and waiting seemed to take the longest time.

Every time one of the small children in the church cried, which was very often, Honi felt like her head was about to burst and her eyes were razors cutting deep wounds into her skull whenever she moved them. Although the church had been without heat the previous night and throughout this day, the breathing and body heat of more than one hundred people had raised the temperature to the sweating point, and the sweat had, in turn, joined with the stench of soiled diapers to cause an odor similar to rotten cheese. Everywhere Honi looked, she was followed by the accusing, hating eyes of those who had been penned up by herself and the female gorilla

Hendrick and forced to spend Christmas in this makeshift jail. And now another night was starting. They had gone to church and ended up in hell.

Finally, Honi approached Hendrick, laid down her rifle, held her head in her hands, and said in a near-pleading voice, "I've got to go outside; I can't take another minute."

Hendrick seemed to be measuring her, figuring out how much value Honi would be if things got rough. She considered most women to be sniveling creatures who had to spread their legs for some man to feel any power at all. She felt disgust for such weak disgraces to womanhood. Disgust, but also deep jealousy, because Honi was someone she had wanted from the first moment she had laid eyes on her. "Go on, if you're not tough enough to stand it, but goddamn it—" she pointed to the M-16 lying nearby—"don't you ever put that rifle down again. Get this straight, you're a soldier now and you keep your weapon with you at all times. If I see you without it again I'll break your jaw. Now go for your stroll, you fucking sissy."

Honi wearily slung the rifle over her shoulder and dragged herself down the church aisle, and to the accompanying swing of glaring eyes, pushed past the doors and into the sweet, cold air of evening.

She walked the deserted dark streets for an hour, trying to clear her mind of the guilt of what she had allowed herself to become a part of. She walked by the banks with the shattered windows and smoke-blackened walls, past the museums with broken doors standing wide open. She reached for the door of the stamp museum to close it, but quickly realized the pointlessness of doing that. She looked up at houses rising on the hills around her and sadly thought of the people behind the dark windows, people huddled with fear, good people, plain people—her people—who had done nothing to invite this desecration of their land. She shuddered and walked on.

Honi could see light shining from inside the police station as the kerosene lamps that had been rigged formed an irridescent glow in contrast to the darkened street. Suddenly, she tensed as she saw on the edges of that glow a huge shape walking slowly toward her. She stepped into the nearest doorway and pushed herself against the building wall as the shape disappeared from view but was replaced by steady, heavy footsteps crunching in the snow. Closer and closer the steps came, becoming steadily louder until a massive shadow crept into view and filled the doorway. Even the dim light of nightfall was blackened by the shape. The steam of a harsh breath felt warm and moist on her face.

Honi didn't open her eyes until he spoke, then almost sagged to her knees in relief. Angus! Only Angus! Dimly she realized that she had allowed the approach of this gentle man to personify all the ugliness and fear that she was feeling and carrying with her. She threw her arms around his neck and cried out, "Oh, Angus, you scared me. Thank God it's you."

He held her a bit awkwardly and patted her shoulder. "I guess we all have some cause to feel afraid," he said in a sad voice that made her pull back and look at his face. The funny man was gone and in his place was a man who had aged years in the last two days. His body drooped like a man who carried a tremendous weight, not on his shoulders, but inside, where the burden presses most heavily. She sighed and gripped his shoulders, not needing to ask the cause of his grief.

"Why did we let this happen, Angus?" she asked of herself as well as him.

"Him, I guess. We both did it because we love the jerk, and he thought he had to prove something by playing soldier again. Sometimes I wonder if he hates the entire world or just himself. We lied to ourselves that we could try and please him without hurting other people. Just one look around here is proof of our stupidity. I guess we just didn't understand enough of what was going to happen." His eyes grew misty. "I don't want to hurt anyone. I'm just a big, fat, funny guy. If I'd had any idea what would happen to that priest, I'd ha—"

Honi felt wire tighten around her heart. She gripped his arms so tight that even he felt the pressure through the heavy coat and his brawn. "What priest? What happened, Angus? Tell me!"

He looked at her blankly. "Haven't you heard? The priest, Hammer . . . Hammer-something, was killed by some of our men when he tried to cross the border. Konrad was really mad when . . ."

His speech faded when he realized her moan of anguish was followed by a dead faint and she collapsed limply into his arms. Clumsily, he laid her in the doorway in a position that looked comfortable and leaned back to try and figure out what to do next.

He wasn't much better off. He closed his eyes and felt the cold sweat drip down his face. He was about to try and revive Honi when his attention was caught by a dim light and what sounded like a whimper from the other side of the door. Curious, he tried the knob. It opened. Silently, Angus stepped inside. The darkened room appeared to be the front of a bakery shop with a large display case

407

running its width and the sugar-yeast smell of baked goods wafting pleasantly through the air. It was empty, but through an ajar door that led to the back, Angus could hear the faint sounds of scuffling. Intrigued, he softly approached the door and gently pushed it open. The only light in the room was a discarded flashlight, the light that had first attracted his attention; it had been put aside, its beam aimed randomly at a far wall, illuminating the entire room in the faint glow of its reflection. At first, Angus couldn't define the strange scene before him because the bits and pieces fit no pattern in his experience. But gradually shapes and motion became recognizable and he shrank back in horror as though he were witnessing the acting out of a Goya painting in the midst of hell. In one corner lay a slim, blond woman of about fifty wearing a baker's white smock. She was gagged and both hands were tied to a water pipe. She was struggling frantically against the rope with such pain on her face that Angus felt like a cold wind had blown over his soul. Her eyes flashed with hatred, but also with a terrible, forlorn despair that made her face twist with the pain it carried. She was torn between having to look and desperately not wanting to. Angus could see the blood running down her arms where she had fought to free herself. He followed her eyes across the room to the source of her agony.

Angus' soul seemed to wither from the evil his eyes exposed it to.

She was a small, blond girl, about twelve, pinned heavily by the bulk that covered her. All he could see was her face, but that was enough to make Angus want to vomit. She was lying on a hastily thrown together pallet of flour sacks and was crying and pushing futilely against the weight that pressed down upon her. No words came from her, but her sobs spoke a language of their own—a pitiful and desperate begging for mercy, a helpless protest against an evil she didn't understand, a prayer that her pain would go away.

On top of the girl, his body covering her like a monstrous leech, was a man. His pants were pulled down to his ankles and he had forced himself between her thin, white legs and was thrusting furiously. All Angus could see was the bulk of the man, but from his sadistic grunts of passion and mutterings of pleasure, and also from a gut feeling he couldn't pinpoint, Angus knew the man was Emil Damser. He listened in paralyzing horror as Damser spoke feverishly to the girl, oblivious to her pain and sobs. "Don't pretend you don't like it, baby. You'll be able to tell 'em you lost your cherry to a fucking machine named Damser. Is it good, baby?"

Angus could take it no longer. "For God's sake, stop it," he shouted. Running over, he pulled at Damser's shoulder, catching him by surprise, and managed to roll the brute off the girl and onto his back. Angus could see by the dim light that the front of the girl was covered by blood from belly to knees. Damser, too, seemed to have been wallowing in it. His genitals were smeared red; his thick pubic hair was matted with blood.

Damser recovered from his surprise in an instant and his fat face blotched with fury. Snarling, he gave Angus a vicious shove and struggled to his feet, trying to pull his pants up as he did so.

Angus was sent sprawling and clattering into baking equipment. By the time he recovered his feet, he could see the thick silhouette of Damser advancing on him, slowly waving the glittering blade of a long, thin knife.

All other thoughts were abandoned as one truth alone bit into his mind like a laser—this man was about to kill him, bury that icy blade into his guts and watch the life spill out. In terror, Angus stumbled away from the methodically advancing specter. He looked for a weapon, but all he could find were some light cookie tins which he clumsily threw at Damser who didn't even bother to duck as he shrugged them off. Then Angus was trapped in a corner, and Damser was right in front of him, his foul breath and mean eyes filling Angus' senses. Then, with a sadistic snarl, he struck. Angus put his hands out to protect his stomach, but the razorlike knife sliced through his fingers like hamburger and into his soft gut. He was surprised a little at how it felt, sort of like a sharp gas pain, but that sensation lasted only a split second; it was replaced by a great, vast malaise, a tiredness deeper than any he had known. He felt his legs get rubbery and holding his eyes open took all his strength and will power. He wanted, needed, to lie down, and so he slid to the floor.

Honi's eyelids fluttered and she stirred as her blood pressure slowly rebounded from the shocking news of the priest's killing that had sent it plummeting and had carried her into unconsciousness. It took a moment for her to clear the mist from her mind and to remember why she was lying in a dark doorway in the snow. As her bearings returned, she looked around for Angus whom she had last seen reaching out for her as the lights of her mind went dark. She still wasn't thinking clearly, but she noticed the door in front of her was ajar, and hearing a scuffling noise coming from within, assumed that Angus was inside.

With the timidity of one reluctant to enter another's door uninvited, she tentatively pushed it open and called softly, "Angus?" She called again, slightly louder, "Angus?" She was startled by a loud, agonizing groan and moved quickly toward the sound and found herself in the back room of the bakery. It took her several moments to comprehend the scene in front of her, but as the sobbing girl, the bound mother, the bleeding Angus, and the leering Damser came together in a montage of horror, Honi screamed in protest, her already battered mind rebelling at this new abuse.

Damser watched her enter the room with undisguised glee, like a glutton awaiting dessert. "Hey, bitch," he gloated, "let's show this brat how two experts fuck." He made a quick move and blocked Honi off from the only exit, then started a leisurely stalk toward her, knowing she had no escape. Honi scrambled behind a long counter, realizing it would give her no safety, but having no place else to run. In an instant, Damser was facing her across the narrow counter top. Every time she would start to move, he would dart in the same direction, howling with joy like a small child with a favorite toy. At any time he could have reached across and grabbed her in his gorilla arms, but he was in no hurry, only wanting to tease his prey and prolong the pleasure.

Damser laughed harshly. "You're going to get fucked to death, you blond bitch. At least you'll know your last fuck was your best." Spittle ran down his rubbery chin in anticipation, then his mind shifted and his face grew hard. "Where's that asshole Konrad when you need him?" He sneered and fingered the side of his head as though it were still sore. "That bastard is gonna pay for

411

hitting me. You're gonna pay for him now, but his turn'll come."

He grabbed across the counter and seized her arms in an iron grip. Inexorably he drew her struggling body closer as though she were a helpless child. She thrashed about wildly as she felt him pulling her onto the counter. His face drew near hers, sickening her with the smell of stale garlic breath coming from his slobbering mouth. Closer and closer he came until their faces were almost touching. In a moment, he would have her flat on the counter, and then it would be all over. In desperation, she butted her forehead into the bridge of his nose and felt the squish of soft cartilage giving way accompanied by a howl of pain. He released her to gingerly rub his bleeding nose, and she threw herself into the farthest corner, temporarily free, but more trapped than ever. As she pressed against the wall, she felt a sharp pain in her back. Instinctively reaching back to remove what was bothering her, she felt the stock of the unfamiliar and forgotten M-16 she still carried on her shoulder. Fumbling with haste and sweat-slippery hands to free the rifle's strap, she watched frantically as Damser started around the edge of the counter and lumbered toward her, his laugh now turned to growls of pained rage. She managed to free the rifle and awkwardly swung it in the close confines of her corner to point at Damser now only a few feet away.

She pulled the trigger. Nothing. She pulled again in desperation. Nothing. He was almost on her, closer by the second. The safety. She remembered that the safety was engaged. She fumbled desperately for the tiny lever. After what seemed like a lifetime, she located and flicked it. But Damser was already on her, his heavy knee crushing her chest and his strong hand pulling the rifle barrel out of her hands. Just before the rifle left her hands she managed to pull the trigger. The gun jumped in her hands and the room lit up with blinding muzzle flashes. The report of the gun in such close quarters numbed her ears and left her head ringing.

In the brief moment Honi had depressed the trigger, a dozen rounds had been fired into Damser's neck and lower face from only inches away. He was thrown back away from Honi, landing in a grotesque heap several feet away. The massed shot pattern had almost decapitated him; his head hung by a few neck muscles as severed arteries drained blood onto the bakery floor instead of into a twisted brain that no longer needed it.

But Honi didn't see the carnage that had been the man who intended to rape and kill her. She only knew the danger had gone away, replaced by the stinging stink of cordite, and she collapsed into a protective fetal position, trying to block out all the evil that had taken over her life.

One of Konrad's patrol cars had been passing within a couple of hundred meters of the bakery when the muffled sounds of the M-16 shots caused the two men inside to skid to a stop and scramble to protected positions behind the car. When no more shots were heard, the driver carefully re-entered the car and radioed headquarters to report the incident. Immediately, Konrad, Otto and several other men came running to the scene, half motivated by wanting to cut off trouble before it spread, half to relieve the boredom of waiting.

Konrad hurriedly conferred with the patrol, and then,

413

after a careful reconnoiter of the now-quiet building, led his men into the bakery, guns at the ready. The shop was deathly still except for the young girl's sobs, muffled now as she buried her face in her still-tied mother's lap, and Angus' gargling attempts to breathe. The beams of powerful flashlights swept through the room, cutting through the drifting gun smoke to reveal the holocaust that had turned a simple bakery into a chamber of horrors.

Konrad knelt beside Angus with a look of shock and disbelief on his face. Laying aside his rifle and flashlight, he turned to Otto and said, pleadingly, "Get that doctor here, quick." He did his best to make Angus comfortable, putting a wadded-up towel under his head and trying to staunch the blood flow with another.

Sensing a presence, Angus laboriously lifted his eyelids and made a futile attempt to focus on the blurred form that hovered over him. But a voice crept through the thickening walls of approaching death and touched what remained of his senses. Konrad. He tried to smile, but hadn't the strength. Falteringly, he lifted his hand to be immediately grasped by Konrad. There was something he had to say to Konrad, an important message he had to give him. Angus struggled to remember, but only one word came to his mind. Straining with all his remaining strength, he managed to whisper it.

"Quit."

Konrad would have given his own life at that moment to save Angus', but to this request he could only forlornly shake his head. "I can't," he said. "I don't know how."

Angus was fading fast and even the tenuous grip he had on Konrad's presence was slipping through the fingers of his mind. The dark form before his eyes slowly dissolved and was replaced by the bright, sharp image of a barroom. It was a dark night and Angus was standing outside looking through the open door. Inside, seated at a table, were Konrad, Imogene and Manny, their laughing faces turning alternately red and yellow by a flashing beer sign behind them. He saw a fourth chair at the table with a huge, frosted stein of beer sitting before it. Angus saw himself smiling with anticipation as he started to walk into the bar to join his three friends. But something went wrong—when he tried to take a step, the ground beneath his feet suddenly turned into quicksand. He struggled to free himself, but the effort only ensnared him more firmly in the clinging mud. In panic, he fought the gluelike ooze, but he continued to sink. He watched helplessly as first his knees disappeared, then his whole lower body, then it was up to his armpits and imprisoned his arms. He saw himself take a final look inside the bar where his three friends were still happily chatting in the red and yellow glow, unknowing of his plight.

The quicksand was up to his neck now, and in desperation he finally managed to cry out. "Konrad, help me!" escaped from his throat with an anguished wail of doom. Then, only blackness remained.

Konrad felt Angus' body shudder and go limp, and his last words lingered in the room like an accusing finger.

Konrad bowed his head and squeezed his eyes shut. He couldn't show tears to the hard-bitten men who silently surrounded the scene. When he closed his eyes, Angus' face disappeared, only to be replaced by Willie Mac Russell's. His long-dead radioman looked up and laughed. "Hi, Lieutenant, long time no see. Hey, you got another one killed! Man, trusting you is risky business. I'm taking

415

poor old Angus' place here for a little while. He went off to dig hisself a grave; gonna put it right next to mine. Old Angus'll fit into a hole real comfortable soon as he gets down to skeleton size."

Konrad opened his eyes in horror, but the mocking black face didn't disappear. "I spoke to the cemetery managers, Lieutenant, they're gonna let me reserve several more graves right next to mine and Angus'. Told 'em we'd probably need lots of room, that you still had plenty of friends who trusted you." Willie Mac winked. "See you real soon, Lieutenant."

Grief and regret washed over Konrad like a flood tide, and he turned his face upward and cried out, "God, help me."

Otto reached down with one hand to the frozen Konrad and raised him roughly under the armpit as the other men looked at each other with embarrassment and doubt. Otto saw with relief that Konrad's eyes were once more alert and clear. If the men thought their commander was a man who would go into a trance just at the sight of a dead man, and they suspected his nerve or backbone, then a mutiny was the next thing that would happen.

As Konrad regained his feet, the local doctor looked briefly at Angus and walked away. "Nothing I can do for that one," he said without regret.

Konrad said to Otto, "I want him buried."

Otto shook his head vigorously and whispered, almost hissed. "No goddamn way. These men aren't sentimentalists, and they're sure as hell not going to dig a hole in frozen ground just to plant your buddy. You'll have a rebellion on your hands if you try to force them." He glanced unemotionally at the body. "He's as well off

416

there as any place you could put him."

The argument was interrupted by the little girl's mother who had been released by the doctor. Her daughter clung to her neck with white-knuckle terror and her sobbing, if anything, was more frantic. The mother's tight lips looked bloodless and there was an ominous glint of hatred in her eyes that surpassed rage. "They tell me you're the one responsible for this." She gestured at the room, her sweeping arm encompassing the wrecked scene, the bodies of Angus and Damser, and the form of Honi still lying in her corner. Th mother riveted a look of bitterness on Konrad's face and clasped her little girl tighter. "You'll pay for this. I don't know how or when, but God won't rest until everything you've done to others is done to you."

Otto motioned for one of the men to lead the mother away, then went over to Honi and helped her to her feet. Honi seemed to have trouble standing. Though she didn't appear hurt, her face carried a dazed, disbelieving look and she meekly allowed Otto to guide her toward the door. Otto motioned for the other men to leave before him, then turned back to Konrad, and said, "We're damned lucky we're almost out of this, it's turning bad fast."

Chapter Eighteen

They struck first shortly after midnight on a lonely, winding road outside the resort village of Steg high in the foothills.

The four men watched the headlights approach in the distance far below them. Two were young farmers standing ill at ease and holding their shotguns like they were covered with germs. They looked expectantly at Walter Stein whom they naturally thought would know what to do. Stein had earned their grudging admiration by convincingly filling the role of oversize town bully whose bragging was made credible by never being challenged. The fourth man, schoolteacher Karl Beckhower, could have been invisible for all the attention he was given.

One of the young farmers didn't help matters any when he said, "I hear these guys are all ex-commandos and have submachine guns." In the next breath, with the innocence of the young, he turned to the bully he held in fear, if not awe, and asked, "What should we do, Walter?"

Stein licked his lips nervously and darted a glance around the group. "Maybe there's nothing we can do. We don't want to go off half cocked in this thing. I think we better wait for reinforcements."

Karl didn't want to be pushy, but no one else seemed to have any ideas, so he squared away his glasses, cleared his throat, and said, deferentially, "Excuse me, gentlemen, may I offer an opinion?"

The others looked at him blankly, which he took for assent. "I guess the first thing we have to do is stop their car." He looked around and saw several logs in a nearby field. He pointed them out and suggested a barricade in the middle of the road. Having no other plans, and seeing no danger, at least in going that far, the others agreed. It took only a few moments for the four of them to carry the logs to the road and arrange them in a random crisscross pattern high enough to easily stop the small Volkswagen that was coming closer and closer.

When the car was almost to the last curve, at Karl's urging, the men paired off and jumped into ditches on opposite sides of the road and waited nervously as the car screeched to a halt at the barricade's edge.

Since the rough mountain winter often tossed logs around like twigs, the two men in the car suspected nothing as they casually left their commandeered police car to remove the obstacle. The driver left his rifle in the car and the other man casually slung his over a shoulder. Together, they started throwing logs off to one side of the road, grumbling all the while about not hiring on as laborers and mindlessly cursing the mountain weather.

Karl huddled in his ditch and felt like he was about to meet a new school principal. His mouth was dry and his hands were shaking as he watched the two strangers work. When they had cleared all but one log, he knew the time had come to act, and since no one else seemed inclined to take the initiative, he uttered a short prayer, checked his old gun, and jumped to his feet at the side of the road.

The two surprised men dropped the log they were holding and for a long moment stared at him in disbelief. Then, just as Karl was trying to find the voice to tell them to put their arms in the air, one man grabbed for his slung rifle. He had it half off his shoulder when Karl pulled the trigger and the shotgun roared and bucked in his hands. The rifle flew out of the man's hands and he cartwheeled into the ditch like a rag doll. The action stunned Karl's companions. Even though they had professed to know what could happen, the shock of seeing a man cut down by a shotgun blast froze their senses and left them staring, mute witnesses to their own violence.

As he examined the dead man, Karl wondered why dead men look so different than live ones. He checked his hands and saw they were no longer shaking and wondered why he didn't feel guilt or remorse. Is this shock, he asked himself, or am I just a natural killer? He realized that all this had transpired without anyone saying a word, but no words seemed necessary to describe the pantomime of death.

Karl walked over to the driver who stood with his hands high and looking at his strange, bookish-appearing assailant with the fear of not knowing if he, too, were going to be lying crumpled in the ditch in a moment. Karl looked at him, sensed the fear and was exhilarated by it. What a great feeling to be respected as a man who can handle himself, he thought happily.

Karl gestured to his three companions who were

standing awkwardly off to one side to come and listen as the shaken driver in a quavering voice explained at Karl's urging the workings of the M-16. After tying the man's hands and detailing a meek Walter Stein to lead him off to captivity in a nearby barn, Karl faced the young farmers who gaped at him as if he had just shed his clothes to reveal Superman. Finally, one of them asked, "What do we do now, Herr Beckhower?"

Karl's answer was fast and confident as he lifted both hands, each holding an M-16. "Let's go find more of them, what else?"

Richard Graff walked several steps ahead of his four companions who willingly deferred to the jaunty young man with the springy step and the gun held easily in his hand like an extension of his body. He looked like a poster for a revolutionary army: wind-burned, rippling muscles, tight-fitting work clothes and the smile of one about to do righteous work.

Richard luxuriated in his private visions of himself as the man of arms, the stalwart who steps forward to defend the people. He grinned happily; the gun felt comfortable and snugly heavy. All that was needed to make his daydreams real were some enemies, the ones whose invasion of his country made it possible for him to learn such great things about himself, to learn that soldiering was his true calling. From long glances in every available mirror, he knew he looked the part, he felt the part, now all he needed was the chance to fill the part.

Richard was engrossed in his fantasies to the exclusion of all else, and so trusting were his companions in this make-believe soldier that they plodded along serenely in the certian faith that his footsteps were the true path.

Their innocence betrayed them. As they ambled through the main street of the village of Ruggell in the revealing light of a full moon, it never occurred to them that other eyes were following their shambling progress, trained eyes, eyes that crinkled in fierce amusement at their amateur plodding. They had reached the town square when the lights hit them like lasers. They stared dumbfounded into the Volkswagen headlights that had suddenly trapped them like rabbits in their glare. They could see the ominous outlines of two people leaning on the front fenders. A voice boomed gruffly out of the loudspeaker, "OK, you damn sod-busters, throw down those guns and raise your hands, and do it fast or we'll shoot."

The men meant to comply, but one of them, a dull-witted carpenter's apprentice named Adam Hossler, suddenly panicked, threw down his rifle and sprinted for the protection of a nearby building. His panic was contagious and the three men standing next to him mindlessly fled in all directions as their discarded weapons clattered in the street. Their stupid reaction caught the two men standing by the Volkswagen in surprise, and the delayed flurry of shots only managed to speed them on their way as they disappeared into the surrounding buildings like squirrels into holes.

Richard hadn't moved because he hadn't the courage to run. He stared into the headlights that seemed to be staring back at him with a malevolent personality of their own. The bravado shriveled in his heart like burning paper. In his soldier fantasies, he hadn't allowed for the fact that guns point both ways. He felt the bitter gall of fear in his mouth, felt it tighten his throat like a hangman's noose. His teeth started chattering and steam rose from the front of his pants as the hot urine from his berserk bladder reached the cold air, but he was unaware; Richard's mind allowed no distractions from the terror that gripped it.

The clammy, tight band of fear encircled him like a powerful snake. He wanted to call out and tell them he was surrendering and please not to shoot, but the tightness took his voice and left only his pleading eyes to tell the story that all he wanted was to go on living, that he would never again pick up a weapon, that if he could only go home to his family, he would never again be a threat to anyone.

But the two men by the car couldn't read his eyes, all they could see was the weapon in his hand, and they called out for him to drop it and raise his hands.

Richard was eager to comply; he wanted nothing more than to please these men, to befriend them. In his haste, his fear-frozen brain forgot about the rifle, and as his arms rose, the gun did also, and pointed threateningly at the headlights.

The clattering of the simultaneous automatic fire from the two men echoed hollowly through the narrow streets, giving harsh voice to the steel-jacketed slugs that ripped Richard Graff apart and left him heaped in a spreading pool of blood, a dead actor in a drama in which he was badly miscast.

In the shadows, lying hidden among the refuse and garbage cans of a nearby alley, two of Richard's companions watched in horror as the man they admired was gunned down in the street. Adam Hossler's own fear was forgotten as he watched the scene with tears in his eyes. He turned to the youth next to him, and said, "Did you see that? Richard took them on all by himself. That was the bravest thing I've ever seen. Richard's a hero; he died for his country." Hossler swallowed hard and said in a shaky voice, "We'll avenge you, Richard."

Glazer and Harndt had been cruising the roads of Liechtenstein nonstop in the police car for more than twenty-four hours playing the same monotonous recording of the prince over and over until they had it memorized. Not a single Liechtensteiner had shown his face other than peering from behind closed curtains, and they were bored and tired. They had tried alternate sleeping, but the narrow seats in the small car plus the droning loudspeaker made the effort fitful at best.

They didn't have much to talk about. Glazer had been a career army non-com until he was pensioned with a bad back and turned to minor crime to help make ends meet. Harndt, however, was a hard-core criminal, a burglar when the opportunity arose, anything else when necessity demanded. Glazer wasn't comfortable with such a hard ass, and Harndt scorned his partner as an amateur. Neither had ever seen combat which was why Konrad had selected them for the errand-boy assignment of checking on Tenelli and Kunst whose radio silence he attributed to transmission difficulty in the mountains.

The driving was slow up the narrow, winding mountain road; in the light of the full moon they could see the glint of ice forming on the pavement as the cold of midnight set in. Their concentration on the road and the drugging effects of hours of boredom provided little opportunity to mentally prepare for whatever they might

424

find as the dark outline of the lodge came into view. Everything seemed quiet and in order as they slowly drove up to the front door and parked, left the car running to retain the heater's warmth, and stepped into their own headlights, rifles held casually at their knees.

Lorenzo and Georgio blinked in disbelief from their hiding places as the two men stood nonchalantly in the glare and tried to figure out which way to turn. Lorenzo called out, "Throw down your weapons and get your hands up."

Both men reacted in panic, swinging their rifles in wide arcs and pouring dozens of bullets into nearby cars and mountainsides, but not bothering to get out of the light.

It was almost with pangs of regret that Lorenzo and Georgio took quick aim on the pair, like hunters sighting in on a wounded deer, but even fools had to be taken seriously when armed with M-16s, so the two gently squeezed off several rounds, all of which found their marks in the bodies of Glazer and Harndt.

The echoes of gunfire died out, and the crunch of snow was the only sound as the men approached their quarry sprawled in the awkward puppet-positions of the dead. They leaned over and picked up the M-16s out of the snow where they had fallen from lifeless hands. Georgio shook his head. "I'm not proud of doing that," he said sadly. "Jesus, that was about as tough as shooting the neighbor's cat. If that's the best they can do, they better stick to making war on farmers."

Lisel Hendrick paced angrily up and down the front of the church, the ring of her footsteps bouncing hollowly off the stone walls and mingling with the fussing of small children and snores of their parents as they tried to sleep on the hard pews.

"Goddamnit," she groused to herself, "where is that blond bitch?" Honi had taken a walk several hours ago and had never returned, leaving Hendrick alone with her one-hundred-plus hostages. Not that they were a problem, the parents were too busy trying to placate their irritable, hungry children to defy Hendrick, but she didn't like being trapped in this creepy mausoleum with squalling brats while that silly broad amused herself. Her irritation was intensified by the fact that she enjoyed being around Honi, liked to watch her ass swing when she walked, like to imagine being burrowed deep in those soft thighs. It really pissed her off that good-looking women like Honi almost always preferred men, would rather have some stupid-looking cock in them than really being loved by someone like Hendrick. She shook her head in disgust. What a waste, she thought.

Her daydreams were shattered by the wails of a small child whose discomfort didn't defer to the mean-looking woman with the gun. "Shut that fucking kid up," Hendrick screamed at the mother who was frantically trying to hush the child. Hendrick swung the rifle menacingly in their direction. She loved this gun; it was better than any cock ever grown. She felt strong and dominating with it, enjoyed the look she saw on people's faces when she pointed it at them.

She resumed her pacing and fumed about such a candy-ass assignment. She was as good as any man Konrad hired, but did any of them get stuck wet-nursing a bunch of fucking kids in a stupid joint like this? Even that cunt Tenelli was sent up to the ski resort.

She reached the stone wall of the church and wheeled

426

to continue her pacing in the opposite direction. Her attention was caught by the image of a stained-glass shepherd in a large window high up the wall. The bearded, robed figure was standing among his flock of contented sheep grazing on a lush hillside, but the shepherd was staring beyond the animals and directly into the eyes of Hendrick. The moonlight softly illuminated his strong face and made his red-jewel eyes glitter as they locked onto hers, an authority figure that made Hendrick grind her teeth in resentment. The ancient man made of glass reminded her of her father with his haughty, condemning manner, demanding that she be something she wasn't, making her feel like shit just because she was different.

Impulsively, she swung the M-16 toward the window and shouted to no one in particular, "This is what I do to assholes like that in real life." She fired a dozen rounds into the window, neatly decapitating the shepherd and blowing away several sheep. The bullets neatly jigsawed the center of the large window, so that a pie-shaped fragment of the heavy glass, about twenty feet in circumference, was broken loose. For a brief moment, the glass seemed to teeter, then with Hendrick looking up in horror, it fell.

To those watching, the glass seemed to take a long time in its tumbling glide. As they would later replay it in their minds, the scene was in slow motion—the glass turning in air, glinting faintly in the soft light of the bright moon, and Hendrick looking up, helplessly trapped by the force she had unleashed.

The glass came down directly on her head and the protective arms she had thrown up in futility at the last moment. The lead edge carved through her skull like a cleaver through a tomato, sounding like heavy knuckles rapping on wood. Her body lay among a million glinting shards of brightly colored glass swimming in pools of blood. An old man shuffled up and threw a blanket over the body to prevent the children from seeing. He stepped back and looked with rheumy eyes at the shapeless mound with blood already seeping through the cloth. He made the sign of the cross with gnarled fingers. "God will not be mocked," he said solemnly, not bothering to conceal the triumph in his voice.

The hate in Hans Haas was the odor of a dead thing in his nostrils and a fire on his brain. He lay still in the snow and let the cold creep into his body like water into a sponge, but he didn't feel it, so great was his concentration on the two men he had been watching for a half-hour. The only sensation he felt was the comforting weight of the big shotgun in his hands. He knew his eight companions were sitting hunched over in a small copse about three hundred yards behind him grumbling about the time he was taking, but he didn't care, he wanted this to be right.

The men being watched by Hans were unaware of anything except their desire to drive away from this spooky place. They had been stationed by Konrad to guard the prince's castle with the royal family confined inside. Not a sound came from the ancient stone structure behind them, and the huge fairy-tale-like building seemed to hover threateningly as though it were watching them, ready to pounce. It gave the guards, two north German hoodlums whose names Konrad never really learned, a sense of foreboding that magnified their isolation as the hours passed. What was left of their spirits was stripped away by the unrelenting cold wind that swooped out of the Alps and chafed their faces and made their bones ache. Their discomfort and self-pity had lulled their watchfulness until their sentry duties were all but ignored. Hans could hear them grumbling loudly about the cold, their assignment, Konrad, Liechtenstein, the world, fate and life. One thing they were not worrying about was the presence of someone like him hiding a few yards away, especially not at two a.m.

Every few minutes, one would get in, start the car and run the heater for a short time to get warm. Hans watched the car's interior light blink off and on with enough regularity to know they were changing places every ten minutes. He decided the next time they changed, he would wait eight minutes and then move, figuring the one outside would be most preoccupied with the cold and the one inside would be most relaxed, giving his approach the best chance to avoid detection.

Hans checked his watch and started to move forward; he didn't signal his companions because he wanted to do this himself. It was the only thing that could sate, at least temporarily, the terrible anger he felt, not only toward these men who would dare rape his country, but against all the frustrations, hurts and disappointments that had for years bedeviled his life. Here was an opportunity to smash back at the world and all the people that had made his life such a mockery of happiness.

He was now only a few feet from the careless and unsuspecting sentries. His fingers clenched and unclenched in anticipation. He felt a growl building in his chest, eager to leap from his throat in fury. He tensed as

429

the car light went on again and the man inside stepped out, holding the door open and framing himself and his partner in the interior light. Hans raised the shotgun. He waited until the men were lined up together down the twin barrels of the gun, then he pulled both triggers.

The deafening blast threw the nearest man over the hood of the car like a strong wind blowing a piece of paper. The man disintegrated in mid-air, the pulpy mess of his head going over the car's roof and the rest of his mashed body falling in a heap a few feet away.

The second man had been shielded from the blast by his unfortunate partner and had only been stunned by a few pellets, but it was enough to send him reeling. Hans never let him recover. As the man stumbled around in shock, Hans closed on him quickly from behind and neatly slipped the shotgun over his head and under his chin. The man grabbed at the barrel, but Hans shifted the long gun to the bend of his elbows and clasped hands behind the man's head giving him a full nelson on the man with the pressure on the gun barrel under his chin. The man would have died a slow death, but Hans didn't wait; one vicious tug and the trigger guard tore out the man's throat. A strangled cry was cut short and the man went limp.

Hans was wiping the trigger guard with a handkerchief when his followers timidly walked up. One of them, Adolph Garn, was an accountant of about fifty, known by few people because he spent most of his free time serving in the Protestant church in this heavily Catholic country. Next to him was his son, Lindo, a lad of barely nineteen whose outlook on life was limited by the demands of a zealously strict father. The two looked silently at the carnage until Lindo threw a hand to his mouth and doubled over retching. His father looked fiercely at Hans, his glasses steaming in the cold but not obscuring the fierce glare in his eyes. He spoke angry words that he spit out like a bitter taste. "I saw the whole thing, Hans. You didn't have to kill them. You had the drop on them; they would have had to surrender. Instead, you killed two men in cold blood. Why? Why couldn't you have just captured them?" His eyes burned with indignation and his lips formed a thin slit in his face. "This can't have God's blessing."

Hans ignored the older man while he finished cleaning the shotgun. Finally, he returned Garn's glare with matching intensity. "I don't have to answer to a milksop like you. We came out here to kill these bastards, and I just showed you how while you were hiding in the bushes. If you don't like my methods, take off, run back home to your old lady."

The elder Garn studied him in silence, then nodded his head. "I think I'll do that. I also want to stop these men, but not by being an assassin. I hope God forgives you for what you've done, forgives and stops you, because I can't do either."

Garn started walking away, his shoulders hunched in defeat and sorrow. When he passed Lindo leaning limply against the car with his face covered in sweat from the strain of vomiting, he said soothingly to the youth, "Come on, son, let's go home."

Lindo stared defiantly at his father and fiercely shook his head. "You do what you want, but I'm not leaving. I'm a man now, and I'll do what I want." Turning his back on his father, he looked squarely at Hans and said, "I'll stick with you, Hans. I won't puke anymore, it just took me one time to get used to it." He shook his small-bore hunting rifle enthusiastically. "Let's go get us some more."

Hans detailed the remaining men to guard the castle, then moved swiftly down the road with Lindo shambling behind while a hunched-over Adolph Garn dejectedly disappeared in the opposite direction.

Although Konrad's gang had the advantage of experience and armament, those factors were offset by the element of surprise, the cover of darkness, and the determination of the Liechtensteiners to defend their homeland during that Christmas night of fighting. Time after time, a patrol car would slowly round a corner on a village street and be met with a head-on shotgun blast from a basement window just a few meters away, or one of Konrad's border crossing guards would be the target of a sniper plinking away from two hundred meters with a small-caliber squirrel gun.

In a rage like that of a bear tormented by a terrier, Konrad's men struck back in fury. The furtive attacks against them would be met with fusillades of automatic rifle fire and outraged curses. On several occasions, the amateurish tactics of the Liechtensteiners caused them to blunder into trapped, dead-end positions where their enemies gunned them down mercilessly.

Within just a few hours, both sides had incurred heavy losses, but with every success, the men of Liechtenstein grew bolder, as though amazed that their adversaries also spilled red blood, felt pain and died.

The second dawn of Konrad's takeover began with gray rays breaking up the shadows on Otto's face and making him look like a Yousef Karsh black-and-white portrait of a tired, troubled old man. He was studying figures he had scribbled and frowning as he slowly walked

432

toward Konrad who was intently staring at a map.

"Doesn't look good, chief," Otto said glumly. "The ducks are shooting back pretty effectively. According to what I can get from radio reports—or radio silence—the guerrillas have killed or put out of action fourteen of our people and—this is even more sketchy—we've gotten ten of them. They've also taken control of the prince's castle which would make it pretty damn tough to take him hostage. So scratch that idea." He released the paper and watched it flutter to a rest on the table in front of Konrad. He mournfully shook his head. "I've fought partisans in Russia and guerrillas in Algeria. People will always fight when you threaten what they believe in. I'm not surprised they're fighting us, just that they're doing it so quickly."

Konrad seemed professionally preoccupied, but one knowing him well would have noticed some little things: His mouth sagged in thin lines of bitterness, his eyes had a red, insomniac look, and there was an overall sense of sadness and defeat about the man, the whole of which exceeded the sum of the identifiable parts. He wasn't a beaten man, only one for whom winning seemed to have lost its flavor.

Konrad squinted in deep thought. "Any sign that the Swiss are moving?"

"Our post at the Fort Sargans border crossing is still intact and they say everything's quiet on the other side."

Konrad nodded. "Good, the operation still looks very positive. The weather report is excellent, as we expected; our force is still cohesive; we've secured the loot we came for."

Konrad motioned for Otto to look at the map with him. "There's no point in continuing our patrols, since the locals are attacking. Let's pull all the men back to a perimeter defense along this stretch of road we cleared last night for a runway. Once we have it totally secured, I'll send the message for the planes and they'll be here in an hour."

Otto nodded vigorous agreement. "With our fire-power, maybe they'll stay a healthy distance until we get the hell out of this place. I'll radio all units to pull back to that point." He paused as though a dark thought had just intruded on his optimism. "I just hope we're not creating a trap for ourselves."

Chapter Nineteen

Andre Wittenburg sat behind his modest desk in the foreign intelligence office and alternately rubbed his red-rimmed eyes and stared at the evidence he had accumulated over the course of Christmas day. It was an impressive amount, thanks to that anonymous phone call. But he knew that no matter how strong the evidence was, unless something was done fast, it would be just so much historical trivia. All he had learned about the strange takeover of Liechtenstein told Andre that the next few hours would be critical. But where to go with the information? Pierre Dumas? He'd just consider it a nuisance and hope it would go away, at least until whatever party he was attending at the moment was over. The foreign minister? Given Gluck's distrust of anyone under senior status in the department, the only thing he would be greeted with would be suspicion, and possibly a stiff reprimand for going out of channels. That left only one avenue open that could produce the speed and decisiveness that might save Liechtenstein: President Franz.

Andre knew if he bypassed the multitude of bureaucratic layers between himself and the president of the country, his career would be finished, even if he were right on all points—especially if he were right on all points. Bureaucrats will forgive almost anything, except for a subordinate making them look bad.

Andre leaned back in his chair and stared out at the moonlit sky. Alone and tired, he was feeling very security-conscious. He thought of his sick wife, Marie, and their two children, Andre Jr. and Katrina, and of the careful and expensive plans he had formed for their education. The smart thing, he told himself, would be to turn off the light, go home for a good, long sleep, and eventually turn his findings over to Dumas who, in his own good time, would give the matter a proper red-tape burial.

He chewed on those thoughts for a while and didn't like the aftertaste. The hell with it, he told himself, I might as well go down with flags flying. He picked up the telephone and dialed. He spoke briefly then replaced the phone and sat thinking for a long moment. Finally, he called the one clerk still in the office and said, "If any calls come in about this Liechtenstein situation, forward them to me immediately."

"Where will you be?"

"The president's private residence."

The moment should have been beautiful instead of foreboding. But as Hanna Moltke tucked her small daughter, Lisel, into bed after a full and tiring day of Christmas celebrating, she knew that what she had to tell her husband, Eric, in a few moments would start the old

436

argument all over again, perhaps for the final time.

Hanna had joined the Swiss customs service as a border guard at a time when women were new to the service and resented by the men they had to work with. But Hanna and Eric needed the money so she tolerated the condescension and prejudicial treatment dished out by her male colleagues. More than once she muttered to herself, "If I didn't need the money, I'd tell them all to go to hell."

But as the years passed, Eric's business flourished and he started putting pressure on Hanna to quit and stay home with their two children. A few years before, she would have jumped at the chance, but when the time came to quit, she could not bring herself to throw away the promotions she had fought for, and the respect that had supplanted abuse from her co-workers. Gradually, a second job to help make ends meet turned into a career for Hanna.

When Hanna heard on the radio newscast that Christmas afternoon of the revolution in Liechtenstein, she instantly thought of the busload of strange people who had gone through her border station several days before en route to Liechtenstein. She especially thought of the cigarettes on which she had made a fingerprint request. She had a hunch that the two things were related; she had learned that hunches are the soft voice of alert experience and not to be casually disregarded.

While her family was celebrating the holiday she slipped away and phoned the head of the crime laboratory in Bern to have her request processed immediately. After a curt reminder that this was Christmas and that others had family plans, even if she didn't, he grudgingly agreed to bring in a lab technician to process the prints. He

437

sarcastically told her that if she didn't have anything else to do on Christmas, she could pick up the results about midnight.

Hanna smiled at Lisel and gave her a gentle kiss while Eric looked on, puffing contentedly on his pipe. "Did Momma's baby have a nice Christmas?" she asked softly.

"I love Christmas 'cause you're always home, Mommy," the child murmured sleepily.

Hanna and Eric turned off the bedroom light and returned to the living room where a crackling fire spread warmth and romantic shadows over the room. Eric ran his fingers softly through her hair and said, "I'll open a good riesling, and we can put a blanket down in front of the fire. Who knows what might come of that." He winked conspiratorially.

She tensed under his gentle caress. "Eric, please don't get mad, but I have some bad news for you—for both of us—I have to drive to Bern tonight."

He stepped back in shock. "Tonight? It's . . . it's Christmas night, for God's sake."

She reached out to touch his arm in sympathy. "I know, dearest, but I have to check out some fingerprints. It could be awfully important, and if I don't do it myself, I'm not sure it'll get done, at least not in time. Please understand. I wouldn't do it unless it was important."

He stepped back beyond her touch, a mask of bitterness etched on his features, his hopes for a fireside Christmas evening with his wife chased away. "Damn you," he hissed. "Don't you ever think of your family? Of me? It's always that goddamn job of yours. Well, I won't try to talk you out of going, you've made it clear what's most important to you. But I warn you, Hanna, if you desert your home on Christmas night, it may not be

438

there when you return."

"What do you mean by that?" she asked fearfully.

Eric had moved to the edge of the room and stood with his arm poised on their bedroom door. "You figure it out," he shouted and slammed the door.

Hanna wiped the tears from her eyes as she hastily wrote the note on the kitchen table while the car was warming up in the driveway.

Eric, dearest:

Please forgive me. You must believe that I wanted this night together as much as you, but please try to understand that I have a sense of duty that goes beyond just the two of us. I need to be a complete person, to be what I can be, which means my needs sometimes aren't always exactly what you would like them to be. But I know in my heart that if I'm successful in my work outside our home, I'll be more successful *in* the home as a mother and wife. Please understand and let me be me. I love you. . . .

Hanna looked sadly at the note lying on the table as she put on her heavy winter coat. It read like a plea, but in that hidden place where the soul keeps no secrets, she knew it was goodbye. She flicked off the light and walked out, leaving the house in silent darkness.

Guilt-ridden and haunted by thoughts of her once-happy home being torn apart by her career, Hanna put down the magazine she had been absently thumbing through and turned to the young technician who approached her through the swinging doors of the crime laboratory.

"Well, congratulations, Inspector, we've got a make. Sorry it took so long, but it was worth it." The technician handed her a card featuring a photo of a man with a nasty scar down the side of his face. "His name is Heine Schultz, and he's a real nasty character. Judging from the times he's been convicted, he's more enthusiastic than effective. Considers himself something of a mercenary, too." He handed her the sheaf of papers. "Have you any idea where he is?"

Hanna studied the surly-looking man in the photo. "I know exactly where he is. Do you have a phone I can use?"

President Franz was a man who didn't stand on ceremony when something he considered important was involved, and at the moment, Liechtenstein was at the top of his list. That's why Andre Wittenburg, within an hour of his call, found himself staring nervously across the shiny, polished surface of the president's desk in the library of the official residence, directly into the unshaven, frowning face of Franz himself.

Franz was a stern ex-schoolteacher known for doing his job like he had run his classroom. He embodied most of the Swiss values: direct, humorless, pragmatic, scrupulously truthful to the point of pain, and honest to the point of nuisance.

"I beg your pardon, Mr. President, for disturbing you at such a disagreeable hour, but—"

Franz impatiently waved aside Andre's rehearsed apology, and said, "Please, no formalities at this hour. I left a very comfortable bed for only one reason: to find out what you've learned about Liechtenstein. Now, let's have it."

Andre cleared his throat and shuffled the papers he removed from his attache case. "Mr. President, in the last few hours I've learned that the 'revolt' in Liechtenstein is nothing more than a clever, well-planned, criminal attempt to loot the country. The leader is an American named Konrad and most of his men are German criminals and ex-soldiers. There are about fifty of them. We also have reason to believe a high-ranking ex-Nazi is the brains behind it."

The president pursed his lips as he studied Andre. "What proof do you have?"

Andre described the anonymous phone call that steered him in the right direction, the admission to German police from Walter Schell of Konrad's recruitment of the mercenaries, and the wringing from Owl of the gun sale to Konrad.

Franz was silent for a long moment, then stood and paced around the spacious room with his hands clasped behind his back, his slippers making little slapping noises on the shiny parquet floor. Finally, he leaned against the edge of a heavy marble table and folded his arms. Andre waited expectantly. "Wittenburg, your evidence is very persuasive to *me*, but would it be to someone who *wanted* to believe these mercenaries are legitimate socialist revolutionaries?"

"Like the Russians, sir?"

Franz grunted his agreement and nodded for Andre to continue.

"Well, I think the key to the whole thing, sir, is that none of these people is a Liechtensteiner. In that sense,

441

it's definitely an outside takeover, naked aggression, and whoever set it up intended to keep everyone in confusion for as long as possible, the Russians included. So the Russians have to be concerned about the same things as we are—making a mistake and appearing foolish. But additionally, they have to worry about how the Americans will react."

Franz appeared to study an original Rembrandt on the wall. "The Americans don't know what to do, so naturally they are doing nothing, the prudent thing. An important election is coming up in the States, so basically they just want the problem to go away and avoid being embarrassed by the Russians." Franz resumed his pacing. "But the big question we have to worry about is what does *Switzerland* do?"

Franz talked rapidly and earnestly to Andre, using him as a handy forum to test his ideas. "Switzerland has her neutrality to protect. We've avoided wars for centuries by steering a cautious course between bigger powers. Are we going to jeopardize that neutrality now over a tiny nation that could disappear tomorrow and not be missed? I have to ask myself, do I want to be remembered as the president who risked—and possibly lost—our neutrality? The Russians obviously see an opportunity to grab a foothold in Western Europe, but they're nervous about the Americans. The Americans don't want the Russians sitting on the banks of the Rhine, so they're nervous about that. It's a good situation for the Swiss to stay out of.

"Still, the evidence you've presented convinces me this is nothing more than a daring, bizarre case of international piracy." Franz waved his finger as though lecturing to an unseen class. "The weak point of your evidence is that you can't conclusively place Konrad or his men at the scene of the crime. We know he bought the guns and hired the mercenaries, but apart from an anonymous phone call, we can't point to any single fact that proves he's anywhere near Liechtenstein. That's the missing key. That's what others—the Russians, namely—would point to."

Franz stared at the floor, adding up pros and cons. "My inclination, young man, is to throw the problem to the bureaucrats like a bone to a dog. They'll gnaw on it, worry it, and eventually bury it. That's the safe way, the Swiss way."

Andre felt fatigue numbing his mind. "I don't mean to be impertinent, Mr. President, but I wish you'd reconsider. Maybe, if—"

"Young man, you don't have responsibility for this nation, I do. And I'm not going to upset the delicate balance of our international posture unless I have conclusive proof of this act of piracy."

There was a knock at the door and a gloved, uniformed aide quickly walked up to the president and handed him a folded sheet of paper. Franz scanned it, then let the paper drop to the desk, gave a deep sigh and turned his back to Andre. Slowly, almost imperceptibly, he crossed himself.

"Is anything wrong, sir?" Andre asked.

Franz' voice sounded very sad. "That was from the commander of Fort Sargarns; those criminals killed a priest, murdered him in cold blood as he was trying to cross the border right under our noses."

The two men lapsed into a long silence, the silence of frustration and defeat. After several minutes when the only sound was the methodical tick-tock of an antique floor clock, the telephone's rude ringing snapped the glum reverie for both men. Franz reached for it and snapped, "Yes?" He handed the receiver to Andre. "It's for you."

Andre took the phone hesitantly. "Hello . . . yes, this is Andre Wittenburg. Oh, yes, I told my clerk that." Andre listened for several minutes, his excitement growing with the conversation. He grabbed a piece of stationery with the president's seal on it and scribbled notes. Finally, he said, "I've got it all . . . yes, thank you, Inspector Moltke. You've done a great service for your country, ma'am, and I'll make sure your efforts don't go unrecognized. Your family must be very proud of your dedication. Goodbye."

Andre hung up the phone with a look of triumph on his smiling face. Excitedly, he told Franz of the efforts of Hanna Moltke and how her digging had placed the criminal Heine Schultz in Konrad's party with a declared declaration of Liechtenstein only two days before the takeover. Franz sat in a nearby chair with his head bowed in deep thought listening and struggling with the burden of decision. Suddenly, he stood erect and went to his desk and pushed a buzzer. When he looked at Andre, the doubt was replaced by determination. "That woman just gave us the key."

The same aide responded instantly to the summons, and Franz took him to a corner of the room where he talked for several moments. Then, the aide, after nodding vigorously, left the room. Franz turned to Andre. "Herr Wittenburg, I'd like you to stay and witness a special emergency conversation I'll be having in a few minutes. Consider yourself the envoy of history; whether what I'm doing is right or wrong, you'll be the only one to witness it." He sat at his desk, rubbing his hands together

444

and glancing nervously at the telephone. He talked almost absently to Andre as he waited for the phone to ring. "I'm waiting for a special hook-up to the leader of the Soviet Union. I've never talked to him, and this is a tough subject to start an acquaintance with. But it's got to be done." Then, in a rare display of humor, he laughed sardonically. "What'll I do if he hangs up on me? That'd be a hell of a fix, wouldn't it?"

The sharp ring of the telephone cut his conversation like a cleaver. He stared at the phone and flexed his hand as it rang a second time. Franz picked up the instrument and spoke with a firm, measured voice. "This is President Franz. How are you, Mr. Chairman? I apologize for the inconvenient hour, but I wish to discuss a most urgent matter with you—Liechtenstein."

Andre watched as the president listened patiently, nodding or shaking his head. All nervousness was gone, replaced by impatience waiting for the translator to finish, a politician eager for the floor.

"Yes, Mr. Chairman, I heard your proclamation on Liechtenstein. . . . Yes, we certainly took it seriously, but my reason for calling is to advise you that something has happened to change the entire picture. We've discovered that these so-called revolutionaries are, in reality, nothing more than criminals and pirates who tried to pass themselves off as patriots to create the very situation we find confronts us, in order to gain time to loot Liechtenstein. There are about fifty of them, led by an American, but the brains behind them is apparently an ex-Nazi. . . . What do I propose, Mr. Chairman?" Franz took an involuntary breath. "I've decided to send in a small force to arrest them."

Andre watched Franz' jaw tighten as the voice on the

other end grew louder. Franz waited for the translation although the inflection left no doubt about the message. "Of course, Mr. Chairman, I know that the Soviet Union can't be trifled with, but let me advise you, in turn, that Switzerland is not without resources herself, especially in international finance. But, please, let's not let our tempers get away from us, too much is at stake here. Mr. Chairman, let me assure you that I gave this careful thought, looking for a way that would avoid bitter feelings between our two countries, both of which prosper, as you know, from friendly relations. . . . Yes, I've considered that; you know how much Switzerland values her neutrality. . . . I would remind you that whom the president of Switzerland confers with is his own affair. Here is what I plan to do: We have a military base just to the south of Liechtenstein; I'm going to instruct the commander of Fort Sargans to send in a small contingent to arrest these criminals under the terms of our customs treaty of 1923 with Liechtenstein. . . . That, sir, is a point of international law the lawyers will have to argue about later. . . . Yes, I understand your misgivings, but let me finish, please. Just as soon as our forces secure Liechtenstein, probably later this morning, a military helicopter will arrive at your embassy here in Bern prepared to immediately fly your ambassador and anyone else of your choosing to Liechtenstein to investigate for themselves that what I say is true. And one other thing, Mr. Chairman: Your proposal of last year for jointly financing the irrigation project in Syria that we rejected, well, I think we should talk about that again. . . . Thank you, I know it's an important project. Please advise your ambassador the helicopter will arrive within a couple of hours. . . . Yes, I would like that also. Goodbye."

Franz hung up the phone and leaned back in his plush chair and exhaled slowly in relief. "Whew!" He grinned at Andre. "He's a tough old bird, but also a crafty politician. Right now he's figuring out a way to cut his losses and pass the blame."

"I take it he'll go along?"

Franz nodded. "With reservations; he's suspicious, but he doesn't want to be an international laughing-stock, either. All I can say, Wittenburg, is that they better not be real revolutionaries."

Andre patted the folder he held in his lap. "You saw the evidence, Mr. President."

Franz pushed a button on his desk and stood up as the ever-attentive aide came into the room. The light of early dawn highlighted the red-rimmed, sleepless eyes of the president and the gray stubble of his beard. He shook Andre's hand warmly. "I'm aware of the chance you took in coming to see me direct. I appreciate it, and be assured I'm going to take a personal interest in your career from now on."

Andre, stunned with gratitude, mumbled his thanks and backed out of the library. The last thing he heard before the big door closed solidly was Franz asking to speak to the commander of Fort Sargans.

The leader of the Communist Party and all the Soviet people felt very old as he replaced the phone in its cradle. He had been through enough international politics to learn that when you gamble, you sometimes lose. He had known that when he OK'd the silly business about Liechtenstein. Maybe he was just getting too old. He grimaced at the thought of one of the world's great powers being outfoxed by a bunch of thieves and he massaged his eyes with two fingers. Well, if it was old age, he couldn't do anything about it; all he could do at this point was what he'd learned to do during the Stalin purges, back when the revolution was young—try to survive.

He opened two manila folders on his desk and picked up the phone again. "Get me General Malinchuk at the GRU. Hello, General, I'm afraid I've got a sad assignment for you. I want you to arrest Serghi Yonolokev and Yuri Terishnikov. . . . Yes, immediately, with no chance of release."

The chairman leaned back and basked in the reflection of the rising sun. Yonolokev would understand, an old politician knew the risks of the game, but poor young Terishnikov would be bitter, confused, and finally, disillusioned. It was the sad fate of the young to believe in justice. But the chairman knew justice to be a leaf in the autumn air, at the mercy of the strange twists of the wind.

Konrad surveyed his men with professional detachment. They were arranged in a broad semicircle about five hundred meters long with the highway and river to their backs. From that position they could protect their designated runway and have the protection of the Rhine. They crouched behind cars and pointed M-16s toward the mountains, across the valleys from where the first light of dawn was emerging and from where they expected the farmers and shopkeepers who had risen against them.

Konrad had selected a command post near the end of the perimeter, where the DC-3s would come to a shuddering halt. It consisted only of the rental truck with

448

a cargo area loaded with untold millions in art, rare stamps, gold and valuable documents. In the front seat Honi sat quietly, still in a state of deep shock from the cumulative effects of learning of the death of Father Hammerschmidt and the horrible happenings at the bakery.

Konrad signaled for Otto to join him at the front fender of the truck. Otto was relaxed, in his natural element. "Everything's secure; those farmers'll pay hell penetrating this defense," he said without being asked.

Konrad had more on his mind. "Did you make sure to bring the radio?" he asked in a brittle voice.

Otto glanced sharply at Konrad. He was worried by Konrad's black mood since the death of Angus. Unprofessional, he thought, a commander shouldn't allow himself to be emotional about his men. "It's right over there," he answered.

Konrad removed a card from his pocket on which he had printed, Every Possession Has Its Duty. "Give this to Ray Mallen and have him transmit it in the open. This will have the planes here in about an hour and also arrange our reception in Germany." He handed the card to Otto, but then stopped him as he turned to leave. Konrad removed a bulky money belt from his waist. "Who knows what'll happen around here before we get out." He glanced quickly at the mountains. "So go ahead and pay the men." Konrad's eyes scanned the length of the defense line which held fifteen fewer people than he started out with. "There's enough here for a healthy bonus for you and everyone else. See to it." He handed the money belt to Otto.

Otto took the belt and fingered it thoughtfully, then looked at Konrad with a worried expression. "Konrad, if there's anything I—"

"There's not," Konrad snapped. "Don't get sentimental, it's unprofessional."

Otto shrugged and jogged over to the waiting radio operator.

They came from the hills and villages; they came on foot, bicycles, even horseback. They weren't organized, they had no plan; goaded on by the snarling hatred of Hans Haas, they were exuberantly following their retreating enemy now gathered on the banks of the Rhine.

Success had swollen their numbers. Each time one of the invaders fell, the ranks of the guerrillas grew by twenty. And as their enemy began withdrawing to their defensive position, the amateur soldiers of Liechtenstein mistook the maneuver for cowardice and even more previously reticent farmers grabbed their shotguns and joined the march, one thousand strong.

The guerrillas stopped five hundred yards away from the long line held by Konrad's men and stared in bewilderment at what confronted them. The way the enemy had positioned themselves, there seemed no way of crossing the intervening farm yards and fields without drawing deadly, overlapping fire. They were too naive to know this was the inevitable consequence of pitting amateur enthusiasm against a trained professional like Konrad, but they intuitively knew better than to throw themselves against the withering fire of the concentrated M-16s.

Every few minutes, one of the more daring of the Liechtensteiners would dart out from behind a barn or stump to test the response and would be sent diving for cover by an immediate hail of bullets. For over half an hour the impasse continued as the guerrillas crouched cautiously and their opponents waited patiently for them to make a move, occasionally spraying the air with bullets as a reminder of what to expect.

Frozen in their cover with plenty of time to consider the inadequacy of their puny shotguns and hunting rifles, not to mention their inexperience, against the hardened mercenaries they faced, the Liechtensteiners started to rethink just how important saving an old painting or postage stamp was, and whether it was worth the agony of a piece of white-hot steel tearing through the guts.

Hans watched his makeshift troops hesitate and shrink back from the guns that faced them. After their hit-and-run success against these same invaders for whom he felt such unbridled hatred, it infuriated Hans to see his men crouched timidly, their eyes wide in fear. Disregarding the rifles aimed in his direction only a few hundred meters away, Hans ran from group to group, urging, cajoling, pleading with them to finish the job, to drive these thieving bastards into the Rhine.

He sprinted into the midst of the most forward-situated group clustered tightly behind a cow shed and belly-flopped behind the barricade as bullets stitched holes in his footsteps closely behind. As Hans gasped for breath, Adam Hossler reached down and helped him to a kneeling position. The youth was still filled with a sense of heroism from having watched Richard Graff's inspiring death, and he welcomed the man who could galvanize these cowardly clods into action against the men who had martyred Richard.

Hans regained his breath and looked with disgust at the men he had risked his life to join. They were huddled like sheep against the building; their weapons were forgotten and leaned against the wall like tools at the end of the day. Hans, in his battle lust, saw them as retransformed from victorious guerrillas to defenseless, despised diggers in the earth. "What the hell's the matter with you men?" he challenged. "We drove them back this far; they're cornered, so let's finish the job. For chrissakes, we were winning, we *had* them. This is no time to stop."

As Hans released his accumulated frustration and hate, it was like pus oozing from an infected wound. He glared at the men who had seemed to quit on him. All but one avoided his look. Adam Hossler, face flushed with excitement, eagerly awaited the chance to demonstrate the same type of heroism he had witnessed in Richard Graff, especially in front of his leader, Hans, the commanding general of what had become the impromptu army of Liechtenstein.

Adam looked around and saw the tight-lipped silence on the faces of his companions, and decided it would be permissible for him to speak uninvited to the man who had become the Napoleon of his small world. "Hans, I think I've found a way to get behind them." Encouraged by a look of keen interest from Hans and stares of incredulity from the others, Adam excitedly pointed out how, by following the contour of the dips and hollows of the ground and cover from farm buildings, one or two men could work their way to the protection of the river bank and sneak along it until emerging directly behind the mercenaries.

Hans looked with approval at the youth he had previously known only as a dull-witted apprentice with a reputation of getting more in the way than helping. "All right, go for it, but don't show yourself until we attack from the front."

Lindo Garn sat nearby and watched the approval on Hans' face while listening to Adam's plan. Jealousy raged through him as he saw the dull-witted youth threaten to supplant himself in Hans's eyes. When Hans nodded his permission for Adam to attempt his encircling plan, Lindo felt he had no choice but to speak up bravely. "I'm going, too. Two men will stand a better chance."

Although a few of the older men may have mused silently about things coming from the mouths of babes, no one spoke as they watched Adam slip off, and then five minutes later, Lindo follow him in the direction of the river.

Thrilled not only that his idea was accepted but also that he was the one chosen to undertake it, Adam cradled his gun in his arm and crept along the field the way he imagined an Indian would do. He wasn't happy that that buttinski Lindo Garn was following, but he couldn't dwell on that. His mind was filled with images of himself as the type of hero he had seen in the scores of war movies he had devoured in childhood. He caught a brief glimpse of himself after this was all over, tired and dirty, surrounded by admiring countrymen, telling them in a strong but quiet voice how he had dedicated himself to the memory of the valiant Richard Graff.

Lindo had crept only a hundred meters along the frozen ground but he was already beginning to feel a sense of isolation. As a small child he had dreaded being left alone, and the fear chose this moment to return. He looked in every direction but couldn't see anyone. Fright welled in his throat and forced his breath to come in short, choppy gasps. Despite the chill of the morning, sweat started to pour into his eyes, stinging and blinding. He was lost. His panic-stricken mind raced, searching for escape. He had to catch up to Adam. Adam knew the way; Adam was his friend, he would help, but first he had to catch him. Lindo jumped to his feet and ran along the field at a low trot, whispering as loudly as he dared, "Adam? Adam, where are you?"

Herman Wellman's sharp, trained eyes picked up the form of Lindo immediately. Wellman's job was to protect a twenty-degree sweep directly in front of his position behind the Volkswagen, and after fifteen years of deadly bush fighting as a mercenary in Africa, that was like asking Picasso to draw a stick figure.

Wellman didn't ask questions. He didn't wonder who was behaving so foolishly by running exposed in the field two hundred meters directly in front of his sights. He figured that was none of his business. His business was protecting those twenty degrees, and that's what he would do. He raised the M-16 and gently squeezed off three shots. The satisfaction he felt when the figure collapsed was very slight; it had been too easy.

No one on either side heard the pleading, "Papa, Papa," coming from where the figure collapsed. It was very weak and wasn't repeated.

As Lindo departed, Hans turned back in scorn to the other men huddled together along the wall. The steam of his breath seemed to come from the fire within him, and he rubbed his red, chapped hands in frustration. "How does it feel to watch young kids do your dirty work for you? Those two have more guts than all of you put together. But you're not going to quit, understand? We're going to attack those bastards, do you hear me?"

454

He stared at each of the men, hoping he could transmit his own rage to all of them. Slowly, it seemed to have an effect as the men returned his gaze and seemed to gain courage from his determination. Hans grunted in satisfaction at what appeared to be an indication of manliness. But intuition told him it would take a more dramatic incident to rouse them from their hiding places. He knew from vague childhood stories that in wartime men usually followed a courageous leader willing to take the initiative.

"Men, I can sneak up close to the sons of bitches if you'll give me covering fire." He motioned for the men to peek around the corner in the direction of the enemy. "See that big log, about thirty meters from their truck? I think I can reach that if you keep them busy. When I get there, I'll signal for all of you to come on the run, and I'll cover you." Hans patted the captured M-16 he carried.

Seeing no signs of disagreement on their faces, he turned in the direction of another nearby group and called softly, "Pass the word to give me cover fire and then attack together when I give the signal."

Hans heard the command repeated in hushed tones along their ragged line, then skittered along the ground toward the objects of his hatred as the men behind him obediently opened fire.

Otto watched with professional curiosity as firing erupted from their clumsy besiegers. "Don't fire until they make a move," he shouted to his men who crouched lower behind the protective cars. "Most of those old shotguns can't even reach this far." Refusing to respond to the random firing, Otto patiently waited to see what the firing was intended to precede. "Take it easy, men," he yelled amidst the rattle of small arms fire. "Mark their locations by the gun smoke."

Using the same ground cover that shielded Adam, Hans stealthily moved closer to the enemy lines, but instead of heading for the river bank, he took advantage of a shallow ravine and crawled unseen to a position behind the big oak log he had spotted in the distance. After catching his breath and checking the M-16, he gave the signal for the others to attack, a short wave and jerk of the head. Nothing. The firing died down and silence enveloped the morning.

Karl Beckhower nervously glanced around; no one was making a move to follow Hans. The men seemed frozen in indecision, waiting for someone's brashness to crack away the ice of their fear. Karl knew it would have to be him; he didn't exactly volunteer, he just knew it had to be done, so he slipped out from behind the protective shed and started running in a crouch, calling for others to follow, his flapping coat acting like a banner as he awkwardly stumbled across the frozen furrows of the field toward Konrad.

A few of the bolder men took a few halfhearted steps in his wake, but stopped in their tracks when they saw what happened. One of the defenders raised above the hood of the car he was crouched behind, took careful but almost casual aim, and triggered a short spurt of bullets toward the weaving Beckhower. Two of the bullets hit him directly in the face; the other hit him in the forehead with a loud *thock*! and tore the top of his head off, sending gray brain matter and his blood-splattered glasses flying behind him to land at the feet of those prepared to follow.

The sight of a man they knew so well flopping to the ground like a beheaded chicken drained the bravado out of the Liechtensteiners like the yolk from a broken egg.

Staring at the heap that used to be a gentle schoolteacher, the men who had emerged into the open took one step backward, then turned and fled in panic back to their hiding places.

Watching them retreat from his concealment behind the log, Hans felt frustration rub at his mind like sandpaper. He wanted to shout, "Come back, you cowards, we can beat them," but was forced to grit his teeth in silence because of the nearness of the enemy.

Hans was on the verge of threading his way back to his men and coaxing them to try again until he saw Honi sitting calmly in the cab of the truck, not more than thirty meters from where he lay. Standing beside the vehicle was Konrad, the one who had caused such grief in Hans' homeland and made Honi forsake her last attempt to win her back.

As he stared at the two he associated with the unbearable grief of his life, Hans was seized by an uncontrollable need for revenge, to strike back at the misery that shrouded his existence like a black curtain. Hans edged the barrel of the M-16 over the top of the log and took careful aim at Konrad standing in full view beside the truck. When Konrad's chest was in direct line with the front sight, he gently squeezed the trigger and awaited the blast of sound and the kick against his shoulder that would proclaim the bastard dead, torn to pieces by a weapon he himself had selected.

The gun betrayed Hans; no matter how hard he jerked the trigger, it stubbornly refused to respond to his demand for the death of Konrad. Not knowing enough about the weapon to quickly clear it, Hans fumed with helpless frustration. The situation seemed just like his life: All that was necessary to insure failure was the teasing glimmer of success.

Hans slammed the jammed gun against the ground in fury. He was about to start back to his own lines when something made him stop and glance back at Konrad. In Hans' eyes, the man who possessed the love of the only woman Hans had ever wanted appeared self-important and arrogant, smugly in control of the situation. The thought of losing again to that man almost made Hans sick. The anger at such a probability built up in his mind like flood waters behind a dam, and as the thought overflowed his brain, the pressure of the frustration burst his sense of restraint and yielded to the irresistible need for revenge.

Bellowing his blood lust, Hans grabbed the barrel of the M-16 and leaped over the log and raced toward the unsuspecting Konrad only a few meters away. The distance closed in seconds and as Hans swung the rifle behind his head ready to club his enemy's brains into mush, Konrad was on the verge of being the victim of the thing every seasoned soldier dreads—the unpredictability of a maddened enemy.

To Otto standing nearby, it seemed a bizarre ballet. The clumsy rush of the man with the clubbed rifle was of a theater he knew well, and he stood for a second in appreciation of the crazy valor that makes men do such things.

As Hans rushed to almost arm's length of Konrad and braced himself to swing the gun with all his might, Otto calmly lifted his rifle to hip level and squeezed off a long burst that caught him in a tight pattern in the heart. Although instantly dead, Hans' momentum threw him into Konrad who, still unsuspecting, was staggered forward as the two-hundred-pound corpse rammed him from behind.

Konrad and Otto approached the dead man as they would a dead rattlesnake: still wary, but curious about something that had almost killed one of them.

Otto looked down and said, "Did you know him?"

Konrad looked at the lifeless eyes and shook his head.

"Well," Otto said with a bitter little laugh that had no humor in it, "he sure seemed to know you."

From his hiding place beneath the edge of the steep river bank facing the backs of his enemies, Adam Hossler had witnessed Hans' charge. "Glorious," he muttered, swelling with pride and feeling privileged at witnessing a second display of heroism. It helped take away the disgust he had felt when Lindo Garn had chickened out and didn't follow him.

The only deaths Adam had observed during these skirmishes had been at a distance where all bodies fall gracefully and impersonally. If he could have been a closer witness and looked into the half-hooded, unfocused eyes, smelled the sweetish, sickening odor of puddled blood and realized that the last act of the dead is to soil themselves, he probably would have formed a more prudent attitude toward war. But he might as well have been playing toy soldiers in his nursery for all the realism he understood. He knew nothing more than a burning desire for revenge and a need to fulfill his sense of destiny to be a man of action and follow the fifes and drums making great music in his head.

Adam didn't think it out very well, but he had an idea that he could surprise the man who killed Hans, then slide down the river bank, hide, and strike again a little later. When his companions waiting safely in the distance realized the lonely, heroic struggle he was waging, they would mount a charge that would sweep these bastards into the Rhine.

Otto wasn't aware of Adam until a warning shot caused him to wheel in surprise. It only lasted a split second, but as Otto stared at the wild-eyed youth pointing the shotgun directly at him, some inner clock told him that this was the moment of his death. In the eyeblink of time left to him, Otto, with the fatalism and grace of the old soldier, accepted what was about to happen as fitting and timely.

Adam felt the gun buck at his shoulder and saw the old man fall backward; he was filled with a sense of omnipotence at having killed his first man. But out of the corner of his eye, he saw a dozen men start to swing their rifles in his direction.

Adam's plan was to jump back down the river bank, but he had formed it with no sense of timing; he had no idea how quickly a trained soldier can react. Unfortunately for his adolescent sense of destiny, it was the only such lesson he would ever receive. He was simultaneously hit with a fusillade of bullets from three directions, and his lifeless body tumbled down the bank and into the rushing river where it quickly floated away from the place of his dreams of glory.

Konrad knelt and supported the head of Otto who lay on his back, his shattered chest heaving in desperation to stay alive, the blood steadily oozing from between his lips and his hands twitching. Otto spoke with great difficulty, gasping and fighting for breath like a man who had just run a long way. "I've seen a lot of men like this, and I always wondered what it was like," he said; he tried to laugh but it came out as a weak cough.

Konrad tried to be comforting. "We'll get you to a

doctor in Germany as soon as the planes get here. You'll make it, Sergeant."

Otto managed a look of scorn. "Damn, don't treat me like a recruit on my last day. I know what . . . what's happening." He made a feeble gesture toward his pants pocket. "The money, take the money, want . . . want you to have it."

Konrad shook his head. "I don't want your money, Otto."

Otto coughed great gobs of blood. "Isn't that what you came for? Take it." He nodded approval as Konrad slipped the huge wad of bills from his pocket.

Otto no longer looked at Konrad, his unfocused eyes stared into the morning sky, not seeing the two lumbering planes cruise lazily into view, looking for the landing flares that would guide them down.

Death was showing impatience, and the words edged falteringly past the blue lips flecked in red. "This is what I . . . what I . . . a soldier's . . ."

He did not have to finish for Konrad to know his meaning. As he reached down and closed the dead sergeant's eyes, Konrad thought, Old man, you'll never again be Old Otto the janitor. Before he turned away, Konrad slipped Otto's money back into the dead man's pocket.

Chapter Twenty

General Henri, commander of the Swiss army base at Sargans, was still stunned by the five a.m. call from President Franz. Despite the general's protests, the order was firm: Send a force into Liechtenstein and arrest the "revolutionaries." Henri was a man who preferred to operate by the book with no surprises, and his unhappiness for the operation that had been thrust so rudely upon him was obvious to the officers he had summoned to this early-morning meeting. Since they took their moods chameleonlike from their commander, the men were about as eager as Arabs in a synagogue. Only Jacques Carpentier sat on the edge of his seat, eagerly following the drawn-out discussions.

Henri was using a long pointer to painstakingly explain a list of procedures written on a blackboard. "Now, gentlemen, we mustn't be precipitous in this undertaking. First, intensive aerial reconnaissance, then a series of small patrols checking the roads for land mines and probing their strength. We should be ready to launch a full-scale attack in three or four days." Henri dusted the chalk from his hands and lowered the pointer. "Any questions at this point?"

Carpentier tried to hide his frustration; Henri was attempting to approach these thugs like they were legitimate soldiers, but he controlled himself and spoke calmly. "Excuse me, sir, but I don't think we have that kind of time."

Henri looked at him with the expression of a man who had just bitten into a lemon. The other officers around the table joined in with frowns of disapproval. "What makes you think that, Captain?"

Carpentier glanced around at his scowling colleagues and plunged ahead. "Well, General, since we now know they're not going to stay, can't we assume they might leave more quickly than we think, like today?" Carpentier continued without waiting for an answer, he was caught up in his own logic and not noticing the stares of the other officers regarding him like an unwanted guest with bad breath. "And if so, shouldn't we move right now? Surely the Swiss army doesn't fear a bunch of crminals."

As soon as the words were out, he realized he should have stopped short of the last remark. Henri bristled at the question which he interpreted as a taunt. "The Swiss army isn't *afraid*, Captain, it just doesn't rush into a situation without making *professional* preparations. I thought you knew that, but perhaps I was mistaken."

Carpentier tried to apologize, but Henri interrupted the effort. "Since you are so enthusiastic about this business, consider yourself in charge of the operation."

Henri meant the detail as punishment, and Carpentier was careful not to show his delight. He wanted nothing more than to confront the men who gunned down the priest and then dismissed his protests with a condescending laugh.

Self-satisfied that he had shifted the work load for such a silly operation to a smart-ass subordinate, Henri turned to the group. "Very well, gentlemen, we'll adjourn until four p.m. at which time our intrepid Captain Carpentier here will update us on his preparations and the latest intelligence. Dismissed."

Carpentier's head buzzed with a hundred logistical questions as he walked back to the motorized reconnaissance unit he commanded. Summoning Sgt. Luigi Giardello, a spirited professional non-com from the Italian section of Switzerland, Carpentier briefly explained the mission, finishing with a promise to personally deal with the border guards responsible for the priest's death.

"Don't know how you're going to do that, Captain," Giardello said.

"What do you mean?"

"Well, while you were in that meeting, they just pulled out, left the border wide open. Some of the men say they've seen others of that gang headed toward Vaduz; seem to be gathering there."

Carpentier was still digesting that information when he heard a faint drone in the sky to the north. Borrowing Giardello's field glasses, he scanned the horizon until two fat, old transports lumbered across his vision and dropped down, quickly vanishing from sight as bright flares marched across the sky.

Carpentier lowered the glasses. "Two old World War II transports; they've landed."

Giardello shook his head. "Impossible, sir, there's no

landing field in Liechtenstein."

"The highway," Carpentier muttered. Suddenly, he knew what was happening. He frantically looked around and spotted a MOWAG SPY reconnaissance vehicle parked in the motor pool, looking like a squat, motorized beetle with its armor plating glinting in response to the first rays of the morning sun, and its needle-point machine gun resting with muzzle pointed skyward.

Carpentier gestured to the machine. "Is that SPY loaded and ready?"

Carpentier sensed action and grinned. "Checked it myself, sir. It's all set."

Carpentier clapped him on the back. "You drive."

Within moments both men disappeared into the SPY, the hatch slammed shut and the fat tires squealed in a cloud of diesel belches as they sped toward the Liechtenstein border.

Konrad turned away from the lifeless body of Otto and looked up at the circling DC-3s. He quickly pulled in the men to tighten the perimeter and shouted orders for cover fire to keep the heads of the lurking Liechtensteiners down, and then signaled for the flares to be ignited.

The pilots grinned with satisfaction as the brilliant red and green flares and the winking flashes of the guns far below gave the gray dawn an unaccustomed hue. They swooped down toward the wide asphalt highway and glided to landings so smooth and uneventful it could have been Heathrow.

The Liechtenstein guerrillas had no further stomach to face the chattering guns of the mercenaries, so they watched sadly as the thieves loaded the crated contents of the truck onto the first plane. The glum witnesses in the distance knew what the crates contained and felt shamed at their inability to prevent the pillage.

After the loot had been loaded, Konrad opened the cab door of the truck and gently helped Honi down and then guided her into the first plane. Then, bracing himself against the prop wash and shouting above the screaming engines, Konrad instructed a nodding Jesse James Jones to have the men maintain cover fire as he and Honi took off in the first plane with the loot, then pull back and make their own escape in the second plane which would take them to a private landing strip outside Frankfurt from where they could melt into the bustle of the city. After a final nod, Konrad wished him luck and ran for the waiting plane.

Carpentier could see through the slotted observation port that the first DC-3 was going to be airborne by the time the speeding SPY arrived. He turned to the controls of the deadly, fast-firing 7.62 machine gun mounted atop the vehicle and gave a quick thought to shooting it down. No, he second-guessed himself, what if the cargo is irreplaceable art? Grudgingly, he watched it gain speed and slowly lift into the air, then disappear into the morning clouds.

A kilometer away, the second plane started to slowly taxi toward them as the last mercenary tumbled through the cargo door. Giardello pointed the SPY's stubby nose directly down the highway-turned-runway and pressed the accelerator. The speeding armored car and the lumbering plane drew together with astonishing quick-ness and the watching Liechtensteiners slowly raised up to stare at the deadly contest that was unfolding before them.

Carpentier knew he had only seconds to disable the plane before it became airborne. He calculated the speed and distance of the plane, then manipulated the controls of the machine gun with practiced speed and fired.

The thin mouth of the machine gun erupted in staccato flame as bullets poured toward the DC-3 at the rate of nearly one thousand per minute. Carpentier felt a surge of satisfaction as the hail of slugs quickly found their target and large chunks of the plane's right landing gear flew off, the tire shredded. The plane wobbled weakly before collapsing on its belly, grinding to a screeching, abrupt halt in a flashing protests of sparks.

With a word from Carpentier, Giardello jerked the wheel and the SPY slammed to a halt only a few meters from the closed hatch of the windowless fuselage. Carpentier unhooked the SPY's loudspeaker, and over the cheers of the watching Liechtensteiners, ordered the plane's occupants to stay put. When, amidst a chorus of shouted defiance from the men inside, the hatch door started to swing open, Carpentier aimed the machine gun at the top of the fuselage and stitched a line of black holes along the length, just a few inches, he calculated, above the heads of those inside. He smiled when the hatch door quickly slammed shut as the gun's echo died away.

Carpentier turned to Giardello, and ordered, "Radio base and request assistance in handling these prisoners. Also, tell them one plane got away and headed into the Alps. It probably can't be tracked in those mountains, but we should notify all airports within range of a DC-3 to be on the lookout."

Giardello picked up the microphone, but hesitated and

turned to Carpentier. "What do you suppose is in the one that got away?"

Carpentier looked at the mountains and shook his head. "God only knows."

As soon as they were airborne, Konrad loosened his and Honi's seatbelts, checked the cargo, then went forward to the cockpit where the pilot, Mike Dawson, turned at the sound of his approach and grinned. "Well, Konrad, we made it," he said and extended his hand for Konrad to shake. Both men were oblivious to the fate of their sister plane, so the occasion was one of unqualified success and should have been one of unrestrained rejoicing. But Dawson noticed Konrad wasn't even smiling and almost said something, but years of living with men under the pressures of combat had taught him to leave such questions unasked. Instead, he changed the subject. "Where to now, boss?" he asked, turning back to the controls as the plane entered the first mountain pass.

Konrad silently handed him an envelope which the pilot opened and studied. "This looks pretty simple to find; we'll be there in about an hour."

Konrad nodded curtly and turned back to the cargo area. Dawson shrugged at his leader's depressed mood. Whatever works, he thought, as long as I get paid.

Konrad steadied himself as he moved carefully back to Honi and the plane hit a pocket of mountain turbulence. Reaching her seat, he leaned over and asked solicitously, "Are you all right?" In the face of her blank stare, he tried again, "We made it; got away clean."

Honi turned a wide-eyed expressionless white face up

to him. "Clean?" she asked hollowly. "Who's clean?"

Konrad suddenly felt very tired and moved back to his own seat. He gazed without feeling at the crates and boxes of loot strapped to the sides of the tube-like cargo area. This was what he had come for; the mission was a success. He, Konrad, had done a thing so daring that all the smaller nations of the world would have to take a deep breath and nervously re-examine existing standards of state security. In truth, Konrad realized he had changed the world, but search though he might among the inner chambers of his mind, he could feel no joy or pride in what he had done; he only felt tired, very tired. His head slowly fell back against the seat, seeking escape as much as rest. . . .

The gentle fingers of sleep massaged Konrad's tired brain and caused it to lay down its burdens and then spread a soft blanket over all his cares, leaving a soothing black void.

But as Konrad rested in the depths of that blackness, an irridescent whirlpool of red and white lights swirled larger and larger, ignoring Konrad's subconscious pleas to go away. Behind the painful lights a voice could be heard, softly at first, in sync with the light, but growing in volume as the lights grew in brightness. It was a familiar voice, a voice that never grew older, never lost the strength of young manhood.

"Hey, Konrad, my main man. This's your bro', Willie Mac. How you be, dude? Tired, huh? Well, you been busy, but you won didn't you, Lieutenant? Yessir, old Lieutenant done whipped hisself a whole country! Whoeee! Let's see now, what'd you get? A bunch of old pictures, some postage stamps, money . . . and all it cost was a few lives. Oh, well, folks is born to get snuffed,

469

anyway, and you didn't lose anyone 'mount to much, just good old Angus and Otto, some farmers dumb enough to try to stop a bad dude like you, and a few guys who trusted you to get 'em out alive. Hah! Well, the chick made it, anyway. Just look at her sittin' over there, don't she look fine? She got the look of someone been hassled half to death. But we know our main man, right? Old Konrad don't fuck around. Get in his way and you gonna have some hurt put on you. Yessir, you sure a hurtin' man. Well, got to go, got to dig some more graves. Folks in hell sure ain't gonna be lonesome with you on the job."

Konrad awoke with a shriek that was soundlessly swallowed by the vibrating hum of the engines. He wiped the sweat from his face with his shirt sleeve and looked over at Honi, still secluded behind her drawbridge of guilt. He was alone, and in the privacy of his loneliness, he wept, the tears streaming down his cheeks like a grieved infant's. For all that he had done and not done, Konrad wept.

Konrad was jarred into alertness by the thud of the DC-3 touching down on the rutted surface of the landing strip. He rubbed his eyes to remove signs of unmanliness as the props gave a final roar and the plane shuddered into stationary silence. Within seconds, the hatch was jerked open and Konrad blinked hard at the light's assault. Framed in the doorway was a silhouette that somehow seemed familiar. As Konrad's eyes adjusted, he saw that it was the same brutish servant, Horst, who had first ushered him into the German's suite in Frankfurt a thousand years ago. Behind him were three young men who stood ramrod straight and unsmiling, their close-cropped blond hair glinting softly in the sun, the Uzi machine pistols in their hands held tightly at the ready. They were all in their early twenties, and obviously regarded Horst as their leader, unconsciously shifting their feet as he did, always maintaining a deferential distance a few feet behind him. On the forearm of one, Konrad could see the sharp blue angles of a tattoo of the Nazi SS runes.

My God, Konrad thought, they're growing a new crop.

Horst gave a grunt and motioned for the occupants to deplane. Konrad guided Honi by the arm and Mike Dawson, keeping a close eye on the pistol in Horst's massive hand, followed close behind. Horst leered at Honi and tried to move next to her, but Konrad subtly shifted her to the other side, interposing his body between them.

Konrad felt a tug at the M-16 he carried at his side. Startled, he turned to stare directly into the face of one of the young Nazi guards. The impasse lasted only a moment as Konrad realized he had no choice and reluctantly released his grip on the rifle.

A few meters from the plane, Horst stopped and turned to the pilot. "You ready to be paid off?" he demanded.

Dawson nodded pensively. Horst held a set of car keys in front of him and motioned with his huge head to a Volkswagen parked in the distance. "Your money's in the trunk. Count it after you get away from here," he ordered. The pilot needed no further urging. He grabbed the keys and set out for the car at a fast trot, not bothering to say goodbye or look back.

Turning to Konrad and Honi, Horst pointed with his

pistol to a dilapidated, dark hangar about one hundred meters away. "You go there."

As they neared the building, the air was shattered by a thunderous boom followed by a scorching wave of hot air that slammed into their backs as if the door of a blast furnace had suddenly been thrown open. Stunned, Konrad wheeled and saw the Volkswagen Mike Dawson had just entered engulfed in a ball of flame. As he watched, it was reduced to a crumpled, glowing steel frame. He could see the cindered shape of what had been a man in the front seat.

Konrad's shock at the scene was interrupted by a chorus of laughter behind him. He turned and saw Horst and his cohorts laughing as though they had just heard a dirty joke.

As Horst's companions joined him in another explosion of hoots, Konrad edged Honi into the foreboding building. The sun's rays penetrated through the cracks in shafts of thin yellow bands with motes of floating dust providing the only movement Konrad could see. He pushed past the creaky door and was suddenly confronted by a hard-eyed man with a machine pistol who slowly stepped aside and resumed a watch at the dirty window next to the door.

Without speaking, Konrad put his arm protectively around Honi and waited, but not for long.

"So you made it," a familiar deep voice came floating out of the shadows across the empty concrete floor. Konrad strained his eyes in the direction of the sound but could see only the outline of a man. "My compliments on a safe return."

Kaltbrunner was silent for a moment, then asked, "What's wrong with her?"

Konrad glanced quickly at Honi. "Oh, she's just tired; it's been a tough time. She'll be all right, though."

Kaltbrunner paused as though unconvinced, then finally asked, "Were you successful? Did you get it all?"

Konrad nodded. "It's in the plane."

"Did you get the Baron?" Kaltbrunner asked anxiously.

"You mean the stamp? No, we couldn't find it."

The German's voice became harsh. "What? One of the most valuable stamps in the world and you missed it? Of all the blundering—"

Konrad interrupted angrily. "One little stamp! Did you think everything would be stacked and ready for us to haul away?"

The German seemed to reconsider. "Well, we can't be greedy, I guess. It was a splendid operation and you've earned your reward, both of you. There it is, over to your right."

Konrad looked in that direction and saw two black satchels standing near the door. As Konrad stared, the German continued, "Those bags contain every penny I promised both of you, enough to keep you in luxury the rest of your lives. It's yours as soon as my man, Horst, checks the plane's cargo, so just stand there and think about spending it for a moment." He gave a short laugh as an afterthought, and added, "You probably feared I was going to cheat you, but I'm an honorable man. Besides, what you're getting is an insignificant fraction of what you brought me."

The voices around her were a dim, meaningless echo, but something was trying to break through to Honi. She

473

concentrated with all her power to comprehend the messenger tapping on the window of her abused mind. Her subconscious seemed to be a hall of mirrors with weird thoughts in grotesque shapes teasing her, making reality seem an illusion among the distorted images. She struggled silently to clear her mind.

As they waited, the German continued to gloat. "This will be remembered as one of the great crimes of history. Think of it, my genius has enriched all of us and stripped a nation of its wealth, all accomplished in a matter of mere weeks."

The curtains slowly lifted from Honi's mind and revealed to her eyes a strange, dark place with shadows that seemed to leap menacingly from threatening corners. Her memory refused to provide the details of her ordeal but furnished instead a dread that came at her like a stalking animal.

"Konrad!" she cried out in a pleading voice that exploded ringingly in the empty building. "Please don't hurt these people! I don't want this; I want to go home! I'm frightened. This is wrong . . . evil . . . don't do it!" Honi leaned against the wall and sobbed loudly, her chest heaving in an agitation that burst from deep within.

Konrad hastened to cover her outburst. "She'll be OK. It's just fatigue. I'll take care of her; don't worry."

A dead silence preceded the German's reply, and then it came in slow, menacing words. "I'd be a fool to turn that woman loose after how far we've come. Look at her, she's out of control. She'd have half the police of Germany after us in a day. No, she has to go."

"Go?" Konrad cried in alarm. "What do you mean? I said I'd take care of her."

Kaltbrunner's voice dismissed Konrad. "You're a fool

474

and a weakling for letting a woman take away your manhood. The woman must die—now."

The sound of a pistol being cocked crashed into Konrad's brain like hot needles. He stood frozen to the floor by the shocking turn of events, but in that instant, the familiar voice of Willie Mac spoke to him, not in its customary mocking tone, but with urgent pleading. "Lieutenant, listen to me, save the woman and everything's square with us. All even. *Do it!*"

"NO!" Konrad shouted as he leaped and gave Honi a hard shove that sent her reeling head-first into the wall. The thud of her impact was drowned out by the blast of the pistol, and she and Konrad collapsed simultaneously to the hard floor.

Kaltbrunner looked coldly at Konrad who was clutching his chest in a futile attempt to stop the blood bubbling out of his shattered lungs. "I was wrong. You're not a soldier, you're a sentimental fool, one who gave his life stupidly, because I'm still going to kill her."

The death drama he had created so preoccupied Kaltbrunner and his sentry that neither was aware of a small door softly opening and closing in the far end of the hangar. He continued gloating to the gasping Konrad. "The bitch is lying there unconscious and won't even know when she dies, but you'll see it, Konrad, you'll know the frustration of throwing your life away for no purpose."

With a condescending snort, Kaltbrunner leveled the gun at Honi's head and started to take aim. He was interrupted by the pleading voice of his guard at the window. "Colonel, please let me do it." The young man fidgeted eagerly with the machine pistol in his hands.

Kaltbrunner smiled approvingly. "It's all yours, Karl.

I like your enthusiasm."

Karl beamed his appreciation and gauged the distance and angle of his target lying against the wall. He didn't want a single bullet to miss.

From the hiding place he had slipped into just inside the building, Riley held his breath and extended the forty-four magnum to full arm's length. Slowly, with both eyes open, he sighted along the barrel and forced himself not to rush.

At the other end of the hangar, Karl was going through the same movements as Riley, except just as his finger started to tighten on the trigger, his head exploded like a melon and his body was thrown into a rag-doll heap by the impact of the powerful slug.

Before the loud blast had stopped ringing in his ears, Riley had swiveled the pistol to where Kaltbrunner had been standing. His trained eye picked up the flash of movement, and he squeezed off several shots at the appearance of a sliver of light that blinked briefly as a door opened and closed.

With a soft curse, Riley realized his shots had just missed the fleeing Kaltbrunner. He resisted the temptation to pursue in the same direction, knowing the likelihood of an ambush, so he lowered the pistol and retreated the way he had come.

The recognizable roar of Riley's magnum stirred Moshe Pritzer into action as he cradled the long barrel of the rifle where he lay hidden in the trees on the edge of the old runway, his hiding place since the two of them had followed Kaltbrunner and his gang to the airfield. Moshe picked up a small battery-operated bullhorn and

476

pointed it in the direction of the knot of men standing around the DC-3 staring in the direction of the hangar from where the shots had come.

As the four men started to walk toward the hangar, Moshe pushed the button on the bullhorn and held it to his lips. "You there, you men! Stand where you are! Drop your guns!"

Horst and his three subordinates stopped suddenly at the sound of Moshe's voice as though frozen in mid-air. The three younger ones looked expectantly at Horst. He glanced quickly in the direction of the amplified voice. "Everyone run in opposite directions . . . NOW!"

At the sight of the running, dodging men, Moshe reached for the rifle, put his eye to the scope with practiced dexterity and quickly lined up one of the figures in the crosshairs. He applied a feather touch to the trigger and watched with professional satisfaction as the man collapsed in a heap. He swept the area in search of more targets and reached for the bolt to advance another shell into the chamber. It didn't work and he had to take his eyes from the fleeing men to struggle with the stubborn bolt. In an instant he realized the mechanism was hopelessly jammed. In disgust, he turned back to the fleeing men, but they were gone, hidden in places he couldn't see, but where he knew their eyes were searching him out. With the tension of a situation gone out of control, he threw the rifle aside, took out a pistol and slipped away.

Riley took cover at the sound of the rifle shot barely in time to see a figure disappear into the hangar he had just left. He stealthily retraced his steps and slipped back into the darkened building.

Inside, he could see the shadow of a man moving silently along the wall. Fearing that it might be Moshe, Riley waited in a dark corner until the man moved into a patch of soft light. He saw that it was Horst, moving like a cautious bull, looking for someone to destroy with the pistol held like a child's toy in his huge hand.

Riley slowly raised the magnum and pointed it directly at the broad chest across the hangar. Riley knew he had only one or two rounds left in the gun because he hadn't had time to reload, and he certainly couldn't do it now. The tension of that fact caused him to move the slightest fraction of a centimeter, but it was enough to make the bullet merely graze Horst's shoulder and slam harmlessly into the wall. Horst wheeled in the direction of the shot and stared toward Riley, raising the pistol in the same motion.

Riley squeezed the trigger again. *Click!* The dull flat sound of the empty chamber thudded into his brain like the knell at his own funeral. Horst heard the same sound and grinned maliciously, realizing Riley was at his mercy. He moved to an angle where he could see Riley clearly and pointed his weapon at the defenseless man, in no hurry to end things, knowing he had complete control. A moment to tease this mouse wouldn't matter.

Riley knew it would be only a second or two until he would be torn apart by the heavy handgun. In desperation, he challenged Horst, shouting taunts across the bare concrete. "Shooting an unarmed man is about all you're good for, you ugly asshole. Why don't you put down that gun and meet me hand-to-hand, you cowardly bastard?"

Horst at first snarled at the insults, then an evil grin

478

spread over his flat face as he thought of what he would do to the smaller man. He slowly put his pistol on the floor, spread his hands in front of him so Riley could see the huge instruments of his impending death, and advanced slowly, a deep, rattling growl coming from between his drooling lips.

Riley watched the brute come toward him, waiting as the distance grew between Horst and the pistol lying on the floor. When he was only a few meters from Riley and the outstretched hands were plainly visible down to the cracks, heavy calluses and gnarled knuckles, Riley calmly opened his jacket, pulled another pistol from his waistband and shot Horst through the heart.

As Horst's heavy body flopped on the concrete like a wet sack, Riley shook his head and said, "When you're trying to kill someone, don't count on them to cooperate."

Ernst Hoffer very gradually allowed himself to breathe freely. He had never been so scared in his life as when he and Horst and the other Nazi Youth were running away from the airplane and the madman was shooting at them. He knew he was lucky to find an open door to this small storage shed; he could only hope his comrades were similarly fortunate.

"Swine!"

The sharp voice of Kaltbrunner slammed into him like a club and he leaped to his feet looking for the location of his leader's voice.

"Cowardly swine, you ran like frightened dogs. You don't deserve to bear the immortal symbol of the SS."

Hoffer saw the outline of Kaltbrunner in his place of

shadowed concealment. "It . . . it wasn't that way, Colonel. I—"

"Don't talk back to me, coward. I know what happened. But I'm willing to give you a chance to redeem your honor."

Relief flooded over Hoffer. "How, Colonel? I'll do whatever you want."

"If I can't have the treasure I worked for years to obtain, then no one else will have it, either." Kaltbrunner tapped two large, full cans of gasoline with his foot. "Take these and dump them on the airplane. Then burn the damned thing. I'll teach them to interfere with me."

Hoffer hesitated, thinking of the man with the rifle. "But—"

"*Do it!*" Kaltbrunner screamed as loudly as he dared. "Do it, or I'll show you how the SS deals with cowards."

Hoffer quickly grabbed the cans and moved for the door.

Moshe's grip on his pistol tightened as he watched the man douse the fuselage of the DC-3 with gasoline about one hundred meters from his hiding place. Even from that distance, the wind carried the unmistakable odor of the fuel to him. Moshe felt helpless, knowing the chances were slim of a killing shot from this distance with a pistol. Besides, one stray shot or ricochet might send the plane and its irreplaceable contents up in flames. He glanced at the gun the guard had left several meters from where he was spreading the fuel. Moshe knew that if he could remain undetected for only a few seconds, he could reach the man before he could grab the gun.

Moshe waited until Hoffer's back was turned and then

480

started running toward him, hoping desperately that he could reach the young Nazi before he was spotted and Hoffer had time to recover his gun. He was within twenty meters when Hoffer heard footsteps and looked back. Startled, he dropped the gasoline can and scrambled for his machine pistol on the ground.

In desperation, Moshe dove for the Nazi and knocked him away from the gun. The two men sprawled awkwardly, both stunned from the collision. Moshe tried to regain his feet, but realized with a sinking heart that his knee had given out. He struggled up like a one-legged man and looked in defenseless fear at his adversary who was stalking him with a long knife held menacingly outstretched.

Moshe reached for the gun in his belt only to discover that it had skittered away when he dived at the young Nazi. Unarmed and crippled he looked around desperately for anything that might give him an edge. He spotted the gasoline can Hoffer had discarded and quickly grabbed it, ready to throw it at his advancing enemy. It was heavier than expected, and the sloshing made Moshe realize it was still about a quarter full. The Nazi's knife was very close to Moshe when he threw the contents of the can in his face.

Caught by surprise, Hoffer took a second to wipe the gasoline from his eyes, but that was all the time Moshe needed. The gasoline can came down viciously with a loud thud followed instantly by the Nazi's piercing scream as he grabbed for his shattered wrist and the hand that no longer held the knife.

Following up quickly, Moshe swung a vicious backhand chop that caught Hoffer on the bridge of the nose and silenced his screams as he sank to the gasoline-saturated ground.

Exhausted and in pain, Moshe hobbled toward the hanger, hurt, unarmed, and in the open.

As Moshe limped toward cover, he wasn't aware of the remaining guard hidden behind the hanger carefully sighting down the barrel of his weapon to line up the killing shot.

Konrad's eyes opened but everything he saw seemed to lack shape and definition, as though he were seeing under water. The pain in his chest felt like his heart was encased in barbed wire. The blood rushing into his lungs gave him the panicky feeling of drowning and he gasped loudly and laboriously for every breath. He couldn't seem to unscramble his thoughts and he felt desperately tired, but an inner sense of need compelled him to start a slow, painful crawl to the open door, the only source of light in his rapidly darkening world.

After long minutes, Konrad reached the body of the guard Riley had killed and picked up the gun that had fallen from that man's hands. He looked out the door and saw the vague outline of the guard's back as he took aim at Moshe. In the distance, Konrad could see an advancing figure. He fought determinedly to clear his vision, and somehow his brain responded and lifted the veil from his eyes. He recognized Moshe as his former inquisitor, a man he realized was about to be killed by the Nazi guard whose back was directly in front of him. Though only half conscious, Konrad's trained mind automatically computed the circumstances of the situation before him, and he slowly but resolutely lifted the gun in his hands and pointed it at the back of the Nazi.

The spurt of automatic fire made Moshe instinctively throw himself to the ground, but when it wasn't repeated, he cautiously lifted up and advanced toward the sound. He discovered the body of the hidden Nazi with his gun still pointed in Moshe's direction but now held in harmless, dead hands. Behind the body, lying in the doorway, was Konrad, trying to hold his head up while his face reflected the pain that beat at his brain with an increasing tempo.

Moshe looked at the gravely wounded Konrad and the smoking gun in his slack hands, and deliberately felt the deep, ugly scars that marred his face, scars that Konrad had inflicted. Slowly, with a wide smile playing across his lips, and with his eyes locked with Konrad's fogged ones, his hand continued to his forehead and he gave a salute to the man who had just saved his life.

Across the airfield, Riley moved like a stalking cat in his pursuit of Kaltbrunner. He could sense his presence, but the old Nazi was proving an elusive quarry. Riley cautiously stepped onto the dirt road between two of the abandoned buildings and slowly turned in a circle, looking for some trace.

Riley heard the powerful engine roar to life, then the loud squeal of tires, and he knew the purpose was his death. By the time the big Mercedes with Kaltbrunner at the wheel came into view, Riley was already moving, desperately throwing himself against the foundation of the nearest building to avoid the onrushing wheels.

Riley felt the car rush past so close that it brushed his clothes, the heat of the exhaust singeing his hair. But instantly he was on his feet. The big magnum bucked repeatedly in his hand as the heavy slugs slammed into the rear tires of the fleeing car. The speeding Mercedes started to weave slightly, then erratically, before finally crashing into a power pole a hundred meters down the road.

Riley approached the smashed car silently with gun at the ready. The car had snapped a pole in two and rested against the jagged bottom half. The only sound was the hissing of the broken radiator. Riley glanced at a sign on the adjoining pole that said: CAUTION! HIGH VOLTAGE—10,000 VOLTS. He backed up and widened the circle of his approach.

On the other side, he saw Kaltbrunner lying on the ground beside the car in obvious pain, one leg pinned at a bizarre angle in the mangled door frame. On the ground close by, dancing feverishly like demented snakes, were the hissing bare wires torn free by the collision. Riley stood well back and exchanged hard looks with Kaltbrunner.

"Who are you?" Kaltbrunner asked defiantly.

"Don't you remember me? I'm the six million Jews who cry out for revenge."

Kaltbrunner's voice softened slightly with scheming. "I have money, a lot of money, millions, and it's all yours if you let me go."

Riley was astonished. "*Money?* You offer me money? Where'd you get it, from the gold you stole out of dead Jews' mouths?" Riley gestured toward Kaltbrunner with his pistol. "In a few minutes you'll be able to explain to those same Jews; they're waiting for you."

Riley walked over to where a rusted piece of fencing wire lay discarded in the grass and started to uncoil it, talking as he did so. "By the way, all that money—" he gestured to the satchels of money intended for Konrad and Honi and thrown out of the car in the collision—"you'll be happy to know that it'll buy a lot of guns for Israel. I thought you'd like to know that."

"You're going to murder me in cold blood," Kaltbrunner said matter-of-factly.

Riley stared down at him without emotion. "I'm an executioner. An executioner doesn't murder, he does his duty."

Kaltbrunner winced as he rose to one elbow, but the pain he felt didn't soften the hatred that exuded from his eyes and voice. "Then go ahead and shoot, goddamn you. I'll not beg a filthy Jew. At least you'll have to tell your kike masters that I died like a soldier."

Riley held the long, straightened wire in one hand and the pistol in the other. "I don't think so, Kaltbrunner."

"Shoot, damn you."

"I'm not going to shoot you." He paused as a barely perceptible flicker of hope crossed Kaltbrunner's face.

"I'm going to electrocute you, like a common criminal."

Riley tossed the fencing wire across a leaping, snapping, high-voltage wire and watched as the other end slowly fell toward Kaltbrunner. In panic, the Nazi struggled to avoid the descending wire, but down it came until it touched his body gently and completed the circuit.

Kaltbrunner's body bucked and stiffened as the burning current smashed through his body and paralyzed his heart. Death was swift but not merciful.

Riley looked down at the blackened body with the eyes turned to glass and mouth puckered like a fish's, and felt a slight pang of remorse. Though he hated what the man had done and stood for, he was still a stranger long removed from the scene of his crime, incapable of being hated personally. Riley carried no satisfaction with him as he turned and walked away.

Riley and Moshe stood over Konrad and silently watched him fight for life as each breath rattled ominously in his torn chest. Riley bent down and examined Konrad's wound; one quick look confirmed that it was mortal. Their eyes met. Riley said, "Thanks for what you did; you're a brave man." He looked ready to say more but kept his lips tightly closed.

Konrad tried to cough but the strength wasn't there. The terrible pain that had been clawing at his chest started to fade, and was replaced by a vast indifference. The man in front of him was badly out of focus, but even so, there was something familiar about him. But it didn't seem important. He and Willie Mac could be friends again, that's what counted.

Riley watched life leave Konrad's body like smoke from a dying fire. The only help or comfort he could give was a deep sense of sadness and kinship that one soldier feels for another, less fortunate one. There are no enemies on the field after the battle has passed. He shook his head at the waste of it. Under different circumstances, he could have liked Konrad a lot. It was a damned shame.

Moshe watched as Riley gently closed Konrad's eyes. "What would you have done to him if he had lived?"

Riley turned to face his lieutenant. "Moshe, don't ask 'if' questions."

Riley went into the hangar to where Honi was groaning

softly and rubbing the large lump that was forming on her forehead. He looked down at her: a beautiful, mysterious woman, one who had struggled against the meanness of life and sought forgiveness by rejecting cruelty and greed.

"You are forgiven," Riley whispered tenderly. He gathered Honi in his arms and turned his back on the dead as he walked away.

Chapter Twenty-One

Honi opened her eyes and stared uncomprehendingly for a moment, the way one does when awakening in a strange place. Then she remembered: She was in the Frankfurt Airport Hotel. She stretched luxuriously in the wide, soft bed then raised herself to one elbow and looked for him.

Riley heard the rustling of the bedclothes and came into the room. "Good morning, Hannah," he said cheerily.

She said sadly, "I don't know if I'll ever get used to that name."

Riley smiled reassuringly. "You will. The difference between Hannah Muller and Honi Miller isn't so great as the difference between the two women—what Honi Miller was and what Hannah Muller will become."

"How do you manage to create a new name just like that?" She snapped her fingers.

"Never ask me how I do things. In my line of work, there's no after-hours chit-chat."

She shook her head in wonderment. "How can I ever

pass for a German-Jewish immigrant to Israel?"

Riley laughed loudly. "Being Jewish isn't that hard. Let the role grow on you; who knows, you might even grow into it. Why do you think I chose that identity for you? In my mind's eye, I can see you in Israel, living, growing, working on a kibbutz. Believe me, you're going to learn to know and like Hannah Muller."

She gripped his arm, an unthinking plea for support. "I've got a long way to go."

He squeezed her hand on his arm. "You'll make it because you're a strong woman. Strong women and Israel go together, my mother was evidence of that, and you're a lot like her. I promise you, however long it takes, I'll be there."

"But you hardly know me." She caressed his maimed hand on her own.

"That's true, and who knows what'll happen? Forty years from now we may be a crotchety old man and his nagging wife, or we may find our differences too great and drift apart to be just friends, seeing each other less and less often but maintaining a memory-filled fondness. But whatever happens, you're a helluva woman that I'll be proud to know I've helped."

She shook her head with regret, her eyes welling with tears. "I feel so guilty about what happened, and the memory of loving Konrad is so fresh and painful. I miss him. I loved him more than any other man, but he still seems like a stranger in so many ways."

She described Konrad's anguished confession to her on the night before they began the attack. "It was guilt. He felt he had let one of his men get killed in Vietnam so he could save himself. Everyone told him he was a hero while he considered himself a coward. I couldn't talk him out of it."

Riley suddenly became remote and gazed beyond Honi's shoulder in the direction of his own memories. "Who can explain what happens to men in war? It's not difficult to train a soldier to kill, but no training can prepare him to live with the memory of it. No one who hasn't been there can fully understand. I think I know, but it's nothing I can share."

She spoke slowly as one lost in thought. "Tell me about him; I feel we were a lot alike."

"No, you weren't. You came back to Liechtenstein to find yourself; Konrad came to lose himself. And as for the kind of man he was, you'll have to find him on your own, but if you loved him, what else do you need?"

"Why did he sacrifice his life for me?"

"No one will ever know that, but I think we can make an assumption." Riley paused and looked searchingly in her face. "When he sacrificed his life to save yours, I think he was trying to say he was sorry."

He cradled her tear-streaked face in his hands and bent low to whisper, "I think we should accept the apology."

Willa Mae Russell clutched the small box like a thing of great value, which, considering it was the only package she had received in years, it most definitely was.

She slowly labored her way up the rickety stairs of the tenement where she had lived for so long in the slums of Chicago's South Side. The stairs had grown steeper with the years and she pushed with her hand on each leg as she laboriously ascended past the odors of frying fish, cheap wine and stale vomit, past the screams of hungry babies and the shouts of harried mothers and drunk fathers. All this had long since soaked into the walls of the

490

shabby building like just one more coat of dirty paint, and Willa Mae was oblivious to it as she unlocked the door to her tiny apartment and slipped inside with her treasure.

With excited fingers she tore the heavy brown wrapping paper off and opened the box. Inside was a small case covered with blue velvet and a letter. She opened the case and stared with bafflement at a small, old-looking postage stamp with funny, foreign writing on it and featuring a sour-looking man with a beard. She shrugged and turned to the letter.

Dear Mrs. Russell:

You may not remember my name, but I was Willie Mac's commanding officer in Vietnam. I was the last man to see him alive. In token of my respect for your son, I am enclosing a gift. The stamp is called the Baron, and it is worth a great deal of money, especially if you follow my instructions.

Wait at least a year, then contact the government of Liechtenstein through the Swiss embassy in Washington; tell them the stamp accidentally came into your possession—that's only the simple truth—and offer to return it for a $100,000 reward. Don't worry, they can afford it, and will be happy to pay. Be certain not to tell anyone where you got the stamp, and don't give it up until the reward is in your hands.

My doing this my seem strange, but I was very fond of Willie Mac and owe him a great deal, a very great deal.

Sincerely,
Lieutenant Konrad

491

Willa Mae studied the strange stamp a while longer then went to a battered, old cedar chest and removed her large, well-thumbed Bible, the framed portrait of Christ, and an old black-and-white television set from the top and carefully hid the velvet case inside.

She went over to the old chair where she rested her hurting legs after a night mopping floors in a big office building downtown and watched the soaps on her little television. Next to the chair was a decrepit but highly polished table with a starched doily on top. There, in an honored place was a double-sided dime-store picture frame. On the left side was a smiling, young Willie Mac in high school graduation cap and gown. On the opposite side was a short letter from Willie Mac's commanding colonel telling her how proud she should be of her son and the sacrifice he made for his country. In the drawer just below was a purple heart, still in its case, and a stack of letters held together by a rubber band and starting to turn brittle and yellow.

Willa Mae had given birth to eight children, had loved them all and cared for them all, even after the man who had fathered them disappeared one day and never returned. But Willie Mac was her youngest, her baby.

She removed one of the letters and reread it. Then, with tears in her eyes, she addressed the smiling youth in the frame. "You were right, son, that Lieutenant Konrad is a good man."

THE SURVIVALIST SERIES
by Jerry Ahern

THE BEST IN WESTERNS FROM ZEBRA

THE SLANTED COLT (1413, $2.25)
by Dan Parkinson
A tall, mysterious stranger named Kichener gave young Benjamin Franklin Black a gift — a Colt pistol that had belonged to Ben's father. And when a cold-blooded killer vowed to put Ben six feet under, it was a sure thing that Ben would have to learn to use that gun — or die!

GUNPOWDER GLORY (1448, $2.50)
by Dan Parkinson
After Jeremy Burke shot down the Sutton boy who killed his pa, it was time to leave town. Not that Burke was afraid of the Suttons — but he had promised his pa, right before the old man died, that he'd never kill another Sutton. But when the bullets started flying, he'd find there was more at stake than his own life. . . .

BLOOD ARROW (1549, $2.50)
by Dan Parkinson
Randall Kerry was a member of the Mellette Expedition — until he returned from a scouting trip to find the force of seventeen men slaughtered and scalped. And before Kerry could ride a mile from the massacre site, two Indians emerged from the trees and charged!

THE LAST MOUNTAIN MAN (1480, $2.25)
by William W. Johnstone
Trouble and death followed Smoke all of his days — days spent avenging the ones he loved. Seeking at first his father's killer, then his wife's, Smoke rides the vengeance trail to find the vicious outlaws — and bring them to his own kind of justice!

GUNSIGHT LODE (1497, $2.25)
by Virgil Hart
After twenty years Aaron Glass is back in Idaho, seeking vengeance on a member of his old gang who once double-crossed him. The hardened trail-rider gets a little softhearted when he discovers how frail Doc Swann's grown — but when the medicine man tries to backshoot him, Glass is tough as nails!

Available wherever paperbacks are sold, or order direct from the Publisher. Send cover price plus 50¢ per copy for mailing and handling to Zebra Books, Dept. 1607, 475 Park Avenue South, New York, N.Y. 10016. DO NOT SEND CASH.